IN THE MIDST OF OMENS

THE LEGACY OF GILGAMESH | BOOK 1

NICOLE BAILEY

Edited by Milly Bellegris and Natalie Cammaratta

Cover design by Stefanie Saw | Cover object design by Modefact

Map design by Chaim Holtjer

"The Epic of Gilgamesh" © 1917 translated by Stephen Langdon

www.authornicolebailey.com

In loving memory of my sister Anna.

And for my readers Daniel and Chera who both requested I write a retelling of the Epic of Gilgamesh. I hope it's all you imagined.

CONTENT WARNINGS

In the Midst of Omens is based on a story that deals intimately with grief, loss, and death. This series delves into those subjects in a detailed manner.

This book contains the depiction of wars and battles including depicted death and mild gore.

There are conversations about lack of consent/dubious consent, but nothing depicted.

The story also contains strong language and sexual content.

I hope readers will find that I've handled these topics with sensitivity. However, I wished to include a note for anyone who may find this content triggering.

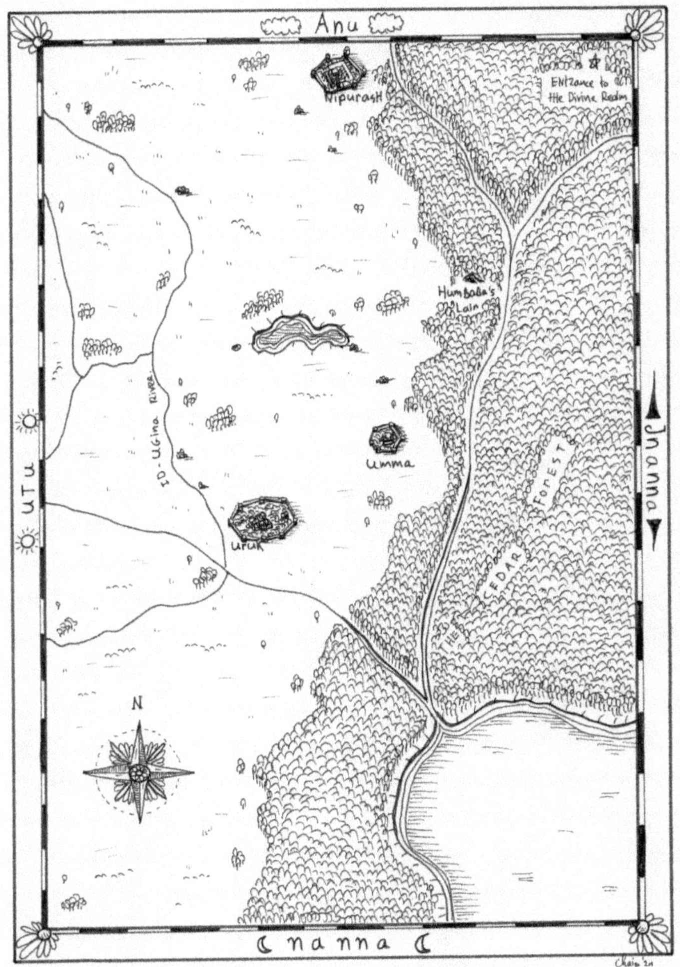

Anu
Nipurash
Entrance to
the Divine Realm
Humbaba's
Lain
ID-UGina River
THE CEDAR FOREST
umma
uruk
UTU
Inanna
N
Inanna

AUTHOR'S NOTE

In the Midst of Omens is based on the world's oldest written story, the Epic of Gilgamesh.

While I've remained true to the epic's heart, I've changed aspects of the narrative to fit this story.

I'd like to make one small note, however. Gilgamesh claims he is two-thirds god. Both of my editors have pointed out that the math doesn't match his mother being a goddess and his father being half god. However, that is directly from the original epic and I've opted to keep it.

I hope you enjoy Gilgamesh and Enkidu's story, a tale four thousand years in the making.

GLOSSARY

- **Lugal**: King
- **Nin:** Honorific for an esteemed woman such as a goddess, queen, or princess
- **Ensi:** Honorific for a prince or governor
- **Dumu:** Son
- **Adda:** Father
- **Ama:** Mother
- **Shed:** Sumerian curse word equivalent to 'shit'

"During my night I, having become lusty, wandered about
in the midst of omens."

-The Epic of Gilgamesh

PROLOGUE

He came into power through blood and violence. The wolf shook his head as he cracked sticks and leaves in his sprint. The forest passed in a blur of gray and green, the cedars' sweetness filling the air.

Usually memories didn't nestle into the wolf's mind, but the blood was still fresh from the attack. Another pack had descended upon his den with gnashing teeth and sharp claws.

His pack overcame.

But at a cost.

His father had died, his thick gray fur matted down under spilled blood.

Protect the pack. Don't forget your duty, he'd said with his last panting breath to the wolf.

The wolf had only lived a few seasons. When the sun lengthened its time in the sky, he'd planned to leave his parents' pack, explore the forest, stretch his legs.

Instead, he stepped into his father's role.

In the mornings, once the pack had bedded down

within the den, the new pups' whimpering silenced by their mother's comfort, the wolf ran. He ran until his breath ached his lungs and saliva oozed past his teeth. Until he could taste the pine sap in the air. Until the birds began their morning squalling as his ears pressed back.

One more lap and he'd return to the den.

To his place in life.

He turned a corner then slammed his paws into the dirt, dragging up moss as he forced himself to a halt.

A human lay sleeping, bare of coverings, sunlight dappling his massive body. The wolf's heart stuttered. He shuffled back a step. Normally his nose would have warned him long before he came across a human. This one didn't have the sharp scent of hunters, though. His grassy, sweet aroma blended in with the forest.

If it were another predator, he'd wrinkle his nose and growl a warning. The wolf was no coward. Already scars marred his body from defending his territory. One lesson he'd learned well from his father, though, was that wolves did not fight humans. They stayed far from them.

The wolf turned. He'd have to send out the pack's strongest hunters to survey the radius around the den. Humans rarely came so deep into the woods and—

"Wait a moment." The voice was light and melodic. It rushed through the trees like a breeze, shaking pine needles free.

Turning back around, he bared his teeth at the human, but the creature slept on.

"It's not him who's speaking to you. It's me."

The wind rushed again, and light glistened through branches. The voice came from beyond the earth. The wolf dropped to the ground and exposed his belly.

"Rise, Wolf. I have a duty for you."

Getting back to his feet, he shook leaves from his coat and stared up at the sparkling sky. The-One-Who-Created-All spoke to him—him of all beasts.

"You are an honored creature, indeed, Wolf. I've seen your loyalty and responsibility. I need you to complete a task for me."

Anything for you, Creator.

"This is my son." Light danced around the human lying on the forest floor. "He needs someone to look after him for a time. To teach him the ways of life. One day fate will pair him with a human king, and he must be prepared."

The wolf heaved a breath, his gaze bouncing between the sleeping human and the Creator's glistening light. *How can I teach a human to be a human, Wise One?*

"He already knows what he will need for his human life. He can speak their tongue. Tell him one day a woman will come bringing food. Once he accepts it, he will be gifted all the knowledge he needs for living among humans. For now,"—the light softened around the man curled in the dark grass—"I want him to learn of duty, of life and loss, and the natural way of things. These are the skills he must gain. Will you accept this calling, Wolf?"

The wolf smacked his mouth and shifted the dirt beneath his paw. He knew nothing of humans and had no desire to learn. The Creator asked him to look after this man and teach him the forest's ways. It was one more responsibility.

But he wasn't one to run away from duty.

I'm honored, Creator.

"Thank you, Wolf." The glistening light transformed into a female human form, though her tresses were as wild as tree boughs, her eyes like stars the wolves howled at. She brushed hair back from the man's face, tucking strands back from the horns on his head. "I know you'll take good care of my son."

The man's eyes opened, and, with a burst of light, the Creator disappeared.

CHAPTER ONE

A VALLEY DARK AND QUIET

GILGAMESH'S AX hungered for blood. For the crunch of bones snapping beneath it and the howling cries of fallen enemies.

And he didn't give a damn what his advisors thought about it.

That didn't stop the advisor who'd joined the campaign from standing before his king with protests. Fuck if some god hadn't bewitched Gilgamesh for him to have allowed Hirin to come with his men.

Most of the soldiers lingered back at their campsite, but Gilgamesh's loyal hundred stood with them on a hill that looked down into a dark, quiet valley. Dozens of animal-hide tents rippled in a breeze which caused torches around the site to flicker.

Gilgamesh's men leaned on their shields or rested hands on their swords. Fine blades were expensive and rare. He doubted the troops waiting for them in the valley possessed many. Every one of his hundred had one, yet Gilgamesh preferred the ax. There was something about the brutal intimacy of fighting so close. The leverage that went into the swing.

When Gilgamesh killed someone, he wanted them to see his eyes as they fell.

"...if we could delay another day and form a strategy, my king."

A sigh built in Gilgamesh's chest. Campfires glowed in the distant valley, golden flecks of moving paint that smudged the not-yet-dark horizon. He'd ignored Hirin's prattling and lost the conversation's topic. The time for action had come.

"What is your concern, Hirin?" His men shuffled behind him. They buzzed with energy, ready to fight.

The advisor, who wore a colorful tunic and beaded shawl as opposed to the practical leather and linen of his soldiers, trembled. "If something were to happen to you, Lugal?"

Gilgamesh scoffed as he chucked his bronze shield onto the ground, causing dust to rise and glow in the dim illumination from the enemy's distant fires. "What could possibly happen to me?" He nodded to his soldiers. Hirin didn't want them to fight tonight. He'd rather they reconvene with the rest of their army to make a strategy, alerting their enemy and allowing them to prepare, and other foolish, advisor-like ideas.

"Not to be indelicate, Your Highness, but you could die." Hirin rubbed his hands together.

Gilgamesh's nose flared. He wasn't some mortal child, incapable of protecting himself. He possessed god's blood powers and he released his hold on them, allowing the magic to flow over the man. One would think Hirin might remember who he stood before as he shivered under their weight. The advisor bowed deeply, and Gilgamesh's teeth clicked. He'd allowed Hirin to come because the man was loyal and well connected. Taking a moment to reassure the advisor wouldn't delay the inevitable.

Hirin bowed again until he touched the ground before scrambling to his feet. "Forgive me, Lugal. You know I am a weak-willed man and not made of the same mettle as your fighters." His eyes dashed to the broad, muscled men. Gilgamesh stood five hand breadths above his tallest soldier which signaled his god-descended nature even without others having to feel his power's weight.

Hirin was attempting to be respectful despite his disapproval, and Gilgamesh needed to keep him on his side. As an advisor, he influenced a realm Gilgamesh couldn't win through might alone. He clapped the man's arm. "Of course." Then he shifted to face the men who waited for his word. At a shake of his head, they'd retreat to the hill's other side and sleep with unbloodied hands. But they had vengeance to take. "I believe our friend and advisor has forgotten who leads our group."

Smiles slipped up their faces. They already knew what he'd say but were eager to hear it again. Gilgamesh rested a palm over the ax's head.

"Is it a mere mortal who leads you, the most loyal men of Uruk?"

"No," they cried and raised their swords to pierce the sky's deepening navy.

Gilgamesh laughed, his chest rumbling with it. "No, Hirin. You need not worry, for it is no mere mortal standing here tonight." Gilgamesh grazed his hand down his beard before grinning. "These fine soldiers will face down this threat alongside the great King Gilgamesh, valorous ruler of the high-walled Uruk,"— battle cries rang out—"son of the great king and half-god Lugalbanda and the mighty goddess, Ninsun!" More cheers rose into a crescendo as the sound echoed. "The man who surpasses all other mortals in strength and deed!"

The men jumped up and down as they hoisted their shields in the air. The noise would wake the sleeping army below. Gilgamesh tightened his grip on the ax and turned towards the slope, directing his men forward. Already soldiers poured out of tents like ants from aggravated mounds. The evening's activity had begun.

"You're not just a god, Lugal," Hirin whispered. His tone caused Gilgamesh to turn towards him, his nose wrinkling in a snarl. The advisor shook his head, his eyes glistening, and it cooled the King's rising anger. "You're one-third human is all I mean, my king. We love you and wish to see you have a long, prosperous reign."

The soldiers ran, their shouts echoing. Gilgamesh remained still and stared at the advisor. It was brave to speak so boldly to the god-king of Uruk. There were many words Gilgamesh might have used to describe Hirin before that night, but brave would not fall among them.

"Perhaps when I walk out of this unscathed, you'll learn to have more faith in me."

The advisor's shoulders dropped with a sigh. Gilgamesh turned and leapt down the hill. His strides were long enough that before his men met the approaching soldiers, he'd reached them.

He roared as he thrust an ax into a soldier who fell with a gasp and crumbled onto the dusty ground. Gilgamesh yanked the weapon free and plowed forward. His men consumed the other fighters like locusts. He'd laugh that this was the army Umma had threatened him with if the cost of their King's pride wasn't lives.

The soldiers fell. They didn't have the ability to challenge his men which sent a quell of disgust curling through Gilgamesh's gut. They couldn't help it. Gilgamesh possessed enough divinity in his blood that mortals grew weak in his presence. As long as his men stayed within half a league, every soldier they fought would tremble and weaken. That, perhaps, was the most frustrating aspect of life for Gilgamesh. Nothing was a challenge.

Yet his own damned advisor doubted him. Foolish man.

He slammed the side of his ax around, knocking down a pair of soldiers, and one dropped a torch that briefly lit a small patch of grass aflame.

Hirin had questioned Gilgamesh in front of his men over this pitiful gathering of so-called soldiers. The advisor was prone to an anxious mind, but Gilgamesh found his perspective useful. He understood battles that happened with words rather than weapons, though his presence annoyed like a fly biting his sweat-dampened back in a spot he couldn't reach.

The enemy soldiers, who'd moved towards them with such bluster and certainty at the start, hesitated. As they made it into the circle that the power of Gilgamesh's god's blood reached, a sheen swept over their eyes and they stumbled, dropping weapons and tripping. They became like lambs led into a temple, their blood splattering the dusty ground of their unirrigated lands.

Gods, this army was a charade, brave men acting as an organized force while their city didn't even have walls or modern record keeping. Gilgamesh wanted to roll his eyes as he shot half a dozen arrows that took down as many men. His body went through the motions mindlessly. He'd spent most of his life with a bow string in his fingers and the wind from an arrow releasing brushing his cheeks. So, his thoughts could drift to political implications and the reason he was out here prepared to end Umma's king, Zage-Si.

Gilgamesh didn't take slights well.

Slights against his queen, even less so.

Zage-Si attempted to cultivate a reputation as the terror of the Lands Between the Waters. But this land was Gilgamesh's. He would work to secure it; then he'd bind his legacy so tightly to the center of human existence that his name would still roll off the tongues of those who lived millennia beyond him. It was the driving force of his life and what caused his heart to beat. This side quest of taking vengeance for Umma's slight aside.

This wasn't a pursuit that would press his name into tablets so that endless years from now, others would speak of his deeds. No, the legend of the slaughter of Umma's army might last a few months or possibly a couple of years as people passed the time over a bowl of beer. It would help further his reputation, but it wouldn't stand against the winds of history. He couldn't bother with that for now, though.

Gilgamesh bellowed another battle cry—a 'hu' that his men echoed—as he plowed another group of soldiers down. Warmth rose through his chest and curled in his stomach. He was god-born and god-blessed, designed for this purpose. And he had a hundred of the most loyal men in the land, fighting without so much as a shudder of hesitation. Who could stand up to him?

Swords clashed as a cool evening wind brought the coppery smell of blood to Gilgamesh, inundating him with the deaths the foolish Zage-Si had wrought. Cries of defeated yet living soldiers rolled through the valley, only overtaken by the roars of success from his men.

Gilgamesh's soldiers functioned as a unit, covering each

other and slamming spears forward with swift movements. The men hinged from the hips and swiveled as they moved, bringing the full weight of their strength into their blows. Gilgamesh had trained these men himself, pulling them aside when he noticed a particular skill or discipline. Once he trusted them, he'd blood-marked them as his, making them immune to the weakness his god powers caused. They were like gems along his crown, small glimmers of all he'd achieved.

"Enough," Gilgamesh roared after his soldiers had cut through hundreds of men. The remaining Umma soldiers stood—firmly, he had to admit—even if their weapons trembled in their hands. His men ceased fighting at once as the other army backed into a mass abutting their encampment's tents. Their numbers had spilled out like a dark tide through the camp, but even for their size, they couldn't stand against Gilgamesh.

He moved forward, his boots squelching in puddles of blood as he maneuvered around downed men. The clang of clashing weapons had given way to an eerie quiet, punctuated by a few lingering sobs and moans of dying men. Gilgamesh would make sure they all received swift ends if his men hadn't handled it once he found who he was looking for. No soldier deserved to die slowly over hours as they imagined the destruction of their city they'd fought to protect. But, first, he had to locate their King. He would be somewhere among the men, despite evading the front lines like a coward.

"Your leader? Lugal Zage-Si?" Gilgamesh asked the blood-splattered soldiers ahead of him. He stood close enough that his powers reached. Men trembled under its weight. Gilgamesh could pull it back, but he didn't. It was difficult enough to wrestle the magic down and even more challenging with his heart thrumming, his awareness of danger.

No soldiers spoke, and he lifted his ax, tossing and catching it before directing it at a man standing in the front line. "One of you will direct me to your leader now, or"—he lifted his shoulder to indicate the group behind him who were still buzzing with exhilaration—"we'll kill our way to him." Still, the men paused, and Gilgamesh had to respect their loyalty. "Do not dishonor your king to believe he'd fear facing me. Is he not as brave as any of you men? Is he not god ordained to his position? Why should he tremble like a coward as you brave souls fight me?"

The Umma soldiers' eyes darted to each other as sweat dripped down their brows. Gilgamesh could imagine their hearts pounding fiercely, yet they didn't jump forward with an answer. He regretted his earlier assessment. Zage-Si had poorly trained his men, but they deserved their reputation. Loyalty burned in their eyes brighter than the torches some carried. However, a hesitation lingered among some; they knew Gilgamesh spoke true. Their gods had chosen their king, and the divine held his life in the balance.

Jaw muscles twitched on some. He understood the trails their minds wandered as clearly as if he could read them. Lugal Zage-Si should be fearless, brilliant, strong, battle-ready, educated, politically savvy, and as handsome as a god. Why didn't Zage-Si stand with them when Gilgamesh fought alongside his men? Gilgamesh understood the demands on a king all too well, understood the workings of these men's minds and the hesitation forming in their postures.

Namtur, an Uruk soldier with a long, sharp nose, shifted towards Gilgamesh. His eyes spoke everything his lips wouldn't say. Gilgamesh's men could take these soldiers. They didn't have to let them weigh things out. They could kill their way to the other king.

Gilgamesh raised a hand to stall his forces. The fight's energy still buzzed around them, their breaths sounding over the winds that flittered sand around their boots. His queen would not like it if this turned into a bigger slaughter. A few hundred Umma soldiers dead, she'd understand, especially after what Zage-Si had done. If Gilgamesh took out their entire force with a handful of men, shamed them to the rest of the world, however, she'd be more than angry with him.

He could imagine the crease that would form between her brows, the words she would throw around. *Diplomacy. Relations. Policy.*

A sigh built in Gilgamesh's chest even while staring down the thousand armed men before him. He loved Shamhat, but at times she was like a nattering younger sister, constantly telling him his sash was unknotted. Like Hirin, though, she made the city stronger for it. Perhaps he viewed his wife strangely. But their relationship didn't possess the romantic or physical interactions most did. So maybe that idea was the most accurate picture or their partnership.

He imagined telling Shamhat he viewed her like a sister. The way her nose would wrinkle, and she'd draw back like she'd taken a taste of rancid wine.

The Umma soldiers parted, creating a funnel into the camp. Wind flapped the animal-hide tents about, crackling them as his soldiers waited for him to decide. Gilgamesh knew an ambush when he saw one. The slight tightening of grips on weapons, the way noses flared to suck in more air.

One of his men—Abgal, the group's oldest and steadiest member—looked at him from beneath thick brows. He felt it too, then. Gilgamesh nodded and turned back towards the Umma forces, tapping his fingers to his forehead. "To our lady in heaven, Inanna."

"To Inanna," his men echoed, and their energy shifted as well.

They were ready to exercise their training, lift spears in swift movements, drop this entire camp of men if required. Gilgamesh couldn't remember when he'd started using a blessing for Inanna as his subtle signal that they were about to step ankle deep into shit and needed to prepare, but a smile touched his lips.

Inanna, the most honored goddess of Uruk—deity of romance, sex, fertility, beauty, war, and justice—could go fuck herself as far as Gilgamesh was concerned.

He stepped into the tunnel of Umma soldiers and sank low into his posture, his feet anchored against the earth, prepared to pounce. His soldiers filed behind him. With how narrow they kept the path, some of his men would be out of touch from his power's protection. Gilgamesh took a deep breath. He'd gladly end this camp to spare one of his men's lives. The rich tang of animal fat burning on torches, the stink of anxious men sweating, and the fresh desert air blending together filled Gilgamesh's sinuses.

His men crunched behind him slowly, their steps steady. They made sure they had the full weight of their body supported before moving forward. This mock army would not take them unaware.

"Now," cried one of the Umma soldiers.

Spears rushed out, bows lifted, men pushed past their weak muscles and trembling bodies.

Gilgamesh's heart thundered as he roared and whipped both axes from his side, slashing them forward in an arced curve that took out a dozen soldiers. They fell to the earth as death cries left their lips, their blood soaking into the dirt that was so far west of their home.

Maybe the men weren't brave. Maybe they were just stupid. His men used their shields to protect each other and fought as the unit they were. Despite the ambush, they pushed through the soldiers, stepping over some as they moved forward.

"Hu," they cried out, "hu, hu."

The sound echoed like a god's judgment coming to fall over Umma. Gilgamesh slammed his axes into place and rolled his shoulders back. "Enough."

His men stopped at once but continued to sneer at the Umma soldiers who'd fallen to the earth. They dug their fingers into the sand as blood slipped down curved muscles to dye the fabric of their clothing.

Gilgamesh addressed the man who he'd made eye contact with previously and who'd somehow survived their onslaught. He almost wished he could recruit him into their forces—mortals who were fearless and loyal were a rare breed.

"Enough," he said again, this time a whisper that scarcely rose over the dying's whimpers. "Do not make us slaughter your forces and shame you before the gods. Where is your king?"

The man glared at him, eyes burning, even as his body trembled then collapsed against the ground. He hesitated only a moment before raising a shaky hand and pointing towards a large tent in the center.

"Tend to your wounded," Gilgamesh said, before tacking on in a grittier tone, "and don't fuck with my men any further unless you wish to feel the breath of the Great Below on your necks tonight."

The Umma soldiers shuddered. Gilgamesh moved past

them and shifted his disposition from soldier to King, his chin raising, his hands tucking behind his back.

Drying blood clung to his skin, and he stretched his fingers to break it as his heart slowed to its regular pace. He doubted one of the Umma men would attempt to attack him again, but gods, he'd love it if they tried. Just once, he wanted to face something that tested the mettle of his strength. He ground his teeth together as he approached the tent that was crafted from pale animal hides. Lifting a hand to stall his soldiers and have them wait outside, he bowed to enter it. Inside, a man stumbled away from the entrance, shifting the rugs that laid on the ground, rumpling them, their different colors folding over each other.

Gilgamesh dropped onto a gritty rug that was nowhere as luxurious as the fine-threaded ones attendants had packed to furnish his tent during the journey. He grabbed a bottle of wine from a low table and poured himself a generous portion into a clay mug, then took a deep swallow. He released a sigh and licked his lips before replacing the mug. "Killing makes a king thirsty, you understand?"

The man had scrambled back against a wall. His hands gripped into the hides, and he looked like he'd gladly tear into whatever attendant had erected the tent edges so tightly that he couldn't escape beneath them.

Gilgamesh leaned back. "Let me tell you two things I know."

"W-what is that?" asked the man, his voice scarcely rising over a whisper.

"First, you are not the King." The man wore a fine, fringed sash over cloth that shimmered even in the greasy torchlight. He had his beard curled, and his long hair tied back in intricate braids beneath a golden band. But

Gilgamesh had met the bastard Zage-Si before and this man wasn't him.

The mystery man raised his chin. "I speak for Lugal Zage-Si."

Gilgamesh snatched a bunch of grapes that sat next to the wine bottle and popped one into his mouth, chewing before responding. "So, Zage-Si truly is a coward?"

"My father's not a coward." The man surged forward, jostling the table and clanging the dishes together. His hands were fisted as if he'd actually fight Gilgamesh.

The King snorted as he chewed another grape and took the young prince in. Neither he nor his father deserved the men they commanded. They were far too honorable and brave. If he had to guess which of Zage-Si's sons this was based on age, he thought Ishme-Ea, his third-in-line. The bastard wasn't even willing to send his crowned prince to join his soldiers. If the boy spoke for his father, then very well. "If he's not a coward, he's at the very least a dishonorable bastard."

Color surged over the Prince's tawny cheeks and he leaned closer, quivering as the weight of Gilgamesh's powers strengthened with the proximity. "That's hypocritical for you of all people."

Gilgamesh stopped mid-chew and placed the remaining grapes back on the table. "Go on, Ensi."

Ishme-Ea looked at the tent opening, like he expected soldiers to flood in and rescue him. When nothing happened and the only sound remaining was the shuffling of Gilgamesh's men who guarded the tent, Ishme-Ea took a fierce breath. "Everyone knows what filth you are; stealing brides from every city of the land, bedding anything that walks, keeping your citizens in hand by working them to death." Gilgamesh stared at him, unimpressed. He'd heard plenty of the rumors about himself, and those weren't even the most interesting ones. The Prince seemed aware that his mark hadn't hit as he intended; he tightened his fingers into fists again. "Do you burden prostitutes and virgins of foreign lands because your whore wife won't have you?"

Gilgamesh's expression stilled.

A grin curled on Ishme-Ea's face, and he threw vengeance into his words. "Everyone says she's more of a slut than even you are, that she'll sleep with anyone and even beasts, but not her king, who disgusts her."

Gilgamesh had an ax off his hip before he had time to think. Its edge rested against the pulse below the Prince's jaw. The man swallowed, and the ax grazed him, nicking him like a copper razor in a shaky hand so that a trickle of blood slipped down the curve of his neck.

"Speak your next words carefully, Prince, or they may be your last. The Queen that you slander has asked me to hold my hand and not destroy your entire city, but currently my patience is like a river running dry."

Ishme-Ea could offend him all he wished—Gilgamesh could bear the heat of wagging tongues—but he would not stand back and listen to slander about Shamhat. Her partners were her business. She was too good for this man and his honorless father. That reminded Gilgamesh of why he was there. "Your father, the great brave man that he is, killed one of our messengers and sent his head back in a basket."

The words fell out of Gilgamesh's mouth like sand, gritty and foreign. It was one of the highest laws not to kill a messenger. Zage-Si had killed not just any messenger, but Shamhat's favorite. Gilgamesh had hired the man because he'd worked with Shamhat's family before their untimely deaths. He'd reminded her of childhood, shared stories about her mother's busy hands and her father's sharp jokes. The throne room rang with Shamhat's laughter when he visited with news and missives. And Zage-Si had not only killed the messenger, breaking Shamhat's heart, but sent his mutilated body home in disgrace. If it wasn't for Shamhat holding him back, Gilgamesh would slaughter his way to their palace and drag the King's entire family through the streets. Diplomacy be damned.

"Everyone knows what you want," Ishme-Ea said, disgust lacing his words even with the blade bobbing against his throat. "All the rulers of the Land Between Waters are aware of your ambitions, Gilgamesh. You want to rule from sea to sea and river to river, destroy all the other kings' thrones. Some of us won't allow it."

Gilgamesh stood, hunching under the tent's draping roof. Ishme-Ea, despite his brazen words, curled into himself. "Let me make this very clear to you, boy," Gilgamesh said through clenched teeth. "I approached your throne with a messenger and gifts in good faith, asking nothing but consideration of an alliance." The Prince looked like he might interject, and Gilgamesh pressed the blade closer to his throat to shut him up. "I could have easily stormed your unprotected city and ripped your family off their thrones, but I did not."

Diplomacy. He could hear Shamhat's ringing voice. *You won't win the world by might alone, Gilgamesh.*

"Let me hear you speak one more ill word about Uruk's queen again, and I will do just that. I'll plunder your city, tear down your temples, and set your palace on fire until there is nothing but burnt earth remaining of your father's legacy. I'll scorch his name so far from history, your children's generation won't know it. Do you understand me?"

The Prince's nose flared.

"You will command these troops to return to your city and you will act as my messenger to your worthless, god-forsaken father. You tell him that King Gilgamesh, ruler of the high-walled Uruk, god-born and divinely ordained, sends him this message: He will pay reparations for the death of our messenger and lend the manpower of labor taxes from five hundred men to our building projects for the year."

"We won't spare a soul for your ceaseless ambitions."

The wind outside howled, a wolf cry of a sound like it mourned the blood seeping into the earth. Gilgamesh leaned closer to the Prince, breathed in the musky oil he wore. A bead of sweat dripped down the man's forehead. "Very well," Gilgamesh said evenly. "Then I shall see you again, Prince, with your conquered city behind me and a blade at your throat, which I won't stall. Send my message to the King, or I shall end you and find someone who can carry your head home in a basket instead. Do you understand me?"

The Prince glared at him but bobbed his head, and Gilgamesh slid the ax back from his neck. "I'll expect these troops out of my valley by sunrise or we shall finish what we began here tonight."

Ishme-Ea wrinkled his nose, probably prepared to argue about whose land they were on, but Gilgamesh didn't wait for a reply. He stepped out of the tent and stretched back to his full height. This issue wasn't over with, and he damned well knew it. Zage-Si had made his move, stacked his pieces, and was prepared to battle. Gilgamesh didn't have time for this shed, but here they were.

He was ready to let it rest for the night. He would deal with the inevitable fallout later. The Prince had been so terrified he'd nearly pissed himself. Perhaps his warning to his father might stall a confrontation for the time. Gilgamesh slipped past the animal hide covering to where Abgal stood at the door. "Lugal."

"Have the Umma soldiers tended to their fallen?"

Abgal bobbed his head.

"Good. Let's retreat for the night."

They lumbered through the dark, over hills, and firmly back into their territory. After making it back to their tent site next to a river that allowed the men to wash and change into fresh clothing, Gilgamesh walked alongside Hirin. The battle's energy still buzzed through him. The night had passed, and the sun waited just beyond the horizon, the great god Utu, ready to stretch up and spread gold over the land.

"We need people in Umma," Gilgamesh said, "the kind Zage-Si and his ilk won't pay mind to. Traders, builders, those who need to fetch supplies from the north and stop at the city for lodging."

Hirin tucked his hands behind his back, but his gaze had gone far off. "To act as informants?"

"That and more." Gilgamesh patted the shoulders of a few of his men who prepared to tuck into a large tent for a few hours of sleep. He turned back to Hirin and walked towards the King's private tent. "You weren't there to see the soldiers. We've planted doubt of their king, and they begin to see him as the coward he is. We need that doubt to fester, to nurture it with some turns of phrases. When we take their city, it will be easier if they accept the shift of power without resistance. Surely some of the palace advisors can concoct a scheme on this matter."

"Of course, Lugal. I'll see to it as soon as we're home."

"Good."

They'd reached Gilgamesh's tent. The rug covering

rippled in the wind. Gilgamesh smoothed his hand over the fine weaving work that came from his mother's temple. There wasn't one other city, not one other mark of human civilization in the world, that compared to the shining gem of Uruk. And there was no leader that could parallel Gilgamesh's rule. Uruk was the center of the world—and every damn person in the land, from kings down to the youngest laborer—knew it. Feared it, even.

"I've arranged a gift for you, Lugal," Hirin said, pulling Gilgamesh out of his thoughts. The advisor gestured towards the tent. "To celebrate your success."

Gilgamesh's lips pinched down. Hirin's expression slackened as the realization of his miscalculation played over the man's face. The King patted Hirin's arm and let his voice go soft. He couldn't risk alienating him or the advisors he influenced—he didn't need Shamhat in his ear to know that. Winning battles was one thing, running a city another. "You honor me, Hirin."

"Of course, my king. I am blessed by the gods to work for one as great and worthy as yourself." The man bowed low to the ground and rose. Gilgamesh nodded good night and ducked into his tent.

The ceiling was higher than in Ishme-Ea's and Gilgamesh could stretch to his full height. He was glad Hirin's *gift* wasn't in the main room. He needed a moment to take a breath and let calm rush over him before he could face dismissing a prostitute. Gilgamesh had no energy to spare for some creature of flesh. For the way their muscles would go slack as he, with his god's blood, drew near. To face the reality that he was nothing more than a mortal meeting low level urges like a beast.

A foul taste had risen in his throat. He smacked it away and brushed fingers over the braids in his hair. He stepped past more colorful, draping cloths into the space where his bed stretched out. Amid plush layers of blankets, a man sat wearing a loose robe. It revealed the smooth, sculpted muscles of his chest. He glistened like a jewel, gold ribbons in his hair shining alongside the bracelets that covered his arms.

The man tucked his chin and looked up at Gilgamesh with massive brown eyes, his lips pursing. "Lugal." He bowed low before rising again. His expression was eager— sleeping with the legendary god-born King held bragging rights for prostitutes. Gilgamesh frequently denied coy offers and broke the gazes of pleading eyes. Everyone wanted to fuck a god.

He longed to sigh again. This man wasn't a prostitute Hirin had found in some lodge. The clothing and jewelry he possessed were far too fine for that. He was a man of Uruk —perhaps from a bathhouse in the northern quadrant.

That meant Hirin, despite his protestations and even questioning Gilgamesh in front of his men, had never doubted him. Hirin had known they'd succeed and pre-planned a victory gift. Warmth filled Gilgamesh's stomach and flooded down his limbs. The man continued watching the King, his shining hair loose on his shoulders.

"Take that robe off," Gilgamesh said, his voice husky, "and lie down."

The man obeyed, removing his clothing and dropping bare into the bed. Gilgamesh joined him and found the jar of oil Hirin must have had someone deliver. He uncapped it, and the rich scent of cedar filled the space. He breathed it in deeply, poured some into his hand, and for half an hour he didn't care about anything. Not that the man became weak despite the attempt to pull his god's powers back, that they'd still have to deal with Zage-Si, that he'd watched good men die, that Inanna ruled *his* city, that Shamhat waited for him with her hopes, that his mother did the same, or that everyone in the world looked to him.

For just a few minutes, he felt every bit the god-born, dominant, unstoppable force that would brand his name into history's memory, no matter what it took.

CHAPTER TWO
IF BLOOD WERE ENOUGH

Gilgamesh woke with a gasp. Sweat coursed down his trembling muscles. He threw the blankets back and swung his legs over the side of the bed to rest his feet on the tent's rugs.

It was dark, and his eyes took a minute to adjust. Wind whistled in the distance, and a quiet murmur of guards speaking reached him. All was calm. It was only his dreams tormenting him, stirring trouble.

Gilgamesh wiped his palms over his face. At least the prostitute hadn't been one of those foolish ones hoping to spend the night. He'd done his job and left, the gods be thanked. Gilgamesh couldn't have others seeing him like this.

If his future was his burning purpose, his dreams were his oppression. Unlike the living fools like Zage-Si, he couldn't attack a dream or force it to submit. Gilgamesh was god-born and god-blooded. His dreams weren't the fantastical conglomeration most humans dealt with. They were prophecies. He'd remembered his first one as a child. He'd dreamed that a snake rose from his food, its fangs dripping with venom. The dream repeated itself until one night a visiting guest dropped dead onto the table over dinner. The cook had been poisoning the food, and Gilgamesh's god's blood had saved him. It taught him to take prophetic dreams seriously.

The one he had that night after the battle spelled his doom.

He hadn't received an omen in some time. Now a new image burned in his mind, a precipice the gods had thrown him off, one he'd not overcome.

Gilgamesh dragged his fingers down the blanket's edge, stretched his toes over the rug's bumps. He was awake in the real world, no longer fumbling through dark omens.

He shivered and stood, then found clothes to pull on. He wasn't going back to sleep. The dream didn't leave him, though. It remained, buzzing through his mind as he sat before a fire in the dim morning light. An attendant thrust tongs into the flames and curled his beard. Still it lingered as another attendant oiled his hands and hair. It buzzed through his mind as they marched home, and even as the walls of Uruk—his glory—came into view, he couldn't shake it.

He'd have to see his mother and ask her what it meant. His god's blood annoyingly gave him prophetic visions but not the ability to interpret them.

It was late afternoon by the time they reached the city. They'd marched through Uruk's undulating farmlands for hours. Once their party reached the slosh of oars in the river and crested a hill where they could see sails fluttering above the river in the distance, Gilgamesh truly felt home.

He paused, and the group stopped with him. Hirin stood at his side and smiled. Everyone seemed to release a collective sigh.

Before them the city's new walls stretched out grandly —a ballast against the rest of the world. They weren't just practical; Gilgamesh had spared no expense in hiring craftsmen and artists who'd carved statues to stand watch along them, etched designs into the bricks, and decorated them with colorful mosaics.

Within the walls, courtyards in the center of each home offered splashes of green that broke up the tan buildings. Inanna's Ziggurat—a steeped stone tower designed to elevate the grandest temple in all the world—gleamed in the sunset as Gilgamesh's palace sat proudly on the city's other side.

Uruk was a gem nestled into the world's heart. The sweeping blue of the Id-Ugina river curled around it like a necklace.

The gods had formed Uruk for their use. They'd wanted a city to live in—somewhere to eat and rest. Then they'd crafted humans to serve them, to keep their temples and make offerings. Gilgamesh wasn't human, though. He was a god, and this was his city.

A grin spread his cheeks wide. "Welcome home, men of Uruk!" he cried, and his soldiers shouted and whistled.

Laughter rumbled his voice as they continued across the massive bridge that spanned the river and reached the city gates. Craftsmen had decorated them in gold, emerald, and crimson tiles so some portion sparkled the entire day. On either side of the gate, massive statues sat, guarding the city.

To the right—Gilgamesh frowned as his eyes swept past it—a statue of Inanna perched with her clawed talons and sweeping wings, her curves accentuated, her gaze looking out over the river. To the left was the statue of Gilgamesh. His likeness had an ax in one hand, and a roaring lion tucked under his other arm. His gaze focused on the path, as if to threaten those who might cross into his city with ill intentions.

Crowds parted as their group passed through the gate's shade. Hirin scrambled next to Gilgamesh, trembling as the god's blood touched him but keeping his voice steady. "You'll visit Inanna before returning to the palace, Lugal? Shall I send others ahead to announce your arrival?"

Gilgamesh stopped walking. He kept his expression even as citizens peered around guards to see their king. All of Uruk worshiped Inanna; he couldn't allow his distaste to rise to the surface despite the way her name made him want to retch. He raised his hand and shouted victoriously. His soldiers echoed his cry.

People cheered and clapped.

Everyone wanted to have a god for a king, to know the safety he could provide.

Inanna didn't do this for the people of Uruk. She didn't fight battles, know their names, or build walls to protect them. She stayed in the city, enjoying people's service which she never repaid. Lutists sang their songs, and her priests had endless stamina for filling tablets with praise-filled poetry. But it wasn't Inanna who won wars or negotiated better trade deals or protected their people.

It was Gilgamesh.

And before he died, that legacy would burn into history's memory.

Gilgamesh started walking again and shook his head. "No. I won't visit her this time."

Hirin's color paled, and he swiped his palms over his crimson robe. "My King, if I may..." He clenched his teeth and wrung his fingers together as they continued along the main road. Gilgamesh met as many eyes as he could, waved at children who giggled, nodded to each guard posted along the path.

His people.

His city.

"It's only," Hirin continued in a quiet voice, "you'll offend Inanna and the people—they will notice."

Gilgamesh ground his teeth together. It was a bad habit—a mortal habit. He couldn't seem to give it up. "I believe a man has a right to visit his mother—who, may I remind you, is also a goddess—and his wife. To let them know he lives before visiting Inanna's temple, does he not?"

"My king I would never suggest... I mean to say, I wouldn't... That is, of course you have the right, Lugal, forgive me. I only mean to advise you as you've asked."

Gilgamesh ran a hand over his beard. His attendants hated it when he did that. Not that they said so. The glint in their eyes, the way they would bite the tips of their tongues as they attempted to fix the twists gave their feelings away. Touching them uncoiled the curls. It wasn't really his problem, but he didn't wish to sit with his attendants fluffing and styling him longer than necessary, so he dropped his hand and vowed to let that habit go the way of teeth-grinding.

"You make a valid point, Hirin."

Gilgamesh kept the nervous man near for a reason. Hirin was loyal, and he had the ear of every important leader in the city. His sibling was a priest for Inanna, he'd married a woman from the city's southern portion, and his family was well connected in the northern quarter. He understood the city's thrumming heart and how gossip coursed through and shaped canals of division. And how to bind them back together.

"Send a group of messengers with formalities on my

behalf. Play up my"—he ran his tongue over his teeth to wipe the grime of what he was about to say away—"mortal weaknesses to Our Lady in Heaven. Tell her I'll visit, but I beg for a rest first. I'll offer sacrifices in thanks for our victory tomorrow."

Hirin nodded. His shoulders dropped and his nervous fidgeting stalled. That would satisfy, then. They continued weaving through the city. News of their arrival had beaten them to the hill where the palace and his mother's temple sat. Musicians played as crowds clapped in rhythm and shouted their praises.

Gilgamesh nodded, kept his shoulders rolled back, gestured around to acknowledge his men who deserved the praise more than him. They didn't have god's blood to protect them, yet they fought valiantly.

When they reached the courtyard, Gilgamesh thanked each of them individually, shaking hands, and offering words of praise.

Maru, your sword swing has improved; I'd love to practice a round together during training.

I don't know how I'd function without your calm approach, Abgal.

On and on, making sure he complimented every one of the hundred. These were his men, his glory. There were no other fighters in the world who could stand against them. That would be true even if Gilgamesh and his powerful blood weren't around. He wanted to impress his respect and appreciation on them until it left permanent indentations. He wanted to make sure that everyone within the palace heard of their feats and bravery.

That done, he stepped towards the group who'd waited through the long process. Dozens of servants and priests and musicians clustered around, but it was the woman standing in the center who drew Gilgamesh's eye.

Shamhat wore a crimson tunic, a single tawny shoulder bare. Dozens of jewels graced her neck, large hoops hung from her ears, and a gold headdress decorated with stars topped her dark braided hair. She always appeared a queen —beautiful and strong and distinguished. If his soldiers and advisors were the blood of his empire, she was the heart. She kept everything in motion and made him damn proud.

He kneeled before her, offering a hand. "My queen."

Shamhat's lips—painted a red that matched her dress —quirked, but nothing else about her expression broke. "My king."

"Would you join me?" He rose and gestured to the hall that led to each of their chambers.

"I would be honored." She turned towards her advisors and whispered something. When she faced him again, he offered his arm which she accepted.

They walked the long halls in silence. Gilgamesh always noticed the palace's beauty more after traveling. So few places in the world had basic irrigation or buildings beyond mud huts. Yet Uruk had pipes to run wastewater away, cone tiles to decorate the halls in intricate mosaics, cloth woven in his mother's temple that was the envy of the world, and private courtyards in every home in the city.

To live in Uruk meant to live in the shade of the gods' blessings.

Servants' and guards' gazes followed him as he walked alongside Shamhat. The King and Queen were the blessed of Uruk, and they guarded their reputation viciously. Once the door clicked in place, Gilgamesh released his wife's arm and dropped onto a high couch, letting his head fall onto the cushion. He scratched at his beard, undoing the intricate coils.

Shamhat smirked and leaned against the wall. "Another victory, I hear? And you managed not to slaughter the entire army. I applaud you."

"Only for your sake. You should have heard the impertinence of the little prince pup Zage-Si sent in his stead. I could have beheaded the bastard."

"A prince needs guidance to learn his place."

Gilgamesh scowled and met Shamhat's gaze but refused to take the bait. It was an old argument and not one he intended to humor. "Did I miss anything of interest while I was gone?"

"Yes, actually. Pharaoh Narmer sent another envoy with gifts."

"Already? Did he send anything good?"

Shamhat's lips twisted. "You know the Pharaoh only sends lovely things, and you also know I've neither opened the gifts nor promised any nobles bounty from them without you here."

Gilgamesh scratched at the beard some more. "You're too good to me."

"True."

He laughed and stretched out farther on the couch. His massive bed was in the next room, layered with dozens of pillows and fine blankets. Despite that, he couldn't find the energy to move. He was finally home and able to release all the roles he played for a few minutes.

"I've already arranged gifts to return once you've spoken with the messenger. I requested more of the woven night sky blankets from Mother Nisun's temple. The Pharaoh especially appreciated those last time according to his messenger."

"Has his daughter prepared a message for him?"

Shamhat sat on a stool then crossed her legs into an elegant line that contrasted with the side-eye she gave him. "Yes, Kara has dictated a tablet for her father as well."

"Good." He grinned until Shamhat sighed and joined him. She hated when he called Meritkara 'the pharaoh's daughter' as though she wasn't technically married to Gilgamesh. As though she wasn't one of Shamhat's cherished partners.

"Speaking of your wives,"—Gilgamesh tensed at Shamhat's inflection. He didn't like that tone—"you have another marriage approaching."

He groaned and jumped to his feet, ripping his shawl off and tossing it on the floor. He walked to the bedroom, and Shamhat followed. Her steady footsteps promised he wasn't getting out of the conversation. Passing the bed, he moved through another carved and painted door frame into the washing chamber and shucked his tunic as well.

If only nudity would make his wife go away. She blanched in the face of nothing, though, and certainly not his immodesty.

She leaned against the doorframe, arms crossed, her dark eyes pinched. He removed his loincloth and grabbed a pail of water from the corner to dump over himself and let the rush of the water drown out life's demands for a moment.

Technically, an attendant was supposed to pour the water, hold the oils, and wash the royal body. Gilgamesh shuddered as he grabbed a bar of soap and started scrubbing. He prayed Shamhat would leave, but she remained steadily at the door until he'd dumped another bucket, washing away the grime of travel.

"You know ignoring me doesn't make this marriage disappear?"

"Are you certain?" He dropped on a bench and stretched his feet out. Water flowed down the angled floor to the drain in the room's center. "It's not a method I've tried yet."

Shamhat clicked her tongue and pushed off the wall so she could place hands on her hips. "You're the one who wants to expand the reach of the city, create alliances—"

"We could do this by shedding blood, but you won't allow it."

She glared but continued speaking as though she hadn't heard his comment. "And leave a lasting impression."

"I'm tired of all these wives. Shed, you act as though I'm a bull good only for fighting and fucking to produce more offspring. I have twelve children—I'd say we've secured the city."

"You have fourteen." Her lips thinned but then spread into a wicked smile. "And as far as political alliances go, that's exactly what you are. If you want Nipurash and their wealth of timber to join your realm of influence, you'll marry this bride and make good on your promises."

Gilgamesh dropped his head to the wall and rocked it towards Shamhat. "Does this girl want a *legitimate* marriage?" Was it too much to hope she'd be like several of his wives who'd happily passed on bedding him and went to live pampered and entertained in the Queen's palace? The only wife who stayed in his palace was Shamhat. Well, and Meritkara occasionally because of her relationship with Shamhat. Their other partner, Akkiru, also stayed because Shamhat, unlike Gilgamesh, got whatever she wanted all the damn time. Gilgamesh rolled his eyes, and

Shamhat frowned at him as though he'd directed the gesture at her.

"She's an adult, not a girl. Her family visited while you were gone and made it clear they are eager to have a blood connection to the great god-born Lugal Gilgamesh."

So they wanted an heir to Uruk's throne which meant he'd have to bed the damn girl. He'd rather spend a dozen moons marching in foreign lands. "Damn the gods; don't they see there are already many in line for the throne? Their ambitions are misplaced."

Shamhat's words turned sharp. "They know you've claimed none to succeed you and that not one of your many children have inherited your god's blood. Perhaps they hope"—she bit through her teeth—"she'll succeed where your other wives have failed."

Gilgamesh stood, grabbed a fresh loincloth, and wrapped it around himself before stepping over to his queen and gripping her shoulder. "If they think my *wife*"—he had many wives technically, but truly only one, and only one queen—"has failed me, it's because they are fools. Uruk would fall without you."

She took a breath, rolling her shoulders back, but something as fragile as untied beadwork glittered in her eyes. "If only our son pleased you as much as I do."

"Shamhat."

She raised her hand to stop his words and pulled away from the touch. "I spoke with the girl while she was here, and I think she'll fit well once she adjusts. She seems amiable and knows several instruments. Akkiru will help her navigate the musicians and find a place in the Queen's Palace."

Gilgamesh wished Usun—their son who had Shamhat's wide brown eyes and the strong slope of her nose—

possessed enough god's blood to stand a chance against the gods should he inherit his throne. It would perfect his plans. He had no control over the child's disposition, and the gods hadn't seen fit to bless him with enough magic to be worthy to them.

Shamhat knew as well as Gilgamesh that every Uruk king coupled with a goddess, and that child became the next king. Their son, for all the attributes Shamhat regularly reminded Gilgamesh he possessed, would never suit.

Gilgamesh could marry as many mortals as he wished.

But divine marriages were distinct.

He could pledge himself to only one divine. That would seal their fates together so their child would rule his city and glorify his mother's name. A divine marriage was irreversible.

Inanna wanted that with Gilgamesh hungrily.

Or, rather, she wanted his vow and his child.

Wanted Uruk for her glory. Then she'd end him like she'd done to his father when the man rejected her. Instead, he'd chosen Gilgamesh's gentle mother, the goddess Ninsun. Inanna wasn't willing to take the slight.

Gilgamesh walked a delicate path in putting her off. The moment they had a child together, his life was forfeit. He didn't mean to give it up until his legacy was so tightly secured into the tapestry of history, fate couldn't pull it loose without unweaving the world. He'd negotiate with ignorant kings, deal with selfish gods, and fight to his last breath. If blood were enough, he'd give every drop he had. It would take more, but Gilgamesh thought he was up to the task.

He'd keep delaying Inanna without angering her too greatly somehow. For the moment he returned his gaze to his wife and grinned. "I win."

Her frown puckered her lip. "You win?"

"You called this new bride a girl." He poked her in the ribs. "I win."

She huffed, snatched his discarded tunic, and flung it at him. He caught it and laughed.

"You're a dick."

"Aw, the loving words every man wants to hear his wife say after he returns home from battle."

She sashayed through his room, the beads on her clothing clattering. "I hope this *girl* is a pain in the ass and wants to grace your bed every single night for months."

Gilgamesh dropped his shoulder against the doorway leading to his sitting room. "You could slap me if you wish to take out your frustration instead of being mean."

She whirled around. "I prefer to actually hurt you."

"Well, you've accomplished your goal."

"Good." She reached the bedroom door then stopped, her fingers spreading over the copper embellishments. Her voice turned soft. "I spoke to your mother about you, Gilgamesh. I requested she intervene on your behalf."

Gilgamesh stood to his full height again. Only gods—including his mother—could alter history, change fate. "You did what?"

Shamhat looked back. All the teasing was gone from her demeanor. Instead, the Queen stood before him. The woman who ruled their city in his absence. Her lips a thin line that meted out judgment. Her chin lifted at an angle that dared another to underestimate her.

"You focus too much on the future," she whispered. "You have everything right now, yet you can't see it. I asked Mother Ninsun to help give you perspective and see all you're missing."

"Shamhat," Gilgamesh said her name like a sigh. She

shouldn't have meddled with gods, not even with his mother. The last thing they wanted was divine beings dabbling in their lives, getting too close, spoiling all their plans.

She raked her eyes down him, flicked them away dismissively, then met his gaze once more. It was the look one bull gave another—a challenge. His nostrils flared with a breath, but she didn't break the contact.

He huffed. "You women are going to be the death of me."

"No, Gilgamesh." She pulled the door open. "You're going to be the death of you if you don't heed the words of those who care. Happiness is here. You have a healthy family, more heirs than a king could want, a city that worships you, the gods' favor, loyal soldiers, the wealthiest, most beautiful place in the world to rule, and you live in the most advanced time in history. Yet you're never satisfied."

"I have to make my name last." Gilgamesh raised his hands as if to show her they were empty, that he had nothing tangible for all his toil. "I'm mortal enough that death will catch me soon, and what do I have to show for it?"

She lifted her face, her jewelry clattering. "The fact that you can't answer that is your greatest issue, my king."

She left, the door clicking shut behind her.

CHAPTER THREE

IN THE FOREST OF INNOCENCE

ENKIDU RESTED his elbow against his knee and set his chin on his hand. His beard itched, but he didn't shift. Before him the lake glistened under the rising sun. Monkeys screeched as they jumped between cedar trees, the massive limbs jostling with their motion.

A wood pigeon moaned, and a turtledove who sounded sorry for the creature, cooed a response. Enkidu sighed as the warm sun splashed over his skin, making the dark hair on it glisten copper in spots.

The snapping of sticks didn't draw his attention away from the soft grass' pleasure, the lake's gentle lapping on the shore. The steps approaching were familiar, and the creature made those noises to announce his approach. The wolf leapt over a patch of grass and settled beside Enkidu.

Are you still here? the wolf asked. His coat always shone red, but in the sun the strands glimmered brilliantly, contrasting the ebony that followed his spine and down his tail. *Do you not plan to find food?*

"I've not hungered yet, and the morning is lovely."

Enkidu leaned on his hands, stretching his spine. "Besides, I'd rather sit and listen to the forest's sounds. The crickets hum so pleasantly."

The wolf flicked his ears back. *The pack has already felled an antelope and feasted well. We rest once our work is complete.* He gave a few lazy licks of his paws as if he could taste lingering fat and gristle before continuing. *It's odd of a human to not scurry constantly.*

Enkidu turned towards the wolf. "What is it that makes me a human?"

The wolf had always addressed him as such but when he spoke of other humans it was with disdain, his lips curling around his teeth.

You look like one aside from the horns on your head. Though, you don't don dead skins and live in holes cut from mud pits. The Creator chose for you to be human.

Enkidu leaned over where he could see his reflection in the water. The warm brown skin of his face was smooth apart from a black pelt of hair on his jaw. Dark strands of hair ran over his arms and legs and across his broad chest, but he didn't have fur that others in the forest possessed. He ran a hand over the short horns that arched back into his thick locks.

"Should I live among humans, then?" Enkidu asked. A frown pulled down his lips. He belonged there among the wild, listening to the birds chattering and helping the wolf.

I cannot say where you belong. You were once not here and now you are.

"When did I arrive in the forest?"

The wolf's ears pressed down again. He wasn't a creature who appreciated time in the manner Enkidu could. To the wolf there was now and later today. There was hunting and den and pack. There was mating and protecting. For him the world centered on the scrumptious taste of still-warm fat or the pleasure of nails long enough to reach an itch. There was survival and territory. Yesterday, though, was difficult. Many yesterdays more so.

For Enkidu, time stretched out like dew along a grass blade, one droplet stacked next to another. His origins were murky, however. He remembered nothing beyond waking one morning in the forest, a cool breeze kissing his bare skin.

Oh. The wolf whined. *There is something I'm supposed to tell you. I suppose I forgot.* A dragonfly flitted by, and the wolf snapped at it but missed. *A female human will come into the forest and offer you food. You must accept it. When you do, you will lose the wild.*

Enkidu sat up and dusted his hands. He regretted starting this dreadful conversation. "I won't accept, then. Better to stay here." He lifted his face to sunshine that streamed through the trees, the warmth caressing his skin. Perhaps he'd take a nap and search for food later. He'd found a bush thick with berries the day before and fish snapped greedily at bugs in the lake. The idea of a thick catfish paired with a clutch of sweet berries had saliva filling his mouth.

It is your duty. The wolf's voice turned grave. If there was anything the creature believed in, it was in obligation to pack, to one's place in the cycle of life.

Something within Enkidu rattled at that. It was warm and sat low in the pit of his stomach. But it was buried, as though a creature had shuffled it under dirt and planned to unearth it later.

"I have no pack." The same warm thing roused at this

idea as well, but just as quickly quieted. "Who do I owe duty to? Where do I belong?"

Enkidu had never had these thoughts before—or at least he didn't believe he had. He possessed brief memories of *before*. At first, he thought he was like the wolf. 'Today' was the only time that mattered. Later, as moons rose and fell repeatedly, he realized he was different—he'd only lacked a *before* for reflection. Now he had many yesterdays to think of—though none of them offered the answers he sought.

You ask human questions. The wolf growled, and flicked his tail against the dirt. *Your duty now is to the forest and the creatures. Later*—the wolf scrunched his nose, like thinking of time beyond the present ached—*your responsibility will belong with the humans. However, it's a simple matter, is it not? Your purpose is whatever lies before you.*

Enkidu snapped a river reed and twisted the stem around his finger. That answer didn't satisfy, though he couldn't explain why. "What needs my attention now? How could I help the forest's creatures?"

The wolf sighed and dropped his muzzle onto his paws. *The greatest issue is the forest's imbalance. Humbaba hungers ceaselessly.*

Humbaba. The woods chittered that name in low, suspicious tones. Every creature knew another who'd met their fate under Humbaba's fearsome claws or beneath its violent jaws. "We hunger and eat as well. Is it wrong?"

It is not wrong to fill a hungry stomach. Humbaba kills without discretion, however. It ends any life that crosses it because it can.

"Where did it come from?"

The wolf sat up again and shook his coat. *It's god-formed, like you.*

"Perhaps that's my role. I'm supposed to kill Humbaba and restore balance to the forest."

The wolf sneezed then cocked his head to the side, his golden eyes skimming over Enkidu as if taking his measure. *No one can kill Humbaba, though many have tried. If you long for purpose*—Enkidu realized he did, that it was the desire he hadn't been able to name that burned his gut—*we have another issue you might handle. A human hunter strains the forest with his clever traps. He takes more meat than is reasonable and creates stress for the pack, for the panthers and foxes and boar. I don't begrudge any hunter his fill. But this one—like so many humans—takes far more than he needs.*

"Will you show me the traps?"

The wolf rose, stretched his paws, and yawned. The creature would probably rather lie in the sun's warmth and let his food digest, but he hopped up and jogged along the lake. Enkidu followed. The forest buzzed, sunshine glistened on water, and a snake slithered through grass, pressing it down. A thousand details existed in each moment.

The world was beautiful.

It would be perfect if Enkidu could get rid of the burning ache that grew with each sunrise.

The wolf slowed when they reached a shady place then stopped behind a massive cedar tree. Moss grew along the side. The forest's rich, woodsy smell filled the grove they'd stepped into. Sunshine fell over the ferns and coppery dried leaves in golden stripes.

A whine left the wolf, and Enkidu followed his gaze to the sleek, black form of a panther pacing a small circle. Its tail flicked wildly, and a growl rumbled its chest. It tugged at a rope that had tightened around its paw. The beast had pulled at it so much that blood crusted the fur.

Enkidu stepped forward, a twig snapping.

The panther whirled, baring its teeth, a scream spilling past long canines.

Enkidu raised his hands. "I'm here to help you."

Help me, the panther hissed. *Your kind caused this.*

The wolf leapt into the clearing next to Enkidu and nodded at the panther. Her golden eyes flicked between the two; she sat with a sigh and lifted the bound paw. Enkidu eased towards her. He crouched on a single knee so he could jump up if needed and unknotted the rope.

The panther pounced away as soon as her paw was free and sank into long grasses, her golden eyes fixed on them. After a moment she raised her head. *I have cubs. I won't soon forget this, Wolf. My children will know it too.*

The wolf bowed his head, and the panther threw her powerful body into the forest.

The warmth in Enkidu's gut brightened. This was something useful, some way he could improve the lives of others. He turned towards the wolf. "Well?"

The wolf sighed—likely still longing to stretch out in a patch of sunlight by the lake and wondering why he'd encouraged their course of action. He rustled his shoulders and led the way, Enkidu following.

Over the course of the day, Enkidu lifted dozens of small nets that held birds and broke six different reed traps to release frightened animals within. A family of rabbits rushed away without a word of thanks. Apparently Enkidu and the Wolf were not a comforting sight.

As the sun started easing down the other side of the sky, a whistle—unnatural and off-key—echoed through the forest. The wolf pressed his ears back. *The hunter is coming to check his traps. We should go.*

"Go?" Enkidu frowned. This human had littered their

woods with snares. Like the wolf said, this wasn't to sate his hunger. He had hundreds of creatures snagged in his machinations. Why would one man—even a hunter for his pack—need so many? He was disturbing the forest's balance. "No, the hunter should go."

The man walked around a tree. He had a tiered, layered fur pelt wrapped around his waist. His dark muscles flexed as he bent over a broken trap and cursed.

The heat in Enkidu's stomach rose, growing until his chest had grown hot and his teeth pressed together. This man didn't belong in his forest. Enkidu burst out of the brush, landing with a pounce on his hands and feet, parting his teeth like the panther and roaring.

The hunter stumbled back, his mouth flying open as color drained from his skin.

"Leave my forest," Enkidu growled.

"Y-you speak?"

"I won't ask again." Enkidu rose to his full height. He'd never seen a human before, but he stood head and shoulders over the hunter who seemed remarkably delicate. His skin was bare of fur, his hands lacking claws, his teeth small, flat things.

"Y-yes." The hunter stepped back, tripped over a rock, and landed with a thud. He stumbled to his feet to move backwards a few additional steps before turning and bolting through the forest so birds jumped out of bushes, crying out amid trembling leaves.

The wolf slunk next to Enkidu and sat.

"There." Enkidu dropped beside him. "We won't see him again."

The wolf snorted. *Humans don't understand boundaries, Enkidu. They get involved in things they should leave alone.* The wolf turned his golden eyes on Enkidu as he snapped his tail. *If there's one thing a human can't stand it's something they haven't yet conquered and destroyed.*

Enkidu sighed and turned towards the empty path the hunter had dashed through. If Enkidu was actually a human, he vowed to never become that sort. He could never respect a creature with ceaseless ambitions.

CHAPTER FOUR

OF MOTHER AND SON

GILGAMESH KICKED up water as he stepped into his mother's temple. It didn't perch on a grand ziggurat like Inanna's, but Gilgamesh liked it far more. Cone tiles decorated the courtyard in a dozen shades of blue. Trees shaded the walk as water ran down walls, pouring over the ground.

It was like walking into the wild, the hum and bustle of the city beyond cut off behind gentle splashing.

As he passed through the temple doorway which was decorated in ivory tiles that formed cow horns, Gilgamesh nodded to a priestess and crossed the threshold into the inner chamber. He blinked, adjusting to the dim light. Water bubbled from the center of the tile floor, spilling across the mosaic of cattle and sheep grazing upon hills. More splashed from the hands of Ninsun's statue, her expression gentle.

Gilgamesh lifted incense to the lone torch. The block caught flame, and Gilgamesh dropped it into a bowl as the herbal smell filled the room. If he closed his eyes, he could imagine himself in the heart of a forest or standing upon a hill with a shepherd looking out at Uruk's vast wealth of livestock.

"Son."

Gilgamesh turned at the voice and smiled as he approached his mother. A strip of cerulean fabric bound her dark curls back, and she wore a layered tunic, her hooved feet dipping in the water below it. The hem wasn't even long enough for royalty, much less a goddess. She'd always been far too humble.

Pulling him into an embrace, she smoothed her hand over his hair. When he visited, he always lingered. He'd done so even as a child when attendants ushered him in, and his mother swept him into her lap, tucking his curls behind his ears.

She stepped back and sat on a bench, patting the side so he dropped beside her. "Shamhat"—she raised her eyebrows—"has visited me three times this week."

Gilgamesh grunted. "You knew she was better than me when you picked her for my bride." He nudged her arm. "And you were right, as always."

Chuckling, she clasped his hand. She was divine yet chose to keep her form delicate and soft, her hands half the size of his. "So, tell me son, what is it you need?"

Gilgamesh readjusted his tunic. The hem dripped water, and he pushed it off his ankle. "I've had a dream."

His mother stilled. She was always reluctant to interpret his dreams. It often felt like she and Shamhat stood against his aspirations more resolutely than his enemies, though he knew they cared for him the deepest. Why they fought him achieving his purpose, he never understood.

She ran her fingers over the rise and fall of his knuckles. "Tell me the dream, and I'll do my best to interpret what I can."

"You can interpret as much as any other god. You guard your words like a king's tomb."

Water trickled, echoing off the sparkling walls. Gilgamesh had asked his mother once if she'd prefer a larger, more ornate temple, and she'd shaken her head. *I would miss this one's beauty. Your father knew what I liked when he built it for me.* So he'd let it go. Compared to Inanna's new home which sat elevated like the sun in the heavens of Uruk, it seemed a slight.

"Chasing these prophecies will only hurt you, son." Ninsun placed her hands in her lap and met his gaze. "Constantly striving, grasping at chaff in the wind. This will be your downfall."

Gilgamesh's eyes shot up, but he forced them not to roll. He wouldn't tease and huff at his mother the way he did his wife.

Ninsun frowned. "What is your dream?"

He could cage the images within his mind, stand and thank her for her time, walk back into the sunshine and the courtyard's false waterfalls. However, the visions had haunted him since the morning after the battle. The same dream had revisited him each night since then, and he always woke with his muscles tensed and a sweat-slicked forehead.

Whatever half answers she might provide wouldn't be more confusing than the images themselves.

He leaned on his knees. "I'm walking in the cedar forest until I feel a pebble in my boot. I stop to dislodge it, and when I do, the pebble grows in size until it's larger than me and begins rolling towards me. Running, I attempt to evade it, but it gains speed. My heart pounds as I try to escape, and all the while it's gaining size. Then suddenly it stops, and it's no longer a boulder but a massive mountain. I climb it, and at the top, I can see the entire world. From up there, it's as though I finally understand the secret to life. Then a storm begins, and lightning strikes the mountain. It cracks and shrinks so rapidly; I struggle not to fall. When I reach the ground, it's nothing more than a broken rock, and I fall upon it and weep."

His words had grown breathless with the telling. His mother remained quiet. When he turned to look at her, he froze. Her eyes were distant, her brow bunched, her lips pale and thin. He'd been right. The dream was about his legacy. It would start as a difficult feat to achieve before growing into something so tremendous he'd believe it would never break. But something would happen, and it would crumble to nothingness. Just like his father and grandfather. History already ate away at their memories.

A shimmering light glimmered across his mother, making her skin as radiant as the palest blue sky, her eyes as dark as deep waters. "You will face a trial, Gilgamesh." Her voice was not his mother's but something far more ancient. "It will test the mettle of your soul, yet you will overcome." At this Gilgamesh leaned closer to her, his pounding heart picking up speed. "You shall gain what you desire but lose that which matters more."

He'd gain his desire. His name would become immortal. Ten thousand moons from now, humans would lift a tablet and see his name scribed on it, his glorious legacy still burning brightly in their minds.

Nothing could matter more than that.

"Then you will—" His mother snapped her mouth shut, and the glowing diminished.

"You stopped," Gilgamesh said.

His mother fluttered her lashes until her eyes returned to their regular inky darkness. "I've told you enough. Maybe too much." She grabbed his hand again. "Perhaps the most difficult thing about being a parent is wanting to give your child whatever they desire, but knowing doing so could hurt them."

He shifted on the bench and nodded. She'd told him the only important thing from the prophecy. Gilgamesh's legacy would last forever. The dream's stone couldn't be his heritage, then. It must represent the trial he'd have to overcome. He sucked in a breath and rolled his shoulders back. His mother already relayed that he'd overcome. Nothing else in life could touch him. He was strong in body and spirit, and his deeds would last forever.

Pacified, he turned towards his mother. "My wife tells me you're conspiring with her against me."

"For you. Not against." Her gaze drifted towards the incense bowl where woodsy smoke curled into the chamber. "Shamhat worries about you, and she's right. You will need a helper." She paused as if to consider her words. "Someone who will enable you to endure the trials coming. Shamhat will receive a sign when it's time to find him; it's her role to bring him to you."

Energy flooded Gilgamesh's chest. He could float. Of course his mother and Shamhat wouldn't stand against him—no, they fought for his purpose even when he was too much of an ass to see it.

"It's something to do with Inanna, isn't it?" Gilgamesh asked. "The trial I'll face?"

Ninsun rose, her hooved feet disappearing in the water which her ruffled skirt skimmed. She moved before the incense and took a deep breath. "Inanna has always caused trouble for the kings of Uruk. Remember, she is Anu's daughter and untouchable."

His mother's voice was small and sad. It was a reminder

of something that shocked the gods—Ninsun, divine and eternal goddess, had loved Gilgamesh's father. He'd been only half god, meaning he was mortal. His human weaknesses had allowed Inanna to end him efficiently.

Gilgamesh shuddered and walked over to his mother, pulled her into his embrace. She rested her head on his chest. "Sometimes I am sad to be divine. I will lose everything one day."

Gilgamesh pulled back and looked down at her smooth face. "You're immortal, Mother. You'll lose nothing."

She swept a thumb over his cheek, avoiding the coils of his beard. "I shall lose you, son. And Shamhat. I'm grateful to have Usun, at least, as a memory of you. I pray your line endures forever."

He raised his mother's hands together and kissed the top of her fingers. "Usun will be a son to you when I'm gone."

"He's a good boy." She smiled. "Now, I have promised to speak with Enki regarding prayers he's received on the flow of rivers for herdsmen. I must go, but send my daughter my love."

"Don't worry, I'll remind Shamhat she's still your favorite."

She chuckled and floated up to press a kiss on Gilgamesh's forehead before disappearing. Gilgamesh turned and walked out of the temple in a daze. Priestesses bowed and sun bounced off the tiles, but he acknowledged neither. His legacy would live on. He'd die, of course, there was no helping that. What mattered about him—the great deeds he'd done, the city he'd crafted, the heroic soldiers he'd trained—that would last.

He was so caught in the thought he nearly passed Shamhat without addressing her. She stood in the courtyard, her purple tunic's hem floating around her ankles. "My king?" She said it in a voice that made it clear it was not the first time she'd spoken the words.

"My queen." He kneeled before her, grabbing her hand and pressing a kiss to it. Weavers that worked in Ninsun's temple meandered through the courtyard and watched their rulers, staying far enough back that Gilgamesh's god's blood powers—which he had firmly pulled in—didn't reach. Gilgamesh wouldn't allow them to see him ignoring his queen or disrespecting her. He rose, water dripping down his leg and offered an arm. As she accepted, he continued, "I'm sorry if I didn't hear you the first time you spoke. My mind was distant."

They stepped out of the courtyard, their hems dragging over stone as they walked back towards the palace. "Did you have a pleasant conversation with Mother Ninsun?"

"Indeed." He couldn't help the smile that stretched over his face. He paused and turned towards his queen. "And I must thank you for the helper you're going to fetch for me." He laughed, gripped her by the arms, and swung her around.

Shamhat's mouth flew open, and she looked around at the guards and various palace workers before returning her gaze to him. "I didn't know she would tell you. You're happy about this?"

"Of course." Something uncertain furrowed his wife's brow. "What do you know?" She didn't speak, and he didn't offer her time to think of sweet words before he added, "There's an ill-omen around this helper, isn't there?"

That would explain his mother's reticence as well. This *helper* was probably part of the trial. Perhaps the man would aid Inanna or betray Gilgamesh. He'd have to keep a distance from him.

"No," Shamhat said. He pulled away and walked towards the palace, turning his back on the teeming city behind him. Shamhat rushed to catch up but kept her voice low. "I never said that. You put words in my mouth."

"Fine, then," he grumbled. "Explain to me what your hesitation was over?"

"It was... It's nothing."

He shifted to frown down at her. "Yes, your voice conveys it's nothing. You know, I actually believed you and my mother were on my side for once." He started moving again.

"For once?" she hissed. "Name a single action I've ever taken against you."

"Besides conspire with a goddess?"

"Who is your own mother!"

A group of musicians stepped onto the walkway, lyres and drums in their hands. The rulers both stopped speaking. When the group passed, Shamhat smoothed her tunic. "I gave up the opportunity to become the high priestess to marry you, Gilgamesh,"—he'd parted his mouth to interject, but she shook her head fiercely, causing her gold headdress to rattle—"and I vowed to stand at your side and to do everything within my power to raise Uruk and its king to glory. Almost every action I've taken since that moment has been true to that and it shall be so until the day they lay me in my tomb. Only once did I make a choice not in that vein, and I discussed it with you first. Even then, I was willing to submit my happiness to your desires if you remember."

Gilgamesh sighed and reached for her arm. She tensed but didn't pull away. The night she'd approached him with trembling fingers and a wobbling voice wouldn't leave his memory. He'd never seen his queen in such a state—even in their early days of rule she'd been as steady as the sun. He'd worried she had something terrible to confess. When she'd shared her feelings for Meritkara, he'd laughed in relief and given her his blessing. It was a comfort to think she'd have someone. The season they'd been physically together to conceive their son was the most uncomfortable of their marriage.

He thrust his hands out. Guards stood along the palace's walls, but Gilgamesh couldn't hold back. "And have I not always given you everything you've desired? Name something you wish for, Shamhat, and if I can, if it's within my ability, I will bring it to you."

Her face dropped. "I know."

"Yet, you keep secrets from me with my mother of all beings."

She clucked her tongue, and a sharpness entered her gaze. "Fine. I have a deal to make with you. Come see your son this afternoon—he's training with your soldiers and excelling above his group." Gilgamesh scowled, but she raised a hand. "Then I shall tell you everything your mother told me, which you know is veiled in riddles. Nonetheless, I'll share what it is."

Gilgamesh considered saying no just to prove he could. He sighed—it was hopeless—and offered his arm again. "Fine."

She walked quietly with him until they turned into the courtyard, out of the guards' sight, and she poked him in the ribs. "Looks like I win this time."

He rolled his eyes and looked up at the starry mosaic decorating the arch above. This woman was really going to cause his end.

They passed the courtyard, walked to the back of the palace, and through another set of gates until they reached the soldiers' training grounds. They lingered behind columns; there was nothing that could disturb an activity as much as the King and Queen walking into the middle of it. Especially with Gilgamesh's god's blood giving him away if he stepped too close to anyone. He had it reined in, but couldn't stop its impact fully.

A group of young boys, who'd lived twelve to fourteen summers at most, stood straight-backed, facing their instructor, Abgal. The man's voice echoed off the surrounding stone walls. "If you're disciplined, loyal, and learn to manage your emotions, you will fight as bravely as your king." At this Gilgamesh smiled and Shamhat elbowed him. "You could even become a hero like the great Utnapishtim."

Gilgamesh groaned. He supposed it was correct of Abgal to keep their history alive, but Utnapishtim was the most annoying of his ancestors. The man's only legacy was that a god instructed him to make a boat before a flood. So, he built a damn boat, saved his family and a bunch of animals and seeds, and thus the entire world, Gilgamesh supposed. For that, for building a fucking boat, his name burned through history and the gods granted him immortality.

All Utnapishtim did with his nearly divine status was get on a raft—his only ability being to build things that floated, apparently—and sail away to some dreadful territory to live alone.

A waste.

If the gods granted Gilgamesh immortality, he wouldn't squander it hiding in some gods' forsaken corner of the earth. No, he'd pour his energy into elevating Uruk and creating the grandest civilization on earth. Never would it fall beneath shifting sands.

But the gods didn't grant immortality anymore.

Thanks to Utnapishtim.

So, Gilgamesh didn't care for the man.

Abgal clapped. He, like all the soldiers, were bare chested, only wearing short kaunake kilts that allowed effortless movement as they practiced. Abgal was one of his older men, his skin stretched taut and shimmered with scars. Gilgamesh's chest burned with pride. Never had mortals as fierce and brave lived.

"We'll start with our strongest student demonstrating today." The group parted before Abgal even said a name. "Usun."

The boy stepped forward. Gilgamesh's grandfather had once told him a good bull marked his calf. He hated that the old man might have been right. Usun was one of the younger students in the class—that year was his twelfth summer—yet he already stood taller than others, his shoulders almost too broad for his lean, muscular frame.

He had Shamhat in the wisdom in his eyes, though, in the fine shape of his lips.

Gilgamesh wished Usun was more like Shamhat than himself. It would serve the boy well.

Usun accepted a weighted practice sword and moved into first position. He thrust then shifted flawlessly to second before dashing into third, his back leg sliding behind him. He moved with a dancer's grace.

The other boys' burning envy radiated from them. Of course, they'd expect the King's son to be flawless. Knowing this was the great god-King Gilgamesh's son didn't change their hearts' desires to execute as perfectly. None of them understood the pressure on Usun—how difficult it was to stand in a king's shadow.

Shamhat watched their child with unblinking eyes, her hands fisted over her heart, her lips curling up.

She truly thought he had a chance to take Gilgamesh's throne. It was impossible, and she wouldn't understand until she saw it.

Gilgamesh took several steps forward. "Abgal, may I interrupt your excellent teaching for a moment?"

Abgal raised his face to the King then bowed low, other soldiers around the court and the boys joined. Gilgamesh stepped into the center and those he hadn't marked with immunity to his god's blood shuddered. He offered a hand to Abgal who accepted it while bowing his head again. "My king."

"What a fine job you've done teaching my son." Usun watched his father with wide eyes. Gilgamesh avoided visiting the child. It only flamed Shamhat's hopes which added to her misery. Furthermore, there was always Inanna sitting in the eaves, watching to see if he favored an heir. She'd kill the child if she believed he did.

"Let me see your skills now, Usun. Face me and let's observe how far you've progressed."

The boy blanched, blinking rapidly and turning towards his peers who'd all shifted from looking like young men to children with their bright eyes and uncertain postures.

"If... If that is what you wish, Lugal," Usun said. His voice cracked. He was still a child, though rapidly becoming a man.

"It is."

The boy swallowed and readjusted his posture, shifting into first position. The crowd had grown so quiet that birds chittering beyond the palace walls and the ripple of flags catching in a breeze reached the square.

Gilgamesh stepped across from his son. Across from the child he and his queen had created—who had her quickness and his breadth, her intelligent expressions and his thick hair. The boy was still smooth-faced and slim with a lingering softness new muscles attempted to push away. Gilgamesh didn't doubt he'd grow into a beast of a man. It just wouldn't be in a body that would sit on a throne.

Abgal offered Gilgamesh a practice blade, and he turned towards the boy. He lowered himself into position and allowed Usun to make the first hit. It was a forceful blow that cracked the swords together.

Gilgamesh slammed forward two quick bursts that drove Usun back. He maneuvered well, keeping his eyes on the King while making sure his feet found firm ground.

He had great potential... for a mortal.

Gilgamesh stopped holding back. He whipped his arm around, directing the practice blade in a series of wicked fast strikes—god-fast strikes. Usun parried three, but the fourth caught him unaware and he stumbled, landing with a thud against the ground.

The boy's chest rose and fell in rapid undulations, his sweaty hair clinging to his forehead. Gilgamesh looked down at the boy—the soul he and Shamhat had brought into the world—and his stomach twisted.

He offered the child a hand and pulled him to his feet. Usun backed away and bowed nose-to-knees in the traditional gesture of ceding a fight. His eyes glistened when he raised his face, but his expression gave nothing else away.

Part of Gilgamesh longed to rewind time, to take back the challenge. However, Usun was the only child he'd ever marked immune from his god's blood. Infant Usun who'd been so soft and small. It hurt Gilgamesh when he made the cut on his arm, spoke the sacred words, and smeared their blood together through the baby's wails.

He'd been a fool to favor the child. It drew the gods' attention as they wondered if he would break the tradition of gods' offspring ruling Uruk. He couldn't help it, though. When Shamhat, dark circles under her eyes, the smell of blood still in the air, handed the baby to him, Gilgamesh had loved him.

It was as though she'd handed him every good thing Gilgamesh wasn't—and never would be.

If he raised him as an heir, a god would kill him.

The most loving thing Gilgamesh had ever done for the child was ignore him.

He squeezed the boy's shoulder. His smallest finger fell to the side. For the time, his hand remained larger than the boy's frame, but it wouldn't be that way forever. "You fought with mind and body, Usun. You give credit to your teacher." At this he nodded to Abgal who returned the gesture. "Keep up your excellent work."

The boy lifted his face, and he almost looked like he might cry, but he rolled his shoulders back and inclined his head. "My king."

Gilgamesh pulled away from the child, though he wished he could explain. It would endanger Usun, and he wouldn't understand. A few other young men looked a bit too self-satisfied, so Gilgamesh met their gazes. "Would anyone else like to duel your king?" A hush fell over the already quiet group. "Usun stood through three solid hits. I didn't go easy on him. If any of you think you could do better, step forward."

No one shifted a muscle. Gilgamesh moved towards a few boys who'd had smug expressions moments before, and they trembled and curled into themselves.

Satisfied they'd learned their place, he thanked Abgal again, nodded to each of his soldiers standing among the group, then walked to the back of the square where Shamhat waited.

She stood tucked behind a column, trembling so the golden jewels on her headpiece quivered. Gilgamesh stepped beside her, beyond the crowd's sight, and braced for her fury. This would hurt and he'd known it.

"How could you?" she hissed after a minute of silence that was filled as the boys began moving through positions again.

"You must understand what your mother's heart will not allow you to see. The boy doesn't possess god's powers. A king of Uruk must be able to stand to any threat—mortal or divine. Anyone who can challenge the King for his throne and overpower him can take his place."

"You could change that archaic law." Shamhat's eyes glistened. "You are the King for Anu's sake."

Her bringing up Inanna's father only reminded Gilgamesh of all the reasons Usun could never rule.

Perhaps the most difficult thing, his mother had said in her soft voice, *is wanting to give everything your child desires, but knowing doing so could hurt them.*

Gilgamesh gritted his teeth. His heart ached, but he lifted his chin. "You're right. I'm king and my word is law. And I'm telling you that while Usun may be strong, disciplined, and powerful for a mortal, he will never be king."

Shamhat's nose flared, and the glistening of her eyes spilled over, a tear falling down her cheek. She jerked away, her tunic flying behind her as she stormed back towards the palace.

CHAPTER FIVE

LADY OF HEAVEN, MAN OF EARTH

Shamhat still wasn't speaking to Gilgamesh. She was the even-tempered one in the relationship, so the behavior was rather immature in Gilgamesh's opinion.

He tapped his fingers on his throne's gilded armrest and refused to meet the Queen's gaze. She sat on her throne doing the same. He'd never paid much attention to the room, but it aided him in keeping his attention away from his wife's simmering fury.

The ceiling was open in the center, allowing sunlight to flood into the space and brighten the mosaics running along the walls in cerulean, crimson, ivory, and gold. Light dappled massive stone creatures with bulls' bodies and faces of Uruk's kings. Gilgamesh was halfway through following the mosaic that told the story of Utnapishtim's stupid flood when Shamhat shifted.

She was close enough to touch, though he suspected she'd make an earnest effort at breaking his fingers if he tried. Their advisors were splayed on either side of them. They joined to offer advice but were spending most of their energy that morning pretending they didn't notice the tension between the King and Queen. Hirin had cleared his throat half a dozen times in less than an hour, so the morning was going poorly for everyone.

Gilgamesh wanted to fix things between Shamhat and himself, but he couldn't give her what she desired. For the first time in their marriage, he thought they'd met a barrier they couldn't surpass.

One of them would have to give ground. With his earned reputation as an unyielding asshole paired with her ability to channel anger into cool relentlessness that had won their city dozens of favorable trade deals, they were in for a long stretch of discomfort.

At least they didn't share a bed, the gods be thanked. Poor Meritkara and Akkiru. They would face her tempest when Gilgamesh had ignited the storm.

Mercifully, the door opened. The relief passed when the person stepped down the hall. Their linen tunic and goat-skin shawl marked them as Inanna's. Fuck. The last thing he wanted to deal with while he and Shamhat were at odds was *Our fucking Lady in Heaven.*

The priest continued in measured strides and stopped a respectful distance from the thrones, bowing low, their painted lids gleaming as they rose back into the sunlight. "My king." They turned towards Shamhat. "My queen."

They lingered a second longer on Shamhat. Gilgamesh's lips thinned. Shamhat sat on the throne in his absence. She knew every priest, scholar, and copper merchant in the city. Without looking at tablets, she could recite the number of cattle and sheep, the amount of beer and wool, the hectares of farmland and orchards Uruk possessed. She was the other leg of their rule and with her pulled away from him, Gilgamesh felt unbalanced. In daily interactions, their people favored Shamhat. He'd always known it, but now it stung.

"You have your king's and your queen's attention," he said.

The priest bowed again, and when they lifted their face, a smile stretched their cheeks. It was rare for someone to grin when they stood before the world's rulers, but they worked for Inanna—the only being Gilgamesh had to prostrate himself before.

"Thank you for the audience, Lugal. Our Lady in Heaven sent me to speak with you today. She's feeling neglected." At this the priest caught the eyes of Kasiru, Shamhat's favored musician who once worked in Inanna's temple, before returning their attention to the King. "While she appreciated your offerings, she found your last visit brief. You didn't even speak with her, my king. Though,"—they added sharply before Gilgamesh could respond—"she understands you were tired after battle and admires all you've done for Uruk. She believes there is no mortal who can surpass you, Lugal."

Advisors who'd frowned initially settled, their muscles loosening. Gilgamesh, however, burned. He knew a slight when he heard one. Every soul in the room looked at him, waiting for his reply. Gilgamesh wanted to say the priest and their goddess could fuck off. His mouth ached with the words. Something grazed his knuckles, and he turned. Shamhat looked at him, her fingers resting on his hand. She gave the smallest head shake.

The fire within him sizzled, and he squeezed her hand before pulling away. If she could put Uruk before her anger, he could as well. This was why his mother wanted him to marry Shamhat. She had much of what he lacked. Fighting armies and tearing kings off their thrones was easy. Maintaining and expanding his rule, keeping the delicate strand of political issues balanced, was not.

Gilgamesh cleared his throat. "Tell your lady that I apologize for any misconstrued slight. I shall visit her this afternoon if it would please her."

"It would, Lugal." The priest bowed again. Could they stop with the fucking bowing as though they held any respect for his throne? At least the visit would please Inanna, because it sure as shed wouldn't please him.

They exited the throne room. As soon as the door closed, it opened again and a man walked in. He was bare chested and wore an un-dyed kaunake kilt and simple leather sandals. He swallowed as he approached the throne, guards following. The man ran a hand through his unstyled beard. When he reached the point guests should stop at, the guards dashed their spears ahead to halt his steps.

The man lifted his face to Gilgamesh then Shamhat. His eyes widened so the whites showed. He dropped to his knees then stretched his hands before him, rising and falling several times before getting uneasily to his feet. "My king," he whispered. "My queen."

Finally, someone who properly appreciated the throne.

Gilgamesh raised an eyebrow. He was tired of sitting and listening to priests complain or city leaders squabble. He'd planned to spend the afternoon training with his men but would have to give that up to visit Inanna. His teeth clenched. A pounding beat in his temple reminded him of the nasty mortal habit that caused the building headache.

"I'm a hunter in the cedar forest's southern portion." The man swallowed and placed his hands together before dropping them at his sides. "I was trapping the other day when I ran across a monster who nearly stole my life."

Humbaba. The creature's name murmured through the room. There was little people feared as greatly. Even deities were wary of the creature. The ill-tempered storm god created it in a pique of anger. Now Humbaba terrorized all, mortal and immortal alike.

Shamhat went rigid beside him, her breath catching. Gilgamesh reached for his wife's hand, and she accepted it, tangling their fingers together. Humbaba had killed her family when they'd traveled the northern route. Gilgamesh ruled the greatest city in the world, possessed god's blood, yet had so little control. It was at his in-laws' death and during his queen's inconsolable grief he realized this life didn't matter. He'd die, and he had no control over how or when. But his legacy—that he could press into history. That could survive forever.

"Humbaba has moved so far south?" Gilgamesh asked. If that was the case, the creature had traveled much closer to Uruk. He and his men may have to face the beast. He fought a shudder.

"No, Lugal." The hunter shook his head fiercely. "It was not the dragon creature." Shamhat sighed but didn't release Gilgamesh's hand. Perhaps she'd forgive him—if not that day, then soon. The hunter continued. "The man appeared as a beast, of sorts, but he spoke our language. He's human, I think, if ferocious. He was, if you don't mind me saying, as broad and tall as you, my king."

A hush of murmuring passed among the advisors. Hirin frowned. There wasn't another human alive that matched Gilgamesh's size or strength. It was a sign of his divine origins.

The hunter brightened at the interest and picked up pace with his speech. "He looked like a human—though naked as a newborn babe—except for one thing, my king."

Gilgamesh waited for the man to carry on and shifted in his throne when he didn't. "What would that be?"

The man leaned away, his shoulders hunching, as if he could feel his king's ire rising. "He had horns, Lugal."

Several people gasped, then cleared their throats. Looks were exchanged. Gilgamesh's heart thudded as his eyes shifted towards the bull statue carved with his face and horns atop its head—the marker of divinity.

There was an uncomfortable shuffle. The advisors knew Gilgamesh evaded Inanna's desires. Perhaps she'd crafted a new man to take his throne, his place, his legacy. Gilgamesh's free hand curled around the throne's arm until the wood bent.

Shamhat, however, smiled broadly and leaned towards the King. "This is my sign," she whispered.

Gilgamesh shifted to face his wife.

"This is the man your mother sends—the helper. I'm to travel and get him alone. It's my prophecy."

She said other things, but Gilgamesh didn't catch the words. Ninsun and Shamhat had conspired against him. His mother crafted a man of his size and strength with a visible marking of the gods' favor. They meant to push him off his throne, to punish him. Long had his mother wished he wasn't king, that he didn't draw the gods' attention and the dangers that went with them. Shamhat believed if he wasn't so focused on legacy, he'd be a better man. Fuck self-improvement. His heritage was the only thing that mattered. A wicked man could perish as long as a victorious mythology lived past him.

He rose so quickly the massive throne wobbled. The advisors startled, and the hunter stumbled back, tripping and landing on his ass. Shamhat stood as well, though her gaze was distant. "I'll leave tomorrow," she whispered as if continuing the conversation Gilgamesh hadn't taken part in.

His headache consumed him, pounding so that he had to squint into the sunlight. "Everyone out."

The people stared at him as if they didn't understand his words. The world blurred and blared. He shifted to Hirin. "I want everyone out of this room at once."

"Of course, my king."

The man ushered others away, but Shamhat called after the guard. "Hold the hunter. I need information on where to find the man."

"Shamhat," Gilgamesh said through gritted teeth. "You can't run off into the wild alone."

She turned towards him, raised her chin, and looked him directly in the eyes. She had the same warm, brown irises as Usun. The same eyes that wobbled with tears as Gilgamesh pulled the boy to his feet.

His head might split.

"I most certainly can, my king." Shamhat said the words with venom, something to sink in and kill. "If you remember, I married you young. I never had a chance to travel with the priestesses. I believe the time for my pilgrimage has arrived."

At that, she whipped around, her shawl flowing behind her in a flash of crimson before she left Gilgamesh alone.

Later, his head still ached when he climbed the ziggurat's endless steps. He'd attempted to dissuade his wife and failed. He knew her well enough to recognize when he'd lost a battle. She planned to go and refused to discuss how foolish it was. She'd only listed a pile of things that would need his attention—his new bride would arrive in Uruk within the week, the message to the Pharaoh needed dictating, and he had to host a dinner for the governors visiting on Moon Day.

If she went off into the woods and died, Gilgamesh didn't know how he'd handle it. Perhaps it was the trial his mother mentioned. Maybe that explained the sorrow shimmering over her, the talk of losing those she loved.

The worst part of having god's blood was having the strength to stand among the divine without the ability to control his own life.

Gilgamesh stormed up the steps, his attendants struggling to maintain the pace. Everything was falling apart since he'd started having the fucking dream. He should have ignored it, never mentioned it to his mother, and avoided Shamhat's urging to visit Usun.

All he wanted was for everything to return to how it was.

He reached Inanna's temple where it sat atop the ziggurat. It stretched above his city, and Gilgamesh could see the entire realm, the swaying palm trees, the milling foot traffic, and the glory of his walls curling around it all.

Approaching the temple, he nodded to a priest, and walked through the door. He followed a hall to the center chamber which was covered in floor-to-ceiling colorful tiles and gleamed like he stood inside Shamhat's jewelry box. It only added to the headache.

He approached an incense basin, lit a block, and dropped it with a clack that shifted the container. He wished it would topple and spill ash over Inanna's garish room.

The bronze statue of her reflected so much light it hurt to look at it, but Gilgamesh refused to bow his face. She stepped out of it.

He fought an eye roll. She loved theatrics.

"Gilgamesh," she whispered through plump lips. She swayed her hips as she walked towards him, ebony curls piled on her shoulders. Her outfit looked nothing like the fashion of Uruk—it was made of two panels that flowed in front of her, revealing lush, flawless skin and ample curves. If she had any interest in Gilgamesh's tastes, she'd take a very different form. Inanna only cared about herself, however.

Stepping over to the King, she looked up at him. She kept herself shorter than Gilgamesh—a veil to lure him into forgetting what she was. Her talons clacking the tiles broke the illusion almost as much as the wings that curled around her shoulders.

"My lady." He bowed.

Before he could rise, she had a hand on his chest, another grazing down his stomach. He steeled his muscles to avoid shuddering at her touch. "You didn't come to see me last time you visited, King of Uruk."

Gilgamesh wished he could shove her through the tile floor, down into the ridiculous ziggurat she'd insisted he build along with the new temple and its hundreds of statues. He was proud to have beautiful homes for the gods, but Inanna's demands only grew.

"Forgive me, I was tire—"

"Interesting. I've never seen you as a weak man." She eyed him like a hawk sizing up a kill. That's all he was to her. A body with royal blood, a means to her end. She wanted his city, but she'd drive it into the sands with her demands. "My priests tell me you have another wife arriving soon."

He sighed, and his displeasure didn't take acting. "I must continue to make alliances for Uruk's sake."

She moved closer so her body brushed his. Revulsion

crawled up his throat as she continued speaking. "A more devoted son of Uruk, this city has never had. There's only one thing lacking, and the time has come."

His heart skipped a beat, the headache easing for a moment. He stared at a glimmering ruby tile beyond her shoulder. "What time do you refer to, my lady?"

She stood on the tips of her talons so her lips touched his as she spoke. "Don't play the fool. You're far too intelligent. We will have a son together. Our marriage will take place during the Akitu festival."

Gilgamesh pressed his tongue to the roof of his mouth to stall words. Akitu, New Year, was after the rainy season —only nine months away. As soon as they had a child, she'd end Gilgamesh quickly and set her son up to rule the city.

"I may not be here during Akitu, my lady. We are currently facing tensions at two of our borders and—"

"You will be here." She bared her teeth, yanked a blade free, and jabbed it against his thigh, very close to a more sensitive region. "You will exchange the holy rights with me, binding yourself to me, and we will conceive a son. Then you shall be free to lead your campaigns as you please. Do I make myself clear?"

Gilgamesh had spent countless hours practicing evasive moves. He wondered if he could catch her by surprise, grab the knife and throw her to the glistening tiles. She was a goddess, though. She'd kill him before he could draw a second breath. "Yes," he said. He wouldn't offer more than he must.

"Excellent." She pulled the knife away and slipped it under the slit in her gown. "Another thing. I've been thinking I'd like to have my temple redecorated."

"Your temple is new," Gilgamesh snapped before he

could stop himself. He needed Shamhat at his side, but she was busy being ridiculous and angry, planning a foolish trip to the cedar forest of all the damned places. She'd left him to face Inanna alone. Gods, that woman needed to straighten out her priorities.

Inanna's eyes burned like flames sparked within them. "Not as new as your wall."

He couldn't help the smile edging up his lips at the jealousy in her words. The wall was Gilgamesh's. He protected his people—not Inanna who sat here in her high temple asking for service and offering little in return.

"It's all anyone speaks of," Inanna continued, her voice measured. "But shouldn't the temple of the city's goddess shine the brightest?"

"Would you burden your people so greatly? We have many building projects currently. The labor tax is also much discussed."

She moved in closer to him, her hips swaying. She looked up at him with doe eyes. "That sounds like an issue for the King to unravel." She turned, walking back towards her statue. "See yourself out, Gilgamesh. I'll have a priest visit you by Sun Day to hear your ideas for elevating my temple."

Gilgamesh parted his lips to argue, but she disappeared. He hissed through his teeth, turned, and stormed out of the damned temple he'd prefer to burn to the fucking ground.

CHAPTER SIX

BREAD AND BEER

Enkidu stretched out before the lake and shook his head. The sun hung lazily in the sky, and he settled with it, ready to take an afternoon nap before joining the wolf on a hunt. The pack had sighted a group of antelope and wanted to give chase before they retreated to their den.

Buzzes and chirps filled the air. The heat tucked around Enkidu, making his eyes heavy. Something nipped his arm, and he swatted the mosquito, a streak of blood smearing over the muscle.

Twigs snapping roused him. Enkidu and the wolf hadn't seen the hunter again since he'd broken the traps. They still lay shattered on the forest floor, plants slowly twining their way around the wood and swallowing the rope.

Perhaps the hunter returned. The wolf felt certain he would—that humans were insatiable. Nothing stopped them when they set their minds on a path. Humans made Enkidu think of the monster Humbaba. Why were such creatures favored to live?

Enkidu jumped to his feet, rising to his full height. He

bared his teeth and prepared to roar when he caught the human's expression. Color slipped from her face, but her wide, brown eyes didn't shift away, didn't blink. She wore such bright coverings it made her look like fruit amid the foliage.

He shrank back, stepping into a shrub. For the first time in his life, he was unaware of his surroundings, snapping twigs and nearly stumbling. "You're the woman coming for me," he said, "aren't you?"

The wolf had told him this day would arrive. That she would offer food, and he'd have to accept. That it would steal everything from him. He stepped back, reeds breaking under his heel.

"My name is Shamhat." She moved forward slowly, readjusting the bag she carried, her covering shimmering like new leaves. "The Goddess Ninsun has sent me to you."

The warmth in Enkidu's stomach—the thing that burned with desire and which he'd managed to mostly ignore—burst to life again. Enkidu retreated farther, though, edging around the shrub. He didn't want the truth. He wanted the cool slosh of lake water on bare skin, the soft brush of moss under feet, the comfort of long, lazy conversations with the wolf.

This woman brought knowledge, and that was a curse.

"Please, don't go." She moved around the tree she'd stood behind and stretched out a hand. Shining loops around her wrist clattered together. They were like sticks but glistened like rocks and clanked like nothing he'd heard before.

"Why must you come?" He had plans. The wolf would arrive before the sun kissed the treetops. They'd run together, hearts pounding and lungs aching. They'd kill and eat and sleep. He didn't need more than that.

The woman frowned. She was the loveliest thing he'd ever seen—not that he was attracted to her. No, she didn't appeal to him like a mate, but she appeared soft and bright amid the scrambling wild around her. Enkidu hadn't imagined feeling attracted to another before. The idea wasn't unpleasant, but this woman with her gentle movements and soft voice didn't attract in that manner.

"I don't mean to frighten you."

"It's not you that scares me." Enkidu shuddered. "It's what you bring."

She grabbed the bag at her side and shifted it to her front. "It's only food. It won't hurt you, I swear."

He shivered as his foot dipped into cool water. He could dive into the lake, swim into its murky depths, come up on the other side, and run. She appeared too gentle for the forest. Certainly he could outpace her.

Duty. A voice growled. Enkidu shifted towards the thick bushes along one side of the lake where the wolf's golden eyes glistened.

"I'll be gone if I do this," he said. "You said so yourself."

The woman—Shamhat—looked where he spoke but didn't appear to notice his friend tucked amid the leaves and shadows.

It is your calling, Enkidu. You aren't a coward to run from it, are you?

Perhaps he was. He whimpered before turning back to the woman and taking a step forward. She gripped the bag tighter and planted herself into the ground as if she was convincing herself to stay.

The wolf was right. He wanted purpose, but something in his gut told him this path led to sorrow. Was he a coward? Enkidu sighed and closed the gap between the woman and himself. He wasn't—even if he longed to act spinelessly to stay in the peace of the forest.

The woman appeared smaller as he approached. Her fingers trembled, shaking the bag she clutched.

"D-do you have a name?" she asked.

The choice was made. He would accept his fate and the misery ebbing around it so intensely he could nearly see it. The need for purpose burned fire hot and lightning bright though him. "Enkidu."

"It's a pleasure to meet you, Enkidu." The woman seemed to have gathered herself. She tilted her chin up, any lingering fear hidden beneath her unyielding gaze was gone. Enkidu had never been so near another human. He'd run off the hunter before he could properly examine him. The wolf said Enkidu thought like a human, looked like a human, spoke like a human. He was more like this woman than the wolf. They had the same upright build, similar eyes though his were wider, the same furless faces and long noses. Yet, something separated them. Where Enkidu was massive, with smooth black hair running down his limbs, callused fingers, and strong feet; the woman was softer, cleaner.

"I've brought you a meal." She opened the bag and pulled out wrapped items. "Well, it's not a feast. It's what Ninsun said to bring, however."

"You worship this Ninsun?"

"Yes, and I love her beyond that. She is my husband's mother and a parent to me as well." She was saying words he had little context for. Husband. Parent. This must be similar to the wolf's pack. Something about it felt familiar, like crossing stones he'd walked before but struggled to remember. She unwrapped the first item and a warm, comforting aroma filled the air. Enkidu leaned closer to breathe it in. Never had he smelled such a thing.

She ripped a piece and offered it. Enkidu accepted the food. It dented when he pressed his fingers into it and didn't fully rise back to its form. Enkidu knew fish and meat, wild herbs and fruit. This was new.

And it held his destiny. He looked back at the bush again and caught his friend's eyes. They widened. This was his duty.

He popped a piece in his mouth and let it sit for a moment, the softness melting. Then he chewed and moaned as the flavor spread. "Bread," he said through the bite. He knew it, then, as much as he understood the rhythms of the moon's phases.

"Yes," Shamhat said in the same tone a mother wolf keened at her pup's first catch.

She opened something—a crock, that word was suddenly there too—and dropped a reed into it before lifting it to him. He cupped his hands around the vessel. It had appeared large in her grip but was relatively small clasped in his massive hands. He breathed in the tangy, sweet-smelling liquid. It was cloudy like water the wolf would tell him to avoid. Enkidu ran his thumb over the crock's smooth surface.

"It's a straw." Shamhat pointed to the reed. "Perhaps you haven't used one before?"

A straw. Something else rattled loose in his mind. Yes, he knew what that was. He lowered his lips and sipped the sweet, tangy liquid. His mouth watered as he took another drink then wondered how he'd ever felt satisfied with creek water.

He swallowed and the ever-present warmth in his

stomach burst into heat that burned through his limbs and flashed across his mind.

Enkidu stumbled back; Shamhat shrieked or said something, but he couldn't hear her words.

Strange images flooded through his mind.

Human knowledge—a lifetime of it—roared through him in a rush of flames that burned hotter than a smelting pot. He knew what smelting was, how copper shifted beneath heat. He understood cities, walls, armies, swords, marriage, temples, offerings, clothing, and— He choked, suddenly, horribly aware of his nakedness and found a shrub to hide behind.

Shamhat eased closer and heat rushed over his cheeks. He was naked, standing around in daylight with his body fully on display before a strange woman.

"Enkidu?" Shamhat asked. Another realization hit him with enough force to knock him over, though he remained standing. He had a name but didn't know who gave it to him. He had no mother, father, or family. There was no god he'd pledged his name to or fire he'd grown up around. He was alone in the world—and what a truly terrifying thought that was.

"Please," he said as she drew nearer. "Don't come closer. I'm unclothed."

Shamhat smiled and dipped a hand into her bag again. Enkidu had words for the things she had on now—tunic, shawl, bracelets, sandals. So many thousands of words that bloomed like wildflowers in his mind.

When she rose again, she held a bundle of clothing. Wind whipped through her braided hair and rattled the emerald leaves behind her as she shrugged it away and took another step. "I can help you, if you don't know how."

"I know how." Somehow, he did. His throat tightened

but he reached for the clothing. His cheeks burned, but better to accept a handout than continue walking around naked. He dressed with nimble fingers, his body going through the motions as though he'd done it thousands of times instead of never.

After he had the rich fabric adjusted over his body, the softness of it brushing his skin with each movement, he stepped closer to the woman who stood by the lake. He startled at his reflection. He'd seen it hundreds of times, yet he looked now with fresh eyes.

The man staring back at him had matted hair and a grizzly beard. He brushed his hands through the tangled strands then slid them over the horns on his head. Other humans didn't have horns. What was he? Did a god have a joke and decide to create a monster, something not human and not animal, then gave him consciousness to become aware of it? What a cruel life he led if so.

"If you'll let me," Shamhat said gently, "I could help with that as well." He seriously doubted she'd be able to soothe the crisis cracking his insides apart, but he nodded and followed her. He'd committed to achieving his duty, had promised the wolf, and Enkidu kept his vows.

She led him to the soft place on the bank where Enkidu had lain so contentedly only an hour before. That was gone —like the last of a flower trampled beneath a herd. He sighed as he lowered to the earth and let her wash his hands and face, oil and comb his beard and hair, trim and style him in a way he'd never experienced but felt strangely familiar.

"I do this for my son sometimes, when he allows me." Shamhat spoke with the gentleness of a dove cooing, with a soothing tone that meant more than the words. "He's growing up now, though. He likes his mother doting on him less and less."

Enkidu never had a mother fuss over him. Where there'd once been warmth in his gut, now hollowness stretched. It echoed through him. He had no family, no one to love and no one to love him in turn.

"There, now. Do you feel better?"

Enkidu turned towards the lake and released a shaky breath. He still had the horns—they were even more noticeable with his hair trimmed, the sleek ebony forms of them tucking back against his head. In some ways it was worse.

But Shamhat had shaped his beard, trimmed his hair to his shoulders, brushed gleaming oils into the tresses so they appeared sleek and smooth. He swiped a hand over his cheeks' newly smooth and tender surface. He looked like a human.

"What is my duty?" Enkidu asked.

Shamhat startled when he spoke. He hadn't said anything to her in some time. She lifted the nearly empty bag and gestured for him to join her. He rose, his toes stretching over sandals. They felt right and wrong at the same time—two ideas that didn't fit together with neither side willing to yield.

"What have the gods told you already?" Shamhat asked as they moved away from the lake. Enkidu looked back. He'd probably never see it again.

His heart ached, but he turned to face the woman. "The gods have told me nothing—except a message through... a friend." He fumbled over words. She'd find his relationship with the wolf unnatural. "I was to accept the meal a woman offered me."

"That's all?" She frowned and brushed a fern aside. "I

thought you'd know more. It was I who prayed for you. My husband needs a helper."

"Is it not typical for one's spouse to be their helper?"

Her lips curled into a thin line. "My husband needs more help than one person can offer. He's a good man... most of the time. He's the King of Uruk."

Enkidu stumbled and struggled to turn back to the woman—the Queen. He dropped to his knees and bowed his head. "My queen." Somehow, he knew this was the right response. A cool rush washed over him. The Queen had groomed his hair and seen him naked. It seemed the day would only continue spiraling into misery with each new reveal.

"Please rise." The Queen touched his face again, her fingers soft and smelling of sesame from the oil she'd anointed his hair with. He stood, and she shook her head as she looked up at him. "I didn't believe it when the hunter said you were as large as Gilgamesh—the King, I mean—but he was right."

Enkidu attempted to hold back a frown, but the flare of his nostrils was beyond his control. "That hunter was over-taxing the forest. He had no sense of modesty or apprecia-tion for the lives he took."

Shamhat grinned. "See, this is what Gilgamesh needs. You're here to balance him, help him see how life can be if he stops striving all the time. I'm sorry no one informed you of this, however. It must be disconcerting."

Enkidu sighed. "You've been gracious to me, Nin."

"Please call me Shamhat. I think we're going to be important to each other."

He didn't know how to respond. He'd only had the knowledge of humanity for a few hours—he didn't understand what it meant to be important to another, much less to a queen. "If you wish."

She affirmed she did and ushered them through the woods. Enkidu played her words through his mind like a harp. Music! He'd never experienced music! He struggled with what she meant. The gods had formed him to balance the King. He barely understood being a human. How could he advise a king?

As they made it to a thinner part of the woods, a gray and copper blur shifted between the trees. Enkidu stopped walking and the wolf paused as well.

"I shall miss you, friend," Enkidu whispered.

The wolf whined, growled, and made several short yips. Enkidu took a long breath. He didn't understand the language anymore. His time in the forest was done.

* * *

They walked until the sun set and they'd reached a place milling with people. A few mud plaster buildings sat together and donkeys and their masters creaked along the road. Someone beat a rug and dust rose. A mother yelled for her children. Enkidu hesitated as he sidestepped others weaving along the path.

Shamhat turned back. She'd slowed on the walk and had grown quiet, but her energy bloomed at the sight of people. "Everything all right?"

"There are so many humans here."

She chuckled. "Wait until you see Uruk. This is nothing. It's scarcely out of the wild, but we can get beds for the night and a warm meal at least."

"Why do you call it that? The wild?"

She pursed her lips, uncertainty tightening her expression. In the short amount of time he'd spent with her, he'd already started to recognize her manners. "Have I offended you?"

"No. It's just—" He didn't finish. The forest made sense to him. It wasn't wild, not in the way she said it. Things grew and died, blossomed and perished. It was orderly. This town they'd reached—the buildings humans had forced from natural materials, the endless amount of clothing they wore. That was wild.

"A warm meal would be welcome," he said instead. Enkidu had never had fresh cooked food, but the concept existed in his mind as though another hand planted it there.

Shamhat nodded and gestured towards a building where guards stood outside the door. A woman stepped out and bowed low several times. "My queen, you do our family a great honor to stay in our humble inn."

"It's a pleasure," the Queen replied.

"There is another here to see you, Nin. Her ladyship, Meritkara. I hope it was right that you wished to see her and—"

"Of course." There was a worried pitch to Shamhat's voice. She ushered Enkidu through the doorway as she spoke with the proprietor. At the entrance, Enkidu stopped. He had names for all the things scattered through the chamber—couch, table, patrons, bowls, stew—but he'd never seen them for himself. His gaze landed on each thing slowly, taking it all in.

Guards shuffled in alongside the Queen and circled around her and another woman who grabbed Shamhat's hands in her darker ones. The woman lifted her face, her eyes widening as she skimmed over Enkidu.

"Meet Enkidu," Shamhat said.

Meritkara frowned at him but bobbed her head. The women leaned in towards each other, earrings swinging. "There's a problem," the new woman said. "It's Gilgamesh. He's saying he won't receive this man in the palace."

"Oh, that stubborn ass." Shamhat cursed. "We have to change his mind." She bit her lip, her eyes dashing to Enkidu, then back to her companion. "And you can help me with that, Kara."

"What do you wish for me to do?"

"There's nothing Gilgamesh treasures more than his reputation. If we give that a shake and make him curious, he'll have to see us or damn his pride."

They continued whispering but Enkidu pulled away, moving between guards. So, the King had no desire to meet him. That was a shared feeling.

Your purpose is whatever lies before you, the wolf had said. In a dark corner, a man sat drinking a bowl of beer alone, the other dozen reed straws in the container neglected. His face was puffy and red even in the inn's dim lighting. Enkidu pushed through the narrow space and approached him.

The man looked up from his drink, bleary eyed and obviously drunk. Drunk—another concept Enkidu now understood but had never experienced. His heart ached for the person sitting slumped and broken. Loneliness was something he had begun to comprehend.

"You drink by yourself?" Enkidu asked.

The man sniffled and gestured to the couch across from him. "Join me, if you like."

Enkidu sat, jostling the table with his knees. His body was too large for this world—as though he was the monster reflected in the lake and not the human the Queen had transformed him into. The man shoved the bowl towards Enkidu, and he took a sip. "Are you hurt?"

"In a manner of speaking." He wiped his nose on his tunic then shifted to look at Enkidu. He slowly raised his face and gaped. "W-who are you?"

"No one of importance, but I'd help you if I could."

"There's no help for me." He sniffled again as he pulled the bowl back towards him. A stack of goblets sat on the table's far side, some still glistening with lingering liquid. Wine. He'd been deep in drink for a long time. The man released a shaky sigh. "It's the woman I love; she's gone."

The wolf had lost a mate once. The pack had howled late into the night and spent many days fasting and mourning. Death was the great divider and the one thing Enkidu hadn't understood even in his innocent forest life. "I'm sorry. Was she ill?"

"She's not dead." He cleared his throat and sat up, shoving the bowl to the side before dusting the tabletop off. "She's being sold off to marry the bastard king." He growled the words, slurring them together.

"King Gilgamesh?"

The man laughed half-heartedly. "Who else? Any other man that attempts to call himself a king is a fool. Lugal Gilgamesh will tear them from their throne and not even offer a proper burial before he burns their palaces."

"Why would he do such a thing?"

"How do you not know about this? Are you a sea person or something?" The man eyed him like perhaps that explained Enkidu's size. "King Gilgamesh does whatever he wants because he can."

Enkidu's heart thundered. *This* was the King he was supposed to help. Someone heartless and filled with ceaseless hunger. Shamhat had called the King striving and said

Enkidu was supposed to balance him. He was a monster like Humbaba—hungry for things he didn't need.

The man seemed encouraged by Enkidu's expression and carried on. "Y'know he has an entire palace of wives? Rumor says he fucks 'em each once then moves on, like... like they're disposable bowls. Tosses them... away... to crack in the rubbish heap after." His voice had grown wobbly, tears entering his eyes again. "Now he's taking my Nissaba from me. My father begged me to not be a fool, but I had to come see the wedding parade. I'm not sure I can bring myself to go into the city, though."

He sniffled again. Enkidu stared at him. If the man's tirade was even partially true, Gilgamesh was Humbaba— the human version, at least. Enkidu fell against the couch, air leaving him. Life was cruel and unfair. He existed solely to help a man who swallowed things like fire burning through the forest. Enkidu wouldn't do it. Just because gods who'd not bothered to speak with him had some purpose in mind, didn't mean he had to follow their plans.

He'd uncover the truth of Gilgamesh then act on what he felt was right. Perhaps what the King needed wasn't a helper, but someone to put him in his place.

His resolve hardened as he made his goodbyes to the man. It solidified the next morning when Shamhat left him with a few clay tokens to pay for provisions and directions to Uruk and the palace, begging her apologies for leaving early. She wished to speak with King Gilgamesh before Enkidu's arrival.

Enkidu thanked her. She'd been nothing but kind, after all. Then he pressed the uneven clay disks into his palm and readied himself to confront the King of Uruk.

CHAPTER SEVEN

THE BRIDEGROOM WAITS

SHAMHAT HAD RETURNED HOME and wished to speak with Gilgamesh, but he hadn't granted her the audience. He had no desire to meet this *helper* she and his mother thrust upon him. Instead, he remained busy with advisors, working through building projects, discussing Umma's lack of response to their demands, and attempting to craft a plan to refresh Inanna's temple that required the least amount of manpower without offending her.

Gilgamesh pressed his stylus into the wet clay tablet on the table before him. He'd growled over learning how to use a stylus as a child, grumbling about how the clay dried too quickly. *Patience, young king,* his instructor had chided him.

He'd never possessed patience, and that hadn't changed. He stood and wiped his hand on a towel before handing it to an attendant. Hirin moved away from the wall like he peeled himself off the mosaic and bowed. "I shall send a messenger to Umma if it pleases you, my king."

"No." Gilgamesh frowned. "I won't risk another messenger to that bastard, Zage-Si." The insult to his queen with the previous messenger—angry with her, though

Gilgamesh was—still stung. "If we don't hear a response soon, I'll deal with him myself."

"As you wish, my king." There was almost a sigh in the advisor's words, but he didn't protest. Even Hirin knew it was necessary. They couldn't allow Zage-Si to make such a slight against them without retribution.

"My shawl," Gilgamesh called to an attendant who brought it and tied it around the King's hips and shoulders, the precious stones clinking together. He needed to dress the part, after all. He had a celebration to throw to welcome the man Shamhat dragged into his court. They'd waste more stores despite also having a wedding soon. Gilgamesh hadn't bothered to meet the girl yet. He'd sent his bride-groom's gift and accepted the present from his father-in-law. It sat unopened in a storage room. He'd open the package before the wedding feast in case he needed to speak of it to the man.

Uruk already buzzed with excitement for the celebration and the palace staff scurried through the halls, preparing food and readying music and dances. More people moved into the city in the time since he'd built the wall, requiring new homes all while battles brewed in two corners of the Land Between Waters. The city strained under the demands, yet Inanna wanted a prettier temple. Fuck her.

Now Gilgamesh had to put on another false show to welcome this man his wife had run off into the forest after. Rumors about them spread through the palace with such a pace, even he'd heard them.

Gilgamesh growled as he approached the table that held his crown. It was crafted after a rolled, felted shepherd's hat but taller, detailed with fine gold filigree and topped with horns to show his divine nature.

He ran a thumb over the wool cap. He was supposed to be a shepherd to his people, but no one else gave a damn. No, Inanna would press for more to exalt herself when the city already grumbled about the labor tax. Zage-Si would lead Umma's soldiers to slaughter for his pride. Even Shamhat would bring some wild man into their home and force Gilgamesh to spend more of their wealth to celebrate the blessed fucking event.

He shoved the cap on and walked out of the room, heading to the front of the palace. The man's name—Enkidu—echoed around the palace and hissed through the city. The rumors about Shamhat were so wild, Gilgamesh knew they were false.

They said she'd fucked the beast for twelve hours—no twenty-four hours, no several days straight!—to make him human. She'd abandoned her throne and husband to chase after a seducer. The gossip wasn't true. She'd never take another lover without discussing it with Meritkara and Akkiru. And probably him, though it wasn't necessary. He'd tried to tell her many times that her lovers were her business. Gilgamesh had always trusted his queen, but she'd never done something like this before.

Regardless, Gilgamesh would have to receive the man or confirm that some aspect of the rumors were true. Damn Shamhat. They'd spent their entire marriage—more than a decade—carefully shaping their image, and she'd not given a fuck that she ripped it all apart with one impulsive action.

More than that, he was angry at the gossipers. When he'd overheard someone speaking about it at dinner, he had them arrested. Then he stood, chalice still in hand, to glare at the others sitting at his table. His and Shamhat's table. "Speak ill of your queen before me again, and I shall have your hands and tongues rather than granting you a few nights in prison. Your queen travels at the gods' behest for a pilgrimage in the interest of Uruk. If anyone takes issue with her actions or sees her as less than perfect, please tell me directly, and I shall address your concerns."

The attendees had gone pale and silent, like ghosts had sprung from the Great Below to take their places. Gilgamesh returned to his dinner, chewing with a vengeance. He dared anyone else to speak with the glares he shot across the table.

Shamhat was the beloved of Uruk. Gilgamesh the terror. If her reputation could falter so quickly over rumors with little evidence, then Gilgamesh had much to fear. That's how the maliciousness of gossip worked. It was the cruelest weapon. Someone could sit at the top of the world one day, and with a few sharp, unconfirmed words, they could fall to the rubbish heap the next. If he wanted a lasting legacy, he'd have to survive the wagging tongues while he lived.

As important, no one in his presence would speak of his queen with anything other than praise falling from their mouth again. The next time someone dared slander Shamhat in front of him, he'd save his voice and draw a blade.

If they couldn't respect her love and wisdom, they could learn to fear his wrath and brutality.

Gilgamesh turned a corner, and his queen stood in sunlight that washed through the arches. She raised her chin. The decorations on her gold headpiece clinked together as her arms folded into the confident pose of a ruler, but her eyes gave her away. She was uncertain.

Good. She'd caused him a great deal of grief.

Attendants and musicians, advisors and soldiers stood around the halls, preparing for the festivities he'd wasted time planning. He approached and bowed to a knee. "My queen."

She offered her hand. He kissed it as she inclined her head. "My king."

He rose, and they walked out to the thrones someone had arranged at the front of the palace. Crowds cheered as Gilgamesh ushered Shamhat to her seat then turned and waved at the people. The crown's grip on his head reminded him of who he was—shepherd. Perhaps he wasn't one who'd recline with his sheep and comfort them with ear scratches. But he'd brutalize any wolf that attempted to attack them and tried his best to shelter them from the gods' tempests.

He dropped beside his wife and kept his gaze on the crowd.

"You're avoiding me," she said.

Hirin walked to the center and began speaking to the people about alliances, the glory of Uruk, the wonderful sacrifices their rulers made for them. Gilgamesh had approved the speech, so it was easy to let it fall into the background.

"How can I ignore you when you're not home?" he asked, a bite in his words though he kept his face placid. Hirin held most of the crowd's attention, but many looked at their king and queen. His soldiers were dispersed amongst guards, helping control the crowd, and they watched as well. He was usually honest with his men, but even they didn't get to see his frustrations with Shamhat.

"Don't be immature." The Queen turned away and waved her fingers at a young girl whose eyes widened before she disappeared behind her parent's legs.

"Oh, yes. Clearly, I'm the immature one in this situation. Do you even know what the people are saying about you?"

A grin—a fucking smile—made its way up his queen's face. "I don't care what they say about me."

"Oh, good." He crossed his arms then forced himself to release them. He wanted to attack something, tear a wall down with his bare hands. Shamhat didn't care about the filth others spewed about her. He fought for her reputation, and she *didn't care*. How wonderful.

"You've arranged a lovely meal for today." Shamhat's eyes were still on the people, but he could feel the tension in her words.

"I used the wedding feast's provisions. We'll go lighter for that instead."

She shot her head towards him, and he smiled back at her. Her lips turned down, and he was glad of it. Let her feel some of the frustration and anger he'd experienced through the week. She'd been glad enough to abandon him and seek this man that surely spelled, if not doom, then hardship for her husband.

Shamhat didn't care about legacy, though. He wished he could press the importance of it into her. Gods, she was clever and cautious and lovely, but she thought the future was a joke. It wasn't. One day they'd be dead, cast into the Great Below, and the only things left would be their names and the stories attached to them.

She'd burn it all for today's happiness, toss it like chaff at the threshing if Gilgamesh would dote on Usun. Foolish.

"If the plans I've created for the wedding"—she emphasized the words—"aren't exactly as I left them, you will be in some deep shed, Gilgamesh."

"It's nice to know that even when we hate each other, we can still tease—albeit with heat that burns."

A dimple formed at her eyebrows. "I don't hate you. I never have."

Gilgamesh turned towards her. He'd never hated her either—couldn't stand the idea that any soul on earth ever would. Yet, her actions didn't align with her words. She'd traveled to the cedar forest—the place her parents died, where she'd vowed to never return. Did so to bring trials into Gilgamesh's life.

"Gilgamesh?" Shamhat's voice was soft.

At that moment Hirin stepped back to join other attendees standing behind the thrones.

"We'll have to discuss this later," Gilgamesh said. "I must go make a speech explaining how very happy I am to have my wife betray me and bring a monster into my palace."

"But—"

He left her with unfinished words, his heart burning as he approached his people.

CHAPTER EIGHT

THE GREAT WALLS OF URUK

THE CITY WAS A TEEMING, breathing thing, and Enkidu understood why Shamhat called his woods the wild. Despite the people milling by like they were caught in currents and carts rattling as donkeys brayed, the city flowed in a logical, orderly, and altogether unnatural way. Noises chittered together like in the woods—vendors called out like monkeys screeching over their territory, and a hum of life surged through the bustling streets—but the sun beat down hard on the ground with no tree boughs to shelter it, and the soothing pockets of quiet or the quaint trickle of a gentle flowing creek were gone.

As soon as Enkidu had passed beneath the massive gate that led into the city, the noise became a buzz in his ear, a mosquito he couldn't swat.

He'd spent his journey productively, talking to people and getting their opinions on the King. At first they'd avoided him, eyeing his horns and stepping back with trembling steps. Others made him offerings as though he was a god. Then he'd purchased a shepherd's cap, a curved wool thing, and while others still balked at his size, they'd eyed his fine clothing paired with the hat and would talk.

Everything he learned only ignited the warmth spreading in his chest, the same feeling he'd had when the hunter became too greedy with his traps. Gilgamesh—according to *his* people—was brilliant, god-touched, and successful. But he hungered endlessly, raising the labor tax to finish his walls, and asked for even more to build a full-time army. Something no other city possessed. Gilgamesh wanted the ability to conquer and destroy even during the farming season. He used his enemies' weaknesses to advantage. He had more wives than he had time to tend, yet he added more season after season.

In fact, another marriage would happen soon. It was the only thing on the city people's tongues. The markets chittered with it, elderly couples sat on front steps wondering about the bride's beauty and the connections she might bring.

They discussed her like she was something for them to possess, not a person with a name. Their king had taught them this behavior. It was the leader of a pack who set the tone, after all.

Enkidu still wobbled on what to do until he passed a stand selling blankets woven with a hundred colors hanging on racks. He walked through them, brushing his fingers over their silky surfaces when someone speaking stalled him.

"Rumors say this new bride doesn't want to lie with the King."

A second voice. "Doesn't matter either way."

"Don't you think the girl should have some say?"

"Most girls, yes. A bride of Gilgamesh? Nah. He gets

whatever he wants and if he wants a young, sweet thing, well—she'd better prepare herself."

Enkidu's fingers curled into his palms. Gilgamesh thought he had the right to take whatever he wanted, abuse anyone, tear down thrones to spread his name, even hurt Nissaba if it pleased him. She was likely more of a person to Enkidu—a man with no connection to humanity—than she was to her future husband.

Your purpose is whatever lies before you.

Nissaba's unfair marriage lay before him now. Shamhat said his role was to balance her husband. Perhaps his position was to bring him down and remind him he was as mortal as everyone he ravaged.

Enkidu's fingers curled into fists as he continued on the path through the city. He stopped to purchase a sack of fresh figs before heading towards the palace.

He'd thought the entrance to the city was crowded, but the palace which sat on a hill above it all—so Gilgamesh could look down his nose at everyone, certainly—had such thick crowds Enkidu struggled to push through. When others caught sight of him, even with the horns covered, they gasped and moved aside.

It was like they were waiting for him.

Enkidu clutched the bag of fruit tighter.

By the time he approached the palace where hundreds of people stood in rich tunics and shawls, their heads crowned with gleaming hats and headpieces, news of his arrival had preceded him. People whispered and pointed and everyone standing before the palace stared.

Enkidu's shoulders hunched, and he tried to avoid meeting the gaze of anyone in the crowd. Ahead, outside the palace, above a set of short stairs, dozens of people stood in an array of bright colors, many with weapons on their hips.

Shamhat sat on a throne among them, straight-backed, dozens of jewels adorning her neck, and he couldn't believe he ever saw her as anything other than a queen. His cheeks burned again. She'd seen him unclothed and filthy. Uruk's queen had brushed his beard and oiled his hair like a child before he had a vocabulary to describe it.

Next to her sat the King. Enkidu's steps faltered. This couldn't be the Gilgamesh he'd heard of. The man looked far too beautiful, his curled beard gleaming in the light, his intelligent eyes meeting Enkidu's gaze without faltering. There was something wolfish about the expression. It made Enkidu both instantly trust him and feel suddenly wary.

The King rose, his rich clothing unspooling around him. The crowd grew silent, all turning their faces towards him as if a god moved among them. Enkidu's stomach twisted.

"People of Uruk," Gilgamesh's voice boomed. It was deep, edged with a growl. Warmth settled within Enkidu. He could listen to that voice forever. Perhaps he'd misunderstood others' perceptions of the King. After all, the drunk man at the inn had been heartbroken and deep in his cups. Maybe this was all a misunderstanding. His grip loosened on the fig bag, tension leaving his body.

"A glorious day the gods have provided for us to meet a new friend of our venerated city." The people cheered. They'd cleared a circle around Enkidu, and many looked at him with the same frenzied devotion they'd shown Gilgamesh. "Rumors spread like fires in a dry season, but look upon another blessing the gods have bestowed on our fine city. Do you think"—something changed in the King's voice, turning sharper—"your king would ever abandon you or lead you astray, people of Uruk?"

"Never, Lugal!" So many people cheered it became a roar that caused Enkidu to cringe.

"It's no mere mortal that leads you, is it?" The people whistled, clapped, and smiled as though they knew what came next. "No." The King rolled his shoulders back, his eyes sparkling. "The gods have blessed our city, giving you a king descended from them. You are led by the great King Gilgamesh, leader of the high-walled Uruk, son of the great Lugalbanda and the mighty goddess Ninsun!" He paused for a round of frantic applause, but his tone lost some enthusiasm with the next words. "Friend of Our Lady in Heaven, Inanna." His tone pitched back up again. "The man who surpasses all other mortals in strength and deed."

The crowd waved their hands around. Some had ribbons they fluttered in the breeze. Everyone smiled and whistled and encouraged the speech, but Enkidu frowned. No beast was that much grander than another, not even a god-born king. He wasn't a wolf, but Humbaba, overtaxing the forest because he believed he had a divine right. This was why Gilgamesh believed he could lord over everyone. He saw himself as a god, able to take as he wished.

When an animal overstepped in the woods, nature or another creature put them back in their place. Gilgamesh had no one to snap sharp teeth and growl at him before the pack, making it clear that he'd surpassed his rights. That's what Shamhat told Enkidu. Her husband needed someone to balance him. The gods had informed him of nothing, but he'd grown wild with the wolves, and he knew what they would do.

He pulled a fig from the bag, its soft warmth yielding to his embrace. He lifted it and chucked it as hard as he could.

It hit the King in the cheek. Its splatter against the royal skin silenced the crowd.

Gilgamesh froze, the fruit falling off him in pieces, sticky juice allowing seeds to cling to his skin. A bee zipped in from somewhere, whirling around his face as bits of fruit dripped from his beard.

Shamhat stood and gaped at Enkidu, her hands suspended like she wished to stop time.

The crowd had grown as still as a mouse caught by a fox, timid trembling replacing the raucousness of moments before. It was an improvement.

Gilgamesh turned the weight of his stare onto Enkidu, his eyes shaded and filled with enough heat to burn, his nose wrinkling.

Enkidu raised his chin. "You are not my king."

"Is that a challenge, beast?" Gilgamesh spoke through his teeth. The mask he'd worn for the crowd ripped away and in its place a *beast*, as he'd called Enkidu, stood, hackles raising.

"I'm sure that's new for you, oh mighty one," Enkidu spat. The King's face turned crimson and every beautiful aspect of him washed away. What remained was a demon —another new word—that would consume the world until nothing remained.

Gilgamesh stepped forward, and people shuddered, hunching away from him. It was like he had magic that pushed them aside. Whatever it was, Enkidu didn't feel it. He remained upright staring the man in the eyes. The King growled, and it didn't warm Enkidu this time. "Are you challenging my throne?"

"I'm here to challenge everything."

Gilgamesh snarled and dove towards Enkidu.

Shrieks and screams broke out. The crowd crushed together to get away.

Enkidu planted his feet and braced for the impact. The

King smacked into him like a storm after a brutally hot day. Enkidu didn't yield. He gritted his teeth, steeled his muscles, and became as unmoving as a boulder.

Gilgamesh's eyes widened, and he skimmed his gaze over Enkidu with the first humble expression he'd donned. It was probably a rare sight. Gilgamesh slammed a fist forward, socking Enkidu in his stomach. Enkidu's breath left him in a rush, and he doubled over.

He wouldn't let Gilgamesh win, though. That would fuel his arrogance and pride. He plowed a knee into the man's gut.

They fell to the ground with a tumble, slamming into each other.

The earth trembled beneath the weight of their wrestling.

Gilgamesh's warm flesh stung Enkidu's fingers. His weight pressing into Enkidu made his stomach twist. It spurred up emotions he'd have names for if he had time to think.

The King rolled them, jabbing a forearm into Enkidu's throat. He hissed at the loss of air but clutched his legs around the massive man and turned him again.

Gilgamesh gasped as his back hit the ground with a thud. Enkidu copied his actions, pressing an arm into his throat and leaned down to whisper. "You bastard. You have no right to steal and brutalize women."

The King's dark eyes widened. "What the fuck are you talking about?"

Enkidu started to respond, but Gilgamesh lunged forward and slammed him into the ground. The crowd had rearranged farther away, and some stretched on their toes to see the fight. Enkidu released a growl of his own.

Gilgamesh would steal forward in an unfair moment, win by cheating.

Enkidu socked a fist into his gut. The King lifted him back to his feet and threw him against a wall that cracked at the impact, plaster falling like rain. Gilgamesh thrust a hand around his throat and pressed a knee between his legs. "While we're busy airing grievances,"—the King spat as sweat dripped down his face—"perhaps I should ask what the fuck you did to cause such malicious rumors about my wife."

Shamhat stood by the throne, her hands fisted and eyes unblinking.

"I've done nothing."

"Really?" The King jabbed his knee forward, and Enkidu shifted in time to miss the worst of the impact. Gilgamesh hit a nerve on the inside of his thigh, though, and Enkidu's leg went numb, buckling his knee. He struggled to maintain his balance on the other foot, and it took a moment to catch his breath. The bastard. He fought dirty. Enkidu prepared to rip the King's flesh from his body, to stop holding back, when the man spoke again, stalling him. "Everyone's saying you fucked her."

Enkidu's lips snapped apart. Fucked. What a crude word, but as soon as he heard it, he knew its meaning. The shock of it was the only thing that could have overridden the pain and fury. "I never touched her," he said through his teeth, "and never would."

"Interesting how rumors can poison minds, isn't it?" The King's face was so close to Enkidu's, his breath brushed his cheek. If his leg wasn't burning so intensely, he might have felt something about that.

"You're implying that this bride isn't stolen. That it's a rumor too."

Gilgamesh grabbed Enkidu's tunic in his fist and jerked the man forward. "Who the fuck are you?"

Enkidu didn't know the answer to that. Instead of replying, he drop-kicked Gilgamesh. When wolves fought, a snarled remark was a distraction. Enkidu didn't intend to let Gilgamesh cheat and knock him down again. The King hit the ground with a thud. The crowd groaned. Enkidu fell onto the royal body and brought his face close to the King's. The motion caused Enkidu's hat to fall off and people gasped. His horns were back on display, but he didn't care. His attention remained fixed on Gilgamesh. "That's for fighting dirty. I should knee you in the groin to repay you, but I'm willing to give you the benefit of the doubt that we've had a misunderstanding."

Gilgamesh's eyes traced over him. Enkidu's heart raced about. Their chests rose with their labored breaths, and Gilgamesh rested a hand on Enkidu's thigh. The sensation was too much, and he needed to say anything to get them to fight again, to move apart. "All the rumors I've heard about you make it seem like you prefer to be on top. Perhaps they're mistaken."

A slow grin made its way up Gilgamesh's face. It was so disconcerting, Enkidu didn't know what to do with himself and his grip loosened. Gilgamesh used the pause and leveraged his weight, tumbling them over so the King looked down at Enkidu. He smiled again. Blood followed the curves of his teeth. He leaned close enough to Enkidu that his lips brushed his ear. "Maybe some rumors are true." Enkidu shuddered as the King rose where he could look him in the eye again. "It seems we should speak." He cocked an eyebrow and it slipped beneath his crown's gold ornamentation. Somehow he'd managed to keep his cap on the entire time.

"I must have misunderstood the situation," Enkidu said. He wasn't sure anymore. Something about Gilgamesh's touch had unmoored him. "I met the man who's in love with your new bride, however. He says the King does whatever he wishes."

Gilgamesh hummed then looked out at the crowd who still watched with lips tugged between teeth and furrowed brows. "We can discuss this, but will you go along with something for me? An act of faith between us?"

Enkidu would do anything if Gilgamesh would stop touching him so he could think. "It depends."

The King chuckled and jumped up, offering Enkidu a hand. He accepted then dropped the contact as soon as he was on his feet. He needed fresh air away from this man who smelled of sweet oils and a lingering scent of something wild that reminded him of the forest. The King slung an arm around his shoulders and addressed the crowd. "I hope you'll forgive us for indulging our theatrical impulses."

The people exchanged looks, and a few quiet chuckles broke out.

"As I said before," Gilgamesh boomed, his hand heavy on Enkidu's shoulder, his touch doing strange things to his body. "Would your King ever abandon you, people of Uruk?"

"Never," the people yelled, though with fewer voices than before.

"You can see our new friend is god-marked, a gift from the divine to honor our city. Rumors have claimed he can overpower your King." Gilgamesh grinned at this and some in the crowd laughed. Enkidu had the urge to shove him away but kept his body still, committed to hearing the man out first. Gilgamesh squeezed Enkidu's shoulder.

"Remember that rumors are just that—exaggerations made bigger than reality. Know that you are secure in your King's competence and the gods' favor. As well as in the favor of my new dear friend."

The crowd clapped and whistled as loudly as the beginning. The wolf managed his clan by snipping at those who challenged him and comforting the frightened. But Gilgamesh's actions were different, cleverer. The gods may have given Enkidu knowledge, but not the experiences to concrete it. He should watch his steps and not lash out so quickly again. That had been a mistake.

"Please, welcome our new friend, Enkidu, to the grand city of Uruk."

The crowd roared, and Enkidu winced at the noise. Gilgamesh looked at him, brows pulling together, but the expression disappeared, and he gestured to the palace. "Come, join the Queen and me for refreshments, and we'll see if we can get to the root of these rumors."

When Gilgamesh's arm dropped, Enkidu's blood rushed back into his flesh, leaving a tingling discomfort. He was unsteady on his feet and not from fighting. Something else had gripped him, something that brought heat to his cheeks and an uncertainty to his steps as he followed the King towards the palace.

CHAPTER NINE

A STUBBORN KING AND CLEVER QUEEN

THERE WAS a moment where Gilgamesh thought he'd have to kill the man in front of his people. As he strode through the palace's front courtyard and passed under an arch towards a hall, he didn't bother to look back to see if Enkidu and Shamhat followed. The latter, he knew, burned with a need to speak, and he'd realized a key detail about the former somewhere amid the two of them pummeling each other.

When Gilgamesh had accused Enkidu of the rumors, the man's eyes gave him away. They were hazel, but unlike any other Gilgamesh had seen before. Brown streaked them before fading to rippling shades of green on the edges. And at the center, a ring of gold circled his irises. When he'd thrown the accusation at the man, those eyes had gone wide and soft, and he'd blinked several times.

The man may share his height and strength—a novelty, indeed—but he was no killer. He might prove to be a threat to his and Shamhat's images, perhaps, but not a real challenge for Gilgamesh.

He opened a door and waved in the two who'd, of

course, followed. They rustled through the doorway as Gilgamesh clicked the door shut, then turned on them.

Shamhat narrowed her eyes at Enkidu. "What in the name of Enlil was that about?"

"An excellent question," Gilgamesh said before sucking blood from between his teeth.

She whipped towards him. "I could ask you the same."

Gilgamesh shrugged before removing his crown and setting it on the table. "Last I checked, my queen, you were the one who prayed for intervention, who went to retrieve this man, and he was the one who threw a godsdamned fig at me. For once, I don't believe you can point a finger in my direction." Gilgamesh swiped over his chest. "He ruined my tunic."

Shamhat smacked the back of her hand against his chest. "You don't know the difference between any of your tunics, so do not start with that." Her voice was sharp but something uncertain wobbled along the edges. Gilgamesh never spoke openly with her before others. They'd always protected their image, but she'd set that aflame with her romp in the woods. Enkidu was now tangled in their marriage and rule. She could bloody well join Gilgamesh in his discomfort.

Shamhat's brow furrowed, but she turned to Enkidu. "I thought you'd agreed to visit as a guest. Why would you shame the King in such a manner?"

Her tone had turned snappish, like a mother shocked at her child's behavior. Gilgamesh's thoughts turned to Usun. Did their son bow his head when Shamhat chastised him, or raise his chin defiantly?

Probably the first; the boy was better behaved than his father.

Enkidu shook his head, hair brushing his shoulders

with the movement. "Forgive me, my queen. I didn't intend to disappoint. You've been kind to me. That said, you never asked what I desired."

"W-what?" Shamhat looked at Gilgamesh as if he'd have something to offer. Gilgamesh had never wanted the man in his city, much less standing on one of his mother's temple's rugs in their palace. Gilgamesh didn't give a fuck what Enkidu desired. There wasn't a person involved in this situation who cared about what he wanted, either. In case any gods wished to know, it was for things to go back to how they were before the damned dream haunted him and Shamhat got divinity involved.

"Enough." Gilgamesh frowned at the two of them. "Lay forth your accusations to the King." He turned towards Enkidu. It disconcerted him that he couldn't look down on him. They stood the same height, and Gilgamesh stared straight into his eyes. He'd never, in adulthood, experienced that.

Enkidu frowned. "The man who's in love with your new bride claims you take wife after wife, disregarding them as soon as you wed, disrespecting the women. People in your city claim you take whatever you want, that you have no limits."

Gilgamesh's nose flared. Enkidu's words struck like a blade into his heart. He was the shepherd of his people. Had he not proved to them repeatedly he would build walls and fight and marry and do whatever he must to exalt Uruk, to guard his people like a lion watching his cubs? Yet they slandered him. It had never bothered him before but since hearing palace staff—those who worked in their very home—whisper about their queen, a fresh worry had bloomed. A man would have no legacy if he destroyed it before his death. Dying was becoming the easy part of his plan to secure his legacy.

A sigh filled Gilgamesh's chest, and he fought against releasing it. "I marry for political reasons. Perhaps if you'd spent any time growing up at a court instead of running wild in the woods, you'd understand this."

"So you don't care what Nissaba wishes?" Enkidu took a step forward, his fists curling. The softness in his eyes drained. A drop of blood glimmered on his jaw. It could be Gilgamesh's. The man had fought him like a demon.

"Who is Nissaba?"

Shamhat frowned but didn't speak before Enkidu bared his teeth. "The woman you're marrying and stealing from the man who loves her? He certainly knows her damn name, at least."

Gilgamesh fisted his hands as well. Shamhat gasped like she worried the two might fall to blows again, but he wasn't that foolish. He couldn't afford to damage the palace with all the other building projects happening. "You think I want to marry this girl? I am as obligated as she is. I assure you, I'd be more than happy to hand her off to her beloved with his loose tongue and leave them to it."

Enkidu released a breath. He shifted towards Shamhat then looked back at Gilgamesh. "Call off the marriage, then."

"Oh, yes." Gilgamesh stepped closer until the man's warmth reached him. "Let me do that and destroy the trade connections between our cities, raise the cost of timber all while the gods demand vaster temples, shatter the road's security between our provinces, and potentially add a third war for our city when their leader hears we've rebuffed them. All so two fools can imagine themselves in love. How romantic."

Enkidu's eyes darkened, and his lips pinched so a dip formed over them. "I can see I owe you an apology. I don't understand how a human court runs." He bowed his head but not quickly enough to hide the color spreading over his cheeks above his beard. "I acted too quickly."

"Your turn to explain," Gilgamesh said without acknowledging the apology. He didn't need it. He gave people one opportunity to cross him and never made the mistake of trusting them again.

"I don't know why there is salacious gossip about me and"—Enkidu dashed a look at Shamhat—"the Queen. I would never—"

"I started the rumors." Shamhat said it like she commented on the weather.

Gilgamesh turned towards her. He lost his grip on his god's blood, and if she were anyone else, any other person in the city who he'd not marked safe from his strength, she'd struggle to stay on her feet. She remained stoic, her hands clasped together, bracelets stacked neatly on her wrists.

"Explain to me," he said through his teeth, "why you would do such a thing."

"Because you were being stubborn."

"I was being stubborn?"

"Yes." She jutted her chin up. On second thought, Usun probably would stare defiantly rather than submit. Both his parents were as obstinate as the earth. He'd likely inherited it. "You just continue to plow forward, never satisfied—"

"We're going to have this conversation here?" Gilgamesh waved at Enkidu.

"Oh, we can discuss my shortcomings before him but not yours? How curious."

Enkidu looked back at the wall behind him like he wished he could sink into it.

"Fine." Gilgamesh swiped a hand out like he could rip the day away, removing it from memory. "I would like you to go get the girl." Shamhat's eyebrows drew together. "The one I'm marrying. Nabba..."

He looked at Enkidu, and the man cleared his throat. "Nissaba."

"Yes, Nissaba. Bring her here but discreetly."

"Her family will have questions," Shamhat said.

"Then it's a good thing my queen is clever and will find a way to answer them gracefully."

Shamhat's expression tensed but she sighed and left the room, the door clicking shut.

Gilgamesh ripped the shawl off and flung it over the back of a couch. He didn't give a shed what Enkidu thought of his appearance, and he'd grown tired of holding everything together. He paced across the rug.

"I believe I owe you another apology," Enkidu said. "I acted rashly and—"

"You've apologized enough."

Enkidu lifted his face and those damned eyes—like gemstones that held the forest's colors—rippled with emotion. "Yes, but I misconstrued the situation."

"You haven't. I'm every bit the asshole you believe me to be, you just didn't understand my reasoning. The situation hasn't actually changed."

Enkidu's eyelashes fluttered. Gilgamesh enjoyed flustering him. He'd felt the same when the man's body had pressed against his, when Enkidu's expression went wide, and those eyes revealed his gentle nature. Gilgamesh had faced many battles; men who would kill, who were inclined to destroy others, never allowed themselves to appear that vulnerable.

"Come, tell me your story." Gilgamesh gestured to a couch. Enkidu sat, though he readjusted several times and perched on the edge, like he'd jump off any moment. He explained his history—what little the man had. Enkidu answered every question, asking nothing in return. He wasn't only soft-hearted, he was a fool. His size and the fact that Gilgamesh's god's blood didn't affect him paired with the sleek black horns curving over his hair would be enough to intrigue Gilgamesh. But he was already exhausted with whatever game Shamhat and his mother played.

Enkidu had, at least, offered him a solution to the marriage problem. Gilgamesh nodded at appropriate moments as the man spoke, but his mind drifted. There were too many issues at hand. This man—beautiful eyes aside—was a distraction. Shamhat meant to destroy his focus. She wanted him to abandon his legacy. Perhaps she believed Enkidu would cause enough chaos in their court to have him preoccupied. She was mistaken.

Some time later, a knock sounded and Gilgamesh tied his sash as the door opened. Shamhat entered with a girl at her side who had dark curls tucked under a gem-lined headband. Gilgamesh and Enkidu rose. At the sight of the two of them—they had to make a frightful duo with their height, Gilgamesh's steely gaze, and Enkidu's horns—the girl blanched, stumbling a step.

Shamhat walked over to her husband and bowed. "My king."

He returned the greeting then gestured for her to stand at his other side. Her lips thinned, but thankfully she didn't lash out in front of the girl. He was sure to hear her thoughts later. For the first time in their marriage, he considered cutting off her access to his apartment.

The girl trembled as she bowed low and struggled to return to her feet. Gilgamesh didn't draw his god's blood back. He wanted to make an impression, to remind her of exactly who she was engaged to marry. "M-my king," she stammered.

"Have you heard about the recent arrival of my dear friend, Enkidu, yet?" Gilgamesh slung his arm around the man and every muscle he touched went as still as stone. Gilgamesh had to fight a grin. Enkidu had no ability to hide his emotions. Life in the palace—for Gilgamesh was sure he was stuck with him now—was going to eat the man alive. He reluctantly dropped the arm.

The woman swallowed as she turned her face towards Enkidu then shook her head. "I haven't. Forgive me, Lugal. I only just arrived in the city."

"I hope you've found it pleasing so far."

Sweat shone on her forehead. Shamhat shifted her body so her tunic covered the gap between her and Gilgamesh. She discreetly jabbed an elbow into his side. He drew back his powers but only a touch.

"It's the finest city in all the world, my king." The woman said it like she meant it. It would warm him if he wasn't aware her lover spread rumors about him to strangers.

"That it is. And you've been invited to become a princess of Uruk. Can you think of a finer position?"

Enkidu looked ready to interject, and Gilgamesh brushed his hand along the man's knuckles. Enkidu took a sharp breath and stopped whatever he'd planned to say.

"No, Lugal." The girl's eyes were filled with tears. "You've honored my family and me greatly."

"Yet, I hear you have another who you'd prefer to marry?"

Color drained from her face until the gold disks on her headband stood out against her skin. "My king, I don't know what you've heard but I've been faithful, I swear it."

Shamhat had practically attached herself to his ribs. He longed to shove an elbow back in her direction. He drew the magic in again and lowered his voice to a gentler tone. "You can speak honestly with me, my dear. We're about to be married, after all."

Enkidu moved forward, standing between Gilgamesh and the girl. "You won't harm her. This is trouble I've caused. She's done nothing."

Gilgamesh pretended he didn't desire to slam the man into the ground hard enough to crack his skull. He spoke around Enkidu's hulking figure to the girl. "See, you even have a god-blessed champion present."

Tears slipped down her cheeks as she stepped beside Enkidu. It was a brave move, Gilgamesh had to give her that much. Side-by-side, the contrast between the two was vast. Where she was all gentle curves and soft, fine fingers tangling into her shawl, Enkidu was broad with hard muscles covered in scatterings of sleek black hair with thick, callused hands.

It had never bothered Gilgamesh before that he preferred the latter over the former. Now he wished he didn't solely to spite the man.

"My heart has rushed away with me in youthful foolishness." She licked a tear off her lip and squared her shoulders. "However, I'm honored you would choose me as a princess of your fine city. I will swear on any god that I've never been touched and—"

"I do not care about that." Gilgamesh scoffed.

"You don't?"

"What's your man like? Does he have any useful skills?"

"Lugal, I don't have a man. I promise you, I've cut all ties."

Gilgamesh turned towards his queen who'd mercifully stopped poking him and waved his hands towards the girl. She studied him for a moment before nodding. She understood his mind—always had. He didn't know why she'd turned against him recently.

Shamhat spoke to the girl. "The King wishes to know if the man you care for has any talents that would render him useful for employment at the Queen's Palace."

The bride looked between both of them then shifted to Enkidu. He fixed his eyes on Gilgamesh, and a promise glinted across them. He'd truly chosen to champion her. If Gilgamesh mistreated the woman, he'd finish what he'd intended when he came into the city. Gilgamesh was disappointed he wouldn't get to see who might best the other in that scenario.

Enkidu nodded at the girl.

"He's an administrator's son, my king."

Gilgamesh brushed his fingers over his beard's curls. "So, he can use a stylus, read, knows numbers, and I'm assuming he knows his history and basic astrology."

"Yes, Lugal, and more."

"Very well. Here's my proposition to you. You will make a blood-vow to me. It will bind you to your words. Should you break them it will cost the life of you and your man." She froze like she'd transformed into a statue. He carried on. "You may conduct a relationship with him if you're discreet and both of you keep it private. I have my reputation to consider. Also, you may have one child. It will legally be mine, of course, but I'll make sure it's educated and well cared for. Only one, however. I can't have my other wives believing I favor you. Have I made myself clear, girl?"

"Her name is Nissaba." Enkidu frowned.

Gilgamesh raised an eyebrow at the girl refusing to acknowledge Enkidu's censure.

"My king, my queen, and..." Nissaba turned towards her champion. "Enkidu. You're very kind. I don't wish for you to believe I've misled you. I intended for this marriage to happen in earnest."

Gilgamesh smiled. It was easy to dredge up a grin after he'd found such a brilliant solution to the issue. "We believe you. All three of us understand our places and the importance of executing our roles." He let his gaze drift to the two in the room who clearly didn't understand that at all. "However, if this arrangement suits you, it pleases me. Besides, I'm growing rather used to inviting men into my home I don't desire to actually have here. What's one more?"

Shamhat gave him such a sharp jab he had to clench his teeth to stall a reaction.

Nissaba hesitated like she wondered if they were testing her loyalty before bobbing her head so her earrings danced. In a short time, Gilgamesh had a knife drawn, her blood fresh on it, and sacred words leaving her lips. Then he sent her away with attendants and soldiers, directing them to offer her and her family additional gifts.

"An attendant will find you a room," Gilgamesh said to Enkidu, dismissing him. He'd played the game long enough. Enkidu looked like he had a hundred things to say, but a breath left him, his shoulders dropped, and he walked through the door.

That left Shamhat and Gilgamesh alone.

She worried her shawl's edge between her fingers, the finery on it clinking. "Gilgamesh, I'm so—"

"Don't." He would manipulate others and act in front of everyone else, but not with her. The one thing they'd always possessed was honesty. He didn't mean to change that even if she'd betrayed him. He thought he understood her reasoning, but it didn't take away the sting.

She paced across the room and readjusted his crown on the table, straightening it before looking over her shoulder. "You're going to let Enkidu stay, then?"

Her voice was quiet. In another time, before all this had happened—before dreams haunted him, Inanna had cursed him with limited time, and his wife who he trusted more than any human in the world had turned against him—he would have comforted his queen. Instead, he remained standing where he was. "I imagine you and my mother would continue to fuck with my life if I didn't."

"We're trying to help you." She whipped around, her tunic a whirl of colors.

"How is that going?"

She jutted her chin up. "It's like attempting to save a drowning fish."

"Leave it to drown then." He turned towards the door.

"What do you intend to do with Enkidu? He's here to assist you, not harm you."

"You know, Shamhat, if I needed to discover how to locate wild honey or learn where to sleep under the stars at night, this man might be useful. However, I don't require that. I'm a godsdamned king of the most sophisticated city in the world—a city we've painstakingly shaped to become what it is. Even a dozen years ago, Uruk was just another eager gathering of buildings hoping to become something more than sand that would eventually shift back into the river. You and I"—he slammed his hand over his heart—"made it into what it is today. But now you've turned away from me." She parted her lips, but he let his voice go dark as he cut her off. "Regarding the beast from the woods, I'm not interested in your ploys. I intend to ignore him. And before you speak"—her lips pressed together—"consider that perhaps you could join him if you no longer care for this relationship."

He left the room, slamming the door harder than necessary, causing it to echo down the halls of the palace they'd built.

CHAPTER TEN
STRANGER IN SPLENDOR

SHAME. Enkidu lay in bed staring at the clothing chest across the room as heat crawled up his neck and spread over his chest. He almost hated having a name for the feeling he experienced. Knowledge really was a curse.

Yesterday, he'd barged into this city as if he knew anything about humanity, about kings and queens or politics. The vocabulary was there in his mind, but he lacked experience to make it valuable.

Instead, he'd done nothing since leaving the forest but shame himself. He clenched his fists into the soft linen sheets and wished he could sink through the clay bricks holding the bed until he landed in the Great Below.

He'd misjudged Gilgamesh—maybe. Part of him thought he was every bit the wicked monster he'd initially assumed. But he'd treated his new bride with kindness, allowing her lover to move into his palace. He was generous and stingy, ambitious and unassuming. Enkidu's head ached trying to piece together the disparate images.

And the way his touch made his heart race? He tried to ignore that altogether.

A knock sounded at the door. Enkidu lurched up and grabbed the tunic he'd hung at the bedside. He didn't intend to be caught undressed again. He pulled the tunic on, ignoring the decorative sash attendants had left him, and answered.

Two people stood in the hall. The first was the woman who'd spoken with Shamhat at the inn. This time her hair was in gemstone-adorned braids. The man at her side had a shaved head and jaw.

He shifted, and the tassels on his kaunake kilt ruffled. "Good morning. The Queen has sent us to give you a tour of the palaces."

Enkidu hesitated a moment then nodded. He didn't understand where he belonged in this world of jewels and furs and glimmering tiles, but he was here, and it would be best to know how to navigate the place. "We've met once, Nin Meritkara." He inclined his head to her.

Her eyes tightened, but she smirked. "You remember my name." She slung a hand over the other man's shoulder. "This is Akkiru."

Enkidu bobbed his head again then walked out of the room alongside the pair. "So," Akkiru said, "is there anywhere you'd like to start?"

The forest I wish I'd never left. Enkidu sighed. He regretted not having the opportunity to say goodbye to the wolf. He lamented accepting Shamhat's food. He didn't belong in this world. Perhaps he hadn't belonged in the woods either, but at least he hadn't known it. Not until he'd eaten the accursed bread.

"Breakfast first," Meritkara said. Enkidu followed along as they chattered about the palace until they reached a small dining room. Their words didn't reach him, though, as they passed hundreds of people moving through the palace. It was like the gods had dropped him into an anthill. The buzz of people and narrow halls made him shudder.

He ate the barley porridge, sweetened with dates and honey and made creamy with a scoop of soft goat's cheese. It was delicious, yet it stuck in Enkidu's throat. The dining room they lounged in had mosaics of lions running along the wall. Enkidu wished he was with the creatures, a breeze rushing through his hair, his feet smashing grass.

"So, you work for the queen?" he asked to break away from his thoughts.

Meritkara shrugged, and Akkiru laughed. "We do her bidding, for certain." He readjusted on his couch. "We're her partners."

"Partners?" Enkidu asked. The word had many connotations, but he didn't know which the man meant.

Meritkara rolled her eyes and swiped a bracelet-laden arm through the air. "We share her life and her bed."

Enkidu took a sharp breath in. Gilgamesh didn't treat his wives the way he'd imagined before. He was comfortable with them taking lovers, but Shamhat had seemed different. Their relationship felt unique, and he suspected his arrival had damaged it. "Does the King know this?"

"Of course."

Shame's heat coursed over his neck again. Obviously Gilgamesh knew about Shamhat's partners. How foolish of him to once again assume otherwise. "I apologize. He seems attached to the Queen in a way that he isn't with his other wives."

Meritkara gestured for an attendant who gathered the breakfast dishes. Once they'd left, she rose, her glimmering shawl rippling down the length of her tunic. "He doesn't pay attention to any of his wives aside from Shamhat. Ask me how I'm aware of this information." She smirked.

Akkiru and Enkidu stood and followed her out of the chamber and back into the hall. "However, you're right. He's always cared for Shamhat, but their relationship isn't typical."

Enkidu didn't think the word typical applied to Gilgamesh in any manner. They meandered forward. His mind wandered to the forest, to his murky origins Gilgamesh had frowned at him over. "May I visit Ninsun?"

She would have answers. Shamhat had prayed to her for Enkidu's creation, after all. If he could speak with her, even for a few moments, she might help him better understand his purpose.

"The goddess?" Akkiru shook his head. "She only accepts visits from those divinely touched and her priestesses—which includes Shamhat. The Queen worked in Ninsun's temple before she married Gilgamesh."

They'd turned a corner into the massive courtyard where palms rustled in the wind. Enkidu grazed his hand over his horns. "Ninsun created me, didn't she?"

Meritkara's gaze lifted to the horns then dropped to meet his eyes. "We're not sure, to be honest. She may have called on another god to craft you, but regardless, you can't visit a god without them summoning you."

Enkidu tried to keep the frown from his face. Akkiru and Meritkara acted kindly, giving up their day to show him around. Yet her words hit like a punch that broke bones.

He didn't know who he was or where he belonged. No one even knew who'd crafted him. He had no parents or history or name. Instead, he flew about like dust on the wind, drifting here and there with no purpose.

The thought gripped into him, talons that wouldn't release. If the goddess who'd desired his creation wouldn't see him or answer his questions, then he'd have to discover them on his own. He was lost in this massive world of grand statues and intricate mosaics. He'd loathed the attendants wishing to bathe and dress him. They'd stood trembling in his chamber, like they'd been sent to attend a beast.

Enkidu tried to push his dark thoughts away as he followed the pair around the palace. He failed and shifted his energy to not shivering as another dozen people passed them. The pair showed him the reception halls, music rooms, kitchens, and workshops. Entire rooms did nothing but house clay tablets that kept ledgers of everything the palace produced. It was a maze he didn't wish to understand.

At the day's midpoint, they walked outside. A fresh breeze swept over Enkidu's face, brushing back his hair, and he sighed. It was a relief to feel some small touch from the wild. Meritkara and Akkiru led him past Ninsun's ivory temple before walking to the Queen's palace. It was more of the same—rooms filled with dyed wools and painted tiles and fine furniture. However, the large courtyard, unlike at Gilgamesh's palace, squealed with noise.

Musicians patted drums, and one created a tune with a bone whistle flute. Children ran around, chasing each other. Others jumped rope or sat in a clump together playing with dolls. Enkidu's heart slowed for the first time that morning. "I didn't know so many children lived here."

"Gilgamesh's." Akkiru shrugged and leaned in towards Enkidu. "Well, they're not all actually his but legally."

"Akkiru," Meritkara scolded.

"He already knows how this works. Shamhat said he was present during the new bride's interview."

She slapped his arm. He groaned and dramatically rubbed it which earned him an eye roll. Enkidu ignored their playful interactions. "Gilgamesh allows all of his wives to have children with others if they wish?"

Meritkara looked out at the courtyard which teemed with giggles, mild arguments, and one round of enthusiastic cheers as someone won a game. "For all his reputation, he's not a terrible man." She twisted her lips up. "He shares a bowl of beer with Hanbi now and then, but he's not evil like that god. Shamhat wants him to find the best in himself."

"Then that's my role," Enkidu said. He wasn't sure he understood it, but he could feel the importance. Gilgamesh ruled the grandest city in the world. The actions he took affected everyone, even the forest's creatures. If he truly had a good heart and needed someone to help him see it, Enkidu would try. "When will I see him again?"

Meritkara's lips curled in. "At his pleasure."

Gilgamesh would desire to see him about the time the moon froze in the sky. Enkidu was back to being stuck without purpose in that overwhelming palace.

"Usun!" Akkiru called and walked into a shaded section where a pair of boys finished a game. Meritkara nodded her head in that direction, and Enkidu stepped over with her. "Don't you have fighting drills at this hour?"

Usun's cheeks flushed. No one needed to tell Enkidu that this boy was born of Gilgamesh's blood. He had his father's broad shoulders and square jaw. He bowed to each of them before answering. "Father decided to train with his men today instead."

"Ah." Akkiru gripped the boy's shoulder. "Your mother tells me I'd best stop teasing you. She says you're becoming such a fierce fighter you'll lose your temper and have me on my back in the dirt."

"Bah." The boy grinned at Akkiru. He was nearly as tall

as the man despite having a child's smooth cheeks. "Even if I get as good as Mother believes I am, you know I'll always let you get away with things."

"What about me?" Meritkara propped her hands on her hips.

"You never tease me, Nin."

She smiled and gestured to Enkidu. "Have you met our guest?"

Usun stepped forward, blinking into the sunlight. His eyes ran up Enkidu's great height then lingered at the horns before he made a hasty bow. "Forgive me. You must be Enkidu?"

Meritkara smirked at the boy. "What if you teach our new friend how to play Twenty Squares?"

The boy looked back at a wooden board covered in squares then lifted his face with a quizzical expression to Enkidu. "It's complicated. Do you have time to learn?"

"I do." He had too much time, in fact. He followed the boy and settled on the ground. Usun, despite his size, folded into a graceful position and kept his posture upright. Akkiru and Meritkara sat on a bench in the sun, and a young girl ran up to hug the woman before jumping into the man's arms. He tossed her into the air as she squealed and Meritkara admonished him to be careful.

Usun explained the game's rules and handed a set of knucklebones to Enkidu. He rolled and moved his pieces.

"Are you enjoying your time in the palace so far?" Usun asked after a few rounds.

Shamhat came out in the boy's refined manners. When she said he'd grown too old to have his mother doting on him, rubbing oils into his hands or combing his hair, sadness had permeated her words.

Enkidu shrugged as he moved a marker. "It's a strange

experience to have everyone already know about me, crafting stories about me, before I've met them." Moving through a complicated palace where he had no role was even more difficult. His throat tightened again.

Usun cocked his head. It was his turn, but he didn't move. "I understand how that feels."

Enkidu placed his hands on his knees and waited for the child to continue. Usun looked around him before sighing. "I am the Lugal's oldest child. Everyone has a story they tell about me—some bad and some good."

Enkidu smiled. "I think you must be braver than me."

The boy's lips snapped apart. "I've heard you fought a panther with your bare hands and wrestle with lions for fun."

He hoped that was the worst rumors Usun had heard. He suspected that if Usun knew the more salacious ones, he filtered them out of kindness. Either that or he still possessed the mind of a young boy that found the idea of fierce battles with wild creatures more compelling. Enkidu snorted and leaned across the board to whisper. "Rumors make a being more interesting than reality, I think."

Usun's expression darkened, and he grabbed the knucklebones. "They definitely make people talk." His cheeks burned with color again. Unlike his father, Usun showed his emotions in the way he held his shoulders and the pinch between his brows. Gilgamesh was angry that Shamhat started rumors about herself. Perhaps Usun had heard them or even faced teasing remarks.

"People only talk about others if they aren't doing interesting things themselves." Usun stopped halfway between moving his chip, and Enkidu continued. "If someone takes a risk and does something different, others might murmur about it. Songbirds squall and cry at each other, but hawks don't announce their presence. They swoop down on the others while they are busy making noise."

The boy blinked at him and nodded quickly before returning to the game. For several minutes they played in silence. The music shifted, and a woman walked up to them, her eyes sparkling. She inclined her head towards Usun. "Ensi."

Usun jumped up and bowed. "Kasiru. Let me introduce you to Enkidu."

The woman tucked a flute beneath her arm. "The man who doesn't need an introduction. I hear even Inanna is curious about you."

"It seems everyone is," Enkidu said.

Kasiru shrugged. "Exciting things happen within the palace every day, if you can believe it." Enkidu didn't comment, but he believed it. It was a restless, anxious place. "Yet we rarely get to meet someone divinely touched."

"Your king walks through the palace every day."

Kasiru laughed, her voice musical. "That's true. Well, it was nice to meet you. Have a good afternoon, Ensi." She nodded towards Usun again before walking away and catching up with another group of retreating musicians.

Enkidu picked up the knucklebones and started playing again. "Inanna is the city's patron goddess?"

Usun reached for a piece but stopped and blinked at him. "I forget you didn't grow up here. It's surprising for someone to not know Inanna. The city exists for her, you know?"

"I don't, actually." He smiled at the boy. Enkidu understood words and concepts, but he didn't comprehend the meaning behind those things. "Would you tell me about her?"

Usun sighed. "I'd like to tell you the truth, but we're supposed to be careful about what we say." He rattled the knucklebones across the board. "Half my parents' jobs are keeping her happy. The only reason Kasiru is Mother's head musician is because she used to work for Inanna."

"Inanna is powerful because she's a goddess?"

"Yeah. She's the goddess of love and war. Uruk is the most influential city in the world because of Inanna." Usun leaned across the board, the sunlight hitting his eyes and brightening them. He dropped his voice to a whisper. "But if you want to know the truth, I think she's a bitch."

Enkidu's eyebrows shot up.

The boy flushed and sat back again. "I'd appreciate it if you didn't tell my mother I know that word."

"Your secrets are safe with me." Enkidu smiled.

Usun lifted his face slowly then returned the grin.

It wasn't until later, when Meritkara and Akkiru returned him to his room, that Enkidu's heart started pounding again and sweat broke out on his brow. He paced his room's confines and tried to breathe. Like for Usun, there was no escape. The palace with all its intrigues and politics and business was their prison, and they were both bound to it by Gilgamesh.

CHAPTER ELEVEN
RUMORS & REPUTATIONS

ONCE AGAIN, Gilgamesh sat on his throne next to his wife while their advisors pretended they didn't notice the tension that strung between them. As each person walked in, Shamhat acted gracefully and spoke with a steady voice. However, she wouldn't meet Gilgamesh's stony stare for more than a moment before her gaze flitted away.

The bull statues along the room with the heads of past kings mocked him. Soon that's all that would remain—statues that others could destroy, bury, desecrate.

He tried to craft something grand out of this life, but his wife had started rumors that burned through the court like lightning hitting dried grass.

They'd burn to death so she could make a point.

At least others had grown wise enough to not speak Shamhat's name in his presence with so much as a sigh attached. He'd said he would cut the tongue out of the next person who spoke maliciously about her in his hearing, and he intended to follow through on that threat. No one had any right to speak ill of her even if it was her damn fault.

The doors opened, and a man wearing a crimson and

gold tunic stepped in and bowed before rising. When he spoke, his accent was thickly curled like those who lived closer to the Idiklat river.

"Lugal, thank you for the audience. My name is Narishal, and I am an uzu." Gilgamesh readjusted in his seat and tried to conceal his displeasure. He had little purpose for diviners and magicians. He'd always hated asking one of Uruk's uzu to divine the gods' signs through animal entrails as if Gilgamesh wasn't a god himself, couldn't confer directly with the gods. "I travel to you from Umma."

At that, Gilgamesh straightened. Zage-Si still hadn't answered for the messenger he'd killed. Gilgamesh's heart hardened like a stone at the reminder of Zage-Si's unforgivable crimes against his wife. He'd always championed Shamhat, fought for her wellbeing, and guarded her reputation. Yet she'd given herself over to foolish impulses.

Gilgamesh hadn't visited his mother since the betrayal. Soon she'd call for him and he'd have to decide how deep this had cut, what other relationships he might sacrifice. With Inanna's deadline hanging over his head like a battle ax, perhaps it didn't matter.

Months left, and he had done nothing worthy to mark his name in history's memory. Perhaps he wouldn't. Shamhat would ensure that his legacy went to dust shortly after his body.

The uzu continued, waving his arms wide so his crimson sleeves rippled. "I have served Lugal Zage-Si all my days. However, more than that I worship Asalluhi, son of Ea, and have always honored the gods' names."

Gilgamesh wished the man would stop with the flowery introduction and get to his point.

"The King of Umma has called for my council

frequently in the last months. He discussed with me something that disturbed me so I couldn't sleep. Night after night, ill omens plagued my dreams. Finally, I took a pilgrimage to Asalluhi's temple and asked for the god's interpretation."

Gilgamesh leaned forward, his feet pressing into his boots. He'd continued having the dream that had him seeking his mother's advice. It wasn't surprising since, instead of easing his suffering, she'd chucked riddles at him while indulging his wife's impulses.

"Asalluhi honored me and appeared to me." The uzu ducked his head low like he bowed before the god again. "He told me that Lugal Zage-Si's actions offend the heavens, and I was to bring a warning to the god-king."

Gilgamesh shifted his jaw to keep a smile from rising. Zage-Si planning something against him wasn't good, but it was nice for someone to appreciate his status. Gilgamesh was the only king who could boast godly origins, he was the only one who had the potential to rule all the Land Between Waters. He expected Shamhat to poke him or clear her throat—somehow expressing that she found his lack of humility wanting. She stared at the uzu, her brow furrowed, and didn't acknowledge him at all.

He was tired of the brokenness between them. When he'd told Shamhat he could ignore her, he'd meant it at that moment. He'd considered informing the guards not to allow the Queen in his apartments, discussing only essential information, no longer sharing meals or burdens. A day of living it, though, and he was already tired.

"Asalluhi wishes for you to know," the uzu continued, "that King Zage-Si attempts to summon demons and hopes to use them to bring you and your walls down, Lugal."

Gilgamesh clenched his teeth, remembered he

shouldn't, then ignored that. He had too much pressure to form better habits. "Has he had success at this endeavor?"

"Not yet, Lugal. However, he believes he will, and he intends to summon Alû."

Gilgamesh breathed a curse. That's just what he needed—a demon of darkness and shadows plaguing him as he attempted to manage Uruk's politics and the gods' fickle desires. "Thank you, uzu. Your endeavors are appreciated and shall be rewarded."

"With respect, Lugal, I do not require a reward. My devotion is to Asalluhi, and he honors my devotion."

"As you wish."

The man left, and Gilgamesh tapped his fingers on his throne's arm. He'd known the situation wasn't handled. Perhaps he'd acted too modestly during the battle. He should have marched into Umma, pulled their blasphemous king off his throne, and strung him up before his people.

Of course he hadn't done that for Shamhat's sake. The woman who sat as still as a statue at his side. Normally she added thoughtful comments between visitors, spoke as much as he did, leaned in to whisper council. Now Gilgamesh had to manage alone. His teeth clacked as he gritted them together.

Hirin bowed to whisper. "One final messenger, Lugal."

He nodded but tacked on a command. "When we disband, inform my men and the soldiers we may march soon." If Zage-Si wished to deal with demons, Gilgamesh would give him one.

Hirin's forehead puckered, but he bobbed his head. "Yes, my king."

Finally, someone who could follow basic orders without complicating matters. Gilgamesh hadn't appreciated Hirin enough. Now time had passed, and he looked into his future demise like he stared at the sun, unblinking but burning.

The doors opened again, and a priest of Inanna's made their way down the room. Gilgamesh bit back a groan. He'd been Usun's age when Inanna killed his father, when he'd taken on the weight of running a city and managing gods. Every time he saw one of her damned priests, that child shuddered within him. Gilgamesh wasn't that boy anymore. He hated the reminder of his weaknesses, his vulnerability.

The priest bowed, smiling at Kasiru as they rose and met the King's and Queen's gazes. Gilgamesh despised having Inanna's rat—Shamhat's favorite musician or otherwise, that's who Kasiru was—among his advisors. She'd started her career as a flutist who frequently served at Inanna's temples. Inanna favored her and had met with her many times. Whether he liked the musician or not, it was wise to keep someone who knew the inner workings of Inanna's temples around.

"Yes?" Gilgamesh growled. He didn't have the patience for Inanna's demands.

The priest was tall and muscular, their eyes glistening with makeup. They only grinned at Gilgamesh's peevishness. "Lugal, Our Lady in Heaven has sent me to ask what colors you intend to wear for your marriage ceremony."

"That is not for some time yet."

The priest raised their shoulders in a shrug, then seemed to think better of it, stalling the movement. "Akitu is not so long from now."

Shamhat gasped, quietly, but it was still a notable reaction in the throne room where she normally kept her emotions trapped beneath a smooth facade. Hirin cleared his throat. Inanna needed placating, and this was easy ground to give. Gilgamesh normally dug his heels in to hold even a finger of ground. However, Hirin was wise. To ignore his council for stubbornness' sake was foolish. "Tell Inanna I shall choose a tunic of crimson and blue, and I'll wear lapis lazuli beads."

The priest grinned widely. Those were Inanna's colors and stone. "I shall inform her, my king."

When they left, Gilgamesh turned towards Hirin and gave a pointed look. The man clapped his hands, his ankle-length tunic rustling as he motioned to others. "Thank you, everyone. You have served your king and queen well today."

The advisors took the dismissal and filed out. Hirin bowed before Gilgamesh.

"Did you tell me once, Hirin, that you have a nephew wishing to join the soldiers?"

Hirin lifted his face, his mouth gaping before he snapped his lips together. "I do, Lugal. He's been informed there is at least a year's wait for the position." Uruk was the only city that held a standing army. Most others recruited among their people during the off season for harvesting. It was expensive to keep an army, but a price Gilgamesh was glad to pay though they kept a strict limit on numbers.

"Send him to Abgal. Tell him I've requested for him to find a place for the boy."

"That's v-very generous of you, my king."

Gilgamesh waved him off. He needed to weave Hirin's loyalty as tight as he could. "Thank you for making Inanna's crow wait until the end."

Hirin chuckled breathily. Only Gilgamesh was foolish enough to insult someone connected to Inanna aloud. "I thought perhaps it would be for the best if your head was clear while speaking with others first, my king."

"You understand my mind, Hirin."

The man's eyes doubled in size, and he bowed several times before retreating.

Shamhat hadn't shifted. She stared ahead at the copper doors as Hirin slipped out of the room. "You've agreed to marry Inanna?" she finally asked.

A foul taste flooded the King's mouth. "Yes. I apologize I didn't inform you, my queen. You were not here when that event occurred."

Shamhat winced. Some part of Gilgamesh bemoaned hurting his wife. Another part, that still licked raw wounds, pushed him to his feet and guided him down the steps.

"Wait." Shamhat followed. When he stopped, she stood before him. "I'm tired of this discomfiture between us. Aren't you?"

She appeared so young with her wide eyes glistening in the sunlight that poured through the open ceiling. Gilgamesh shook his head. "Of course I am." Everything in his life crumbled like sand against a tide, their relationship most of all. She'd always been his steadying hand, his most trusted counselor, his queen. "But what would you have me do? You conspire with my mother, drag some strange man into my court, spread salacious gossip about yourself, and I have to pretend I'm friends with him to try to keep our reputation—"

"Oh, yes, gods forbid we sully your name." She snarled the words and her eyes had gone as dark as coals.

Fuck his name. His ambitions were likely ruined, anyway. Inanna would win—she was who history would remember. But in this lifetime—this godsdamned present moment Shamhat always wanted him to appreciate—no one would speak ill of her. She sacrificed everything for Uruk. He didn't doubt she'd have been made a high priestess in his mother's temple if she'd continued serving there. She'd have become one of the most influential people in the world without the court's gossip and watching eyes. In the temple, she would have remained insulated and happier. Gilgamesh's heart ached.

"This is about *your* name, not mine," he growled. "I've always withstood wagging tongues talking shed about me, but I won't have it for you."

She moved closer and thrust her chin up. "Oh, so this about *my* reputation?"

"Of course it is! No one has any right to speak ill of you."

She clenched her fists. "I never asked you to safeguard my reputation."

"You didn't have to," he roared. "I love you!"

Shamhat's features smoothed as she released a breath that sounded over the room's quiet. Birds chirped somewhere in the distance and the quiet murmur of palace workers hummed. Shamhat's fingers loosened, and her gaze skimmed her husband's face.

He let his posture loosen, and his words came quietly. "I love you... and I know our relationship isn't that of a typical man and wife, but I do care for you deeply. You're my queen —yes—but beyond that you've always been my counselor, my co-ruler who I trust explicitly, and my friend." He sighed and turned from her, his voice wavering. "Yet you conspire against my dreams."

That's what hurt, really. He'd always had a vision too massive for a lifetime. He thought he could achieve it or die trying. Through it all, Shamhat stood at his side. He had his men—his most loyal soldiers—who he trusted with his life. However, they had lovers or families they returned to. They had warm bodies to fill their beds and soothing hands to rub their backs as they recounted a battle's stress.

Gilgamesh never had that. But he thought he had something as good—better, maybe. His relationship with Shamhat was the most honest thing he'd ever experienced. He'd liked her from the moment they met when she'd placed her hands on her hips and said she would prefer to remain a priestess instead of becoming his queen. He'd replied that he'd prefer a man in his bed, but sometimes one must sacrifice for the good of the people. Her eyes had glittered, and she pinched her lips to suppress a smile. After that, they sat side-by-side in Ninsun's temple and spoke freely about everything. He left that meeting knowing he'd met his queen if she would have him.

"Gilgamesh." Shamhat gripped his arm. "Of course I don't wish to destroy your dreams. I spoke with your mother and asked her to intervene because I worry for you." Her eyebrows pinched. "You see nothing but the future. You're missing your entire life and—don't shake your head —it matters. Don't you think you can have both? Your mother sent this man to help you, not to destroy your legacy."

"How could he help me?" Gilgamesh's voice rose, but it lacked heat. He only wanted an answer. Why did his mother send this man who had no useful skills, no political savvy, and no godly connections?

Shamhat's shoulders dropped. "I don't know. I wish I understood—he's not what I expected, but he's not what you fear. He didn't grow up immersed in political implications and the gods' drama and family connections like we did. I tried discussing politics and the importance of your rule with him on our walk back to civilization, and he barely listened. He's not here to challenge your throne.

More than that, I believe he's a good man, like you." She placed a hand on Gilgamesh's chest, and he cupped it beneath his palm.

They stood like that for a moment. His heartbeat thudded through her hand and into his. She looked down. "Usun met Enkidu. He liked him."

Gilgamesh's throat tightened. He couldn't keep doing this with Shamhat. He gripped her fingers and grabbed her free hand, looking her in the eyes before he spoke in a whisper. "You know I'd crown him if I could."

Shamhat took a shaky breath and her eyelashes fanned her cheeks with her rapid blinks. "He's an amazing young man, Gilgamesh. I don't just say that because I'm his mother. He's clever with numbers, popular among the boys his age, and so strong and quick on his feet."

"I don't doubt he is; he's your son after all."

A pained smile crept over her lips. "He's your son too."

"I know."

They remained frozen like that for a moment, like they'd transformed into one of the room's grand statues. Neither could say the truth they both understood: Inanna meant to have her son on the throne. If Gilgamesh favored Usun, it would condemn the child. He loved him too much to do that.

"Do you think," Shamhat said, enunciating each word carefully, "it's good for Uruk to have the divine on a mortal throne?"

At another time he might have grown offended, his pride stinging, but he understood. He and Shamhat had fought to change Uruk, to build something new. The gods created people to serve them. Humans had evolved; they had their own desires and wishes and needs. Gilgamesh didn't mean to abandon the gods—he was two-thirds one, after all. But together, he and Shamhat dreamed of a world where people held as much value as the gods they served.

Gilgamesh ran his thumb over her finger's smooth length. "I think angering the gods is a dangerous game that mortals cannot afford to play."

She winced. "When does it change, then?"

"When someone is willing to endanger themselves. However, it won't be our son, Shamhat, and do not ask it of me. Usun is too good to risk."

Shamhat exhaled, her body crumpling. Gilgamesh did something he never did. He folded his arms around his wife and pulled her into his embrace. She rested her head on his chest. Her breath rose against his body, and he rubbed her back. His hand was so large compared to her. Sometimes he forgot his wife was mortal. She'd always exuded so much majesty. With her tucked beside him, though, she felt smaller, her bones fine, her heartbeat reminding him of just how breakable she was.

"Maybe Enkidu's purpose," she whispered, "is to help you look."

"Look at what?"

She leaned back but didn't pull out of his embrace. "He's lost too, Gilgamesh. He's also god-marked, also worries what his purpose is and wishes to make a differ- ence but feels stymied by how the gods have used him. Maybe he isn't here to make you stumble but to deepen your purpose. If you look at him, see things about yourself in him, it will help you craft the legacy you long for."

Gilgamesh sighed but, for once, didn't argue.

CHAPTER TWELVE
SECOND IMPRESSIONS

It had become a habit for Gilgamesh to pace the courtyard at night. His omen-filled dream haunted him too much, the pain of the pebble biting into his heel, the thunder of his heart as the stone grew into a boulder, the surge as it raised him so he could see the entire world spread below. Then finally the wracking sobs when it broke.

He'd never cried like that in life—but he knew whatever grief would cause it tracked him like a wolf. He could almost hear the snapping of twigs, feel the warm breath of fate on his neck. Tension filled his body, preparing for its teeth to sink into his flesh.

Now he had Umma and Zage-Si to deal with. He'd march his soldiers as soon as the wedding was over with. More wasted time. He had so little of it, yet something always demanded more. The gods siphoned it from him so he'd never achieve his goals. He'd become like his father— buried, his name lost.

Flickering puddles of torchlights rippled over his shawl as he reached a wall. He turned to go back but stopped.

Something drew him towards the yard's shadowy side. Ornamental grasses tangled together, rustling and blending with Gilgamesh's clipped footsteps.

He rounded a corner and stalled. Enkidu walked along the wall, his fingers tracing over a mosaic of stretching cedar trees, galloping beasts, and the wild's cacophony of greens. Enkidu's hand froze before curling into a fist. He turned and slid down the wall, his eyes closing.

Gilgamesh scoffed. He couldn't even have a decent night of insomnia without this man ruining it. Enkidu clacked his head on the tiles and released a trembling breath.

He's lost too, Gilgamesh.

The scab forming over the wound between him and Shamhat was raw. One snag and it would come off, fresh blood welling. She wanted him to speak to the man. It might preserve his marriage, make Shamhat happy. Still, he remained tucked behind the shrubs, unwilling to move.

Enkidu reached up and slid a hand over the sleek ebony horns that tucked into his hair. He shivered again, his lips pulling down, his fingers lingering. Shamhat said Gilgamesh and Enkidu were alike in that they both worried what their purpose in life was. She'd been wrong about that for him. Enkidu may wander around aimlessly, but Gilgamesh had a plan. Every day he lived in the city destined for him since birth, walked by the ivory form of his mother's temple, and looked out at the walls he'd created. All he needed was some act that could seal his name in history, and he'd fulfill his purpose.

There was something in the way Enkidu touched the horns, like his markers of godhood revolted him, that shifted Gilgamesh from his hidden place. If Enkidu had arrived to steal his throne, he wouldn't hate those horns, he'd boast about them.

He stepped closer. "Enkidu?"

The man snapped his eyes open—those eyes that burst with color even in the shadows. Then he stumbled up. He wore only a tunic, his feet were bare, his long toes curling over the tile's grout. Enkidu's cheeks had warmed—he truly had no control over his emotions. What god crafted this pitiful creature?

He was a capable fighter though. Gilgamesh had called their wrestling 'theater' to influence the crowd, but the King had met his match and knew it. It still sparked in him. How could a man with so much strength, with a body designed to brawl, with legends already forming around him, not desire more? How could he sit in the courtyard with his nose flaring and his cheeks pink?

Shamhat thought he'd look at Enkidu and see himself. That just proved how little she understood him.

"Lugal." Enkidu bowed. The word rushed from him, wobbling.

"Are you all right?" Gilgamesh did this for Shamhat. Appeasing his wife was worth it. It had nothing to do with his curiosity about the man—and zero to do with those damned eyes. He'd speak with him so he could tell Shamhat he'd done so. He wouldn't mention that he didn't see a damn thing that reflected himself.

Enkidu shifted away, like he longed to run from the courtyard. "I apologize if I shouldn't be out here. I couldn't sleep."

Gilgamesh frowned. Okay, one thing. They had one thing in common. He scraped his fingers over his beard. He'd long since untangled the curls into a wavy mass. "Neither could I."

Enkidu didn't reply or move. Gilgamesh wished he would tell him to fuck off. He'd gladly do so. *I tried, Shamhat. The man is unapproachable!* Instead, Enkidu stared at him, and damn the god that gave him those blasted eyes.

"I have nightmares," Gilgamesh said. It surprised him to hear the words leave his tongue. He'd only ever shared the dream with his mother, and that was so she might interpret them. A foolish desire. One would think he'd learn.

However, Enkidu seemed so damned vulnerable. He pressed against the wall like he needed the support, his muscles trembling.

"My nightmares aren't typical ones," Gilgamesh said when he received no response. He could admit he now acted from curiosity. This man who'd thrown a fucking fig at him in front of his entire city and fought him with a god's strength and a demon's conviction wouldn't make eye contact in the courtyard. "Or, I gather they aren't typical. I've never experienced a normal human dream."

Enkidu's eyebrows pinched together. "What are your nightmares about?"

The stars above glistened—the torches' glow dimming their shine. He shouldn't share, but he'd told Shamhat he would try. "I possess enough god's blood that my dreams are omens—prophecies that will come true. Right now, I have the same one repeatedly. Oh. Can you interpret dreams?"

His question came out eager. Perhaps Enkidu with his divine horns and immunity to god's blood might possess divine abilities. The man gushed emotions like a waterfall; he was the opposite of most gods with their manipulative words and tricky actions. Enkidu would interpret his dream without the subterfuge his mother used to keep him from true understanding.

Enkidu frowned, his face scrunching before he lifted it towards the sky then met Gilgamesh's gaze again. "I'm not entirely sure, but I don't believe I can, my king."

A beat of disappointment pulsed through Gilgamesh, like a rock dropped to ripple through him. It settled quickly, though. He'd already processed that disappointment. He raced towards tragedy, but no one would spare him by explaining what it was.

"Don't call me by my title." Gilgamesh didn't know why, but he didn't like the man using formalities with him. Maybe it was because Enkidu was so honest—there was nothing veiling his emotions or intentions.

Enkidu's gaze dashed towards the arch leading into the palace. He wanted to escape the interaction. But, no, Gilgamesh wouldn't be dismissed. He'd end the conversation when he was through with it, and trying to put together Enkidu's incongruent pieces was more intriguing than mulling over the damned dream for hours.

Enkidu's eyelashes fluttered against his cheeks' smooth surface. His skin had to feel as soft as Ninsun's blankets. Enkidu pressed to the wall, steeling his muscles like something cornered him as sweat dripped over his brow. Gilgamesh had seen this in soldiers after battle. The fight would haunt them as badly as Gilgamesh's ill omens followed him about. They'd tremble and struggle to remain in the present.

"Something is wrong," Gilgamesh whispered.

"F-forgive me. I should return to m-my room."

"Enkidu." Gilgamesh stepped back to give him space. "What is it?"

Enkidu licked his lips. "I'm not used to the..." He

stopped for a rattling breath then straightened, like he attempted to force control back over his body. "The city is... the noise. It's all very..."

Uruk had to overwhelm someone who'd grown up in the cedar forest. Even with it so late that the moon had risen overhead, the occasional hooting yell or donkey's bray reached even the palace elevated above the city. "You miss the forest?"

"P-please." Enkidu turned his face away. He wanted to leave but Gilgamesh needed to help him. The sight of such a finely formed man—his height and muscles doing justice to his divine origins—shivering and struggling didn't sit right. When he'd had soldiers who struggled, he'd always remained with them himself, checked on them, made sure they had what they needed. A man shouldn't be alone in that state.

"Come with me?" he asked.

Enkidu released a breath. Even the wind held still so only his exhale, long and heavy, filled the space between them. His forehead furrowed, and a pucker formed above his lips as he pinched them. "All right."

The words were more capitulation than eager offer, but it was enough. Gilgamesh gestured towards the front of the courtyard and started walking, Enkidu a few paces behind. They passed through the palace's gates then down the hill towards the city. Enkidu stopped, a grimace twisting his features.

"Please," Gilgamesh said, "trust me."

Enkidu raised those damned eyes again. Fleeting glimpses of sorrow rippled across them. Enkidu didn't speak—it was like he couldn't—but nodded.

Gilgamesh led him onto a street, and went the long way, ignoring the busier paths that might overstimulate. It wasn't fear for their safety or concern that others would recognize him. His god's blood made even the fiercest people little trouble. He wove them farther from the palace until they reached a quiet section, the houses all closed for the night, laundry whipping about on some roofs.

When he arrived at his intended house, Gilgamesh spread his fingers over the door. He'd never forget visiting it for the first time. It had surprised him that he could feel nervous when approaching mortals. Humans were one thing, meeting one's father-in-law for the first time, another.

He opened the door, breaking the seal. He had guards inspect the house daily. If he ever found someone defacing it, their punishment would be brutal. Enkidu stepped into the dark with him. Their knuckles brushed, and Gilgamesh took a breath. He wasn't used to having someone his size nearby. Most people stood several cubits shorter. Gilgamesh found Enkidu's elbow to steer him through the dark. Years had passed since lamps had graced the place, but he could navigate it without sight.

Enkidu tensed. Gilgamesh wanted to slide his fingers around his arm to discover what reaction he could pull from the man. Enkidu was overwhelmed though, shutting down, so Gilgamesh kept his touch light.

They stumbled together through another door that led to the inner courtyard. It was desperately overgrown—Shamhat couldn't bear gardeners changing her parents' home. This seemed to be just the thing for Enkidu, though. He released a shuddering breath and stepped towards the trees, and shrubs until he stood among them. They swallowed his legs, hugged his hips. Enkidu reached for a leaf and slid his thumb over it. For being so large, his hands were graceful. They moved with a weaver's finesse.

Enkidu remained still for a long time. His breathing slowed. The shadowed form of his shoulders was somehow elegant among the scrabbling plants. Gilgamesh had seen him as a wild man, but as Enkidu lowered himself among the plants, he realized he'd been mistaken.

The forest with its tangling poisonous plants, gnashing beasts, and Humbaba's lair—it was wild. Enkidu was something else entirely. He didn't belong in the city, didn't long for a throne, and understood nothing of politics. Yet, sitting in an overgrown courtyard, draped in pale moonlight, there was something so beautiful about him—strong and fragile, mysterious and transparent. Gilgamesh couldn't tear his gaze away. Perhaps he had judged him too quickly.

Gilgamesh ground his teeth together.

He was not willing to admit to Shamhat he'd been wrong yet. The gods could incinerate his legacy before he'd give that quickly. Damn him for marrying someone who always saw straight through him. He crossed his arms, feeling like a petulant child.

After a time, Enkidu's posture eased, and the trembling stopped. He looked back at Gilgamesh, and that's when he joined him, sitting over a broken tile where weeds sprouted.

"Thank you," Enkidu said as though he struggled to form the words, wished to say more but couldn't craft it.

"We all have moments, Enkidu."

He turned to look at Gilgamesh. "Including you?"

The way he asked it made the preening part of Gilgamesh straighten itself, spread its feathers. Even Enkidu—the man who'd thrown a godsdamned fig at him, which he'd never get over—saw him as fearless. Gilgamesh had crafted the perfect image of a god-king. However, sitting there in his family's home, their ghosts lingering as the elements slowly took over, cracking pots and climbing walls, he couldn't lie. Sweat broke out over his body like it had the first night he'd had the nightmare. His muscles tensed, struggling to shake him from the omen's grip.

"Yes, including me." Then, to avoid discussing that further, he added, "This is Shamhat's parents' home."

Enkidu's gaze flowed over the walls where dirt caked the bottom then passed over chipped pottery. "It seems a long time since anyone has lived here."

"They died a decade ago." Gilgamesh slid his teeth together.

Usun had been a toddler still sleeping with his mother. She was tired but appeared in the throne room—that was the detail that stuck with him about the day. She had shadows under her eyes. He'd once suggested Usun sleep with a nursemaid, but she'd refused. Then the messenger walked in with the news.

Shamhat kept her perfect image intact. But he could feel the cracks slowly spreading over her. He'd stood so quickly his stone throne had shifted with a screech. *Everyone out at once.*

He held her as she wailed. As she asked why the gods had allowed her parents to die in such a vicious manner. Gilgamesh hadn't possessed answers. All he had to offer was the strength of his arms, like he might hold all her broken pieces together.

It was the only time she'd grieved before him. The next day she'd appeared in the throne room wan, dressed in a plain goat-hair tunic with no adornments or makeup. But she raised her chin as if she dared Gilgamesh to question her actions.

They had no bodies to bury, no rituals to help them process.

So, they moved forward. Shamhat became the priestess-queen force of nature she now was, and Gilgamesh grew to understand how little certainty life offered.

"They were traveling the northern road," Gilgamesh continued, transfixed on a vine that curled its way around a palm tree. "Humbaba left its lair, apparently. There were not even bodies left to bury. I had"—his voice grew thick, but he was so lost in the memories he scarcely noticed—"nothing to offer Shamhat."

Enkidu curled a hand around Gilgamesh's arm, and it broke the trance. Gilgamesh turned towards him. "Death is a curse," Enkidu said. "It takes from us, leaving only questions we can't answer."

Gilgamesh's stomach fizzed and the place on his arm where Enkidu's hand draped warmed, like all the blood in his body rushed there. He pulled away. It was too much, an unfamiliar sensation and one he didn't wish to parse out.

"You might have been made a priest if you'd grown up in the city." Gilgamesh meant to speak with levity, but his voice remained heavy.

Enkidu chuckled and raised his face to the stars. "I doubt that. Meritkara and Akkiru showed me your mother's temple. The priestesses seem to buzz here and there all day, so busy."

"It's good for a man to be busy, isn't it?"

Enkidu shrugged. "If the work is meaningful, yes. If not, he's just toiling to fool himself that he has purpose."

Gilgamesh released a breath and leaned against his legs. So much of his life was toiling at unimportant matters, chasing chaff on the wind as his mother had called it. How did one find their purpose, though?

"It was good of you to bring me here," Enkidu said. "I can see that this is a personal place for you. It's helped tremendously. The palace—it's too much." His voice deflated. "I suppose I'll adjust."

Gilgamesh wanted to snatch the defeat from his voice. He knocked their shoulders together and pointed at the sky's sweeping ebony. "Did you know the stars indicate what to hunt and gather in the wild at different times of the year?"

Enkidu's eyebrows shot up, and he raised his face to look at the crystal specks. "I suppose I do know that. I have many things in my mind that I have the words for, can describe, but don't truly understand."

Every sentence that came from the man's mouth seemed profound. Men—even god-born men like Gilgamesh—grasped at the world like they swung a scythe before rye. As if they could thresh about in the darkness and find meaning by slicing blindly. But not Enkidu. His words flowed like a quiet river, like he had all the time in the world to understand things.

"I suppose that's true for us all in some ways." Enkidu shifted closer, his head cocked which revealed a stretch of more smooth skin. How such a rough man who'd lived among the wild had such perfectly unmarked flesh, he didn't know. Fine, dark hairs ran over his arms and legs and even they appeared too soft.

"Come with me to the roof and I'll teach you some about interpreting the sky."

Enkidu blinked—gods if his eyelashes weren't long. Gilgamesh couldn't understand this man, or find a category that fit him. Enkidu nodded and jumped up with the finesse of his youngest soldier, his feet scarcely making a sound despite his bulk.

Gilgamesh stood as well, aware of how brutish his movements were in contrast. That's how a man the size of

Enkidu should sound when moving, like a being that made an impression on the earth. Instead, Enkidu was graceful and nearly silent.

Gods, Gilgamesh was tired of the paths he'd let his mind follow that night. He led the way to a ladder and shook it several times to ascertain its stability before gesturing for Enkidu to climb.

CHAPTER THIRTEEN

UNDER THAT SPLENDID SKY

AT THAT DARK part of the city where torches were put to rest for the night, the stars sparkled almost as brightly as in the forest. Enkidu had spent the evening spiraling into a panic. When Gilgamesh found him in the courtyard, he felt as low as a grub attempting to burrow in dirt.

Then the King had brought him to that quiet house so he could stand among plants and find his breath. Gilgamesh had listened to him, touched him gently.

Enkidu didn't know what to make of it. Gilgamesh embodied everything a person could, all the good and bad. Perhaps that's what it meant to be part god—having too much of everything to exist as merely a mortal.

"You see there." Gilgamesh pointed, his shoulder brushing Enkidu's so that it tingled. They lay side-by-side on the roof, and Gilgamesh had spent the previous hour explaining how to read the sky with so much passion, he'd drawn Enkidu into a topic he'd never cared about before. "The bright one near the bottom. If you look closely, it's not a full circle like the others. It's almost a crescent."

Enkidu squinted. He'd never observed the stars so carefully before—they'd been like pebbles on the lake shore, a beautiful mass. He wasn't sure if Gilgamesh had better sight than him or if he'd studied the skies so much longer. The King spoke of the heavens with a child's enthusiasm. Enkidu froze when he found the star. It had a sliver missing from its edge. "I've found it."

"That is the star of Inanna. I think that covers the basics of tonight's sky, but perhaps that's what is so fascinating. It's always changing. In a month I could show you an entirely different arrangement."

Enkidu shifted, and his arm scraped Gilgamesh's again. Warmth swept down his limbs and clenched his stomach. Before that night, he could ignore what spurred the feeling. The palace's chaos kept his mind occupied. Out here, far from the politics and buzz of thousands of people moving through the halls, the quiet on the roof allowed for the same in his mind.

Which left room for him to process the emotion.

He was attracted to Gilgamesh.

A normal response. Anyone might find Gilgamesh attractive, and Enkidu couldn't control his body's responses. But it was a disaster for him. Gilgamesh was the King of Uruk—the most powerful and revered human in the world. Why would he bother with someone like Enkidu? A man who had no past and no purpose.

Enkidu couldn't lie there and share interesting things he'd learned in childhood—he didn't have one.

He also wasn't sure how he felt about Gilgamesh as a person. Everyone kept saying things that confirmed the gods had created Enkidu to serve a self-absorbed demon. Then Gilgamesh would do something compassionate and thoughtful. He possessed more layers than a practice tablet, and Enkidu didn't know how to navigate his own mind, much less unravel Gilgamesh's.

According to gossip, the King had favorite temple prostitutes, and he'd sired many of the children who lived in the Queen's palace. Enkidu didn't think it was wrong to approach sex casually, but he knew bone-deep it was wrong for himself.

All of that combined made the gooseflesh that rose every time their skin brushed unwelcome.

Enkidu moved away and turned his attention back to the star. "Do you dislike Inanna?" Usun did, and every time Gilgamesh said her name his inflection shifted darker.

Gilgamesh stiffened, his breath catching. "Inanna is our city's patron goddess." He said it as though he read it from a tablet.

The King shifted his face. Enkidu had seen Gilgamesh draped in fine clothing, his beard neatly curled as he towered over his people and dripped fine words. The authoritative leader handing out commands like clouds giving rain. This Gilgamesh, though, his eyes rippling with emotions, his beard wavy and untouched, was new.

Gilgamesh licked his lips, and Enkidu hated how his gaze traced the motion. "Sometimes," the King said, "one must be careful with their words. They never know who might listen."

So, Inanna could overhear their conversation. That explained a great deal of Gilgamesh's reticence to speak true. Enkidu shifted back towards the sky, finding the star of Inanna solely to break free from the contact that had his heart racing.

Enkidu laced his fingers over his chest. "In the forest, the creatures discussed Humbaba in the same way. They whispered its name like speaking it would summon the dragon." Enkidu shifted back to find Gilgamesh focused on him, not with derision for his unhuman-like past, but with fixed interest. "There are wolves and panthers and lions—fierce but able to coexist and share the wild. Then there is Humbaba who destroys everything it touches, who kills when it doesn't need food, or harms for no reason. Its demands surpass reasonable even for a predator."

Gilgamesh took a breath that caused his nostrils to flare and nodded. He understood what Enkidu meant. Gilgamesh might be a wolf—vicious in some ways, deadly, but not destructive like Enkidu had originally thought. From the little Enkidu had gathered from others, the actual monster of Uruk was Inanna.

"The difficult thing about creatures like Humbaba"—Gilgamesh stretched the name out; they weren't actually discussing the cedar forest dragon—"is who can control them? They are too powerful, and so the rest of us must meet their demands or perish." His jaw flexed. "Shamhat isn't the only one who had a monster kill her father, if you gather what I mean."

Enkidu moved closer. Inanna had ended Gilgamesh's father's life. He reached out to drape a hand over Gilgamesh's arm and found his wrist instead. He froze. Before he could pull back, the King grasped his fingers. Enkidu shivered, his body caught somewhere between frozen and rushing with every imaginable feeling. Two things that shouldn't exist together yet did. The sensation matched Gilgamesh perfectly.

The King had massive hands, slightly bigger than Enkidu's even, with smooth calluses.

"W-what demands must a king give to a wild creature?" Enkidu choked out the words. Gilgamesh's flesh burned against his between their clasped hands. His shoulder tingled where it touched the King's.

Gilgamesh chuckled, but the smile faded quickly. "Every King of Uruk must marry and vow themselves to a divine."

"You're already married, multiple times in fact."

Gilgamesh rose onto his side, dropping the hand. That would provide a break in the tension except he leaned over Enkidu. He blocked the moon's light with his broad shoulders and brought their bodies even closer. "I thought we'd already discussed this topic." Gilgamesh smirked, his dark eyes gleaming. "We won't fight again, will we? I'm afraid I can't allow us to damage this house."

I'd fight you solely to feel your body pressed against mine again. Enkidu slammed his eyes shut, willing the thought to drown. "Of course not," he said. "I acted foolishly when I came into the city. I wish I could take my actions back."

"I don't." Gilgamesh shifted close enough that his breath brushed Enkidu's cheek. "Describe a more epic meeting than ours."

"It's about the story, then?"

"What isn't about the story? What do we leave behind besides our names and legends?"

The answer might be the way his heart pattered as Gilgamesh's body loomed over his. Here was something no one would ever understand, regardless of stories. Enkidu didn't comprehend it himself. "You leave behind a son."

Gilgamesh released some sound between a scoff and a laugh and dropped to sitting, stretching his long arms over his bent knees. Enkidu sat up as well. The moonlight draped over Gilgamesh's muscles, following the curves like a lover's fingers.

"Did Shamhat put you up to speaking with me about Usun?"

Enkidu frowned. They'd shared some odd intimacy tucked away from the city under that splendid sky. It rushed away with the conversation's turn. "Shamhat didn't ask me to discuss anything in particular with you. I've met Usun, though. He favors you."

Gilgamesh grunted. "Damn the god that cursed him with that."

A breath puffed out of Enkidu. How could Gilgamesh think that? He preened like a haja-bird half the time. Surely he knew how beautiful he was. His body was humanity perfected—all strength and muscle and height. He had thick, dark wavy hair and sharp eyes that observed things so directly they cut.

Everyone who met him had to fear him, desire him, or feel inadequate compared to him. Possibly all three. Enkidu had certainly experienced the entire range.

Physical beauty meant nothing without the heart to back it, though. Gilgamesh had killed, led battles, and possibly overtaxed his people. But he also loved his wife, cared about justice, and had helped Enkidu.

There was good in his heart even if a dusty layer covered it.

"I can marry as many humans as I like, but I can only vow myself to one divine." Gilgamesh picked back up the previous topic like he wished to avoid discussing Usun. "A promise made to a divine is unbreakable. It lasts"—he released a breath that joined the wind, rushing over the city he led—"forever."

Forever.

He'd have to vow himself eternally to the goddess who killed his father. What a damning position. Enkidu wished he could shield him, longed to stand between the goddess and this man, not allow her to abuse him.

He wished he knew how he could help.

Ninsun had sent him for this purpose. If only he understood what he was supposed to do.

Gilgamesh shook his head. His eyes were fixed ahead. The city had quieted in the time they'd spent studying stars. Only a few lingering lamps glistened here and there aside from the line of torches that followed the palace's perimeter. Behind it all, Inanna's temple stood atop a massive ziggurat, like a hawk's perch where the creature sat and decided where to strike.

"Perhaps you're right," Gilgamesh whispered, as though he didn't mean to speak aloud. "Maybe stories become dust with time anyway and we'll all succumb to the cruel fate of death, forgotten and buried."

Enkidu's lips snapped apart, but words wouldn't form. Something delicate stretched between them, a spiderweb that brash movements would rip apart. He wanted to hold it. He longed to see it in every light, watch beads of dew glow orange across it at sunrise.

Instead, he moved closer so their arms brushed. Gilgamesh shifted and some of his weight rested on Enkidu.

"I don't agree with that, actually," Enkidu finally said.

Gilgamesh looked at him. With how close they sat, his beard prickled Enkidu's flesh. His eyes rippled with feelings that few others probably got to see. Perhaps not even Shamhat. He grabbed the King's hand again. This time his focus didn't fix on their touch—that was there, a slow burn —but more than that, he wanted Gilgamesh to know he wasn't alone.

"I've found words to feel inadequate," Enkidu said. He'd

spent hours running through the vocabulary stored in his mind. *Tablet, boat, drought, cousin, mother, lover.* He could define them but didn't understand them, not truly. "However, words strung together, pressed into clay in a certain manner or told around a fire with the right enunciation, can bring a man to tears or cause a grieving widow to laugh. I don't think the most important stories are ever truly lost."

"What do you think are the most important stories?" Gilgamesh's eyes traced over Enkidu's features with such intensity he shivered.

The answer to that question might have something to do with Gilgamesh's lips, or the weight of their hands clasped. He cleared his throat and attempted to keep his voice steady as he responded. "Maybe stories about love."

Gilgamesh scowled and pulled back, though he let his fingers linger in Enkidu's. "Love? Bah. Is this why you were so eager to jump to Nabba—the girl's defense."

"Her name is Nissaba."

"You're a romantic." Gilgamesh ignored the annoyance in Enkidu's response. "That explains a great deal about you, I think. I'm afraid a king can't prioritize love."

He squeezed Enkidu's hand before pulling away and jumping to his feet. Enkidu followed him but his body felt heavier than a mountain.

Gilgamesh found love worthless. Perhaps Enkidu was a romantic, because even though he only grasped the concept by the tips of its wings, he thought it something worth facing monsters for. And Gilgamesh had all but laughed at it.

Enkidu shoved down the desires that had unleashed themselves the entire night. He'd lock them away. Helping Gilgamesh he could achieve, but they clearly could never be more.

The King didn't believe in love.

Something about it was a hunter's rope, snagging his leg and wrenching a limb loose from its socket.

"Unfortunately,"—the way Gilgamesh said that single word made Enkidu's heart prickle with possibilities again—"we must return. You don't know the state Hirin will get himself in if I'm missing in the morning." He rolled his eyes. "As if someone could damage me."

Enkidu chuckled uneasily. He didn't even know who Hirin was. Time to return to the palace he didn't belong in, the place where Gilgamesh ruled and shoved love and dreams and interests under his duties and ambitions.

"I want you to become one of my advisors." Gilgamesh cocked an eyebrow.

Enkidu threw his hands out. Gilgamesh's gaze followed the length of his arm before returning to his face. "What would I offer a king? I don't even know what advisors do."

"They listen to people complain about their troubles then say things that piss off their king. You'll be brilliant at it."

Enkidu held his breath until Gilgamesh laughed.

"Please. Help me." Gilgamesh ran his hands over his hair, weaving fingers through his thick tresses. "Everything you say is nonsensical and makes perfect sense at the same time. I don't understand it, but I want to hear more."

Enkidu tilted his head. That's how he saw Gilgamesh too. Rational and illogical all twined together. He'd vowed to take up his duty, to care for whatever stood before him. Now a king—*the* King—stood wrapped in indigo light imploring him to help. "All right. I doubt I'll have much to offer, but I'll do what I can."

Gilgamesh moved closer. His fingers flexed like he'd

reach out, but he curled them into a fist. "I'm glad to hear it."

They climbed down the ladder and stepped through the peaceful shadows of Shamhat's family home. Outside Gilgamesh clicked the door in place, then slid a hand down it before kneeling and opening a crock at the base. He pulled out a pinch of wet clay and spread it over the space where the door and wall met.

The light had changed, edges of lilac blending in with blues, the sun rising on another day. Gilgamesh pulled a cord from his neck that held a cylindrical stone. He pushed it to the clay and rolled it to impress an image.

"What's that?" Enkidu asked before his mind provided the answers. Already the concept flooded into his thoughts —*seal, stone, king's marks*—but the question was out.

"It's my signature. We seal Shamhat's house whenever we visit. If it's broken when we return, we'll know someone has entered."

Enkidu bent closer to the seal. A man who had to be Gilgamesh stood on a hill in the center, a lion cub tucked under his arm, sun rays stretching behind him. On either side, cattle grazed. Beyond them people bowed. Enkidu's lips pinched. He'd add Gilgamesh's seal image to the "arrogant" side of his attributes.

Then Enkidu's gaze caught on something. He hovered his hand over the impression. "Why does your crown have horns?"

Gilgamesh remained quiet long enough that Enkidu finally rose to find him staring at him, his eyes sparkling. "Horns signify divinity. Notice any statues of gods around the city—you'll see horns there too."

Enkidu slid his fingers along one of his smooth horns.

Gilgamesh's gaze followed the motion, and Enkidu dropped his hand like he touched a flame. "I didn't know."

Though now that Gilgamesh explained it, he realized the concept had lingered in his mind, waiting for him to discover it.

Gilgamesh laughed and knocked his shoulder into Enkidu's. He walked past him before calling back. "I'm glad I was there for the moment you discovered you're divine. Your expressions have yet to disappoint."

Heat pooled across Enkidu's cheeks, and he vowed to learn to cover his emotions better. He turned and followed the King back to the palace.

CHAPTER FOURTEEN
MARRIAGE & MURDER

ENKIDU STARED at the gold tiles on the wall. Sunshine spilled in from high windows and caused them to gleam like a golden river, the color bubbling and swirling in every shade. Hours had passed with advisors sharing news then arguing over minute details.

Shamhat stood at the front of the room perfectly composed, her hands resting on her arms as she watched the conversation, occasionally interspersing comments. Gilgamesh's eyes rarely remained on the person speaking. Instead, he looked around the room, stared at the windows, and occasionally glanced at Enkidu.

His heart would trip over itself each time he caught the King shifting attention towards him. Enkidu wished he could drag those feelings down, push them into a crock, and bury it deep within the earth.

He wanted to sit next to the King watching stars brighten in the night sky again.

He wanted to leave the city and never return.

The warring emotions filled him with misery. Joining the advisors didn't help. He had nothing useful to add. He felt as bored as Gilgamesh appeared, though the King would snap his attention back to the group when he added comments every few minutes. It was obvious he paid careful attention despite his wandering eyes.

A sigh built in Enkidu's chest, and he released it slowly.

"I believe we should advise the foresters to harvest only from the cedar forest's southern portion." An advisor frowned down at a clay tablet. "Humbaba's aggression grows. They could carve out sections of the forest and cut all the trees in that area."

"No." The word left Enkidu's mouth before he could stop it. Every face in the room turned towards him, and he shrank back towards the wall.

Shamhat cocked her head. "Do you have thoughts you wish to share, Enkidu?"

The King's gaze upon him felt like the sun beating down on him, burning until it marked. Enkidu swallowed and stared at the floor again. "You cannot clear an entire section of the forest. Everything is interconnected. It will damage more than just the area you raze."

The advisor shrugged and clapped his ring-adorned hands together. "The cedar forest is large. It will recover."

"Perhaps it would." Enkidu couldn't stop the words now. They spilled out, burning with passion. "However, there are other lives that would be affected."

The wolves' haunting howls streaked across Enkidu's mind.

Hirin cleared his throat like he would speak, but the first advisor scoffed before he could. "And why should we listen to you?"

Enkidu's anger left him in a great breath, and heat swept across his cheeks. He couldn't answer that. The gods had sent him, but for what purpose he didn't know.

Standing there advising a king was foolishness. Enkidu had nothing to offer.

Gilgamesh rolled his shoulders back, and thunder filled his voice when it came. "Are you questioning my appointment of Enkidu?" His nose flared. "Do you question the gods who sent him?"

The advisor's sneer washed away, and his eyes darted among the others before he shook his head. "Of course not. Forgive me, Lugal."

Gilgamesh kept the weight of his glare upon him for another dozen heartbeats. "That's enough for today. I have a wedding to prepare for."

The advisors bowed and shuffled out. Shamhat nodded towards Gilgamesh then left.

The room felt larger when it was empty. Enkidu's heartbeat seemed to echo off the high ceilings as it pounded in his ears. Gilgamesh walked up to him, his bejeweled shawl curling around his hips, tucking against his shoulder. It outlined his form and highlighted his muscular arms.

"I fear I'm making a terrible advisor," Enkidu said when he approached.

Gilgamesh grazed his knuckles over Enkidu's hand, and his heart stopped pounding for a moment. The King grinned at him. "I already trust you more than half the people in this room." A well of feelings dipped in Enkidu's stomach. "I'll see you in a few days."

"A few days?"

Gilgamesh sighed. "The wedding will have me preoccupied."

"Right." Enkidu forced a smile on. Something new snaked within him, though. It chipped at him like a stylus pressing into clay, marring him. It burned and blistered. If the feeling rested in his hands he'd drop it with a howl of pain.

Gilgamesh gripped his arm, causing the heat to flare within him, then turned and walked out of the room.

Days later, he watched the wedding parade from a distance—the bride winding her way through Uruk towards the palace, ribbons tossed around, colorful fabrics draped over everyone—with his heart clenching. He couldn't explain why; Nissaba's future and happiness were secure, and it wasn't an actual marriage. He hung back during the feast despite Gilgamesh's gaze darting to him from across the room throughout the night.

Hundreds of unnamable feelings swirled through him, leaving him with an aching head. He asked Meritkara how long he needed to stay and left as soon as she deemed it appropriate.

The moon had risen in the sky and Enkidu found himself sleepless once more. He passed through the palace's arched doorway. He couldn't risk going to the courtyard and running into Gilgamesh. If they ended up alone again beneath a silky dark sky, Enkidu might do things he'd regret once Utu stretched golden and bright across the morning sky.

Gilgamesh saw love as a joke. But love might mean everything—to Enkidu at least. He couldn't give in to the physical burn between himself and the King because Gilgamesh would tire of him, and Enkidu wouldn't be able to bear it. He'd rather have nothing than risk everything.

So, he walked past Ninsun's temple, the stars sparkling above. Gilgamesh's low voice explaining their names slipped across his mind. His arm had scraped his and bled warmth into Enkidu's body. The King had pulled open his heart that night.

Enkidu swallowed and passed a guard with a nod. The palace grounds were quiet after the wedding feast. Gilgamesh had shared enough wine to leave half the people who lived in the palace drunk and the rest stumbling to their beds from exhaustion.

Enkidu was tired, but not able to find the release of sleep. He walked to the Queen's palace, passing more guards, before finding the empty children's courtyard. Abandoned signs of them lingered everywhere—a pile of slingshots sat on a bench, a basket of rattles and bells were tucked in a corner, and the Twenty Squares board remained beneath the roof's shelter.

The children's courtyard wasn't as peaceful as the wild, tangling garden at Shamhat's family home, but it came close. Enkidu leaned on a wall and raised his face to a cooling breeze.

A scrape drew him out of his contemplations.

In the hall beyond the courtyard, someone moved, a dark shadow slipping along. Enkidu frowned but remained still. Guards lined the palace, after all. That was likely who it was. However, the burning in his stomach had turned into an inferno. He'd vowed to serve whatever lay before him. If his intuition proved wrong, he could return to the quiet in a few moments.

He pushed off the wall and stepped through an arch then turned down the hall. His feet scarcely echoed against the tiles as he walked down the dim corridor. He hadn't lost the silence he'd learned in the forest. Only the occasional torch lit the hall. Everyone slept. Typically, at night he'd pass one or two people, but after the wedding preparation and feast, only guards remained awake.

He turned a corner. A man in a guard's leather and helmet slumped on the ground. Enkidu crouched and raised the man's face. He held his breath to still his racing heart. The guard didn't rouse, so Enkidu pressed fingers to his neck. They plunged into something warm and damp. Enkidu pulled back glistening, crimson coated fingers.

His hand trembled. The guard was dead; his throat slit.

Enkidu jumped to his feet and ran. Footsteps echoed ahead. He stopped at a corner, attempting to remain hidden in the shadows. A person wearing some sort of head covering that obscured their face fiddled with a door. Something clicked, and they pulled a sword from their side and walked inside.

Enkidu gasped then cursed himself for the pause as he threw himself towards the door.

A shout tore through the night.

He was too late!

A clang of metal sounded as Enkidu stepped through the doorway. It was dark, the bodies shadows, the blades they brandished ebony lines. The two fought, grunts and heavy breathing echoing. Enkidu didn't know who the attacker was. He wasn't sure how to help.

One shadow turned its face towards him. "Enkidu!"

The voice was the same one that requested he not tell the Queen about his coarse language. Enkidu stood in Usun's bedroom, witnessing an attack on Gilgamesh and Shamhat's son.

The yell cost the boy. He stumbled back, his sword flying out of hand.

The assailant raised their blade with both arms.

Enkidu roared and tackled the fighter. They fell to the ground with an oof. Enkidu had them on strength, but they whisked a blade out. He jerked aside, but the blade cut across his arm. It stung as blood spilled.

Usun had recovered his sword and jumped back in to engage the assailant.

"Usun, don't," Enkidu cried. "Protect yourself."

The boy scoffed. So, he wasn't just like his father in appearance. Enkidu couldn't stand there and let the child die. Ignoring his injured arm, he darted towards the pair, caught the assailant, and crushed them against the wall. He slammed an arm across their throat. Many of Enkidu's musings of the last day had left him wondering if he could kill if needed. Now he didn't doubt it.

Usun released a sigh before lighting a lamp.

The fight had destroyed the room. Blankets had sword slashes, a broken gash in the mattress wept goats' hair and linen stuffing, and a shelf had tilted, leaving tablets scattered and broken on the floor.

"Enkidu, watch out!" Usun pointed.

Enkidu turned just as the assailant thrust a knife towards his gut. He released them, and they dashed from the room like a rabbit evading the wolf. Enkidu debated chasing, but staying with Usun and ensuring his safety seemed the priority.

"Shed," Enkidu cursed. He shouldn't have let the assailant go. Now they'd continue to pose a threat for the boy. More than that, he didn't understand *who* would risk their life by murdering Gilgamesh's son. The King would kill anyone who threatened his family—vindictively. It was part of the constant push and pull of attraction and wariness Enkidu felt for the man.

Usun's eyes widened as he walked up to Enkidu, but he didn't tremble. "You saved my life."

"You saved your own life. I assisted." It was true. Enkidu had been a few steps too slow. If Usun hadn't parried, hadn't possessed a sword and knew how to use it, his blood would be cooling over the broken mattress.

Usun's mouth gaped when his gaze dropped to Enkidu's cut. "That's bleeding a lot."

"It'll be all right."

A clattering of dozens of feet rang out as guards poured into the room. They took in the space, the mattress cut right where the prince's neck would have lain, Enkidu who held his injured arm, and Usun with his sword still in hand.

They surged towards Enkidu. "Get away from the Prince."

Enkidu opened his hands in front of him and took a slow step back.

"It wasn't Enkidu," the Prince said, but no one acknowledged it. The guards approached him like they circled a wild creature, weapons brandished and eyes unblinking.

"As long as guards stay here to protect the boy," Enkidu said, "I'll go with you. I don't wish to fight anyone."

Usun stormed forward, pulling a guard aside. The man startled. Usun appeared to be a child—his features soft, his skin yet unblemished by life. But he'd inherited at least some of his father's strength. "I said it wasn't him."

The guard frowned and looked at the others.

"We need the King or Queen," one replied.

"My mother is in Meritkara's room tonight."

"That's closest," the guard said. "Someone, run and get her."

An awkward dozen minutes passed where the guards kept weapons raised at Enkidu. He attempted to appear non-threatening. It wasn't a simple task with his bulk and blood-covered clothing. Usun passed the time glaring at the soldiers, his arms crossed.

Enkidu's cut dripped blood with an occasional plop

against the tile. The wound had already begun sealing, but he didn't dare attempt to tie a makeshift bandage around it. He feared any movement would set off the guards.

The Queen swept into the room. Her gaze trailed the damage like she followed the fight then landed on her son. She released a startled cry as she ran over to him and pulled her into his arms. "Oh gods, Usun. Are you okay?"

"Ama, I'm fine." He pulled away like a wolf cub trying to escape his mother's clutches. "But Enkidu isn't guilty. He saved my life. He wasn't the one who fought me."

Shamhat's eyes tracked over to Enkidu, her eyebrows gliding up her forehead. She'd washed her makeup away and her hair was loose on her shoulders, no headpiece decorating it. She appeared mortal for the first time.

"Release him," the Queen said in her scolding voice.

The guards looked among themselves before lowering their spears and bowing. "Apologies, my queen. We didn't wish to risk the Prince's life."

"Yes, and I thank you. But I doubt the Prince would spare him if he was the being who... d-did this." She surveyed the room again with thinning lips. "Usun, do you know who it was?"

"No, Ama. They had their face covered."

A guard stepped forward. "We should inform the King the palace is under attack."

"No." Shamhat cracked the word like a whip. She swept her gaze around, meeting every eye in the room before she took a deep breath and rolled her shoulders back. Despite her lack of adornments, she was a queen again, her actions not requests but commands. "King Gilgamesh leaves in three days to face Umma. We cannot have him distracted. I want guards roused and security doubled. You two,"—she pointed—"run now and alert all the nursemaids and mothers who have children with them, but nothing to inspire panic. Say only there's a drunkard from the wedding causing trouble and they are to stay in their rooms. And you,"—she gestured to another—"go inform Nin Meritkara the truth. I want a trio of guards around every room any child of Gilgamesh sleeps in tonight. Am I understood?"

"My queen." The guards bowed, the three she'd spoken to rising to scurry out of the space.

"Not a word of this to the King. We'll inform him when he returns from Umma."

"Yes, Nin." The other guards bowed and exited the room.

Shamhat reached out and cupped Usun's cheeks between her hands, ruffled his hair, and drew her fingers along his shoulder. To the boy's merit, he remained still for the exam and didn't push her away. "Will you sleep with me tonight, dumu?"

Usun's lips tipped down, but he cleared the expression quickly. "Of course, Ama."

"Good." Shamhat's shoulders dropped. She raised her face to Enkidu. "Thank you for helping save my son." Her gaze was as intense as staring into the sun. "You aren't to tell Gilgamesh either."

Enkidu's stomach twisted. If he knew anything of the King, he'd be furious that someone harmed his son within his household. He'd want retribution. Gilgamesh would likely thresh through the staff one-by-one until he had answers. Shamhat had a point, though. If he didn't find answers before he left with his soldiers, he'd be distracted. Gilgamesh had his god's blood, his strength, his abilities. But maybe he could get killed if he wasn't focused.

He nodded stiffly. "I'll keep it quiet until after Umma."

He couldn't lie to Gilgamesh, even by omission, beyond that.

"So loyal to him already," Shamhat grumbled, but tucked her arm into Usun's as she continued speaking. "Would you join the guards in walking us to my room?"

"If you'd allow it, I'll join those guarding your door tonight."

Shamhat's eyes rippled with emotions that contrasted against her queenly bearing. "I'd like that," she whispered.

"I'd be honored, Nin."

Usun pulled free from his mother to grab his sword. "In case we need it again!" He bounced on his toes, a young boy eager for another adventure.

"Let us hope not. And you can't share this story with any of the other children or the boys in your training."

"But, Ama, this is—"

"You cannot. It's a matter of security. Do you understand me, Usun?"

Usun puckered his lips out and bowed his face so he suddenly appeared very much a child. "Fine."

They met half a dozen guards who waited in the hall, crossed back to the main palace then to Shamhat's apartment. It was close to Gilgamesh's and Enkidu couldn't help the way his gaze trailed down the hall to where the King slept. Lying to Gilgamesh crossed a boundary. He understood Shamhat's reasoning even if it twisted him like a wolf ripping into its prey.

Shamhat ushered Usun into the room, then turned back and grabbed Enkidu's hand. He gasped. Her small hand fit like an acorn within his palm, though far smoother. "Thank you, Enkidu. I cannot say how much."

Her eyes glistened but before he could respond or

decide how to react to a crying queen, she slipped into her room and shut the door.

Guards clogged the space. It seemed unlikely someone would attempt to harm Usun again with the level of security. Plus, the child now slept in his father's hall. Enkidu remained, regardless. He found an empty stretch of wall, sat, and ripped a piece of his tunic to bind his arm. It had mostly stopped bleeding, but when he moved, the skin puckered.

Someone entered the hall, and the guards all straightened, spears coming out.

"It's just me."

The guards relaxed. Akkiru walked down the hall, stopping before Enkidu to gesture at the space on the floor by him. "Do you mind?" Enkidu moved over, making more room, and Akkiru dropped beside him. "Quite the night. How's Usun?"

Enkidu cleared his throat, but clearly Akkiru knew the reality of what happened. Shamhat hadn't forbidden him from speaking to Akkiru, only to Gilgamesh, the man he was supposed to help. "Usun was scarcely phased. His mother, though..."

"I'm sure." Akkiru dropped his head against the wall. "Do you mind if I keep watch with you tonight? I doubt I'll sleep more."

"Of course. Where is Meritkara?"

"She's with her daughter and has joined a few friends. The children are finding the excitement delightful."

Enkidu smiled. Children held the wild in their heart— they knew the only moment that truly existed was the present one. They didn't strive to leave legends about themselves or get caught on previous mistakes.

"You're a musician, aren't you?" Enkidu asked. They

had a long stretch of time before Utu's rays kissed the sky, so he might as well make conversation. An occasional guard looked their way. Otherwise, they sat alone in the dim hall, the glittering artwork all hushed in shadows.

"I play the lyre, the harp, and the lute. Occasionally you can get me behind a drum, too, but you'll have Kara on my ass saying I'm off rhythm." He leaned in closer to whisper to Enkidu. "She's mistaken. I'm never off rhythm."

Enkidu chuckled. "You didn't play at the wedding feast, and I've never seen you with the other musicians at dinner. Do you perform at a temple?"

Akkiru pulled away with a sigh. "No, I perform little anymore." Silence stretched between them. The guards scarcely made any sound, and for a few moments that section of the palace was the quietest place in the city. It was so silent, Enkidu's heartbeat throbbed in his mind and he cleared his throat.

"Have you ever been in love?" Akkiru asked.

Enkidu shifted towards him. He didn't know how much of his past Shamhat might have revealed to the man. Enkidu scarcely understood what the word love meant. He hadn't lived long enough to experience it, but some part of him wanted to. Another part still longed to return to the forest, to the wolf's sense of duty and simplicity. "No."

"Ah, well, it tips you off balance. You give up things you could never imagine."

"You gave up music to be with Shamhat and Meritkara?"

"Not directly." He shrugged. "They are Gilgamesh's wives, though, and Shamhat is the Queen. I've attempted to join musical groups, but they always have their spots filled. They won't tell me directly—wouldn't want to anger the Queen." He chuckled, but the edges of it felt brittle.

"They don't want someone so close to the rulers in their groups."

"Shamhat has a favored musician—Kasiru. Why didn't she choose you for that role?"

Akkiru kicked his feet out and crossed his ankles. "Kasiru serves Inanna. It's political as much as anything. Shamhat choosing her lover over many other wonderful musicians would weaken others' view of her."

"I'm surprised Shamhat isn't upset on your behalf."

"She would be, if she knew the full extent of the situation." Akkiru rolled his face towards Enkidu. "I've told her I'm happy to play for the children and to spend my energy on them now."

"You've lied to her." Enkidu said the words softly. The guards likely couldn't hear them. He didn't understand. If Akkiru loved Shamhat, why did he keep the truth?

"I've not lied, exactly. It's true—I enjoy spending time with the children. I even teach some of them. However, yes, I've downplayed some details that would hurt her. She's the Queen, her focus can't stay on her partners. Kara and I understand that."

Enkidu slid his finger over the smooth tiles. Lying was always wrong, wasn't it? Then again, Usun had asked him to not share something that would hurt his mother as well. Gilgamesh never spoke his true feelings on Inanna. Perhaps lying was necessary and Shamhat was right when she asked him to keep the attack from Gilgamesh.

"Do you ever regret it?" Enkidu asked. "I don't mean your relationship with the Queen and Meritkara, but the consequences?"

Akkiru smiled widely, his eyes twinkling. "I couldn't have one without the other. And no, I've never regretted it. The thing about love tipping me off balance is it made me realize I don't want the normal before I found it. I've sacrificed things for Shamhat and Kara, and I'd do it again without hesitation."

Enkidu chewed the edge of his lip. That idea—love—hooked through him like talons, dragging him towards itself. He wanted to find something worthy of sacrificing for, someone who'd make even the hardest life choices feel worth it.

He spent the night's long hours wondering about that.

The next day when he stood before the King, his heart lurching into his throat with the lies he concealed, he managed to keep his mouth closed.

"Enkidu," Gilgamesh said from where he lounged against a dining couch. "We leave for Umma this week. I hope you'll join us."

Enkidu hesitated, meeting Shamhat's gaze. She bobbed her head. He turned back to the King, the man he lied to, the person who made his heart ache. "I'd be honored to join you."

CHAPTER FIFTEEN

AN OFFENSE, UNFORGIVABLE

TRAVELING with his most loyal soldiers and all of Uruk's trouble left behind, had Gilgamesh filled with fresh vigor. Dust floated around their ankles like mist, and a fresh breeze brushed his face. That was where he belonged—out having adventures, crafting legends about his name. Not stuffed and pressed in the palace.

When they'd stopped to make camp, Enkidu had gone into the forest with a few others then returned with two large bucks.

Gilgamesh rose to meet them. "A good catch tonight, Namtur?"

"No, Lugal. We didn't see shed in the forest. Both of these"—he dropped a buck—"were Enkidu's catches."

Gilgamesh shifted his gaze to Enkidu who shrugged. "I couldn't have brought them back without the others."

The men who'd joined him grunted. Namtur jostled an elbow into his arm. The group smiled as they began the work of preparing the animals for the supper pot.

As they ate dinner around the fire, soldiers told stories

that made everyone laugh—even Enkidu. He was different away from the city.

When it came time to turn in for the night, Gilgamesh approached Enkidu and grazed his fingers against his elbow. Color flushed his cheeks above his beard and Gilgamesh struggled to bite back a smile.

"You'll join me in my tent."

Enkidu jerked his face upright, and the color flooded his skin, even the tips of his ears darkened.

Gilgamesh chuckled. "If that suits you. My tent is a large, segmented space. You'll have your own room within it."

"Ah. Y-yes."

Gilgamesh grinned as he gestured for him to follow. The man was hopeless, and it was endearing. He could fight like a demon, hunt like a god, yet blushed like an adolescent.

They ducked past the rug together. Inside, Gilgamesh lit a lamp. To the left, beyond another rug, his bedroll lay. Part of him wanted to invite Enkidu to join him there—he might say yes. Gilgamesh had never been with a man who was immune to his god's blood before, and the idea intrigued him. He was a physical man but had never had an equal sexual partner. Enkidu fascinated him. Perhaps that's why he hesitated. Something about Enkidu felt like a clay jar, still unfinished. If he grabbed at it too roughly, he'd damage it before it set.

"I didn't know you could hunt," Gilgamesh said.

Enkidu, who hadn't made eye contact since they'd stepped into the tent, shrugged. "How did you think a wild man fed himself?"

There was a sour note to his words, and Gilgamesh stepped closer. "Why do you say it like that? A wild man. Like it's a bad thing."

Enkidu raised his face. Damn the gods—he'd thought those eyes couldn't get more alluring. He stood close enough that awareness of the man's thick shoulders and long limbs prickled at him. The lamp's orange glow gleamed over his eyes, making the colors richer than ever. Gilgamesh could look into those eyes forever.

"Everyone says I'm wild as though it's a bad thing. Even the guards looked at me like I was a beast when—" He clacked his teeth together.

Gilgamesh frowned and moved even closer. Enkidu had slammed a topic closed. If he found out palace guards heckled the man—his god-given helper—within his home, he'd have their heads. Enkidu had found the palace uncomfortable. Gilgamesh had never considered that the talk might bother him. He had always embraced rumors as king —even the ones that burned his gut. After all, his name passing on tongues only helped achieve his aim.

He stretched his fingers out over Enkidu's elbow again. His purpose wasn't to tease him as he often did, to watch his skin darken, but to offer support. "People who stir up rumors are usually those too afraid to step into the forest. They'd rather criticize the hunter's bounty than face their own shortcomings."

Enkidu tilted his head. He didn't speak for a long stretch. Instead, he ran his eyes over Gilgamesh's face. "And you say I'm the one who shares profound things."

Gilgamesh chuckled and moved closer, so only a breath of air separated their bodies. "It seems you're rubbing off on me. Maybe that's what you're supposed to do—sand down my rough edges. I pity you for that task."

Enkidu smiled and looked Gilgamesh straight in the eyes. It was still strange to be around a human who could do so. His voice came out soft. "I don't." His gaze dropped to

Gilgamesh's lips before lifting again. "Perhaps, for the first time, I'm starting to understand I'm where I'm supposed to be."

Gilgamesh released a sigh that sounded more like a groan, and Enkidu leaned closer. Their eyes met again, and Gilgamesh closed the distance. Their chests grazed, their knees, their hips. Enkidu released a shaky breath against his cheek.

Gilgamesh swept his hand around to the dip in Enkidu's back. He didn't push for more, though, simply waited to see if the man pulled away.

This wasn't a prostitute or some governor's son eager to fuck a god. Enkidu didn't care about the King's status. The man was divine in his own right, in fact. Gilgamesh had never fucked a god before. Interest sparkled through him from a hundred points, but Enkidu trembled beneath his palm, so he remained still.

Enkidu shifted so their noses grazed. Gilgamesh swallowed—he'd never moved this slowly before. It was excruciating.

He loved it.

Their lips brushed, not quite a kiss, but somehow more searing. It was the most intimate touch Gilgamesh had ever experienced.

Enkidu jerked free from his grip, stumbled back over the rugs.

Gilgamesh's chest rose and fell in a rapid clip. His arms felt empty as they never had before. He'd give anything to have Enkidu next to him again, to rest his hand on his warm back.

"I can't," Enkidu said. "I'm sorry."

Those were words Gilgamesh hadn't heard before. He was the one who turned down partners, not the other way around. Enkidu had every right to do as he wished, of course. A flame of a feeling licked in Gilgamesh's chest regardless, a spark of injured pride. It smothered when he met Enkidu's gaze. The man's eyes were wide, his body pressed against the tent's wall as though he could sink through the fabric. Like when Gilgamesh had found him in the courtyard trembling. That night they'd lain next to each other and discussed the heavens.

There was something about this man that was so different from anything he'd ever experienced before.

"That's all right." Gilgamesh's voice hummed low, a whisper against the howling wind beyond the tent. "I shouldn't have pushed you. I've misread things." His mouth felt strange admitting weakness. Part of him wanted to swallow it back, another part felt lighter to have the truth sitting between them.

"You haven't." Enkidu hunched into himself. "I just... I can't."

"All right." It was enough for Gilgamesh. His body still hungered, and rejection's sting still smarted, but he wouldn't push anyone, much less Enkidu. He'd go to bed sexually frustrated, having to meet his own needs—that wasn't atypical for him, anyway. For the first time since he'd married Shamhat, he worried about hurting a relationship with sex. "Forgive me, Enkidu. I don't want to change things between us."

No, actually that was a lie. He'd like very much to change things between them. If he had his way, Enkidu would be bare and sinking into his blankets. He didn't wish to harm their relationship though. Something about Enkidu settled him. Gilgamesh was a tree thrashing about in a desert beneath the gods' tempests. Then this man arrived, a pillar the gods had yoked him with. He didn't realize how much Enkidu soothed him until he imagined losing him.

"Forgive me, Lugal," Enkidu said without meeting his gaze.

Gilgamesh frowned. He moved closer again, and Enkidu leaned back, his head brushing the animal hide. Gilgamesh stopped moving and raised his hands as if to show he didn't have any weapons. He didn't mean to invade Enkidu's space and didn't intend to touch him again. As much as he enjoyed teasing the man, he didn't wish to harm him.

"Please," Gilgamesh whispered, "don't use titles with me. Forgive me for tonight."

"You don't need forgiveness."

"Can we move forward from this? I won't touch you."

Enkidu frowned, his posture righting some. "I didn't ask you not to touch me. I'm just not ready for..." His cheeks darkened, and for the first time since he'd met the man, Gilgamesh didn't relish it. He wanted to hold him, comfort him. He never did that with others. The past week had been the first time in a decade he'd done so for his wife.

Gilgamesh didn't know how to be close to another. He fought his way through everything—even with Shamhat. His method of expressing care was to yell *I love you* at her. Gods, he was a fuck up in relating with anyone. As a child he'd only had his distant goddess mother, servants who feared him, and a father who died. He couldn't form bonds, understand them. He crossed his arms. That line of thinking was as exhausting as walking a road he'd never seen before.

"I've caused this trouble." Enkidu still pressed against the wall like he'd become one with it. "It's I who should apologize."

"You don't owe me any apologies." Gilgamesh shifted his feet. "No, actually you do, for throwing that fig at me."

Enkidu's shoulders dropped. "You're still upset about that?"

"You threw a godsdamned piece of fruit at me in front of my entire city."

Enkidu's lips snapped together. His eyes took on a twinkle, and he shook his head. "I'll never apologize for that. It didn't hurt you, and I think you needed it."

Gilgamesh splayed his arms out. "I needed to be shamed in front of the world? It hurt deeper than the physical."

Enkidu stepped closer to him. His awkwardness had washed away. Gilgamesh, despite the contrary expression he wore like a mask, was relieved.

"You said I'm here to sand away your rough edges."

"Could you do it in a manner fitting for a king?"

Enkidu frowned. "That is part of your roughness."

"Being aware that I'm a king?" Gilgamesh scowled. He'd always defended his position, his rights, the glory due to him. Enkidu left him feeling uncertain. He wanted to get snappish, but he stalled himself.

"Believing you deserve more than anyone else because you're a king. After all, you didn't choose this life. You were born for it. You haven't earned your god's blood, your title, or your city. They were all given to you." Gilgamesh's mouth gaped. Enkidu gestured behind him. "Is this where I'm supposed to sleep?"

Gilgamesh nodded, and the man disappeared.

The King craved to follow him. Demand he retract his words—but Enkidu was right. That sank into Gilgamesh like a boulder, so heavy it crushed him. The only thing he could claim was his wall. Even though it was the grandest in all the world, he was no fool. Centuries would swallow each other, and men would craft finer walls, higher towers, grander temples.

Soon his contributions would mean nothing.

Like all other kings, his deeds were nothing more than circumstance. He could have been born like Usun—lacking god's blood and forgotten. Or, worse, he could have been born outside the palace or the temples at all. Gods what if he'd come squalling and bloody into the world in some mud hut far from the city?

It was a line of thinking he'd never traversed, and it left him so shaken he forgot all about his sexual frustration. Instead, he ran his mind around the truth in Enkidu's words until sleep took him. It wasn't until later that he realized he didn't have his nightmare that night.

* * *

Umma was a squat city of unpainted mud-brick buildings. It had grown in the last decade, though. The road had shifted, making the city a favorable stop for traders. It had little reputation or interesting gods to guard it yet. Its one temple sat half-neglected in a corner.

An oversight Zage-Si would soon regret. Gilgamesh and his army marched onto the main street. People stared or stumbled back. If they moved too close, Gilgamesh's god's blood reached them and they tumbled over.

He was a shepherd to his people. But these were not his people—not yet at least. If they didn't respect him as a god, they could fear him as a demon.

His men walked behind him, their steps rhythmic as they pushed into the city. They damaged nothing. That wasn't how Gilgamesh's forces worked. His offense was with Zage-Si, not these pitiful humans who trembled and gaped. Destroying things wouldn't instill loyalty when Umma fell under his authority.

Enkidu's words from the previous night crawled through Gilgamesh like ants. He could have been born some priest's son, a shepherd's child, a scribe's adoptee. A million roads could have happened to him circumstantially, but he'd landed on a throne in the greatest city in the world.

Enkidu walked alongside him, his gaze roving over Umma's dusty buildings and dull fabrics. Only Uruk boasted the colorful blankets and rugs. They were so common there that color splashed around the city. Umma appeared drab in contrast.

Things had still felt awkward with Enkidu that morning, but for the time being he had to shove it away. They were here with a purpose—a god-ordained one. Zage-Si had angered the divine, and they'd sent a prophecy to Gilgamesh so he could enact punishment.

His axes shifted along his hips as he moved. His hands itched for them, but first they'd be diplomatic. He'd assured Hirin, and he meant to mind his advisors a bit more.

When they reached the palace, Gilgamesh's eyes narrowed. The building was a vast ivory mass, lined with statues and covered in sparkling tiles. It gleamed like Utu himself lived in it compared to the dingy hovels that made up the rest of the city.

Gilgamesh frowned. He lived in a beautiful palace himself, however he also lived in a beautiful city with rich temples. Even the lowest citizens had well maintained homes and color to brighten their lives. Zage-Si truly thought himself a god—as if it was the people's job to keep him and he didn't need to give anything back.

Shed. Gilgamesh clenched his teeth against the pounding in his temple. He *was* a god, and he didn't demand as much. Perhaps, he wasn't divine after all. Enkidu had been right—he had nothing to credit to his name. He didn't even expect as much as the worm Zage-Si did.

Hirin would end up choosing the name for the year. It would be something like *The Year King Gilgamesh Defeated his Enemies, Destroyed their Palace's Defenses, and Ended the Reign of Zage-Si.*

It would be his most notable act of the year.

And in five hundred years—in a hundred, even—who would care? No one.

It was with that sour thought he approached the guards lining the front of the palace. Abgal broke free from the group and bowed—more deference than needed for these men. "Lugal Gilgamesh requests an audience with your king."

The guards, who'd begun to sweat, flicked their eyes towards Gilgamesh. He pushed his powers out, reveled as the men trembled. The first straightened as best he could. "Lugal Zage-Si says he will not hear any messenger from Uruk."

Abgal's eyes darkened. "It is no messenger who has traveled here. It is the great god-king Gilgamesh. Son of Ninsun and the half-god Lugalbanda. Ruler of the high-walled Uruk and servant of Our Lady in Heaven, Inanna. A man who surpasses all others. Surely your king will see him."

The guard swallowed like he wished to Enlil that the King would. "Lugal Zage-Si will not receive your party."

Abgal turned back towards Gilgamesh. The King nodded. His men drew swords, and the guards fumbled for weapons, but his men cut them down before they could reach them. Their bodies fell broken on the ivory stone, crimson blood pooling around them.

Enkidu released a breath, his mouth gaping.

Gilgamesh didn't have time to parse out the man's thoughts. He couldn't figure him out in a calm moment, much less when his heart pounded with hunger for blood. He loosed the axes and spun them.

"Will we let Zage-Si slight us so, men of Uruk?"

"No," they roared.

"To Our Lady in Heaven," Gilgamesh roared.

"To Inanna."

They surged forward into the palace's front courtyard. Workers and musicians screamed and scrambled. Gilgamesh didn't need to instruct his men about Umma's people. They didn't harm innocents.

The men, aided with Gilgamesh's powers, took out guards. Others arrived, better armed but just as poorly trained. Gilgamesh and his men moved through them like locusts swarming a field.

Enkidu fought as well, dragging guards down, knocking their heads together.

He didn't kill though. Gilgamesh fought a groan but nodded towards the men Enkidu had felled then met Namtur's gaze. He nodded and went to finish the job. They couldn't risk guards rousing and attacking them from behind.

Screams became the palace's music, blood its decoration.

They moved through the building, clearing room after room.

It was so easy—comforting even to have his axes sinking into human flesh, to do something he was good at.

They approached a room surrounded by a hundred guards.

Gilgamesh looked at Abgal. The man dripped with blood. It coursed down the wrinkles on his cheeks as he nodded. Zage-Si and his family were likely in there hiding like cowards. Shamhat would defend her people despite not having god's blood or weapons training, but this royal family hid. The King, and his bratty-mouthed son, were Gilgamesh's to take.

They pushed forward. The world became rife with yells, with the clank of metal engaging, the slippery spill of blood over tiles.

A clean death for anyone we face, Gilgamesh had reminded his men that morning. Enkidu had frowned but not interjected. *We leave no one to suffer.*

It was a vow they kept, as solemn as a god-bound oath. They didn't maim; they gave opponents quick, honorable ends.

Zage-Si, however, would not be as lucky.

They finished the last of the guards, and Gilgamesh reached the door, giving it a shake.

Locked.

He lifted his ax, sticky with drying blood, and slammed it into the wood. It splintered, and he hit it again and again. The door groaned on the fourth blow, then cracked open on the fifth.

A dozen people sat at the back of the room, cowering.

A few were children, and Gilgamesh turned towards Abgal again. He bowed and gestured to a few men who would remove them before things got too dark. Gilgamesh wasn't there to traumatize children. He was there for—

"Zage-Si." He said the name calmly and met the gaze of his adversary. The man trembled, his shepherd-style crown cocked at an odd angle over his ebony hair. Gilgamesh smiled wolfishly as he strode into the space, his boots leaving bloody prints that traced his path. "I'm here to call you to answer for your crimes."

Zage-Si bared his teeth. "May you die unremembered, Gilgamesh."

Gilgamesh's fist clenched tighter around his ax. Zage-Si turned to a girl standing at his side and gestured. She dropped to her knees and spoke in a language Gilgamesh had never heard. She was the demon-summoner.

"Enkidu," he said. "Stop her."

The man startled at being called on. He was the only one of their group not covered with blood. He was the best choice for interception without the girl getting hurt.

Enkidu grimaced but moved towards the girl. A few people near Zage-Si attempted to intercept, and Gilgamesh's soldiers disarmed them. Enkidu reached the girl and pulled an arm around her throat, cutting off her breath. She struggled against his thick arm and her eyes dashed to her king who did nothing but frown at her. She passed out and Enkidu eased his grip.

Other soldiers grabbed the children and the young women clinging to them, escorting them from the room as more of his men guarded the exits.

Gilgamesh stepped forward and gave his ax a lazy swing. "Zage-Si, the gods have appraised your rule and they've deemed it unworthy."

The man growled and pulled a sword. Others in the room—his family by the quality of clothing they wore—did the same. Gilgamesh grinned and met the King's blow. Zage-Si was an adequate swordsman but no more. He clearly didn't train regularly. Gilgamesh parried him twice before slicing into his hand so the sword dropped with a clang. Zage-Si screamed, and Gilgamesh kicked him onto the tile floor.

His soldiers had subdued the weak king's sons as easily. What a bunch of fools, playing at gods, flirting with powers they didn't know how to control.

"Someone take him," Gilgamesh cried. "And bind his damn hand. I won't have him bleeding out before he watches his name catch fire."

Enkidu had lowered the girl gently to the ground and fixed his eyes on Gilgamesh. His gaze was like a lamplight that poured over him.

Gilgamesh stood over the King as his men bound him, then jerked his hair so he looked up at the god-king. "Apologize for killing our messenger."

Zage-Si glared at Gilgamesh, his eyes burning. He had nothing to back up his expression though. An unprotected city and untrained army and descendants who Gilgamesh would soon thrust into the Great Below.

"Apologize," Gilgamesh growled.

"No."

He backhanded him; the crack rumbled like thunder.

Enkidu seemed to hold his breath. He'd stopped blinking.

"You will apologize, or I will pull it from you through your sons' pain."

Zage-Si looked back at his children, all kneeling, wrists bound, with Gilgamesh's soldiers standing over them.

He could have formed an alliance with Gilgamesh and saved all this trouble. For fuck's sake, he could have politely told him no, exchanged a few meaningless gifts to keep friendly relations up between the cities and moved on with his life. Instead, he'd insulted Gilgamesh, hurt his queen, and garnered the gods' attention.

Gilgamesh strode over to Ishme-Ea, the prince who'd called Shamhat a whore. Gilgamesh swept his ax forward, stopping just short of the prince's neck. A woman screamed —his mother if her pleas indicated anything. Gilgamesh leaned close to the Prince and whispered, "Did I not tell you, pup, that if you didn't heed my words, the next time you saw me it would be in your city with a blade to your throat?"

The man swallowed, the ax bobbing against his skin. Blood trickled over it, but it wasn't Ishme-Ea's, not yet at least.

"Your father won't lower his pride enough to spare your life, boy." Ishme-Ea's dark eyes darted to his father who watched but said nothing, his lips a thin line. "How about you? Will you apologize for the messenger?" Gilgamesh looked up at the others in the room. "I demand an apology from everyone in this room."

Another man raised his chin. His nose dripped blood so he must have fought when the soldiers took him down. "You will not get one from us."

Gilgamesh walked over to the man and glared down at him. He swung his ax, arcing it forward. The man jerked back. Gilgamesh slashed through his tunic, the material draping down his chest. "Someone had better start speaking."

"We're sorry." Gilgamesh turned towards the voice. Ishme-Ea stared at him, trembling, but with his chin raised as he had in the tent months before. Others glared at him, and he shook his head. "Is it worth your lives?" He shifted back to Gilgamesh. "We disrespected you, and we're sorry."

Huh. Gilgamesh hadn't expected the pup to be the one to find reason. He turned towards the other dozen in the room. "Anyone else?"

Zage-Si trembled over his ruined hand. Others stared at Gilgamesh, noses flaring. A few wouldn't meet his gaze or wept silently.

"Fine, then. Take him." Gilgamesh gestured to Ishme-Ea. Godsdamned fate that would have him continuing to work with the boy, but he needed an Ensi to run the city beneath him. Someone of Zage-Si's line would make the easiest transition, and if the boy could find some manners, he'd do fine.

Namtur grabbed the Prince and moved him out the back way the children had gone. "No," Ishme-Ea cried. "Wait. Please."

Gilgamesh turned back to look at the sorry group of nobles as Ishme-Ea's cries quieted. He frowned. "Strip the rest of their clothes and jewels. We can mete out punishment in the palace's entrance before marching them through the city."

Zage-Si raised his face, his eyes finally wide and sorry.

Too late.

The King didn't need to be fully intact to parade around the city. Gilgamesh stepped forward and lifted his ax, but Enkidu dashed in front of him.

"No." His voice rang around the room.

CHAPTER SIXTEEN

QUESTIONING A KING

"No," Enkidu said again, the word echoing around the room as he stepped in front of Gilgamesh.

He'd stood frozen during Gilgamesh's interrogation of the royal family. He'd understood their purpose for coming into the city, had helped take guards down, but it had twisted his gut that Gilgamesh and his men ended lives like it was nothing.

There was a brutal beauty in it—they moved like a pack, dropping enemies like they swatted at flies. With the way they functioned, no creature in the world could stand up to them.

At least Gilgamesh had his soldiers remove the children and had spared the man who apologized. Enkidu stood with his feet planted on the tiles as Gilgamesh threatened and humiliated the family.

He understood it. Zage-Si's pack had offended Gilgamesh's. He'd crossed territory that wasn't his. Actions had consequences just as they had in the wolf clans.

But Gilgamesh had threatened to drag the family out naked before their people. He intended to defile and shame them, go beyond retribution, so Enkidu had surged forward before him.

Now the god-king of Uruk stared at him, his eyes dark and flat, blood trickling along the curve of his nose.

He'd seen Gilgamesh, the man, speak of the stars and his dreams and Gilgamesh the ruler who could bark and snip. However, Enkidu had never seen him bloodthirsty and vicious before.

Part of Enkidu wanted to back down, to remove himself from the situation. Fury rippled from his king in waves, but Enkidu planted his feet and spoke again. "No."

Gilgamesh's lip curled. Gods, Enkidu had nearly given in to his lust with the man. How had he ever found him attractive? It turned out he was everything the rumors had suggested—brutish, violent, and wanting more than he should have. Gilgamesh had told him as much himself. He'd said he was everything Enkidu imagined.

Gilgamesh snatched Enkidu's arm and directed them behind a column. The King's touch had been a flame in the previous days, burning down to Enkidu's bones. Now he wanted to wrench himself free and demand he never touch him again.

"What are you doing?" Gilgamesh growled once they'd moved out of sight. Blood had dried on his lips, emphasizing the lines on them.

Enkidu yanked his arm loose and lifted to his full height. He may have acted the fool around Gilgamesh—trembling and blushing—before. Not anymore. "I'll ask you the same."

"You understood why we came here."

"Yes, for retribution and to achieve the gods' desires. But you go too far, Gilgamesh."

Enkidu says dishonoring your legacy doesn't please the gods."

Enkidu tucked his hands behind his back and clenched his fingers together. Gilgamesh shaped the story as though Enkidu spoke for the gods. Enkidu wasn't a soothsayer, though, he only told what he believed was right. Gilgamesh's soldiers watched him with tightened eyes. Gilgamesh had to maintain his reputation before these men. It still felt like lying to Enkidu, but he kept his mouth shut.

"For this reason alone," Gilgamesh continued at a measured pace, "I'll offer you two options, Lugal. You may apologize and officially vow yourself in service to me as Ensi or you may receive a death of honor." Some of Gilgamesh's soldiers frowned at their king. Gilgamesh tensed next to Enkidu but didn't otherwise react. "This is not because you deserve it, Zage-Si,"—he looked around at his men—"but because the gods demand it, and I am nothing if not a loyal servant to them."

The soldiers loosened some at the end of the speech, but many of their eyes darted to Enkidu. On the trip the men had joked with him, hunted at his side, listened to his thoughts on navigating the forest. They'd ignored the horns crowning his head. Now they appraised him anew. If he worked for the gods, then he wasn't one of them. He was other—dangerous. After all, the gods were fickle. They could flood the world on a whim, destroy a city, choose to side with an enemy. People had little control which they commiserated and bonded over. But Enkidu wasn't a human. He was divine. His connection with the group slipped away like a leaf caught in a tide.

Zage-Si's nose flared as he raised his narrowed eyes at the King. "I will never vow to serve you."

Gilgamesh clenched his jaw before nodding to his men. "Honorable deaths it is, then."

* * *

Enkidu remained silent as Ishme-Ea made a begrudging vow to Gilgamesh, sealing his city's fate. Ishme-Ea's mother stood at his shoulder weeping. Gilgamesh spared all who'd apologized. Only a few remained. Gilgamesh left half his soldiers to oversee the transition of power and promised to send resources from Uruk to the people. The rest of the group didn't linger—by the next day they traversed dusty roads again.

Gilgamesh had ignored Enkidu the entire day of travel. The whole group had. He'd started to feel not quite that he belonged, but that he'd found a place he could fit. Enkidu wasn't human, though, and he wasn't a god. He was some outlying creature.

Gilgamesh was too.

He scraped after legacy like a dying wolf swiping at his opponents to make them bleed. Neither had a place they belonged in the world. Perhaps that's why Gilgamesh was so fascinated with the heavens.

As they walked back into the King's tent together, Gilgamesh stopped and stared at Enkidu. He stood straight to meet the man's gaze but didn't speak. The tent's fabrics shrouded them, making the space uncomfortably intimate. If Gilgamesh had an issue with him—and he definitely did —he could start the conversation.

Gilgamesh rolled his jaw around, his eyes fixed on Enkidu like he imagined a hundred ways he could kill the man. "If you take issue with something I do, speak with me about it, but never disrupt me in front of my men again."

Enkidu scoffed. They were back to his injured pride. Enkidu wished he had another fig—an entire bag of figs. The man would never learn humility. "All right, then explain to me how the next time you're acting brutish and making a fool of yourself in a room of people how I should intervene quietly?"

Gilgamesh stepped closer. Like he had before in the tent, when their bodies had touched and everything within Enkidu felt alive. He'd wanted desperately to do more but couldn't. This man didn't have the ability to love or even to see beyond himself except in limited glimpses. Enkidu wished he could paint it for him, help him see just how much he already possessed. The issue was, Enkidu could speak until his lungs emptied of breath, but if Gilgamesh wasn't ready to hear it, he'd do nothing but waste words.

Gilgamesh was close enough that his grinding teeth echoed between them. "It's easy for you to judge me. What rests on your choices? The world's fate is on mine. My people look to me for protection and abundance. The gods have expectations I must fulfill. The nobles and priests and soldiers and workers all rely on my decisions."

Enkidu no longer cowered before Gilgamesh—he never would again. He'd seen some broken thing within him. If Gilgamesh would slow down enough to notice it, he might achieve more of his desires than he realized.

"All of that is on me too, then," Enkidu answered.

Gilgamesh frowned. His eyes roamed over Enkidu's face intimately, as if he sought something. Enkidu had the urge to cover himself, to back away. He tensed his muscles to fight it. His role was to push back on the King, this man who had potential but couldn't see the mountain he stood upon because he spent all his time carving away at a solitary rock.

"My responsibility is to you," Enkidu said. "I'm here to keep you accountable. You said yourself that my role is to sand your edges."

"Perhaps I've changed my mind about that." His lips thinned, and he shifted away. It was a dismissal, like he'd escort Enkidu from his palace and life in the way he would a common worker. But Enkidu didn't work for him, and he wasn't about to be dismissed.

"You're demanding and capricious, and that's half your issue."

Gilgamesh turned back. "You're obnoxious and speak when you shouldn't."

"Perhaps consider the gods created me specifically for you." It stung—the truth of that. He didn't have his own purpose. They wrapped his entire reality in this man who acted like a spoiled child. "So, what do you think that says about you?"

"All it says," Gilgamesh said through his teeth, "is that every aspect of my reality is unbearable. I'm attempting to make a notable life, but at each step there is something stopping me."

Enkidu wanted to grab him by the shoulders and shake him until the teeth he kept grinding rattled. Here was a king—beautiful and clever and compassionate. And he was as stubborn and conniving and self-focused as Inanna. He almost shared that just to see anger's flush sweep across the King's skin, but he snapped out something else that had eaten away at him during the trip.

"You're out worrying about your name and your gods-damned legacy while there are people in your palace attempting to kill your son."

Gilgamesh's tensed expression washed away, and his eyebrows jumped.

"That's right." Enkidu growled. He wanted to be the wild beast at that moment—growling and acting on instincts. Enough with the politics and parading about. "Someone attempted to assassinate Usun. I saw it myself. If the boy wasn't so capable—so strong and intelligent like his foolish godsdamned father—he'd be dead. I vowed to keep it from you until after you handled Zage-Si. As his blood is now cold, it feels appropriate to mention that he's not the only person who had some brute coming into his home to execute his children."

Gilgamesh stared at Enkidu like he was a dropped bowl, cracks slowly rising, the entire thing about to shatter.

For once, Enkidu didn't care. Let him feel something besides arrogance for once in his godsdamned life.

"I'm going to bed." Enkidu didn't even meet Gilgamesh's gaze as he turned and slipped beneath the rug.

CHAPTER SEVENTEEN
SHATTERED

GILGAMESH ROSE EARLY and slipped out of the tent while night still hovered over the valley. He'd scarcely slept, and his dream had invaded what little rest he found. He couldn't escape tucked under night's wings any more than he could during daylight. Always something haunted him but nothing as much as Enkidu's words.

You're out worrying about your legacy while someone else is attempting to kill your son.

He hadn't known.

He never would have left if someone—anyone—had told him Usun was in danger. Shamhat might be at risk or his other wives or children. Gilgamesh wasn't attached to most of them. His distance kept them safe—or so he thought. Despite that, he would do anything to protect them. He meant his vows when he'd made them; it was his place to protect those under his roof, yet he'd failed Usun, failed Shamhat.

He hissed through his teeth as he stood up beneath the sparkling sky.

Abgal jumped up from the fire, a sword drawn. One of

his best soldiers of the army he'd created. He still felt pride for his men, appreciative of Abgal who slid the weapon back into his sheath when his gaze met Gilgamesh's.

So much of his life was sand the gods tossed into the wind to watch it rush away.

He was only one among millions of grains.

Soon that would be gone too.

"I leave for Uruk this morning," Gilgamesh said.

Abgal nodded. "I can rouse the men."

"No. I wish to go alone. You'll make sure Enkidu returns with the others today?"

Abgal's brows drew together, but he left it at that. "I will."

Among the other soldiers, Abgal would have addressed him as Lugal or king, but only a few stood as guards at the camp's perimeter. Abgal's tone was humanizing and Gilgamesh needed that. He offered a nod, slung a sack over his shoulder, and stepped out of camp.

His thoughts plagued him on the journey home. By the time he reached Uruk's gates, his head pounded. He didn't fight the ache but leaned into it instead. He needed to remember he was human, that he'd die, and he would leave nothing to show for it.

When he stepped up to the gates, others veered away. Normally he'd wave and meet his citizens' eyes. He couldn't do it, though. He stopped before Inanna's statue where she looked out over the river's blue water.

She would win.

Gilgamesh had always fooled himself that he could be strong enough, that he could make a mark on history. How he ever thought he could best the gods at their own fucking game was beyond him.

Enkidu had hammered in the finality of his crumbling

purpose. He saw Gilgamesh as foolish, chasing after meaningless pursuits. Thought he didn't love Usun. Gilgamesh ground his teeth until his jaw ached.

He'd loved Usun by ignoring him, and still it hadn't been sufficient.

With a sigh, he readjusted his pack and walked into Uruk—the city Inanna would scrub his name from in a short time.

Throughout the streets, people stopped to gape at him with wide eyes, to bow low to the ground, but he couldn't bother responding. His heart ached too deeply to care about his image.

Perhaps the dream was what he always believed. The pebble was his legacy. He'd built it until it seemed possible to stand among gods. However, then the lightning stuck—the omen, or Shamhat's intervention, or Enkidu's arrival. It didn't matter what it was specifically. It cracked his efforts, left them shattered beneath him. He wished he could weep like he did in the dream, but it wouldn't come.

When he made it into the palace, the sky's hazy pink had given way to the gleam of sunrise. He trekked down the halls of this place he'd expanded and beautified. One day it would all lie beneath sand, crumbled and forgotten. Like his life.

He reached Shamhat's favorite dining room and stopped before entering. Dozens of guards surrounded it. He'd wanted Enkidu's words to prove false, but he'd never seen Shamhat use so much security. A guard lifted his face as if to speak to the King, but Gilgamesh shook his head. He didn't want his presence announced yet.

A door sat ajar, and laughter rang out from within. Gilgamesh stepped closer. Usun was chasing Meritkara's daughter around, the little girl squealing. The boy caught and tickled her.

Beyond, Akkiru and Meritkara sat on a couch together, grinning at the spectacle. Shamhat's arm was stretched towards them from the adjacent couch, her fingers tangled with Meritkara's. Her lover whispered something to her that brought a hint of a smile to the Queen's face.

"If it pleases you," Shamhat said to her partner, "I'll have the dancers return for dinner again tonight."

"Stop teasing me." Meritkara tucked her face but tightened her grip on the Queen's hand.

"All right, Usun." Shamhat returned her attention to the children's rowdy play. "You're going to have your sister too stirred up for her lessons today."

"He won't!" the girl cried. "Please let us play longer."

Meritkara clicked her tongue. "Is that how you address your queen?"

Usun set the girl carefully on her feet, and she bowed. "Apologies, Nin."

Shamhat shoved Meritkara who grinned as she knocked into Akkiru. He bumped her in return, sending the motion back down the line. Gilgamesh remained frozen watching his family live life without him. He'd always felt so at home in Uruk and within the palace. Now he felt like a ghost, roaming the halls, haunting them.

He stepped into the room.

Shamhat snapped her face towards him, met his gaze and must have seen the darkness in it. Her expression dropped, and she jumped up. "Everyone please excuse us."

Akkiru and Meritkara ushered the children away, all of them bowing before leaving and shutting the door with a thunk that cut off some of the room's light.

"My king." Shamhat bowed.

She was a gem among the desert sands, her crimson and gold tunic glimmering among the room's finery. But he was no matching jewel, and he couldn't play the role anymore. She stared at him, her brow furrowed.

"Why wouldn't you tell me?" He'd wanted it to come out loud, laced with anger. Instead, his voice was low, draping along the floor and gathering dust as it dragged its way to her.

She released a breath. "Enkidu?"

"Yes, Enkidu." The anger he'd wanted returned with a rush. "Everything is about godsdamned Enkidu lately, is it not?"

She took half a step forward then stopped, pressing her hands together. "I didn't want you distracted and—"

"I have a fucking right to know what is happening in my own home. How dare someone threaten my child—our child. You should have fucking told me. I would have dealt with it."

"You couldn't go to Umma angry and unfocused. You are mortal, Gilgamesh." His nose flared. He was fucking aware. That mortality was a wolf panting against his neck, stretching its sharp claws on his heels. "I have it handled for the moment and planned to discuss it when you returned."

"By handled it, do you mean you're a prisoner in your home?" he yelled and gestured to the walls where the guards had hovered.

Shamhat fisted her hands into her tunic. "I'm sorry my actions displease you. We don't all have the power of god's blood to protect us, and my pride must come second to keeping everyone here safe."

He bared his teeth and shouted through them. "Keeping everyone here safe is my job." He slapped a hand to his chest. "Everything doesn't fall on you, Shamhat. We are supposed to be partners."

A moment passed where his heavy breathing echoed, then she whispered, "Supposed to be, but rarely are anymore."

The anger he'd wanted to summon moments before bubbled within him, rising to the surface. He whirled around and slammed a fist into the wall. Tiles cracked, a few falling onto the ground. A split crawled up the wall then across the ceiling so dust rained down.

Shamhat jerked back, her eyes wide as they dashed to the ceiling then stared at her husband. She shivered, her earrings trembling. Color had rushed from her face.

She was afraid of him.

It was perhaps the only thing that could have drained the pounding fury that sliced through his body.

For a moment they looked at each other. Gilgamesh's arms went heavy by his sides as he turned and walked out of the room.

Not only did she not trust him enough to share vital information about their child's safety and the integrity of their home, but she feared him. He stepped out of the hall and into the courtyard with its manicured plants and gleaming tiles.

Gods, he hated all of it. Wanted to rip it apart with his hands rather than allow the divine to do it. Nothing mattered.

Workers bowed. One musician stumbled and hit their knee as he passed.

He had no control over his god's blood powers at that moment, and he didn't care. Life was meaningless and there was no hope.

He stormed through the back of the palace, ignoring the reverential words, the bowing, the damn show of it all.

When he reached the gate he sought, he stopped. Inanna was carved into the stone, her wings' feathers rippling along it. He spread his hand over her form for no other reason than to block her image. He didn't need the reminder of who this city truly belonged to, whose name history would record.

He stepped through the gate into the back courtyard that only gardeners and spiritualists ever visited. Gilgamesh's father—Lugalbanda—had loved that quiet, small space. Gilgamesh could remember visiting his father there, the man looking at him from under his heavy brow.

They had the same relationship he and Usun had.

Formal.

Distant.

Walking into the garden he never visited swept up the coals of his anger, breathing it back to life. He turned towards a vase and kicked it. It hit the walkway and shattered, pieces flying everywhere.

A gasp drew him out of the white-hot fury of his thoughts.

Usun stood down the path next to a palm tree, his wide eyes staring at his father. When he noticed the attention, the boy bowed. "Lugal."

Gilgamesh stepped over the vase, his boots crunching a piece, and approached the boy. "What are you doing here? Surely your mother has guards assigned to you presently?"

"Forgive me, my king, but I evaded my guards." Color washed across the boy's nose. Gilgamesh wanted to conjure up sternness, but it was exactly what he would have done as a child himself, and Usun had a weapon on his hip. He wasn't incapable of defending himself. Unlike Gilgamesh.

"It's quiet here." Usun offered as if that explained everything. He met his father's eyes and didn't cower away. Usun didn't fear him—respected him, yes, but didn't have the same reaction to his strength that Shamhat did.

Usun's wide, brown eyes remained fixed on him, waiting obediently for orders or dismissal. His mother had raised him well. The boy had never once addressed Gilgamesh as Adda, as Father. He'd lost his child's entire life to try to keep him safe and an attack happened within their home anyway.

Just once he wanted to feel the weight of the boy's flesh in his arms, hear his breathing, bury his nose in his dark curls. If someone might kill him regardless of Gilgamesh's distance, perhaps it didn't matter. He moved a step forward.

The boy stiffened as if he understood Gilgamesh's intentions and didn't know how to interact with him as anything other than Lugal. All the roaring heat within Gilgamesh left like steam hissing from a doused fire. It was too late for him to become a father to that stranger-boy. He remained standing a distance away.

"Enkidu tells me you were attacked but defended yourself honorably."

Abgal needed thanks. He'd trained the boy—not Gilgamesh—and was the reason the child had survived a fight. He'd have to make sure he shared that later with the man, thanking each of the soldiers who spent their time working with the adolescents.

"Enkidu stopped the attacker. Not me." Usun frowned and his chin dropped.

"Look at me," Gilgamesh ordered. If Usun could only approach him as Lugal, then he'd speak to the boy as the King. The child raised his face, and Gilgamesh could see

Shamhat in the lines of his profile, the depth of his expression. "Don't downplay your successes. It's difficult being the King's son. I know. I grew up similarly to you."

Except Usun had a human mother of flesh and blood who held him at night when the shadows became great. He had siblings to tease. Aunts and uncles to play games with and learn from. Perhaps their lives were more different than alike—Gilgamesh had always been brutally alone.

"Except you have god's blood," the boy whispered. It was the first insecure moment the child had shown.

Gilgamesh gripped his son's shoulder. "God's blood is a curse, Usun. You stopped that attacker not because of divine powers, but by your own strength. That's something you can take pride in."

Enkidu had exposed that truth. Most of what Gilgamesh had to claim was handed to him. The city, the crown, and even his damned strength and abilities weren't earned. It was no wonder his legacy was so fickle, that it would crack and crumble over the dry earth.

Usun, though, was still a boy and only a human. Yet, he'd fended off an attacker. That was the making of a legend—not the easy kills Gilgamesh had taken. It meant nothing if it cost little.

Shamhat was right. God's blood in a mortal—in a ruler—was a curse. Something that shouldn't exist. It made power unbalanced. No humans could stand up to Gilgamesh. He could only pride himself if he fought a god, something he wasn't foolish enough to try. Perhaps his son, this boy, was braver than his father.

He moved his hand away from the child, but it ached. He wished to know him, to reclaim the lost years. Return to the first time he held the warm, squalling bundle and treasure every moment since then as deeply.

His fingers grazed the boy's cheeks. Usun fluttered his eyelashes but didn't pull away as Gilgamesh spoke, his voice full of gravel. "Know that I'm proud of you."

A breath escaped the boy. For a moment they remained still, a statue of a father and son both longing for things they didn't have the capacity to name. Then Usun pulled back to bow. "Thank you, Lugal."

The moment was gone. Gilgamesh straightened. "Now, where should you be at this time? Breakfast has passed, and a prince doesn't have a free schedule, does he?"

"No, my king." He bowed again, but when he rose, his eyes lingered for a moment. Then he passed Gilgamesh and dashed towards the gate like someone free of burdens.

Gilgamesh moved through the courtyard he hadn't visited in years. Usun liked the place. Perhaps he could speak with Shamhat, see if there were any amendments he could make to it for the boy's sake.

He followed the mosaics along the wall. Bushes had grown, edging against the images of his father's deeds. They'd swallow them if the gardeners didn't keep the plants trimmed. A year without human intervention and the wild would overtake what little remained of his father's life.

Gilgamesh ran his fingers over the rise and fall of the tiles, tracing them like a harpist plucking strings. His hand stopped. The mosaic had changed. A massive dragon stared at him from the wall, its fangs dripping blood, its snake-head tail curling around its body.

Humbaba.

The monster watched the King, taunting him.

Gilgamesh ground his teeth.

His life stretched before him with a path he could already sketch out. He could stay in Uruk, continue his work, and allow Inanna to use him then kill him when her son grew strong enough to take the throne.

He'd help create another child with god's blood, another terror that didn't fit among humans or gods, who restlessly sought enemies to have something that might prove a challenge.

The only way to change it, as he'd told Shamhat, was for someone to endanger themselves.

He'd meant he wouldn't risk Usun's life by crowning him.

But.

Gilgamesh sucked in a breath and met the dragon's gaze again.

If he died, Inanna couldn't use his god's blood to create another child. The people of Uruk would never accept someone from a different line. They'd have to take one of his existing children. The gods would need to support that to keep Inanna from having her way. He thought they might. His mother had mentioned grumblings from other gods about the divine mixing with mortals.

If he killed Humbaba, he'd do something truly legendary.

Even the gods feared the monster.

If he died trying, he might end the god-blood reign in Uruk.

Gilgamesh slid his hand over Humbaba's face, down his gleaming neck, and for the first time that day, he smiled.

CHAPTER EIGHTEEN
WHEN A GOD FEARS

ENKIDU APPROACHED the palace with weary steps. Abgal informed him the King desired his return, but the soldiers had otherwise ignored him. Whatever connections he'd created among the men during the journey and hunt were gone.

A few even glared in his direction.

Being called a prophet could do that to a man.

Being viewed as a spineless spy for the gods could do that.

Enkidu returned to a gleaming, chattering world but with even fewer connections than he'd had the last time he'd been there.

A guard left his post and approached. "The King wishes to speak with you. Follow me."

It wasn't a request. Enkidu didn't bother fighting it. Facing Gilgamesh again was inevitable. He'd angered a king and would face punishment. He couldn't find it within himself to care. Perhaps Gilgamesh would send him to the Great Below. It would be preferable than spending years aimlessly milling through the palace's fine halls.

The guard led him to an empty sitting room Enkidu had never seen before. Lattice stonework allowed sunlight to fall over the floor in geometric whorls. The cushioned couch was appealing after days of travel, but he remained on his feet. He wasn't sure what version of Gilgamesh he'd face.

He'd now seen Gilgamesh the haughty king, the compassionate ruler, the vicious conqueror, the curious scholar, the desirous man, and the hurting soul.

The last still ached. It had been no pleasure to throw cutting words at Gilgamesh, but he couldn't see what remained out of his vision. The gods had sent Enkidu to bring him clarity.

The King stepped through the door then pulled it shut. He wore a tunic and shawl in a trio of bright colors—crimson, cerulean, and gold. Curls adorned his thick beard again, and he gleamed.

Enkidu released a slow breath. It was so different from when blood had dripped from his face, his eyes so dark they scarcely reflected light. And it differed from when they'd stood chest-to-chest in Gilgamesh's tent, their lips brushing.

Gilgamesh had arrived as the King.

The man had so many layers. Enkidu wanted it to bother him, to make him hate Gilgamesh. It didn't.

"I've had a great deal of time to think in the last day." Gilgamesh moved forward, his sandaled feet peeking out beyond his tunic's hem. When he reached close enough to touch Enkidu—though not as near as they'd stood in the tent—he stopped. His gaze ran up Enkidu's form, sending a shiver through him before stopping at his eyes. "I've realized why the gods must have sent you."

Enkidu lifted his chin. He'd longed to know his purpose

since Shamhat had brought him bread, beer, and the bitter taste of knowledge. They were closer now, warmth building between their bodies. Gilgamesh's carefully arranged expression flickered with interest before he rearranged it back to neutral.

Enkidu wanted to throw harsh words and finish their fight.

Enkidu wanted to kiss him and see what the King of Uruk tasted like.

The grappling opposition of those desires kept him stuck in place, his body still though his heart hammered.

Gilgamesh cleared his throat and looked away, as though he couldn't keep the act up when meeting Enkidu's gaze. "We're to go together and kill Humbaba."

Warmth drained from Enkidu's face then followed down his shoulders and sides until his entire body turned cold. Finally, words found their way to his tongue. "They say even the gods fear Humbaba."

"That's true but think it through. You made me realize everything I've accomplished has been through divine powers or appointment. Even my godsdamned walls I could only build because I'd been born a prince. To accomplish something meaningful, I'll need to take on a divine problem. Only then can I say earnestly that I've tested my merit."

Enkidu wanted to interject. He hadn't meant Gilgamesh did nothing meaningful. Fine walls that protected his city had purpose. The children he provided for had meaning. Thousands of people worked in his palace which supported their families. Palace workers kept sheep and cows and crafted wool to help form the temple's blankets. They farmed and made beer. He'd seen all of this when Akkiru and Meritkara had given him a tour of the palace. It wasn't that

Gilgamesh's work didn't matter; it was that he missed the important parts. He missed the devotion of the people who loved him and the impact he already made on the world.

Gilgamesh continued before Enkidu could say anything. "The more I thought of it, the more it made sense to me. I mean, what do you and I both care about?"

Love and power. The former for himself, the latter for the King.

Enkidu didn't get to say that aloud either. He might not have done so even if given the chance.

"I want to see the Land Between Waters prosper. You care for the beasts in the cedar forest. We help both if we do this."

Hairs on the back of Enkidu's neck rose. If they killed the dragon, they would help. He remembered discussing Humbaba's terror with the wolf. How the creature overtaxed the forest and made life hard. It wasn't likely they'd achieve killing Humbaba, though. Perhaps this was the gods' plan all along. Use Enkidu to lure Gilgamesh away, killing them both. They'd employed Gilgamesh's viciousness to punish Zage-Si, perhaps they'd use Enkidu's gentleness to do the same to another king.

Gilgamesh's eyes sparkled, and the edge of a smile sat on his lips. He thought it was possible. He had god's blood, Enkidu had divine strength.

"All right."

Enkidu's voice sounded like it belonged to someone else. It echoed. An hour before, he'd dreaded spending his life trapped in that palace. He didn't realize he would walk away from it and into their doom.

Gilgamesh gripped his shoulder which made his stomach dip. He couldn't process so many emotions at once. Then Gilgamesh said something that made him feel even more nauseated. "I want you to meet my mother."

Ninsun's temple blocked the sounds of the city. Within the inner rooms, water trickled from the walls in the dimness. It was like the waterfall hushing in the distance at the lake, twilight stretching across the sky.

Gilgamesh lit a block of incense and dropped it into a copper dish with a clang. His mood had shifted again since entering the temple. His lips pinched down, and he crossed his arms as the incense smoke trailed through the space, filling the room with the rich notes of cedar.

A deep breath drew more of the scent into Enkidu's nose. It had always comforted him, but a new feeling twisted alongside that. Something that picked up his heart rate and made his mouth dry.

They'd go to the cedar forest to fight Humbaba, and they'd die.

Wind rushed through the temple, and a woman appeared, her features delicate, her dark hair piled on her head.

Gilgamesh only tilted his head to the side, but Enkidu bowed.

Here was the goddess who had requested his creation. He had so many questions. Through his sleepless nights, he'd imagined getting to ask them. Now she stood before him, her hooved feet in the temple's waters, her gaze fixed on her son.

"It's been some time."

"Have you heard someone tried to kill my son?"

Gilgamesh spoke the words like he bit each one off with his teeth.

Ninsun batted her eyes and looked away. Trickling water filled the quiet. "I am not the only god. I control limited aspects of this life, Gilgamesh. If I could protect you and Usun, I would. Your lives are not within my realm, however."

Gilgamesh's nose flared, but he didn't answer his mother.

She turned to face Enkidu. "I'd hoped to meet you soon."

He'd longed to meet her since the day he learned of his origins. Something hungry within him ached to stand before her. She could have sought him out, explained things to him. Shamhat had been surprised she hadn't. So the avoidance must have served some purpose. Maybe she wanted him to interact with Gilgamesh naturally without her guidance.

She smiled and winked at him.

It left him so shaken he couldn't think of anything to say; apparently she understood his thoughts.

Gilgamesh looked over his shoulder towards the door like he wished to leave. "My companion you've had crafted for me,"—he glanced at Enkidu whose emotions tumbled —"and I are going to fight Humbaba."

"No." Ninsun snapped towards her son. One moment she stood across the room and the next she was beside Gilgamesh, her light gleaming over his muscle's curves. "You must know how senseless this is. It is divinely crafted and will kill you. Even if you make it to its lair, its breath is poison, and it's far stronger than you." Gilgamesh didn't answer her, and she stared into her son's eyes before frowning. "It's a fool's plan."

Gilgamesh scoffed and turned his face away. It reflected in the water, the corners of his eyes wrinkling as they closed, his nose flaring. Enkidu had never seen this side of Gilgamesh—the hurting son.

"Does it matter," Gilgamesh whispered, "since my life has no meaning?" Ninsun looked ready to reply, but Gilgamesh lifted his face and shook his head to swing loose locks of hair over his shoulders. "I go to protect my people. I'm a king, a shepherd. My duty lies there."

Ninsun kept her gaze fixed on her son whose jaw jumped. If Enkidu stood closer, he'd hear the clicking of grinding teeth. Ninsun gripped Gilgamesh's arm. "Please, my son. I know you're angry with me. Don't leave a mother for a foolish quest without a goodbye, at least."

A sigh slipped from Gilgamesh's lips, then he bent down and embraced his mother.

"Now," she said as he pulled away, "I'd like to speak with Enkidu alone."

Gilgamesh turned towards Enkidu and raised an eyebrow. There was an offer of escape in his expression. Gilgamesh still hadn't discussed the brutal things they'd thrown at each other in his tent, and words had become gummy, difficult things. They'd always felt awkward in Enkidu's mouth but now more than ever when Gilgamesh looked at him with soft eyes, willing to defy a goddess' desires if Enkidu asked for it. He nodded though. Even if he couldn't conjure words, he wished to speak with Ninsun.

Gilgamesh's jaw shifted again. Then he bowed to his mother and left the chamber, his feet kicking up water as he went.

When the noise settled, Ninsun retreated to a bench. She sat and patted the space beside her. Enkidu pressed his tongue hard to the roof of his mouth. Ninsun didn't seem dangerous—she offered a gentle smile, her eyes twinkling. And her son had been casual with her. Then again, she was his mother and Enkidu was nothing more than a disposable helper who'd already failed.

He sat.

"You're not disposable, Enkidu. I want you to look after my son." Within her eyes, colors pooled together. Lakes and rivers crashing into pale brown fields.

A breath left him. She could read his thoughts which made this meeting even more intimidating. "I'm not as strong as your son. It's a hard task."

She closed her eyes then raised her face towards the tiled ceiling. "You're stronger, you just don't realize it yet."

"We've fought." Enkidu struggled against squirming. He felt like a child confessing to his mother—an experience he'd never actually had. "We're equally matched."

"I'm not speaking of physical strength. You see how much my son needs you, don't you?"

Enkidu took a deep breath of humid air and leaned on his legs. The King needed help, but he didn't understand how it could be him. He'd done nothing but cause tension and issues since arriving.

"Don't you see my son needs that?" Ninsun rubbed her hands together. They were so smooth her knuckles lacked wrinkles. "He's sailed through his life like a boat with a strong wind. If he wishes to achieve his goals, he must get off the boat, tie up the ropes, and walk it back up the river against the current."

Enkidu nodded. "As you know my mind, you must understand I'll do whatever I can. But please, would you tell me my purpose?"

Ninsun rose and moved, her tunic skimming over the water like a petal blooming. She wouldn't answer and he'd be left with his endless questions. When she reached the incense, smoke wreathed around her. "Gilgamesh has asked me that for himself many times. I've never revealed it to him."

Water shifted as Enkidu stood. Gilgamesh had spent so much of his life alone, lost in omens with no one to guide him. How unfair that he had god's blood thrust on him, a city on his shoulders, and no one to help him hold it all together. Enkidu hadn't considered the burden he held as a divine king.

Ninsun turned back towards Enkidu. She was short and slim with fine features and sharp cutting eyes. How she birthed Gilgamesh, Enkidu couldn't understand. Ninsun stepped through the water without shifting it. "Your purpose, Enkidu, is to love my son."

A breath rushed from Enkidu's lips. "He hates me."

Enkidu longed for love the way Gilgamesh sought a legacy. He wanted to know the emotion, feel it until his bones ached. Loving Gilgamesh, though? The man had laughed at love. He didn't even care for his wives. Besides, Enkidu was a wild man pulled from the woods. A king would never love him.

"He doesn't know how to express love or fear," Ninsun said. "He's had that driven from him by other gods. You are divinely crafted, Enkidu. Why do you disdain the wild? I am the goddess of cattle and dreams—wild things. Do you despise me?"

"Of course not."

"Then know you're blessed, not cursed, by your origins. You are a lesser god, even if you're mortal. Because of that, you can help my son reclaim things other gods have stolen from him."

"I would if I could manage. He doesn't listen to me."

He blinked, and Ninsun stood near him again. "Do you really believe that?" Enkidu hesitated. Gilgamesh had readjusted his plans in Umma because of Enkidu's words and had changed Nissaba's situation because of his interjection. Perhaps the King did listen to him.

Ninsun smiled. "He heeds you more than any other, much to the chagrin of his wife and mother, I assure you." Enkidu chuckled. "You're changing my son's heart. I'm sorry for the hardship it's cost you. I suppose I forgot in my love for my son that you would be a person of your own, someone needing love and guidance as much as him."

Enkidu took in a ragged breath. He wasn't supposed to exist. He wasn't natural. Ninsun had him crafted to fix the broken aspects of her son. Cold flooded through his body. Who would love someone with no purpose? Of course, she hadn't said the aim was for Gilgamesh to love Enkidu in return. Enkidu's purpose was to love the King. He teetered on the edge of it already. If other emotions—fury, disgust, anger—hadn't gotten tangled up with it, he might already have arrived there.

The wolf had told him his responsibility was whatever lay before him.

What lay before him was a goddess requesting that he love her son.

"I'll do everything I'm able, Ninsun. I'll protect him as much as I can."

"I know you will." Still, her shoulders dropped. "Let me tell you something about your purpose. When I asked Aruru, the mother goddess, to create you, she designed you as the opposite of my son. Sometimes he is more fierce than kind. Often, you are more compassionate than violent. Together, you're complete. Do you see the perfection in that?"

Enkidu released a breathy laugh. He hadn't moved past the fact that his purpose was to love the most stubborn ass in the Land Between Waters. He didn't have space to muse on completing him in some mystical way. He didn't have the ability to think about this new goddess, Aruru, who'd formed him.

"You'll understand in time." Ninsun grasped his hands. Hers, unlike her son's, were smooth as a river stone. "You are not my son, but I will interfere for you as though you are. I'll speak with Utu and ask for his divine protection for both of my boys."

Enkidu's heart leapt. He'd never been anyone's child. Words caught in his throat like moss on rocks, blocking all the meaningful things he wished he could say. "What about Usun?"

If he could choose to protect anyone, it would be Gilgamesh's son, not himself.

Ninsun smiled, a wispy thing, like a spiderweb blowing in the wind. "Usun is a good boy. Tell me, Enkidu, do you think the good are rewarded?"

In his limited life, he'd seen cruel and merciful things. When he tried to imagine someone he'd label as good, the thought became slippery. Every person he'd met so far had positive attributes and damning ones. "I cannot say, Nin."

"Take some time to think about it. This life isn't everything. Keep that in mind as you consider."

With a rush of chilly air, Ninsun disappeared.

Enkidu stumbled back against the wall, water gliding down his neck, as he tried to piece it all together. Tried to decide what it meant to love a god-king.

CHAPTER NINETEEN
AMBITION

A RUSH of activity filled the palace over the next week as the King prepared for his trip. Gilgamesh interviewed every person who worked or lived in the palaces. The attack had happened after the wedding feast, which meant it could have been a visitor, but he was meticulous and wouldn't take risks.

He assigned his loyal hundred soldiers to protect the Queen's palace where his wives and children lived. Except for Abgal who he asked to train Usun to use a dagger which the boy could keep on hand. Abgal also recreated the attack with Usun then reported to his king. The attacker fought in the style of Gilgamesh's men. They'd used certain sword stances that Gilgamesh had created. Which meant the attacker was someone close.

Irritation buzzed through the King as he pressed a stylus into a clay tablet, arranging his affairs should he not survive.

He likely wouldn't.

But he'd die trying to do something great.

Later the sun beat down on Gilgamesh as he sat on a

throne on his mother's temple steps. Sweat beaded down his back. He'd asked attendants to bring fans and silks to divert the intensity off Shamhat who sat at his side, however he didn't want the treatment for himself. No, he wanted to burn. Wanted Utu to watch him and see that King Gilgamesh would look defeat in the face and not quit.

He may not be eternal, but he was just as much a god. Perhaps he couldn't control his fate. His legacy might crumble. But no one would say it happened because he didn't try.

Kasiru rose from her bow, her gaze meeting Shamhat's before flicking to Gilgamesh. "I pray for Inanna's protection for Uruk's leaders every day."

Gilgamesh's lips pulled down. He'd saved interviewing his advisors for last. Something in him fought against the idea that a person who stood at Shamhat's and his side every day, who benefited from their blessings and were privy to their devotion to ruling Uruk well, would betray them.

Abgal's discovery made it seem likely it was someone near, though.

Shamhat's cool fingers draped over his arm, though her gaze stayed fixed on the girl. "We thank you, Kasiru."

She rose and walked down the long steps, her shadow zigzagging over them. From where they sat, the Id-Ugina river glimmered and curved in the distance. Ivory birds swooped over its form and men hauled boats upriver with ropes. The city milled about, thousands of people weaving within Gilgamesh's walls. Safe and supported.

Gilgamesh had wanted to perform these interviews at his mother's temple to remind everyone in the palace of a detail some overlooked.

Gilgamesh was a god as well.

Enkidu climbed the steps. He moved with such grace, his large body looked like water in motion. Someone had given him a royal tunic, and he wore a navy strip of fabric around his head that pulled his thick curls away from his face.

He reached the top and bowed.

"This is only a formality," Gilgamesh said before the man made it back up. He needed to explain things to Enkidu so he could understand his perspective. He'd kept Enkidu at a distance, but it no longer mattered. If Humbaba ended him before the new moon, he had no reason to hide things anymore. "We know you didn't conspire against us."

"Thank you again," Shamhat added, "for your intervention."

Enkidu swallowed. "I wish I could remove the burden altogether."

Shamhat bobbed her head, her earrings wobbling. But Enkidu didn't keep his focus on her. Instead, he slid those color-flecked eyes towards Gilgamesh. For a moment, the city faded, the walls disappearing, the clattering noises gone.

Then Gilgamesh readjusted in his seat and looked away. "Thank you."

Enkidu bowed again and retreated.

Last of all was Hirin who made the trek slowly. "My king. My queen." He bowed low to the step. "I pray every morning and night that your rule is long, your names last forever, and your children remain safe."

"Where did you hear that this has anything to do with our children?" Gilgamesh shifted forward in his throne. They'd kept Usun's attack quiet. All they'd asked during the interviews were basic questions about the wedding night and for a reaffirmation of their loyalty.

Hirin readjusted his tunic then tangled his fingers together. "Only, rumor, Lugal. Forgive me for inferring."

Godsdamned rumors. People always had things to say. They longed to speak ill of anyone if it meant they could avoid facing their own lives' lack of meaning. Perhaps it helped them ignore fate's hot breath on their necks.

Shamhat's fingers grazed his arm. She smiled at Hirin. "If I remember correctly, you stayed during the entire duration of the wedding feast?"

"Of course, Nin. I'd never dishonor the King by leaving early."

The interview carried forward, Gilgamesh scarcely listening to Hirin's words. The man was his closest advisor. He often went with him to drills, if only to pester him into addressing more dull tablets and political questions. It was difficult to see him as a fighting man, but not impossible. He could have observed the fighting stances and practiced them later. He had the financial means to purchase a blade.

When Shamhat excused him, Gilgamesh chewed his lip. "Did he seem suspicious to you?"

Shamhat waved off the attendants who retreated. The sun sank low behind buildings; the sky burning flame red. "You've suspected everyone who's approached today."

Gilgamesh gripped the throne's arm and fought the inclination to break the stone. "That's because someone attacked my family in my home."

Shamhat removed her glistening headpiece and set it in her lap. She fiddled with a golden disc on it so that light reflected and bounced around between the two of them.

"I leave in the morning," Gilgamesh said when she didn't respond. "If you need anything in my absence or suspect anything while I'm gone, Abgal is at your disposal."

Shamhat's fingers stilled. "You know this mission is foolish, don't you? Your mother is right."

"My mother and you are always right and I'm always stubborn. We're playing out our roles perfectly."

A puff of breath left his wife. "Gilgamesh—"

"I've arranged things for you in case the worst happens. There's a tablet I've pressed my seal to that expresses my wishes. Hirin knows where to find it, though I'm now going to assign one of my soldiers to guard the room as I don't know who I can trust." Sinking back into the throne, he frowned. Hirin was his most loyal, proven advisor. If he'd arranged to kill Usun, Gilgamesh would have no one politically to rely on. His soldiers were dependable. Though now he suspected even them. He'd still take a man of earth over someone who kissed royals' asses any day. *You can't rule this city through might alone.* Shamhat had said that to him years before. She was probably right, but it wasn't something he'd need to worry about unless he survived Humbaba.

Her eyes brightened. "You don't think you'll survive this, do you?"

"I can't say." He found it unlikely, but his queen stared at him with such fear in her eyes, he couldn't offer her honesty.

"Gilgamesh, we need you. Uruk needs you. Damn it, I need you."

"You're afraid of me." He met her gaze as her lips snapped apart. "Tell me I'm wrong about that."

Her skin glistened in the evening's coral light. Sweat illuminated her brow and shimmered over her dark hair, but she held herself upright. Always a queen. "I'm not afraid of *you.* You're a good man. But you are a god. When you lose your temper, your strength and abilities are more than mortal and it's frightening."

He'd been right then. She was afraid of him. Had she imagined he'd hurt her—*her* of all people? No one had seen him as intimately. He'd laid out his flaws for her like offerings, allowed her to tease him, given her access to every part of his reality. Yet all that time she had felt afraid he'd damage her? Never would he do such a thing. He'd accept death first.

She blinked rapidly, her eyes glistening, but didn't say it wasn't true. He sighed. No one had ever been able to handle all of him, not even his wife. "Let us hope Humbaba finds me as intimidating."

He rose, but she grabbed his hand, stalling him. For a moment they stayed like that. Birds called in the distance and water rushed in the temple's courtyard beyond. She squeezed his fingers tighter. "I love you too," she whispered. "Before you go, I want you to know that."

The stone encompassing Gilgamesh's heart crumbled. He leaned over his wife and pressed a kiss to her temple.

* * *

But you are a god.

Shamhat's words rushed through Gilgamesh's mind as he walked towards the cedar forest alongside a quiet Enkidu. They'd packed simple bags with a handful of necessities. When Enkidu asked about it, Gilgamesh replied he'd intended for them to survive as Enkidu once had— with their wit and skill. Enkidu had frowned, as though it was an insult rather than the compliment Gilgamesh had intended. Then he'd descended back into an uncomfortable silence.

What haunted him more? His omen-filled dreams or the aching loneliness of his actual life?

When they reached the edge of the cedar forest the next morning, Enkidu finally spoke. "Has Humbaba come so far south?"

"No. I wished to see your home, and Shamhat says this is where you lived. Is that correct?"

The notch between Enkidu's brow deepened. "My home?"

He'd always acted squeamish about originating from the woods. Gilgamesh respected a man of the earth, though. Someone who knew how to hunt and trap, how to live and die by his own means. Gilgamesh was a city man from birth, but his mother was as wild as the wind, and her blood coursed through his veins.

"I want to see it. And surely you can understand a man wishing to delay his death by a day or two?"

Enkidu stopped walking. "You think you'll die?"

Those beautiful eyes once again fixed on Gilgamesh. In the last weeks, Enkidu had kept his head down, his face turned away. The enchantment his gaze cast over the King had been lost. Standing under their spell again, Gilgamesh's heart skipped a beat. "It's possible. I do not expect you to sacrifice yourself with me. If I should fall, return to Uruk and report what happened."

Enkidu's long lashes fluttered, a dimple forming beneath his lower lip before he shook his head. "I was created for you." Something lingered in his voice—perhaps sadness. Gilgamesh wished he could name it, but it was like trying to capture wind. "Should you fall, I'll go with you. I will not abandon our task."

Moths flitted through long grasses. Everything was still golden and hazy with the promise of a fresh day. A wind blew in, bringing the sweet smell of cedar with it. It made

Gilgamesh's stomach tighten as he stared into Enkidu's eyes.

"There's something I wish to tell you." Gilgamesh shook his head to break the trance. "I don't know why. I've never felt the need to justify myself before. This seems different though." He took a breath. "I love Usun. Should I die and you live, I'd like you to tell him that."

The man's damned eyelashes batted his cheeks like rowers fighting a storm. "You don't spend any time with him."

Stone piled over Gilgamesh's heart again, making his chest heavy, his shoulders sagged. "If a wolf knows Humbaba seeks to destroy him, he would not be wise to lead the monster to his den, would he?"

Enkidu's dark brows drew together. His thick lips frowned. Gilgamesh wished he could stop feeling so much attraction for the man. "Oh," Enkidu said. "I didn't understand before."

"I've cultivated a certain image as the terror of the Land Between Waters. I need it. But now we go to face our potential deaths together and everything has changed." Most of all, Gilgamesh had accepted the foolishness of his desires. The likelihood of leaving a legacy was like hoping a stone would float over a pond. This task was as senseless as his mother said, but it was all he had left. Ninsun had sent Enkidu possibly to distract him or to knock him from the stars he grasped at. Whatever her purpose, she'd succeeded. The man was loyal though. Gilgamesh trusted him as much as his soldiers—more, maybe. "Ask me anything and I'll give you an unfiltered, honest answer."

Enkidu shifted closer. Hair rose on Gilgamesh's arms, and he reached out so their knuckles scraped. Enkidu sucked in a breath at the motion but didn't pull away. This man was a splinter slipped under his nail, constantly aching. He was a flower that bloomed only once a century, so beautiful and unique Gilgamesh wanted to hold his breath so he didn't miss a moment.

Enkidu took another step forward. Their arms scraped, and Gilgamesh looped a finger around Enkidu's thumb. His heart thundered. He wanted to consume Enkidu. Wrestle and best him. Pin him beneath him. Follow the muscles of his legs—

"Answer me this, then," Enkidu said, his voice thick as though his mind had followed the same trails. Gilgamesh nodded and finally found himself able to ignore his damned eyes, because the thick line of his lips was far too captivating. Enkidu parted them to speak. "How does a god-king, indomitable and fierce"—Enkidu paused before continuing—"get so very offended over a bit of thrown fruit?"

Gilgamesh snapped his face up. For a moment they stared at each other, then Enkidu chuckled. Gilgamesh laughed and shoved him hard enough that the man tumbled back. "Let's go." Gilgamesh rolled his eyes but couldn't pull the smile away. "Show me your forest, then we face our destinies."

CHAPTER TWENTY

IN THE FOREST OF LONGING

TWIGS SNAPPED beneath Enkidu's feet. He'd spent the morning pointing out familiar spots to Gilgamesh, sharing stories of hunts that went wrong or misadventures. Gilgamesh listened as though it truly interested him and laughed at appropriate moments.

The King walked through the city of trees wearing only a loose tunic and soft boots. His beard was free of the careful curls he wore in the city. There he was attractive, slicked and polished, and garbed in shimmering colors. But something about seeing him in the woods, his clothing simple if still fine, his skin flushed with exercise, made the warmth in Enkidu's core spread until his entire body burned.

Occasionally Gilgamesh bumped into Enkidu, grazed the back of their hands together, or walked close enough that their hips brushed. The first few instances, Enkidu brushed it off to being caused by the narrowed path. But it kept occurring. Twice, Gilgamesh even looped a finger around Enkidu's for a moment, making him catch his breath.

It was a relief when the sun finally began its descent down the sky and kissed the treetops.

"What should we have for dinner?" Gilgamesh asked. Wind rushed through his hair, and he raised his face to the breeze, closing his eyes. Enkidu wished someone would make a mosaic of Gilgamesh like that with his hand wound around a tree branch, his body swinging forward, his expression as peaceful as the leaves gently rattling together.

"I could find honeycomb," Enkidu said. "It's later in the season now, but there should still be some berries you could pick. Then we could catch fish."

When they'd finished the first half of the plan, Enkidu placed the honeycomb next to the cloth bundle of berries Gilgamesh had gathered. He placed his sticky fingers into his mouth and sucked the sweetness off them.

Gilgamesh watched, his eyes darkening.

Enkidu went still, a flush running over the back of his neck.

"You enchant bees?" Gilgamesh asked, but his gaze remained locked on Enkidu's fingers.

He dashed his hand behind his back. "I used to hear their language. Not anymore, though. I think magic or speaking with them is irrelevant, anyway. It's more about remaining calm so they don't feel alarmed enough to sting."

Gilgamesh stared at him. It had to be the same expression a wolf donned when it had cornered prey and prepared to sink teeth into its flesh. Enkidu's heart hammered. "Are you ready to fish?"

Gilgamesh's eyebrows shot up, and his body loosened. "What traps do you use?"

Enkidu laughed as he raised his hands again. "These ones."

After securing the first portion of the meal to make sure some creature didn't steal it, they meandered down to the lake. It was exactly as Enkidu remembered. Water from distant falls rushed into a hazy mist that spread along silver boulders. Bugs skated across the surface. Plops and splashes echoed around as frogs jumped and fish leapt.

It was peaceful.

Yet Enkidu wouldn't remain. Even if he could have his memories erased and return to his life in the woods, he wouldn't abandon Gilgamesh. Instead, he'd stay at the King's side, face a monster.

Gilgamesh still smiled as they reached the water, his eyes twinkling. Something had transformed in the man. Perhaps facing his death had allowed him to shuck all the worries and stressors in Uruk. Here in the forest, he was as wild as a haja-bird, and twice as joyful.

Gilgamesh rubbed his hands together as he leaned over the water. "All right. How do we do this?"

Enkidu pulled his tunic off and hung it on a branch. He wanted to avoid getting his sleeves wet. Gilgamesh dropped his arms and raked his gaze down his body. So much hunger lit his dark eyes that Enkidu shivered.

"S-sorry. I just thought, we only have one change of clothing and—" And he'd forgotten he wasn't in the woods alone. That he was no longer comfortable walking around nearly naked.

Gilgamesh let his gaze linger as it traced back up Enkidu's body, then he shrugged and removed his tunic as well.

Enkidu's mouth went dry. He'd known Gilgamesh was broad and muscular—he'd had the man's body pressed against his, after all. But seeing him nearly bared, the scattering of hair over his chest gleaming in fading sunlight, was another experience.

His nipples were hard, his stomach undulating with his breath. He had his loincloth tied to leave little to imagination. Enkidu mumbled but didn't form actual words. He wanted to find a compelling reason for them to dress again.

Gilgamesh grinned with all the arrogance he'd shown during their initial meeting then turned towards the lake. "Are we going to catch fish or not?"

Oh, shed. Enkidu wasn't sure he was capable. He kept his eyes fixed on the water and crouched. Gilgamesh lowered beside him so their skin gilded together. Enkidu closed his eyes, swallowed, attempting to remember how to breathe.

He moved over, creating space between them and ignored Gilgamesh's laughter.

"We're at a deep, calm part of the lake." Enkidu tried desperately to remember they were catching dinner, that he was hungry... for food. He swiped a hand over his sweaty forehead. "There are rocks here where the fish like to hide."

Gilgamesh's voice turned serious. "So, we'll just reach in and catch them."

"Essentially."

With a grunt Gilgamesh stretched an arm out towards a massive catfish. Its slick body slipped through his hands, and Enkidu refused to think anymore about that. They were catching dinner.

Gilgamesh leaned forward to stall the fish's retreat, and it slapped its tail against the surface, spraying him with water. He sputtered as he dropped the creature and fell to his knees. "Gods damn it."

Water dripped from the King's nose, trailing down the dark strands of his beard. He furrowed his brow and spat lake water. A laugh bubbled in Enkidu's chest then spilled out of his mouth.

With deliberate slowness, Gilgamesh lifted his face in Enkidu's direction. "You can't actually catch fish with your bare hands, can you? This has been a bunch of shed to play a joke on me. Enjoying your laugh?" But he smiled, his words filled with too much levity to convey any censure.

"I'm sorry, but you should see yourself. Gods, if your advisors saw you right now. You look—"

"Ridiculous." Gilgamesh's lower lip puckered into a pout, and Enkidu's heart did strange flips. Fading sunlight gleamed over the King, drops of water coursed down the planes of his chest, and his thick brows were low over his eyes.

"Beautiful," Enkidu whispered without truly meaning to say it aloud.

Gilgamesh raised his chin. Droplets still slipped down his cheeks and caught in his beard, but the intensity in his expression pulled the smile from Enkidu's face. Perhaps the forest was enchanted, stripping all the misunderstandings and distance between them away when they'd stepped into its embrace.

"Let me show you," Enkidu said. He turned towards the lake and stretched out on his stomach over the bank. A moment passed before Gilgamesh joined him, lying close enough that their shoulders touched. Enkidu kept his gaze focused on the lake as he plunged an arm into the water's chill bite. That's what he needed—to dive into the lake until his body cooled. Gilgamesh dipped a hand in too and cocked an eyebrow.

"Now we stay still for a few minutes." The King—Gilgamesh—lay so close, his brown eyes kissed with gold from the sunset as he looked unabashedly at Enkidu. A shiver ran down Enkidu's body and he struggled to follow his own directions. "Some things in life you can't fight your way through. Sometimes it's patience that wins. If you remain still long enough, a fish will swim between our hands and these rocks. Press it against the rock then scoop it up. Be mindful, though. Many have teeth or sharp gills."

Gilgamesh grunted and turned towards the lake so the angular lines of his face reflected in the dark water. "All right. Be still. I guess I can try that for once." After a moment he snorted. "If you'd asked me how I thought I might spend my potential last days alive, I never would have said freezing my arm off in a fucking lake in the middle of the woods."

Enkidu smiled. "What would you have done with the time if you could choose anything?"

Gilgamesh's smirk dropped. "I don't know the answer to that."

Enkidu parted his lips, but he couldn't find words. This was what Ninsun had asked another goddess to create him for—to help Gilgamesh discover that answer. He knew it like it was part of him. Enkidu was happy spending what might be the end of his brief life next to Gilgamesh, their bare arms warming each other, laughing and exploring the forest.

A fish swam by, and Enkidu did as he'd instructed Gilgamesh. He slammed his hand, wedging the creature against the rock, grabbed it, and tossed it behind them.

Minutes later, Gilgamesh attempted to do the same, but the fish flapped out of his grip and landed in the water. "Damn the fucking gods."

"Does that include you?"

"Me most of all," he grumbled as he lay down again.

An hour passed. Enkidu caught half a dozen fish and Gilgamesh grew increasingly flustered as they continued to evade him. A massive catfish swam up then tucked itself behind Gilgamesh's hand. Enkidu could just make out the form of it beneath the murky water.

Gilgamesh took a slow breath, slammed his hand back, then grabbed the creature, pulling it out of the water as he jumped to his feet.

For a moment he stared at it while the fish thrashed about, water flying everywhere. He stumbled back, and a smile spread across his face. "I caught one!"

Enkidu stood and chuckled as he watched the valorous King of Uruk, son of Ninsun and the mighty half-god Lugal-banda, he who owned countless cattle and led the fiercest army in the world, smile like a child as a massive fish thrashed dirty water over his bare chest.

He wore the same expression he'd donned while explaining the night sky—his eyes wide with wonder, his body free of the stressors for a moment. Enkidu pulled his tunic off the tree to wipe his arm over it and smiled. "Well done, Lugal."

* * *

A fire crackled, flames jumping up to kiss the trees' dark shadows. Fireflies flickered, lighting the branches and glistening vines. The forest had shifted to a tired, navy mass. Crickets and night creatures whistled at each other, and a dove cooed somewhere in the distance.

Gilgamesh finished his last bite of roasted fish, tossed the stick into the flames, and lay back beside Enkidu.

A log shifted and sparks danced before them. Enkidu was full and warm, stretched out beneath the trees' canopies where twinkling stars peeked through. He yawned. Gilgamesh readjusted, the back of their knuckles scraping, and every drop of exhaustion evaporated from Enkidu's body.

Gilgamesh slid his hand over Enkidu's, then gripped his fingers. "Is this okay?"

Enkidu tried to form words, but they were like honey in his throat. He swallowed them down and nodded. Gilgamesh chewed the last bit of honeycomb, all the while running a thumb over the rise and fall of Enkidu's knuckles.

"I've never had honey so fresh before," Gilgamesh said.

Enkidu forced his voice to work, though it came out husky. "What do you think?"

Gilgamesh dropped his hand so he could lean over Enkidu and smile down at him. The firelight flowed over his form, making his muscles bronze, his hair golden. He was a statue of strength and desire staring down at Enkidu. "It's delicious."

Gilgamesh moved closer, and Enkidu stopped breathing. Their ribs grazed. Gilgamesh's face came so close, his breath warmed Enkidu's lips.

There was a voice in Enkidu's head warning him that while they'd achieved peace, they still disagreed fundamentally on many things. But the weight of Gilgamesh against him, the curve of his mouth drowned it out. Enkidu raised his head and brought their lips together.

Gilgamesh groaned and wrapped a hand around the back of his head, sinking his fingers into his hair. He parted his lips, and Enkidu followed his lead until their tongues touched.

Enkidu gasped and Gilgamesh used the opportunity to kiss him deeper. He shifted more of his weight on him. It was a dam breaking, a flood that rushed through Enkidu until it drowned everything else.

His fingers found Gilgamesh's beard—the hair was coarser than he'd expected. He traced the line of his jaw, letting his free palm follow the shape of his neck. All the while it was teeth and tongues and lips. It was the shared warmth of mouths.

And Enkidu learned something he'd long wondered.

The King of Uruk tasted like golden honey and smoke.

Gilgamesh's hand wandered over Enkidu's chest, tracing against his collarbone then down his tunic. Lower. His fingers reached Enkidu's ribs then swirled across his stomach, dropping with each sweep. They'd become lost to the touch, fingers clenching flesh, Gilgamesh tangling Enkidu's hair and grazing a horn. A shiver coursed along Enkidu's spine.

Gilgamesh's hand moved lower again, and Enkidu froze, pulled back.

He stopped. "This isn't okay?"

A sigh left Enkidu. It was wonderful. Yet... he couldn't do it. He couldn't be Gilgamesh's last night—a meaningless experience. Gilgamesh might find that acceptable, but Enkidu didn't. His body screamed at him, his muscles tensed and wanting. Words sat ready on his tongue. *It's fine. Don't stop.*

They weren't true.

He would regret it if they moved forward because he couldn't do this without more. And he still didn't know if Gilgamesh could offer more.

Something had shifted for Enkidu. A new feeling

blooming within him for the man, but he needed it returned.

"I'm sorry," he breathed finally. "I'm not ready."

Gilgamesh remained still for a moment, like Enkidu's words froze him. Then he sighed and leaned down to kiss Enkidu softly. Coarse fingers drifted across Enkidu's cheek once more, then rose to glide over a horn before the King rolled over and dropped back against the forest floor.

Enkidu's body ached with need. Gods, he was an idiot. He should apologize, start things back. They were both ready, their bodies had been close enough to make that very clear.

But he knew he'd regret it.

He closed his eyes and breathed slowly through his nose.

Gilgamesh laughed, causing Enkidu to open his eyes again. "Is something funny?"

The King shifted, tucking his arms behind his head. "Do you know, I've never been turned down for sex before."

"No one has ever turned you away?"

"Most people find the idea of sleeping with a king fairly appealing."

Enkidu couldn't argue. He found the idea of doing so extremely enticing. However, if it was nothing more than a physical release for Gilgamesh, a last grasp at life, it would crush him. "Even your wives?"

Gilgamesh smacked his mouth. "Shamhat discusses things with my brides before the ceremony. If they insist on"—he grimaced—"consummating the marriage, then I follow through." He rocked his face towards Enkidu, his eyes darkening. "However, I've never kissed someone I can't take my eyes off, who I'd kill for solely to taste his mouth again, then had him turn me down. That's a different feeling."

Enkidu's heart pounded in his throat. The King stared at him like he saw into his soul. No one had looked at him like that. Physical attraction wasn't love, though. Enkidu needed the latter before he could give in to the former. He'd had some level of desire for the man since the moment they'd met when the only thing sitting between them was animosity.

It didn't matter anyway as Enkidu had ruined the night. He shifted his voice to teasing, attempting to break the tension. "You've discovered my purpose."

Dark eyebrows slid up the King's brow.

"It's to torment you and keep you distracted."

Gilgamesh laughed hard enough that it vibrated against Enkidu. "Well, the gods have never been so successful before." He shifted then grabbed Enkidu's hand. "Is this okay still?"

As he slid their fingers together, Enkidu wished he could express that it was more than okay. When they touched, the heavens kissed the earth. Those words were too much since Gilgamesh didn't feel as deeply. Perhaps Enkidu clung to the man because he'd been crafted for it. No others needed him, desired him, or would mourn him if he died. Gilgamesh had that.

"Would Shamhat mind that we…"

"Didn't have sex?" Gilgamesh asked, a smirk sliding his lips up. His grip tightened though, like he'd clasp them together. "Shamhat and I have always had other partners. I love her but not in that manner. I'm glad we had Usun quickly." His voice turned dry, his eyes widening. "That was a very uncomfortable period of our marriage."

"You love her?" Enkidu hadn't gotten past that. This

from the King who had laughed at the concept. He'd been protective of Shamhat, affectionate even, but he'd said a King couldn't love. "I thought you said you couldn't choose love."

Gilgamesh's lips pinched. "I said I can't prioritize it. Of course I love. Maybe I was wrong about that, anyway. Keeping myself separate from everyone, not showing affection, it hasn't given me control over their fate at all."

Enkidu's heart ached. Here was a brokenhearted father, a loving husband, a man who brutally fought armies but jumped with childish joy over a caught fish. Never had there been as beautiful of a sight as his eyes glistening in firelight, his long, powerful frame tucked against Enkidu's. The world could go on for ten thousand years and nothing would ever top it.

The definition of love had evaded him, but a willingness to sacrifice for another was part of it. Akkiru had shared that much. Just like Gilgamesh sacrificed his relationship with his son to protect him. How Shamhat gave up her husband's support to protect him.

Enkidu would give anything for Gilgamesh—his life included.

His feelings could no longer be doubted.

He loved Gilgamesh.

Stupidly and irrevocably.

He'd follow him to death's lair and never hesitate a step.

If this was love, it was the most foolish, precious thing in the world. It was honey in a famine, rain in a desert. He'd drink it down greedily even if it caused him nothing but pain and sorrow once it was gone.

Gilgamesh lifted their hands and pressed a kiss to

Enkidu's fingertips. His breath caught. Of everything they'd shared that evening, that was the most intimate.

"Sleep now," Gilgamesh said. "Soon we will face Humbaba."

Enkidu shuddered. That night he'd sleep beside the man he loved in the forest of his origins. Then they'd face their fate.

CHAPTER TWENTY-ONE
SEVEN TERRORS

WIND RUSTLED tree boughs and swirled through Enkidu's hair, causing locks to curl around his horns as he slept. Gilgamesh flexed his fingers. He wanted to slide them over the smooth surface of those horns again, capture the man's mouth, and press their bodies together.

Days passed of them traveling the forest into the ancient, darker portion. Enkidu had taught him dozens of skills during that time. The man could sense the wild in a way Gilgamesh was certain he'd never achieve. It made him feel like, for the first time in his life, he stood beside an equal—someone who could match his strength and skills and desires.

"Wait," Enkidu said one morning, grabbing Gilgamesh's hand to stall him. "Listen."

Gilgamesh stopped and lifted his face to the breeze. Leaves crackled and birds chittered as they always did in the forest. "I hear nothing."

Enkidu tightened his hold on his hand. "Try again."

Gilgamesh frowned as he attempted to push his hearing to the limits. Water rushed somewhere in the distance, a faint hush. Some birds had shrill calls while others cooed in low, dulcet tones. And— "Monkeys are crying out somewhere far from here."

Enkidu smiled, and it wrinkled the corner of his eyes as sunlight sparkled in them. "Right. That's to the northeast. They're shouting warning cries which means other hunters already move through that section and have the animals stirred. We should move north-west for our best ability to catch breakfast."

Warmth filled Gilgamesh's chest. This man in his element was something else. He didn't bite his lip or avert his eyes. Rather, he marched them forward purposefully, constantly pointing out plants and animal trails, explaining how certain things were best to eat in the morning and others at night, or why they shouldn't impede on another predator's territory.

He was beautiful in the cedar forest. Wandering with Enkidu in woods more ancient than language, by trees that made them both appear small, it was easy to forget he was a king.

Instead, they were men surviving, seeking food, drinking water, washing in streams, and touching each other every moment they could.

It always ended the same as the first night, though. Enkidu was comfortable with their touches up to a point, but pulled away before they did anything more. After another night of sleep, Gilgamesh's body ached with the lack of release. Sunlight filtered through branches, splotching over Enkidu's arms and making the fine black hairs along them glisten.

Gilgamesh had never endured rejection before. The most surprising thing was that it didn't bother him. Something in Enkidu's eyes had stalled him the first time, making him catch his breath. It almost looked like fear, but he knew the man wasn't afraid of him. He couldn't push this man who could fight gods and navigate the wild but found a palace overwhelming and worried about every soul he'd ever met. There was something sacred about him— holier than any deity Gilgamesh had begrudgingly worshiped.

He would sacrifice in Enkidu's name and do so gladly, though he couldn't explain why.

He shifted so their bodies touched. Enkidu took a breath but didn't wake. Gilgamesh had never slept at a lover's side before. He'd woken, peeling his groggy eyes open, to find Enkidu's face soft in sleep next to him. It was funny that Enkidu was considered the wild man between the two of them. Gilgamesh had the mannerisms and polish of a city-born man, but Enkidu's heart was gentler.

Asleep, Gilgamesh could see his soul. The lines on his face had all gone soft, his long lashes fanned against his cheeks, and his lips puckered.

He was beautiful lying amid the woods, resting peacefully.

For the first time in months, Gilgamesh had multiple nights of sleep without his damned dream disturbing him. He missed his bed's plush embrace, but he'd give it up without hesitation and stay in the forest forever if he could do so at Enkidu's side.

A dimple formed beneath Enkidu's lip. He frowned and his face scrunched. Muscles twitched, and he mumbled.

"Enkidu." Gilgamesh grabbed the man's arms and gave him a shake. When that didn't rouse him, he gave a harder one.

Enkidu didn't wake, just continued to moan and shiver.

Gilgamesh tucked over him, like he could take the

tempest's beating instead. A drop of sweat dripped down Enkidu's forehead and Gilgamesh swiped it away then let his thumb linger at his brow.

Enkidu's eyes snapped open.

They were the colors of the forest—cedar brown, grassy green, golden sunlight. They widened until they met Gilgamesh's gaze and Enkidu released a breath.

Gilgamesh helped him sit up. Their hands remained clutched, Enkidu gripping his fingers like he held onto earth by the roots.

"You received an omen?" Gilgamesh finally asked. Part of him didn't want to know. He wished the gods would leave them alone and stop offering pointless prophecies no one would interrupt.

"No," Enkidu breathed, his voice gravelly with sleep. "Your mother spoke with me."

Gilgamesh's breath caught. Ninsun could infiltrate dreams, but she'd never done so with him. Not even when he'd fought battles or faced death. Yet, she'd twined herself into Enkidu's sleep to send him a message. A sharp pang thudded in his heart.

"She wants you to know, first, that all is well with Usun and Shamhat."

Gilgamesh pressed his lips to fight a frown and slid his thumb over the rise and fall of Enkidu's knuckles. His mother wouldn't speak to him directly, but at least she watched over her grandchild. He couldn't piece her out— she was a god and too far removed from mortal troubles to understand their plights and priorities.

A bird cawed and Enkidu bowed his head, his lips brushing against Gilgamesh's knuckles before he raised his face again. "She says Utu is pleased with our choice because Humbaba embodies darkness. Even his rays cannot fully reach the dragon's lair. However,"—he swallowed—"Humbaba can radiate seven auras of terror before we reach the lair. We'll have to make it through all of them before we fight the dragon. We'll reach the edges of his territory today."

A breeze rustled through, tangling Enkidu's curls together. He looked steadily at Gilgamesh, and the King's heart seized. This man would follow him and risk his life. He hadn't considered Enkidu's predicament before. He'd been created for Gilgamesh—with whatever machinations his mother had concocted but wouldn't share. Enkidu had no say over where his path led him. It had taken him to a king who was ready to die if needed to stop Inanna's plans. The idea of this man with his hard hands and soft heart dying as well left Gilgamesh's mouth dry.

"You shouldn't go."

Enkidu blinked rapidly. "I won't leave you." He wrapped his fingers around Gilgamesh's. "I told you—I'm by your side until the end."

The sincerity of his words echoed off cedar trees. Gilgamesh wanted to beg him to retreat. That man whose mouth had tasted like purpose, whose fingers along his skin felt like hope.

He wouldn't stay back unless Gilgamesh did. And Gilgamesh, as much as he wished to protect Enkidu, couldn't allow Inanna to win. If she used him, she'd put a child with nearly all god's blood on a mortal throne; it would only continue the unbalance in the world. He had to outsmart her. If he died fighting Humbaba, he would win. If they killed the beast, they'd do something legendary. He only hoped Shamhat could work with his mother and execute the plan he'd left to try and protect Usun from his same fate.

Regret had his tongue sticking to the roof of his mouth as he formed the words. "I must face Humbaba."

"Then I must go as well." Enkidu didn't hesitate. The fear that had furrowed his brow and flashed in his eyes at the palace was gone. He looked steadily at Gilgamesh the way a wolf raised its face to the moon.

Gilgamesh had never had this level of responsibility before. He ran the world's largest city, but he'd had Shamhat to balance him. He led his soldiers but had Abgal's wise counsel. He politically maneuvered but had Hirin's worried voice and cautious suggestions in his ear.

Never had the weight of someone's life laid fully in his hands alone.

And it wasn't just anyone, but Enkidu.

Gilgamesh couldn't hold back from touching him anymore. His palm curled around the man's neck, his mouth met his. Enkidu's lips slipped apart, and he leaned closer. The kiss warmed Gilgamesh into his bones. He forced himself to pull away, stand on his feet, and offer a hand to draw Enkidu up as well.

He grabbed his bag and removed a sword to give to Enkidu. The man accepted it like a piece of fabric, scarcely weighing it out before tying on a sheath and putting it away.

He would face the world's greatest terror for Gilgamesh's sake.

Gilgamesh placed a trembling palm on an ax at his side, took a deep breath, and nodded for them to walk. This was his destiny, and he had to face it. However, he couldn't force words, couldn't beg Enkidu to remain or plead with him to stay at his side. He wanted both things so much the sentiments tangled his tongue. Instead, he remained silent and more haunted than any omen had ever left him.

* * *

The change in the forest started with shadows that grew long and menacing. They stretched out like spilled bitumen, black and sticky. Gilgamesh weaved himself and Enkidu around them until it grew too dark to avoid them. The first time his foot pressed onto a shadow, he half expected it to grab and suck him into the earth's belly.

A scream shot out in the quiet.

Hair rose on Gilgamesh's arms; he gripped his axes and smoothed his fingers along the wood.

Another cry rang out, and Enkidu snapped his face in its direction. The cry turned into a trumpeting howl, like some creature was being torn apart piece by piece without death's mercy.

A third shriek echoed, higher pitched, like a younger animal was caught by whatever ferocious thing still tormented the previous beast.

Enkidu jerked towards the sound and bounded forward. Gilgamesh dashed after him and wrapped his arms around the man's shoulders.

"Do you hear that?" Enkidu cried. "They're hurt. They need help."

"It's not real, Enkidu." Gilgamesh spoke the words into the man's thick hair, letting his lips linger against the curve of his neck. "This is the first terror. Humbaba wants you to run into the darkness and be lost forever."

Enkidu relaxed and allowed Gilgamesh to take his hand. They moved forward through shrieks and screams and brays that had every muscle in Gilgamesh's body tensed. Tears welled in Enkidu's eyes. He didn't brush them aside but let them pour down his cheeks, catching in his beard.

Gilgamesh once again wanted to beg him to leave the adventure and return to safety. Occasionally Enkidu pulled away, shifting towards a pitiful cry. Gilgamesh locked their grips together, refusing to let him wander off.

Enkidu whimpered, and the King wanted to beg mercy of the gods if it would ease the man's suffering.

They pushed through, hands clasped so tightly it ached.

The forest's gray light reflected on Enkidu's wet cheeks. He was so compassionate—too good to spend his life foolishly following Gilgamesh. Selfishly, Gilgamesh couldn't let him go. Instead, he clung to him, keeping them on the path through the woods.

The screams softened and finally stopped.

Enkidu released a trembling breath.

Thick, pale mist rolled in over their ankles. Gilgamesh braced for whatever might happen, but nothing else occurred. The woods had grown so silent their breathing was as loud as battle cries.

The mist continued growing, reaching their waists, then shoulders, and finally covering them.

It blinded Gilgamesh. He couldn't see his feet. He stopped.

Enkidu squeezed his hand. "We have to keep moving. I know how to navigate the woods without sight. Stay with me."

Always, Gilgamesh wanted to respond as Enkidu had once said to him. He couldn't find his voice. The mist filled his throat and nostrils and eyes. Enkidu tugged him forward, navigating them steadily through the path, around trees, over rocks and stumps.

They wandered endlessly in that mist.

Through it all, Gilgamesh could sense only one thing.

The weight of Enkidu's hand in his.

And it was enough.

The mist dispersed in layers. At first, Gilgamesh felt certain it thinned, then chided himself for giving in to false hope. A stark form of a tree rising through the pale air caused him to gasp.

Soon they'd reached a point where they could make out the woods again, though they remained as quiet as before. Their feet snapped twigs, and it seemed to echo against the heavens.

You'll be forgotten, something whispered. Gilgamesh shivered as the voice's silky brutality returned. *You'll gain what you want but lose what matters most.*

You're nothing.

You're mortal.

Your bones will rot here.

Your son suffers at home while you strive for foolishness.

You're lost forever and so is your name.

You'll kill the only man who's ever truly seen you.

Enkidu loosened his grip and pulled away. Gilgamesh jerked towards him, grabbed him by the arms, and attempted to ignore the voices. "What are you doing?"

Enkidu's head hung. "I'm going to harm you. I'm not the help you need. Me arriving is probably a punishment. I'll never be enough. I should let you finish this alone."

"No." He brushed fingers along the man's jaw. "That's just the terror. It's playing on our fears. Try to ignore the voices."

Enkidu's jaw shifted beneath Gilgamesh's touch, but he bobbed his head. They moved forward together again, and Gilgamesh cemented their hands.

The voices continued screaming his greatest fears, but Gilgamesh shoved them aside. Another thought burned too brightly.

Apparently, some of Enkidu's greatest fears were that he wasn't enough for Gilgamesh. The King wanted to laugh at the absurdity. Enkidu had already helped him more than he had words to express—he was as loyal as his finest soldiers, as beautiful as Uruk at sunrise, as peaceful as the lake. He was perfect. How he couldn't see that, Gilgamesh didn't know.

Enkidu slowed, like he longed to pull away, and Gilgamesh found his authoritative voice—the one he used when he led his men into battle. "Hold on to me and do not let go. You vowed to stay at my side. Do you keep your vows?"

Enkidu lifted his face slowly then tightened his grip. "Always."

"Good." Gilgamesh's fist ached from holding onto the man, but he wouldn't let him go.

The whispers finally sloughed off like mud, clinging as long as possible until they reached a darker portion of the forest. The quiet had grown so painful it was as though the forest held its breath, waiting for whatever might happen next.

Gilgamesh took a step.

"No!" Enkidu grabbed Gilgamesh, his fingers digging into his arms, then threw him. His back pounded into a tree with a bang that knocked the breath from him.

Gilgamesh gasped as he slid onto the ground. His spine radiated with a burning ache.

If Humbaba could turn Enkidu against him, if he had to fight Enkidu to succeed, he wasn't sure he'd achieve it. It was perhaps his one true weakness in that forest.

A tree branch snapped above them and landed over the path then sank slowly into it. It pulled leaves down that had obscured the sludge beneath.

"Quicksand," Enkidu said as he offered Gilgamesh a hand and pulled him back to his feet.

The silty sand had already swallowed the branch. It was deep and moved quickly. Gods, if Enkidu hadn't thrown him, he'd be under it right now as well.

What a miserable, pointless death.

"You saved my life," he whispered.

Enkidu dropped his face but not quickly enough to hide the warmth surging onto his cheeks. "Follow me. I can tell where solid ground ends. I can get us through this."

Gilgamesh moved one foot after another while his heart raced. He couldn't have done this without Enkidu, yet he'd brought them here, dragged them into this danger.

He was still ready to face his death, but he couldn't bear Enkidu's harm.

They'd passed four terrors.

Only three more stood between them and the dragon.

CHAPTER TWENTY-TWO
IN THE FOREST OF FEAR

ENKIDU GUIDED Gilgamesh through the paths slowly, his gaze fixed on the speckled variations of dirt between mulch. He tried very hard not to think about everything that had happened. One misstep and the ground would swallow them.

Gods, it had nearly happened to Gilgamesh.

He'd been halfway to pressing a foot down when Enkidu had thrown his body at the man and prayed to any god that might hear. He hadn't cared if he lost his life. All that mattered was protecting Gilgamesh.

He shuddered and twined their fingers tighter as his feet snapped sticks. Their linked hands felt like the sun kissing the earth while the moon rose in the sky. Like two things that shouldn't belong together shared the splendors of heaven.

The paths widened enough for Enkidu to pull Gilgamesh to his side. They kept moving forward as a cool breeze reached them.

It curled through Gilgamesh's loose hairs and swirled over his braided chignon. The King's nose flared as he surveyed the forest that had changed once more. Trees grew tall and stark, the ground muddy and slick.

"We've passed the fourth terror," Gilgamesh said. He raised Enkidu's fist and pressed a kiss over his knuckles. Enkidu's stomach clenched.

Another blast of air hit them, cold enough to cause his muscles to seize. They pressed on, icy winds picking up and battering them until Enkidu's cheeks ached and his eyes watered.

Gilgamesh stopped so they could pull extra clothing out of their bags. They dressed in everything they had but it wasn't enough. Still they shivered and bowed against the wind.

"Here," Gilgamesh said. He wrapped an arm around Enkidu's shoulders which dropped as the King's heat seeped into his body. Enkidu tucked his arms around Gilgamesh's waist. They leaned into the ice and burrowed together into the warmth they created.

About the time Enkidu wondered how quickly freezing occurred and if they'd even realize it was happening, the winds lessened.

Enkidu straightened, and Gilgamesh released a shuddering breath.

They continued, and with each step the trees darkened.

As they stretched stiff arms in the warming air, they walked through shadows.

Gilgamesh's eyes darted back and forth across the stony path ahead of them. A massive tree, larger than Inanna's temple-topped ziggurat even, reached out with craggy dark arms. Nooks curled like a howling face within it. Beyond, everything stretched gray and misty.

Gilgamesh hesitated as he looked up at the enormous tree.

It made Enkidu feel small, like a speck of dirt staring at the night sky.

"Just two more terrors, right?" Enkidu asked.

Gilgamesh tore his gaze away from the tree and nodded. "Well, aside from the monster itself."

Enkidu slid his tongue along the back of his teeth and grated his boots into the ground.

He pulled them forward.

A crackling snagged their attention, and they both turned towards a bush. A trio of massive men stood there, bows lifted in their direction. Enkidu slid his sword out, but Gilgamesh grabbed his hand. "No, they're not real. Try to look them in the face."

Enkidu had been focused on the weapons in their hands, but he lifted his gaze and found he couldn't make out the details of the men's faces. Whenever he tried to look, they blurred into ebony shadows.

They continued forward together—the god-created man and the divine king. They moved shoulder-to-shoulder, each watching a side of the path, their fingers brushing while their other hands rested on weapons.

The entire time, men appeared in the mist with weapons raised, beckoning them to fight.

Despite every intuition that screamed for him to do so, Enkidu remained on the path next to Gilgamesh.

Finally, the men stopped appearing.

The world grew darker and darker with each passing step.

Enkidu didn't know dark had so many shades. First was a deep gray that allowed him to make out Gilgamesh's broad shoulders, the curve of his lips. Then came black that made his eyes ache to find the path. Lastly, ebony took over

—a dark so intense his eyes searched restlessly but found nothing to grip onto.

Gilgamesh stumbled and landed with a thud. Enkidu dropped beside him. "Are you all right?"

"Tripped on a rock. I'm fine."

He helped Gilgamesh back to his feet. His sight was gone, but Enkidu had never feared night. It was a time of midnight creatures like the wolves and owls. Normally stars speckled above, the moon glistened on tree limbs. However, this didn't feel so different. He was good at navigating things with all his senses. He needed to stop relying on his sight so much. City life had left him unpracticed.

Gilgamesh's heart thundered against his hands as he helped him to his feet. His breathing came weighted.

Enkidu let his hand linger on the man's back. "We have to move through this slowly, but we will make it past this, together."

"I can't win everything by fighting my way through it, is that what you're saying?" There was a tease in Gilgamesh's words, but the breathiness of fear lingered around it.

"Right." Enkidu chuckled and didn't let him go. He never would. "We rely on each other as we have the entire journey so far and this will pass."

"Yes." Gilgamesh scarcely breathed the word but leaned in closer to Enkidu. They wrapped up together again, but not to fight the brutal cold. It was for the comfort of the other's touch, the spark of hope that they were not alone despite facing a dark world.

Gilgamesh's hand found Enkidu's and traced over his knuckles. Back and forth.

Enkidu swallowed.

He wished he hadn't stopped him when they'd lain tangled up on the forest floor together.

He wished he had that memory to hold onto in the darkness.

Finally, the dark swept away like fog dispersing. They stepped out over stones into a clearing. Before them a massive, ancient tree rose to scrape the heavens. Enkidu lifted his face to take it in. Gnarled dark branches grappled at each other, knots forming in enormous lumps. Limbs stretched out, leafless and jagged, like they clawed the earth.

On the trunk, a gaping hole like a cavern spooled with the same darkness they'd just walked through.

A puff of smoke rushed from the opening.

A scaled nose slipped out of the tree. Then fiery-red eyes appeared. The dragon's entire face stretched out, larger than Gilgamesh and Enkidu paired together.

Enkidu trembled and fought the urge to step back.

The creature had the countenance of a lion but with a dragon's scaled exterior. Its face was jumbled and gray like entrails. Its eyes glowed, and it parted its enormous mouth to reveal hundreds of glistening teeth.

It moved out of the tree in a massive sweep forward, landing so the earth shook beneath its clawed paws. A tail whipped around with a cobra's head and the end, fangs dripping venom.

Gilgamesh and Enkidu remained frozen.

Staring up.

Their eyes fixed on fate.

Humbaba roared. Trees shook and limbs broke from them, clattering against the forest floor. The creature charged.

The vibrations pounded into Enkidu's feet, tingling his bones.

Gilgamesh whipped his axes off his side and planted his feet into the ground.

Enkidu struggled to pull his sword free. His palm was slick with sweat, and his mouth had gone dry.

Humbaba's tail swung forward and smacked into them. Enkidu fell with a bang to the stone, his sword falling free from his grip. Breath rushed out of him in a painful burst. Gilgamesh barely hit the ground before he jumped back up, axes raised. He swung one and lopped off the tail's end, the snake head screaming as it slammed into the earth. Enkidu's heart warmed with dueling feelings—pride at Gilgamesh's boldness, shame at his own weakness, and a fiery need to get back on his feet.

Humbaba's cries echoed through the forest. Enkidu cringed, grabbed his sword, and pushed up to his feet, but he struggled to get his balance. The creature turned and yanked a massive cedar tree up by the roots to fling it at them. Enkidu dove towards Gilgamesh, knocking them out of the projectile's path.

The creature ripped up another tree and threw it. Then a third.

They dodged the massive trunks, throwing themselves onto the hard ground. Blood dripped from their skinned knees, and Enkidu's body ached from newly forming bruises.

Trees landed with thuds that made the earth vibrate through their feet. The ground dimpled and scarred where the trunks fell.

After hitting the ground another time, Enkidu jerked to jump up. Humbaba slammed a paw to the earth and vines wound around him, holding him against the earth.

Enkidu gasped. Humbaba had control over the elements.

They grabbed Gilgamesh too, crawling over his body and covering his mouth. The King fought, his axes slashing away the vines as quickly as they grew.

Enkidu sliced his sword free from his side. Dozens of vines ripped away but just as many replaced them.

Humbaba prowled closer, its steps shaking the ground.

Gilgamesh growled through his teeth, his face as fierce as Humbaba's. He escaped the plants, dashed towards Enkidu, grasped an arm, and yanked him out.

Enkidu's shoulder popped, and warmth drained from his face.

"I've hurt you." Gilgamesh's forehead furrowed.

"I'll be all right." Enkidu raised his sword. Thankfully, it wasn't his fighting side that got wrenched, but the pain left him trembling. Gilgamesh's eyes darkened as he kept his focus on Enkidu rather than the massive dragon thundering towards them.

He leaned over and brushed coarse lips over his brow.

The touch was delicate, intimate; it made Enkidu shiver for a different reason.

Gilgamesh jerked away, turned, and charged Humbaba with his axes raised.

Enkidu's breath caught as the man he loved ran towards his death like he threw fear behind him, had shucked it in the cedar forest, and had nothing holding him back.

Gilgamesh lunged so quickly, Humbaba didn't have time to react.

His ax found a paw, slicing off a toe.

Humbaba cried out and a gray mist left its mouth, hazy and glimmering.

"Enkidu, get down!" Gilgamesh cried.

Enkidu threw himself to the forest floor before the mist

reached him. It crept along his skin, burning the hairs off his arms. Enkidu held his breath and closed his eyes, but the poison crawled over him.

As soon as the blazing abated, Enkidu jumped back up, cradling his injured arm to his chest. Gilgamesh stepped beneath Humbaba's body, rolling to avoid the creature's slamming paws. His axes slashed the creature so that it howled but didn't seem to inflict much damage.

Humbaba slashed claws at Gilgamesh. Knocked him into the ground.

Gilgamesh lay still, staring ahead but not moving.

The monster raised its paw.

Enkidu's heart tripped.

A shoulder-high boulder sat beside him.

He could use the same strategy the monster had employed.

Enkidu grunted as he lifted the rock, his injured arm straining until his muscles shook. He threw it as hard as it could.

It hit Humbaba's side with a crack then fell to the ground. Humbaba didn't shift but turned to face Enkidu who already had another boulder in his arms. He chucked it again.

It hit Humbaba's snout, and the creature reared back with a hissing howl. Gilgamesh scrambled back to his feet and used the distraction to swing an ax into Humbaba's leg.

The creature roared and stumbled back, turning to seek Gilgamesh.

Enkidu found another pile of heavy rocks and threw three of them in rapid succession. The creature whirled around again, and Gilgamesh landed another blow.

They moved in unison—the King and the wild man— keeping Humbaba too confused to attack.

Gilgamesh landed a vicious whack on the leg that caused blood to well from the beast as it howled. The sound was so sharp, Enkidu stumbled back, tripping and landing on the ground.

Gilgamesh was nearer, and he cowered into himself. When he lifted his face, blood dripped from his ears. Humbaba's scream had damaged him.

The dragon turned, glowering at Gilgamesh.

At the man who gave Enkidu the stars' names.

Humbaba stomped, and vines dashed up from the earth. They held Gilgamesh down. The monster raised a paw.

No.

Enkidu threw himself forward. He'd always been fast— he'd spent the first part of his life running with wolves.

He threw himself over Gilgamesh's vine-wrapped body just as the paw landed.

The creature's claws ripped into Enkidu's side. He gasped and tumbled away. Rocks and sticks shredded his skin as he rolled across the clearing.

He took a breath, and it hurt so much the release came shaky.

The world blurred. He touched his side and drew back a crimson-painted hand. The warmth of him gushed out. Every breath was too much.

But he'd fulfilled his purpose.

His duty was to stand at Gilgamesh's side, to protect him.

He'd done that.

Enkidu was brought to life in the forest. Now he'd come to the same forest to die.

There was poetry in it.

He released another shuddering breath and turned his face into moss as his life drifted away.

CHAPTER TWENTY-THREE
A DIVINE DIES

GILGAMESH'S EARS POUNDED, and a keening ring echoed. He could barely hear, but it didn't matter.

Enkidu had fallen.

Gilgamesh yanked his axes loose and pushed all his strength into slicing free of the vines.

He stumbled up.

Humbaba leered over Enkidu who had a massive slice through his back and along his side. It gushed blood like a waterfall. Enkidu breathed raggedly and slowly peeled his eyes open.

Gilgamesh gaped as Enkidu smiled at him—he fucking smiled as he lay dying. Dying because he'd thrown himself over Gilgamesh, spared him.

No. Not this gentle-hearted man with his forest-colored eyes and fierce heart.

Gilgamesh wished he could unwind time and trade places. He should be prostrate and bleeding into the earth, not Enkidu.

A realization hit him harder than the cedar tree denting the earth.

All the nights he'd spent wandering about reflecting on the dream crashed into him.

"It's you," he said as he stared into Enkidu's eyes.

The man lifted the corner of his lips once, then closed his eyes and went still.

"No!" Gilgamesh roared.

The creature turned on him, shifted away from Enkidu's broken and bleeding body.

Gilgamesh couldn't focus.

His omen was about Enkidu.

The pebble that entered his boot, irritating him, was the man showing up at his court. Then he ran as the stone grew in size. He'd felt like he couldn't escape Enkidu. *Everything is about godsdamned Enkidu,* he'd yelled at Shamhat. Then they'd soared together. That wasn't about his legacy—but how Enkidu had made him feel alive and purposeful.

Now the man lay broken, just like the boulder in his dream.

Gilgamesh didn't want to weep—not yet at least.

Fire burned in his gut and rushed down his veins.

Dizziness had him unsteady, but that didn't matter. Retribution was the only thing left. Humbaba had stolen family from him, security from his people, and now this man—the only good thing the gods had ever freely given him.

Humbaba raised his paw towards Enkidu. The King tightened his grip on his axes and took a deep breath.

His heart thrummed with the anticipation of every battle he'd faced, his body shifting into a fighter's stance, his nose flared.

With a roar, Gilgamesh threw himself at the creature and sank an ax so deep into its stomach hot blood gushed out, flooding him, clogging his nose and spilling into his mouth until the tang had him gagging.

The dragon hissed as it jerked towards him, abandoning the broken Enkidu.

Gilgamesh no longer felt fear.

He'd always had a bite of it he held back, but now it was gone. Because Enkidu had—Gilgamesh's thoughts stuttered, and he swallowed against the feeling. Enkidu had sacrificed himself. He would honor the man's life with Humbaba's death even if it killed him to achieve it.

Gilgamesh had been hesitant in his approach, avoiding the poisonous breath and sharp claws. He no longer cared. He wanted those claws to peel him open, to see if gods bled as violently as mortals. Gilgamesh longed for the taste of pain, for the rush of pushing through it.

Hesitation shucked, he dove at the creature, attacking more viciously than he ever had.

Humbaba knocked him down, trampled over him, slashed an arm so Gilgamesh had only one left to fight with.

Live as a god, die as a god.

Gilgamesh grabbed scales on Humbaba's side and dragged himself up with his feet and single working arm as the creature thrashed and bucked. By the time he made it to the monster's shoulders, Gilgamesh felt like his spirit walked outside his body. He was too beaten down. Never had he realized how mortal he was.

With slow movements to keep his balance, he crawled along the thrashing creature. It slammed him between ridges of hard scales. If he lived through this, he would be unrecognizable from the bruising.

Not that he had any intention of surviving. He only needed to finish this then die.

When he reached Humbaba's neck, he rose onto his knees. His right arm was completely useless, hanging limply at his side.

"For Shamhat's family," he whispered. His eyes stung, and a tear dripped past his lashes and trailed down his cheek. "For Enkidu."

He jumped to his feet and threw every bit of strength into a blow. Light and darkness exploded. They rushed together then formed again. Gilgamesh drew from powers he didn't know he possessed as his ax slammed into the creature, snapping tendons and crunching bones.

The creature gave a cry that shook leaves from trees.

It was a howl of the earth dying. The world coming undone.

Everything shook and went dark.

Then Humbaba fell to the earth, Gilgamesh dropping with the creature.

He slid down its damaged body and tumbled into a tree trunk, wincing at the impact. For a moment he'd been a god—indomitable. He'd returned to his mortal body once more and pain pulsed within him. A tide that would lap at him until his end.

The dragon gave a final shudder then lay down and died.

Gilgamesh turned towards the creature.

He was a god of sorts too—divinely formed. How easily a divine could die in the end.

Gilgamesh attempted to stand then fell into the dirt. His jaw hit a stone which clacked his teeth together. He was too damaged to rise, so he crawled, dragging himself one painful bit after another.

When he reached Enkidu, his eyes ached again. He

turned the man's face towards him and touched his cool cheeks.

"Enkidu," he whispered. "Do not leave me yet. Please."

Enkidu remained unmoving, his body as broken as Gilgamesh's felt. Across his mind, visions of his life floated. Shamhat's twisted lips, her hands propped on her hips, bracelets sliding down her wrist. Usun, tears in his eyes as his father helped him to his feet. Pressing a stylus into wet clay before leaving. Preparing for this moment—the one where he died and left them Uruk.

Shamhat could handle things, though he hated leaving her alone.

If only he could tell them both he loved them.

He dragged broken fingers over Enkidu's beard. If only he could say as much to this man.

An ache seized his heart. He closed his eyes and tears pooled in the corners.

"Mother," he whispered. Or maybe he shouted it. His hearing still rang. "Mother, please." It was a prayer without content, a dying plea.

She wouldn't come—she never had. He didn't wish to live if Enkidu died. Perhaps he simply longed for his mother at this moment of his death.

"My son." A voice as peaceful as water trickling down a stream came clear in his buzzing mind. "I'm here."

* * *

Enkidu couldn't open his eyes or move.

He wasn't sure if he breathed anymore. The pain had stopped, though, which was a mercy.

Gilgamesh touched his cheek with fingers as warm as the sun.

Enkidu swam through the realm of omens and memories, swirling through the dark, trying to find his way back. He was lost, tumbling through warm sunlit days by the lake, the wolf's steady voice in his mind, birds whistling in trees.

"Help me, please," Gilgamesh said, and it yanked him free from his dreams.

Pressure built on Enkidu's palm, almost painful. He thought it was Gilgamesh holding his hand again, but it hurt so much. He'd pull away if he had control over his body.

"I saved you because you're my son." Ninsun's melodic voice. "You know I'm not supposed to interfere in mortal lives. The gods have forbidden it since Utnapishtim."

"You're the goddess of dreams. Just put him into a sleep, take his pain, so I may attempt to heal him. Please, Mother." Gilgamesh's voice broke over the last plea, and Enkidu longed to reach for him.

"He's too far gone to heal."

"There must be something you can do."

Silence filled the space and Enkidu swirled back into the golds and emeralds of his forest again until Ninsun's voice shattered his mental wanderings.

"What if I told you that if I interfere you'll lose your reputation? That no one will remember you killed Humbaba. That if I do this for you, the cost is erasing any knowledge of your successes, and your legacy may burn to ash."

"Fuck my legacy," Gilgamesh yelled. His voice roared but pain rippled through his deep tenor. "I do not care about fucking Humbaba or any of it, but Enkidu cannot die. You can take it and my name may die on your tongue if only you'll spare him."

Enkidu's mind grew still.

Gilgamesh would sacrifice his legacy to spare Enkidu's life.

He'd give up the thing that mattered most to keep him—a man with no past, no glory, and no abilities—alive.

Gilgamesh loved him.

Enkidu's heart picked up again, as though it had gone to sleep and once more found the strength for a few painful beats.

He wanted to speak, to clench Gilgamesh's fingers. To tell him he didn't need to sacrifice so much.

Enkidu would choose his wellbeing.

Before he attempted to muster the strength to do anything, a heaviness drifted through his mind, mist clouding his thoughts, ushering him into the realm of sleep.

CHAPTER TWENTY-FOUR

FALLING UPON HIM IN EMBRACE

RAIN FELL OUTSIDE THE HOUSE, clattering on the ground. Gilgamesh stared at the empty mud-packed wall as he lounged against a couch. The region Ninsun had moved Enkidu and him to was green and lush. The weather was cooler than home, and a breeze swept in through the small window that was tucked by the ceiling.

Enkidu lay asleep in the bed, his lashes fanned over his cheeks. In the forest, Gilgamesh had studied him before he rose in the mornings as well. How he wished he'd flutter his eyes open now.

"It could be weeks before he rises," his mother had said before leaving. "I'll let Shamhat know."

Gilgamesh had only nodded. He couldn't find words. His injuries were gone—though phantom aches still seized him. Occasionally he'd pull his right arm up and was surprised to find it functioning.

Weeks had passed.

Gilgamesh had readjusted Enkidu, paced the dirt floors, eaten meals he'd paid to have brought from a village nearby, written Shamhat. His body burned with the still-ness, his ears throbbing from the quiet.

Occasionally he spoke to reassure himself he could still hear.

But Enkidu continued sleeping.

He was beautiful at rest, his features soft, his lips pursed. Gilgamesh wouldn't mind sitting and looking at him if it didn't worry him so. He should have woken already, shouldn't he? Gilgamesh wasn't desperate enough to beg his mother to appear again. Not yet at least.

She'd saved them, and her warning that it would cost him his legacy of killing Humbaba turned out to be a lie.

The villagers who arrived twice daily at the cottage to bring food and usher up messengers acted as though they approached a god. They spoke reverently to Gilgamesh, bowing at his feet. They'd praised him for ending Humbaba. One even brought incense and left it burning in a bowl outside. The sweet scent trailed in through the window and filled the house for a day.

Yet Enkidu slept.

Gilgamesh swallowed and shifted again.

He'd always been a restless soul, but now it was painful. This man—this beautiful, foolish, wonderful man—had laid down his life for him. Gilgamesh leaned closer to Enkidu, smoothed his blanket, and grazed his knuckles.

Even if not a single person had remembered the defeat of Humbaba, he'd have no regrets. Gilgamesh would have sacrificed his soul, his legacy, anything to save Enkidu.

He needed him to wake. Until that happened it would continue to feel like he wandered through an omen rather than living and breathing in real life.

Enkidu huffed a breath and Gilgamesh stilled.

The man opened his eyes, and something as big as the

sun grew in Gilgamesh's chest, warming his entire body. He wanted to grab his hand, or yell at him for doing such a brazen ridiculous thing, or press their mouths together and let the protestations die beneath lips.

He loved him.

It was a strange realization.

Gilgamesh had grown to love Shamhat slowly through a hundred moments of trust and connection. Through years of marriage and friendship.

His feelings for Enkidu had seized him like a lightning strike.

And it burned as intensely.

"Enkidu." Gilgamesh spoke with a gravelly voice. The man turned towards him, and a smile spread across his face. It was the catching-a-fish-together and discussing-the-stars smile.

Enkidu's expression faltered as he winced. "Is this the Great Below?"

Gilgamesh laughed, but it came out choked, and his eyes prickled with tears. Never in his damn life had he come close to crying so often. Somehow, he'd subverted the omen—he wouldn't weep over a broken Enkidu. No, he'd get a second chance, and every moment felt precious to him now, stolen. "I'm afraid you're still here in the land of the living with me."

Enkidu rose slowly to sit. His eyes sparkled, and they were full of life again—full of swaying grasses and coppery trees and glittering sunshine. "I longed to return to you—fought to stay. So, I'm glad to hear that's the outcome."

Gilgamesh held his breath.

Rain filled the silence.

"What happened?" Enkidu ran his gaze down Gilgamesh's body like he searched for injuries.

Gilgamesh curled his fingers around Enkidu's and traced his knuckles. "A moon has passed. Utu and Ninsun helped heal us and brought us both here. It's not a luxurious house, but it's allowed you to rest."

Enkidu released Gilgamesh's hand and pushed the blanket back from his bare chest. His fingers grazed the scar that curled over his hip then trailed around to his back. The flesh was silvery and rippled. Enkidu frowned. "I should be dead."

Gilgamesh leaned forward and clasped his hands again. He needed to touch him, to know that he was very much alive still. "I would not allow it. If Nergal wants you, he'll have to fight me and take my life first."

Enkidu's eyelashes fluttered and warmth swept across his cheeks.

He was the most beautiful damned thing Gilgamesh had ever seen.

"Let me get you some food. There's little other furniture in this place, so stay in bed. I'll bring it to you."

He slipped out and gathered crocks of porridge and honey the villagers had brought. His heart was too full, and he didn't know how to find words to explain the sensations bounding through it. He busied himself preparing a bowl for Enkidu then brought it back to him.

With the first bite, Enkidu groaned. He downed the food. Gilgamesh led him to the room with a bucket of fresh water and gave him time to clean up. Then he urged him back into the bed. Enkidu seemed fine, his posture straight, his strides steady. But Gilgamesh didn't wish to take chances.

When he had him back in bed again, those damned eyes staring up at him once more, Gilgamesh felt better. They could stay at that house as long as he needed to recover. A voice in the back of his mind told him that Enkidu was at full strength again, but he wouldn't risk it. They had weeks of travel to make it back to Uruk and they wouldn't go until Enkidu was ready.

"Shouldn't you be in Uruk?" Enkidu asked as though he could read his thoughts.

Gilgamesh shifted back into his couch. "Undoubtedly. Shamhat is used to handling the city in my absence, though. I'll owe her when we return. I've left a great deal of work on her this year." Gilgamesh took a deep breath. Shamhat really was too good for him. He wondered if she'd always known it and why she'd married him if so. "We've exchanged messages. I believe us living through Humbaba has her in a forgiving spirit. Then again"—Gilgamesh clicked his tongue—"if he'd killed us both she'd probably feel even more compassionate about the situation."

Enkidu closed his eyes. "Right. I'd forgotten about Humbaba. So, the creature is dead?"

"Yes, may the gods be thanked," Gilgamesh whispered. But the gods had no hand in ending the dragon. Enkidu and Gilgamesh had achieved it. They'd both nearly paid with their lives.

"I remember your mother appearing."

"Do you?" Gilgamesh had thought the man was already gone at that point. Gilgamesh had been frantic with grief and pain, willing to beg for the impossible. "I prayed for her to come."

Enkidu's eyes tightened, their colors darkening. "Is what you said to her true?"

With the way the man looked at him, Gilgamesh thought he understood the question. He grabbed his hand. "That I'd rather have my legacy go to dust than lose you?"

Gilgamesh ran his thumb across the man's knuckles. "That I realized I'd missed everything in life, and it wasn't until I saw you dying that I understood how futile it all had been?" Gilgamesh shifted closer, until his knees touched the bed. "Or do you mean that which I didn't say? That I love you."

Enkidu stared at him, his lips parted, his body statue-still.

"Yes," Gilgamesh said. "What I said to her was true."

Enkidu leaned up, moving closer. He reached out and traced a hand over Gilgamesh's beard. Breath ceased for Gilgamesh, and he remained still as the man ran his calloused fingers across his skin. Enkidu brushed his lips over Gilgamesh's. It was a gentle touch until it wasn't. Gilgamesh curled his hands around the man's broad shoulders and tilted his head to fit their lips together.

Mouths and lips and teeth found each other. Gilgamesh could devour the man. He wanted to pull him apart with his fingers or hold him in his arms and dare the gods to touch him.

Leaning over Enkidu, Gilgamesh pressed him back down on the bed. Their mouths were frantic, and Enkidu gripped his fingers into Gilgamesh's spine.

Gilgamesh rested a knee on the mattress to pull back. "Am I hurting you?"

"The opposite." Enkidu yanked him between his legs until his full weight rested on the bed. The mattress groaned beneath their bulk. Gilgamesh shuddered at the relief of Enkidu being alive, at the pleasure of their bodies gliding against each other.

He found the warmth of Enkidu's mouth again and let his hand trail down his arm's silky hair, along his side, then over his chest. Gods, he was glad Enkidu hadn't donned a tunic. He needed to touch every piece of him he could, possess him, die for him. Prove to himself that Enkidu was whole and healthy. It was like walking a precipice above fear and passion. And he was ready to dive in.

Enkidu lifted his hips, grinding against Gilgamesh, and the King hissed. He'd never been with someone who could bear the weight of his god's powers, who didn't grow soft and weak in his arms. It sent an inferno burning in his gut.

Raising his hips again, Enkidu peeled part of Gilgamesh's tunic down, revealing his chest. He brought his mouth to his nipple and flicked his tongue over its hardened surface.

Gilgamesh bowed his head to Enkidu's and groaned. He forced himself to freeze. "I thought you weren't ready."

He breathed the words, pushed past the desire fogging his mind. Doing something Enkidu would regret wasn't a risk he'd take. He'd meant what he said. Gilgamesh loved him. He wanted him by his side forever, whatever that involved. Even if sex wasn't part of it.

Enkidu's beard scraped his chest again, then he looked up at Gilgamesh. For a moment, they both stilled. Enkidu kissed him gently. "I'm ready now."

Gilgamesh's body screamed with desire and want as he growled through his teeth. Oh, he'd gladly accept getting to physically have the man too. He kissed Enkidu's neck and let his hand trail down his chest, over his abdomen, then reached the hard length of him.

Enkidu's hips bucked as he ground into Gilgamesh's hand. He shuddered a breath against Gilgamesh's bare chest.

Gilgamesh nipped his ear then began gliding his hand up and down. Enkidu groaned and moved with him. Men always softened beneath him, and he'd taken physical release as quickly as possible. Now he wanted Enkidu's satisfaction more than his own and his heart seized.

He pulled his hand back and kissed Enkidu. "What do you like?"

Enkidu fluttered his eyes open again and there was fear in them. It reminded Gilgamesh of facing Humbaba, of the terror of almost losing him. Color flushed Enkidu's cheeks, and he shifted his gaze away. "I know about sex—the mechanics and how it works, I mean. But I've never..."

Gilgamesh tilted Enkidu's chin towards himself. "This is new for me, in a way, too. Tell me if it's good for you, please?"

He was scraped bare, his soul stretching out. Enkidu could shatter him. Instead, the man kissed him and brushed their noses together. "I'll tell you."

Gilgamesh nodded, then lowered his mouth to Enkidu's chest and kissed there. Silky hair grazed his lips as he made his way down the perfectly sculpted body. Enkidu shivered and Gilgamesh slowed his pace.

They had both dived into something neither understood.

Gilgamesh would embrace drowning to stay in Enkidu's presence.

His tongue traced down the lines of his abdominals and his lips pressed against the scar. Gilgamesh said a silent prayer to the gods for saving Enkidu's life then dragged his teeth over a hip bone. Enkidu's breathing deepened, over-taking the rain's clatter.

Gilgamesh untied Enkidu's loincloth and pushed the fabric aside. His breath caught. He'd always known the male form attracted him. But this—being with a man who stayed hard and desirous in his presence—it was a pleasure he'd thought he would never experience. Gilgamesh ran his tongue up Enkidu's length and the man gasped.

It was better than music.

Gilgamesh put his mouth around him and took him deep. "Slower," Enkidu whispered without opening his eyes. Gilgamesh obeyed. He'd never done this before, never been able to, but thankfully Enkidu wasn't afraid to ask for what he wanted, and Gilgamesh was eager to give. For several long minutes, he followed his directions as he'd done in the mist and darkness, letting Enkidu guide.

When Enkidu clenched his hands into Gilgamesh's shoulders enough to ache and his body tensed, Gilgamesh pulled back. He wasn't ready for it to end yet. He wanted to see Enkidu scrunch his face up, wanted to hear him pant and whisper his desires, wanted to have his hands on him for hours, days, months.

Enkidu rose and kissed him. "What do you like?"

Heat rose to Gilgamesh's neck. He'd only ever known sex as a basal need to be met. It made him feel like a beast. He wanted Enkidu's pleasure more than his own and didn't want to do anything to hurt him.

Enkidu glistened with sweat. "If I remember correctly, you told me the rumor is true that you enjoy being on top?"

Gilgamesh huffed a breath against his chest. "I want you to enjoy this."

"I am. A great deal." Enkidu grinned at him. "Well?"

Gilgamesh sighed again but rose and grabbed his bag. He removed the crock of cedar oil he'd packed. Gods, he'd been a dick when he brought it on their trip. He'd hoped this would happen, but it was purely driven by lust. Now he wanted more. So much more he couldn't even name it. It felt bigger than legacy or history, something that stepped outside the bounds of time.

He returned to the bed which whined beneath his weight again as he uncapped the crock.

Enkidu took a deep breath. "It smells like the forest."

Gilgamesh poured some into his hand. "Cedar has always been my favorite scent."

Enkidu's eyes flicked up. They stared at each other, oil dripping between Gilgamesh's fingers and onto Enkidu's chest. He didn't seem to notice. His expression had changed to something that made Gilgamesh hold his breath.

They were created for each other.

The truth of that sat between them.

Gilgamesh found Enkidu's lips again, tasted the man as he let his oil-slicked hand glide down his body. Enkidu breathed against his mouth, pressed into his hand, whispered pleas for more.

Everything became the motion of their bodies together, the warmth of lips touching, the smell of sweat and cedar tangling. Gilgamesh moved carefully, watching Enkidu's face with each step, making sure he'd not done something wrong, that he was still enjoying it.

Enkidu kept his eyes closed and groaned and bucked his hips.

Gilgamesh could fall apart, his body could turn into pieces and slip into the Great Below, and it would be worth it to have seen that alone.

When he finally prepared to slide them together, he met Enkidu's gaze one last time, a question in his eyes, an uncertainty in the way he'd draped his fingers over the man's knees.

Please, tell me to stop if you don't want this.

Enkidu smiled and grabbed his hips, pulled him forward.

Sinking into a man who didn't crumple beneath his powers made Gilgamesh groan. It was heaven. And to be that close with Enkidu, that was more than heaven, more than divinity or legacy. It was truth. It was holy.

Enkidu drove his hips up to meet him and Gilgamesh growled at how good it felt—how right.

He fumbled then found Enkidu's hard length so he could glide his hand up and down again.

"Like that, yes," Enkidu whispered.

Gilgamesh hissed.

They moved together like they'd fought together—an understanding of the other existing without speaking. Gilgamesh didn't think there would be words that could describe it anyhow. Poets often made sex seem crass or furled out phrases that had it sounding lighter than clouds. Neither described making love to Enkidu.

It was hot and sweaty and slick. But it was also pure and beautiful and divine.

Enkidu shuddered, his rhythm breaking. He came undone with a moan that made the hair on Gilgamesh's neck rise. He gripped Enkidu's hips and finished with a final, fierce thrust.

Gilgamesh remained trembling on his knees for a moment before dropping beside Enkidu onto the too-small bed. He grabbed the man and pulled him into his arms. With a sigh, Enkidu leaned closer, his horns grazing Gilgamesh's beard.

Hands intertwined, they lay together, and Gilgamesh reveled in the silence.

He kissed Enkidu's head and let his eyes drift closed as

he breathed in the sweet and bitter smells of the messes they'd made of each other.

Sometime later he roused. Enkidu was awake and smiled at him then brushed his hand over the King's beard. Gilgamesh grinned back despite feeling like an idiot. Perhaps he'd feared waking and finding Enkidu had regrets. The man kissed him, though, his body warm against Gilgamesh's.

Gilgamesh shifted so his body covered Enkidu's again and their chests scraped each other and warmth pooled in his stomach. A knock sounded. Enkidu froze and Gilgamesh laughed. "Villagers here with food. I'll get it. Then we should get cleaned up and eat."

Enkidu sighed and dropped back onto the bed. His eyes followed Gilgamesh all the way out of the room.

They took turns washing up with the villager-provided buckets of fresh water. Gilgamesh finally missed home—how he'd love to have his lavish washing chamber. He imagined having Enkidu there with him. Imagined dropping to his knees on the wet floor...

He clenched his eyes shut. Damn, the man was a distraction now. A beautiful, glorious one, but Gilgamesh had to think about the future as well.

For the first time in his life, he did so begrudgingly.

He hadn't expected to live through fighting Humbaba. Now that Enkidu had recovered, they needed to return to Uruk. New Year arrived soon. Inanna would use him and put another child with god's blood on the throne.

Gilgamesh sighed. He couldn't let it happen, but now he feared death in a way he never had before. He wanted time with Enkidu, longed to explore his body and his mind. Time dashed around him regardless.

If there were any divine he'd willingly vow himself to, it would be Enkidu.

His breath caught.

"So,"—Enkidu interrupted his thoughts as he leaned on the wall—"we've cleaned up and eaten." He licked his lips and his eyes sparkled as he raked them down Gilgamesh's form.

Gilgamesh huffed a laugh, rose, and kissed him, then walked him backwards to the bed. They dropped together and, for an hour, forgot the future.

As they lay panting in each other's arms again, Gilgamesh's fingers lazily tracing over one of Enkidu's horns, his previous thoughts returned to him.

His idea would solve the issue, though it would likely cost his life.

Unlike when facing Humbaba, Gilgamesh wasn't willing to give it up so easily now. But he knew what he must do.

"Enkidu?"

"Hmm?" The man's reply was slow and drowsy.

Gilgamesh readjusted, causing them both to shift. He stared up at the ceiling and tried to steady his breaths. He felt exposed like he'd never been before and afraid of what Enkidu might answer. "Do you remember when I told you that a mortal can vow themselves to only one divine?"

"I do." Enkidu turned to look at Gilgamesh, his eyes brightening out of their sleepiness.

Gilgamesh furled his lower lip between his teeth and released it. "If I were to ask you if you'd make that vow with me, what would you say?"

Enkidu didn't answer. Gilgamesh's body grew as heavy as stone, and he wished he could find the strength to rise off the bed, walk away. He couldn't look at Enkidu if he rejected him. Couldn't survive it.

Enkidu gripped Gilgamesh's chin, forcing the King to meet his gaze. He smiled and the sound of it permeated his words. "You want to marry me?"

"It's a divine vow. It's not exactly the same thing, but..." Gilgamesh swallowed. "Yes. What would you say to that?"

Enkidu chewed on his lip for an excruciatingly long moment. "Won't it anger... Humbaba?"

He wasn't speaking of Humbaba—a word now tainted as well after facing the monster. Enkidu asked about Inanna of course. Gilgamesh scraped his tongue along the backs of his teeth and focused on the ceiling's dimpled corner. Inanna would kill him. Enkidu would refuse if he knew that. However, it would secure the city from having a ruler with almost all god's blood. For the first time since they'd met, Gilgamesh lied to Enkidu. "After speaking with my mother and Utu, I have a plan for handling that."

He nodded, then a grin spread across his cheeks as he whispered, "Well then, in response to your question, I would say, oh great King Gilgamesh..."

Enkidu bent over and kissed Gilgamesh's neck which picked up the pace of his already pounding heart.

"Valorous ruler of the high-walled Uruk..." Gilgamesh pinched his lips to fight a smile as Enkidu kissed his chest then peered up from beneath his long lashes. "Son of the great King and half-god Lugalbanda and the mighty goddess Ninsun..."

Enkidu pushed covers back so he could kiss Gilgamesh's hip.

"He who surpasses all other mortals in strength and deed..." He rose until he was mouth-to-mouth with the

King again, his laughter dancing over Gilgamesh's lips. "Yes, I will."

Gilgamesh chuckled and captured the man's mouth. He deserved the teasing, and Enkidu had said yes. He'd vow their souls together. Gilgamesh wanted that—wanted to live long enough to enjoy it.

He doubted he would.

Enkidu kissed his collarbone and Gilgamesh decided that for a moment he didn't need to worry about the future. He could just be right there. He might as well enjoy the man while he could.

CHAPTER TWENTY-FIVE

HOME AGAIN

GILGAMESH'S HEART thundered as he and Enkidu reached the hilltop that offered a view of Uruk. Below, the gates he'd crafted sat beneath a golden day. Boats drifted around the city along the river. Flags rippled.

It was beautiful and he'd never appreciated it.

Not until Enkidu had come into his life and shattered everything, pushing him past his boundaries. He lifted the man's fingers and kissed them.

Enkidu's cheeks warmed, and Gilgamesh's body buzzed with desire but also with something deeper, something consuming. Attendants who'd met them outside the city had already cleaned them both up. Gilgamesh had sighed as he sat to have his beard curled, and Enkidu shrugged the treatment off, stopping at having his hair oiled and lotion rubbed into his skin.

Gilgamesh had grumbled once the treatments finished which resulted in Enkidu laughing and, when the attendants left, kissing his face a dozen times though carefully avoiding his curls.

Heart warming, Gilgamesh had gripped fingers into the man's hips and pressed a soft kiss to his mouth.

Now they walked together into the city he and Shamhat had built. He'd never taken the time to appreciate its glory, its security and beauty. He'd always viewed those aspects through the lens of his legacy. Now that he'd released that—allowed it to flitter out with Enkidu's near death—all he could see was the world's wonders.

How he'd been blessed enough to rule that glorious city he'd never appreciated. He'd married someone as strong and lovely as Shamhat, had a son as brave and fierce as Usun, and fallen in love with a man as kind and passionate and beautiful as Enkidu. More importantly, the man returned his affections, though he didn't deserve it.

King Gilgamesh was blessed among men, and he wouldn't soon forget it. Then again—a wisp of fear flitted through his mind—he likely wouldn't live long enough to do so.

He tightened his grip on Enkidu's hand, vowing to enjoy every second he had, and led them down into the city.

As they passed under the gates, people cheered and waved colorful ribbons. They bowed to the King and his god-given partner. Called their names. Tears streamed down cheeks and children clapped chubby hands together.

Gilgamesh couldn't help the smile that peeled across his face. For once, his city matched his mood perfectly. He and Enkidu had defeated Humbaba, they'd found each other, and returned home. He grabbed Enkidu's hand and thrust it in the air.

The crowd cheered so loudly it was like Uruk was a living thing itself, roaring in victory. Humbaba was defeated. That would open new trade accessibility and provide more cedar for lumber and—Gilgamesh's stomach warmed—other things like the oil he loved.

Enkidu's cheeks colored as the crowd swarmed them. Throughout their journey home, Gilgamesh had watched that blush as he explored the man's body, while he'd learned different ways he could make him catch his breath or whisper his name. Gilgamesh liked that a lot. His name was sweeter than honey rolling off Enkidu's tongue, guttural and breathy. He lapped it up and didn't care if it ceased to exist in the future, as long as that man continued to speak it during their lifetime.

Crowds pressed in around them—as close as they dared. Gilgamesh had pulled his god's blood power back as much as he could. His gratitude for having a man at his side who could bear the weight of it was infinite. A man who could see him at his worst, most arrogant, and most ridiculous, and love him anyway. Vowed himself to him anyway.

Enkidu's grip on his hand tightened as the crowds thickened. Gilgamesh pulled him up a set of steps, away from the milling crowd that caused Enkidu distress.

The people lifted their faces, smiling up at their king and Enkidu, waving and jumping. Musicians had arrived from somewhere and played a triumphant melody.

Enkidu's hand unclenched as they pulled away. Gilgamesh brushed a thumb along his knuckles but couldn't turn from his people. He was a shepherd to them until the gods forced his death. He'd be the best damn one the world had seen.

"Citizens of Uruk," he called. The joy bubbling in his chest demanded to spill out. The noise dropped, and he grinned so widely it hurt. "Humbaba the fierce is dead."

The responding roar would have caused even the

dragon to jump. Enkidu tensed again, and Gilgamesh traced a finger over his wrist. They'd make it back to the quiet of the palace soon. The part of him that longed to protect Enkidu wished to retreat immediately, but he needed just another moment to speak with the people.

"Long have we hoped for this day, and I thank the gods who blessed and enabled us to defeat this monster." Clapping joined the cheering.

"With thanks to Inanna, the patroness of our city." He didn't even feel bitter to say that because he'd already defeated her as well. "To my mother, the mighty goddess Ninsun. To Utu who blessed our journey and saw us through the dark. And finally, to Anu who watched over all."

People chanted the gods' names. It was so loud that the deities had to hear it. For once, Gilgamesh didn't mind sharing the glory. "And most of all to Enkidu."

Enkidu sucked in a breath which reminded Gilgamesh once again of the man's body bared and molding to his. He forced his attention back to the crowds as he thrust their joined hands into the air again. "Divinely formed and my given companion. Enkidu is the bravest of men, as strong as a god and just as compassionate." More so, really, but Gilgamesh wasn't trying to anger any gods that day. "It was Enkidu who killed the dreaded dragon and spared us all."

The crowd exploded with noise. Enkidu leaned into the King, their skin grazing as he whispered. "I didn't kill Humbaba, you did."

Gilgamesh met his gaze, those godsdamnned forest-wild eyes. "I couldn't have done it without you. You deserve the credit, Enkidu. You deserve everything."

Enkidu stuttered over a breath, and for a beat of time the entire damned world faded.

The roar became the waterfall's rush, stone beneath their feet shifted to the forest's rocky path.

Gilgamesh loved Enkidu.

Loved him so fiercely he'd do anything to make him happy, to exalt him.

He turned back towards his people. "We will celebrate this more than any previous victory. In two weeks, we'll have a feast so indulgent your great-grandchildren will speak of it! I will open my finest wines to share with every person living within the city. Blessings on Uruk!"

"Blessings on Uruk!" the crowd cheered.

"Blessing on Inanna!" Oh, how easy it was to say those words and to hear them repeated now that he'd bested the goddess.

"And blessings on my dearest companion, the god-formed Enkidu!"

"Blessing on Enkidu!"

The man in question's skin burned with more color than ever which cemented the stupid grin Gilgamesh had worn all morning.

He pulled Enkidu forward and urged them in a near run towards the palace. All the while, he waved at people, met as many gazes as he could, repeated the message that Humbaba was gone. Here is what he could do with his life —secure the city, shepherd his people, and love those closest to him.

It was enough.

When they finally reached the palace and made it into the courtyard, Shamhat stood waiting among the advisors. She'd always been a gem in the desert, but his breath caught at the sight of her. She wore gold and crimson, her chin raised high, her dark appraising eyes dropping to his and Enkidu's intertwined hands before dashing up again.

How he'd ever gotten lucky enough for that woman to marry him, he'd never understand.

He released Enkidu's hand to approach his wife. Here he wouldn't cheer and beam. Humbaba's legacy still hurt, and she needed gentle words, not victory cries. He bowed before her, accepting her outstretched hand then kissing it and smoothing his thumb along her wrist. Her lips snapped apart, but he didn't care. No longer would he hold back on showing affection for those he loved.

"My king?" she asked like it was a question.

"My queen." He rose, not releasing her fingers. "Humbaba is dead."

She swallowed and her eyes misted, but she batted the tears back then nodded. "Do you wish for respite after your travels?"

"No, we should eat, and you can tell me all I've missed in my absence." He leaned down to whisper. "And just how much you hate me for it."

Her eyes dashed to the advisors who watched with raised eyebrows, but she chuckled. "Breakfast it is then."

* * *

Enkidu's mouth was soft and warm. They'd already had sex and lay tangled and sprawled out in the plush comfort of Gilgamesh's bed. Yet he couldn't get enough of the man's touch, his taste. If the gods had any mercy, they'd let him die there. Let him perish as he listened to Enkidu's groan of release, let his last smell of earth be sweet cedar and salty sweat.

His fingers swirled around the pattern of Enkidu's chest hair which gleamed with oil. Gilgamesh nuzzled his nose into his neck then began kissing and sucking on that as well.

A knock sounded, and Enkidu jerked away. Gilgamesh grinned down at his bright eyes and mussed hair. He pushed another kiss to his lips. "Wait a moment. I'll send whoever it is away."

Enkidu pulled a blanket over his naked form, and Gilgamesh laughed before he rose and smoothed his beard which Enkidu had knotted his fingers into. He dressed, leaving off the decorative sash. He hoped whoever stood at the door would get the message that he was rather busy at the moment.

He answered. Shamhat stood in the hall and took a step forward, but he eased out and shut the door. She frowned and waved her fingers to dismiss guards farther down the hall. Words didn't leave her until they'd moved out of hearing range.

"I'm not allowed in your apartment anymore?"

He reached out and traced a finger over her arm. Her eyes brightened. She apparently didn't know how to approach an affectionate Gilgamesh. Well, what was life if not for learning new things?

"Of course you are, but I currently have someone else there and he'd probably be embarrassed to be found naked by the Queen."

His queen's painted lips parted into a gape. It wasn't often he could surprise her, and some wicked part of him that apparently hadn't died with Humbaba reveled in it.

"In fact, he told me meeting you naked is a memory he wishes he could remove."

Shamhat shifted so the beads on her outfit clattered. "Enkidu is in your private chambers?"

"Does that bother you?" He hadn't considered it might.

She'd always understood his taking partners at the temples. However, perhaps she felt differently about Enkidu.

"Not at all," she said before his thoughts could fester. "I just—you hated the man not long ago. And you've never allowed others this close."

"I've changed since leaving. Pursuing Humbaba made me realize the error of my ways. You've been right all along. I'm too focused on the future instead of enjoying what I have presently."

And presently he had a very desirable man naked in his very comfortable bed and he'd very much like to rejoin him.

Shamhat's brow furrowed. "You're making a joke at my expense, aren't you?"

It was understandable why she'd think that. They'd always teased each other, and Gilgamesh had run forward with ideas even when she didn't approve. Scarcely would he return from one campaign before starting another, but not this time. "I've never been more serious."

Her frown deepened. "And what is this you mentioned about a party you're throwing for the entire city? You didn't go into details but I'm hearing rumors."

"Right. It got lost in all the bustle of this morning. Don't worry, though. I'll handle all the planning." His thoughts drifted back to Enkidu. Gods, this conversation was going on forever.

"Is it true you're throwing a feast for all of Uruk— opening our palace's finest wines?"

"As you said, my queen, we should live for this moment. We have no control over our fate." When Inanna crushed him beneath her heel, he would fight, but she was divine. Not divinely crafted like Humbaba but truly a god. He couldn't defeat her, not physically, but had destroyed her aim. That would have to satisfy. "We should enjoy this moment we have now."

"This party sounds like a wedding." She said the words carefully, her eyes burning into his. "Not a victory celebration. You've mentioned only a brief plan for sacrifices at the temple from what I've gathered."

Gilgamesh fought the smile forming on his face. He wished to shout the truth in her speech for the world to hear. Enkidu had told him yes. He'd vow himself to the King. If only they could celebrate for a month. Even then it wouldn't be enough. "You've always been quick at inferring the truth of things, my queen."

Shamhat shifted, her bracelets clattering. "Who the fuck are you and what have you done with my husband?"

He bent down to kiss her cheek before raising his face again. "I am King Gilgamesh of Uruk, two-thirds god and crafter of fine walls. I've ventured to kill Humbaba the fierce and achieved it. I'm married to the finest woman in the Land Between Waters. She's raised a son who gives me more credit than I deserve." His voice dropped, softened. "And I'm in love with the world's finest man."

She released a breath, and her expression softened.

"No longer will I waste my days." Gilgamesh shrugged. "I'll find the joy in each one, as you've advised."

"If you're implying what I believe you are, then you're going to anger the only being we've ever feared within this city."

"Perhaps so." Gilgamesh swallowed and took half a step closer to his wife. "As I told you before I left, I've arranged things. And I'll use the days I have well. Now, is there anything else you need of me before I return to my bed?"

She looked back over her shoulder, down the long hall with its ornate mosaics, towards the throne room and their offices where all the work waited. "You're going back to your bed?"

"Oh, yes. I need rest from a long journey home." He smiled which she met with an eye roll. It was nice to return to their regular pattern.

She gripped a fist into her shawl, though. "Gilgamesh, please be careful. I meant it when I said we need you. If you could have seen me when I got the news you survived— how I wept with relief for your sake, perhaps it would change your heart."

Gilgamesh pulled her into his arms, hugged her tight. She clenched her fingers into his back like she'd hold him in place. When she finally softened, he leaned back. "I will not be used or threatened anymore. Once I told you that someone had to risk themselves if anything would change. It's me, Shamhat. I'm so sorry for what it may cost you, but you are strong. You run this city in my absence frequently, and you can continue if fate demands it. In the meantime, no more talk of sad things. The next few weeks are for celebrating. That's what I want you to do."

"And who is going to run the city if we're all celebrating?"

Gilgamesh grinned down at his wife. "Perhaps Kasiru? She always seems to have opinions."

Shamhat pulled free of his embrace and slapped his arm. "Fine," she huffed past a laugh. "Enjoy your day. But tomorrow we get work done."

"I promise you, my queen." Gilgamesh spoke so quietly his words didn't even echo in the hall. "Tomorrow I will begin catching up on anything that's burdened you and binding up loose threads. I won't leave you unprepared again."

Shamhat's brow furrowed, but she sighed and reached

out, scraping her fingers over her husband's beard before turning to walk away.

Gilgamesh hesitated a moment. He wished he could offer her false comfort. However, they must both face reality.

He took a deep breath, turned back towards his room, and let the worries slough away as he sought the man waiting for him.

CHAPTER TWENTY-SIX

TRAITOR

Enkidu sank onto a couch as Gilgamesh tied on a purple sash lined with a gold fringe. Enkidu couldn't tear his gaze away from the King's thick curved muscles. Even draped in finery in his richly decorated bedroom, his body's muscular form was obvious to Enkidu now that he'd explored it so intimately.

Heat spilled over his face, warming his nose. Gilgamesh was thankfully too busy sliding in earrings to notice or he'd tease him for it. Then again, teasing usually resulted in them kissing which often led to...

Enkidu swallowed and pressed his eyes closed. His beard smelled of sesame, his skin of myrrh, but cedar lingered around him, filling his sinuses with every breath. He'd wanted to be with Gilgamesh since the moment they'd met, but he'd never imagined how perfect it would be.

A part of him felt selfish for taking so much of the King's time since returning to the palace. Another part longed to ask him to stay, just another day. He'd want the same thing tomorrow, though. Enkidu wondered if the hunger for him would ever cease. He hoped it wouldn't.

"I've gotten an idea from something you told me," Enkidu said, forcing his mind to move in a different direction.

Gilgamesh slid golden bracelets on his arms. Soon attendants would come in to coil his beard and tend his hair. The King would scowl like a petulant child. Enkidu pinched his lips to fight a smile.

Gilgamesh turned towards him, eyes sparkling. He'd been just as desirous as Enkidu, just as eager to touch and explore, just as unwilling to sleep or let go. His gaze spoke of that, but something deeper lingered in his expression as well.

Love.

Enkidu would never get past it.

"It must have been a rather foolish idea, then." The King grinned at him. "You should disregard it at once."

Gilgamesh slid rings onto his fingers. He was beautiful, dressed in his royal fabrics, but Enkidu had found him just as attractive in a simple tunic wandering through the forest. Enkidu had seen Gilgamesh in so many variations—in darkness and light. He loved every one of them, now. Even the parts that angered him before, he could love those as well. Love the man who was becoming something more.

Enkidu cocked his head, his stomach warming as Gilgamesh traced the gesture with his gaze. It was such an intimate expression, Enkidu could nearly feel Gilgamesh's breath on his skin, his teeth. Enkidu cleared his throat. "You said if you were a wolf you wouldn't want to draw Humbaba's attention to your children's lair."

Gilgamesh frowned. "If you're concerned about... Humbaba..."

"That's not what I meant." Though, perhaps he should worry. He'd taken Gilgamesh's word that he'd worked with other gods on a plan to deal with Inanna. Something dark flitted across Gilgamesh's expression, and Enkidu's breath caught. Gilgamesh making his sole divine vow with Enkidu would anger the goddess. She'd retaliate. Perhaps there was no plan in place to protect this man. Losing Gilgamesh after he'd just gained him caused Enkidu's stomach to dip, reminding him of diving from a cliff into water. Bile surged into his throat, and he forgot how to breathe for a moment.

Gilgamesh walked over and pressed a kiss to his forehead. "We cannot control our fate, can we?"

"No, but we don't have to march into the cedar forest and taunt it, either."

"As I remember"—the King's lips found Enkidu's, molding to his mouth in a searing kiss—"we succeeded at that."

"As I vaguely remember, we both nearly died in that pursuit."

Gilgamesh's nose flared, and he brushed knuckles over Enkidu's cheekbones. "Let us pray we continue having success, then."

Worry poured through Enkidu, a rush of a feeling that swallowed all the previous weeks' happiness and pleasure. Enkidu wanted to grasp Gilgamesh, force him to stay at his side, vow to protect him as he had in the cedar forest. However, Inanna wasn't defeatable. Unlike Gilgamesh who had god's blood or Enkidu and Humbaba who were divinely crafted, she was a goddess and immortal.

He could only solve the issues in front of him so, reluctantly, he returned to his original point. "I'm speaking about Usun and rooting out who might have attacked him. What if we choose to lead Humbaba to your lair?"

Gilgamesh frowned. "Why would I do that?"

Enkidu stood and grabbed his hands. "I could remain in Usun's room from early morning through the night. You could reduce the guards back to the standard amount before the attack. I'll stay with Usun to set a trap for whoever it is. With this celebration about to happen,"—Enkidu squeezed Gilgamesh's fingers, and the King's intense expression softened—"and New Year is coming soon, perhaps the person might come out again."

Nuzzling his nose into Enkidu's neck, Gilgamesh scraped his teeth along the dip. "The only person's room I want you waiting in at night is mine."

Enkidu groaned and curled his fingers around Gilgamesh's hips. He wanted that as well, especially if Inanna may threaten his life. However... "For Usun's sake?"

A sigh spilled past Gilgamesh's lips and his breath's warmth bloomed across Enkidu's collarbone. "Of course." He released Enkidu and something about the cool spreading over his flesh felt like heartbreak. "You're fond of the boy, then?"

Enkidu wished he could find words to address all the conversations not happening between them. They moved slippery and unformed in his mind. Failing to come up with anything solid, he answered. "I would protect any child of yours with my life. But, yes, I like Usun."

Turning away, Gilgamesh's voice went quiet. It was a candle's final sputtering attempt at staying aflame despite fate's breath. "Do you think, were something to happen to me, you might look out for him?"

Enkidu's lip quivered. He wanted to scream to the gods, demand justice. Forming Enkidu for Gilgamesh only to threaten to take the man away was vicious. "I will."

It was all he had to offer. He'd gladly look after the boy

in his father's memory if it came to that. But gods, he hoped and prayed with every drop of blood in his body that he wouldn't have to face that reality.

* * *

Enkidu twisted his neck around. It was his third night of spending most of his hours in Usun's room and sleeping reclined on a trunk by the door. His body twinged with dozens of little hurts. Usun tossed in his sleep, turning over on the mattress.

Sliding his hands over the rug, Enkidu attempted to still his body. He didn't wish to wake the Prince; he was just so damn restless and his thoughts plagued him.

If he wasn't worrying about the future, he was remembering Gilgamesh's coarse hands, his warm, wet mouth, the weight of his body on his.

Enkidu readjusted again and clenched his eyes shut.

He longed for sleep to swallow him.

Damn it. He wouldn't spend the night in Usun's room the evening of the party regardless of how things went. They could up the guards again for one day. He wanted to spend that night in Gilgamesh's chambers, warm and bare and happy.

The last time he'd attended a celebration at the palace was also a wedding, and he'd had to stand back from Gilgamesh, watch him marry another. This time was about them—their victories and their relationship. He wanted to celebrate with him, but even more so he longed to commemorate the event privately.

Gilgamesh loved him and asked him to make a vow that would endure past this life.

Enkidu had never felt so purposeful as when Gilgamesh requested it, the King's words a whisper.

The door rattled, and Enkidu jerked his face towards it. Beside him, he curled his fingers around a blade as he sank deeper into a shadow. Another rattle, then the door opened.

Someone stepped in.

A blade in their hand gleamed even in the dim light.

Enkidu dashed forward, throwing the person to the ground. They landed with a grunt and dashed their sword forward.

It found skin and muscle, tearing through them.

Enkidu scarcely flinched.

He'd experienced far more painful injuries from a creature much fiercer than some human assassin. Usun was up, light spilling in and glowing over his mussed curls.

Enkidu yanked the sword from the person's hand as Usun lit a lamp.

The child's eyes were wide and searching. Gods, he was so much like his foolish father—looking death in the face with wonder instead of fear. Enkidu held the writhing assailant tight with one arm as he pulled the mask off them.

Usun and Enkidu both gasped at the face that appeared.

"Kasiru?" Usun asked, his voice appropriately wobbly at last. "You tried to kill me?"

She didn't answer the Prince, only bared her teeth as guards stormed into the space.

* * *

A few of Gilgamesh's soldiers had lit torches around the throne room, and the glow of them blended with the silvery moonlight that washed through the rectangular opening in the ceiling.

Enkidu had released Kasiru to the soldiers who held her where guests stood when they visited.

Gilgamesh stood before his throne, dressed in full regalia, as he looked down at Kasiru. Shamhat was at his side, her arms crossed, her eyes as dark as night skies.

Enkidu shifted to leave. This was a private matter, and he wasn't sure he belonged there. Gilgamesh turned his face towards him, his eyes softening, and Enkidu stopped. The King needed him, wanted him to stay. He clasped his hands together and tucked against the wall.

That was his role—to balance Gilgamesh, to soothe his crackling, tempestuous personality.

Gilgamesh turned back towards the musician who'd given up fighting the soldiers who held her. "Explain your-self," he boomed.

She didn't reply, didn't look up.

"Now." Gilgamesh's voice was cedar trees thundering into the earth. It was a scream so loud it made ears bleed. It was the voice of an angry god.

Still the woman didn't reply, and Shamhat stepped forward, her fists clenched. "Your king just demanded something of you. Speak at once."

Kasiru lifted her face. "It was never personal, my queen."

"You attempted to kill my son," she spat back, her head-piece trembling. "Do not tell me it wasn't personal. What have we ever done to prompt this from you? We invited you into our home, promoted you to the highest position among the musicians, and invited you to join our personal advisors."

"You both sneer in the face of Inanna." Kasiru thinned

her lips, and Enkidu's heart seized at her words. The woman was right—Gilgamesh had always despised Inanna and had done little to hide it. Enkidu's chest tightened until it ached. If they'd angered gods, and no other divine stood to speak for them, they'd face immortal wrath.

"You act as though you are more important than Our Lady in Heaven." Kasiru's words became louder and more intense with each one. "I know you mean to promote some mortal child to Inanna's son's throne. I'm devoted to the goddess and could not allow such a slight to happen to her name."

Shamhat's nose flared as she marched closer to the woman. She pulled an arm back and slapped her. Her head jerked. Enkidu shuddered but remained in the shadows. A mother wolf would have ripped out the woman's throat already—Shamhat was showing restraint as far as he was concerned.

Gilgamesh stepped forward next to his wife. He looked at her and some silent war played between the two of them before she released a breath and took a step back.

The King approached the musician and leered down at her. Enkidu's stomach twisted. The last time he'd meted out punishment in a similar situation, he'd acted so cruelly Enkidu hadn't known him.

"So, you do not trust your goddess' judgments?" Gilgamesh asked.

Kasiru frowned. "Of course I do."

"If she took issue with us or our children, don't you think she'd handle it herself?"

The musician fluttered her lashes and finally seemed at a loss for words.

"No," Gilgamesh continued. "You don't have faith in her. Instead, you thrust yourself into a position of the gods, making judgments for Our Lady in Heaven, when you've been so respected amongst our court and the gods' considerations. You've damned yourself."

"This city is Inanna's." She strained forward, but Abgal clenched her tighter, forcing her still. "She will live forever —long after you're dead."

Gilgamesh leaned towards her so that his face was level with hers. She whimpered and slumped, the soldiers having to hold her up. Gilgamesh had released his god's blood powers. He'd explained it to Enkidu during the journey. He was immune to it. The musician clearly was not. She sagged and her skin grayed.

"I know," Gilgamesh whispered.

Enkidu traced his fingers over the mosaic behind him. Gilgamesh had changed. When they'd met, he wanted to fight his fate with his bare hands if he must. Now he stood beside his wife in his palace, accepting it. Enkidu wished he could wrap the man in his arms. He knew the cost of that admission.

"How did you learn sword work?" the King asked.

Kasiru didn't even lift her face, but one soldier holding her looked at Abgal who nodded. The soldier cleared his throat. "If I may speak, Lugal."

"Of course."

The soldier frowned but carried on. "She's been seeing Naram-Sin, my king."

Gilgamesh released a breath loudly enough that it echoed from the stone. Once again, Enkidu had to force himself to remain in place, to not stride across the room and touch the man.

The King turned towards another soldier along the wall. "Rouse Naram-Sin and have him brought here."

A stretch of time passed where silence reigned aside

from Shamhat's rustling clothing as she paced across the floor. Finally, Naram-Sin stepped into the darkened hall, his brow furrowed. He bowed deeply to the King and Queen then gaped at Kasiru being held by his fellow soldiers.

Naram-Sin had gone hunting with Enkidu. He was quick-witted and kind. He'd been one of the first soldiers to accept Enkidu despite his god-marked past. It stung Enkidu that he might have conspired against Gilgamesh's family.

"Kasiru attempted to murder my son tonight." Gilgamesh didn't waste time with flowery words. Shamhat stood at his side again, both of them looking down at the soldier.

He whirled on Kasiru. "What? Tell me this isn't true."

She wouldn't meet his gaze.

Naram-Sin lifted his face to Abgal. "This happened?"

Abgal nodded, though his eyes held the compassion of a father in them. He mentored the younger men and worked with the palace's children. Naram-Sin was scarcely more than a youth. Enkidu longed to help, but there was nothing for him to do.

The King stood as still and stony eyed as the room's statues. "Did you teach her sword work?"

Naram-Sin gasped as he turned back towards the King. "I did, Lugal." He stumbled forward and bowed to his knees. "I didn't know she would use it maliciously. I swear to you, will vow it to you, my king. Nonetheless, I've betrayed you most grievously. It will never be enough, but I offer my neck to pay for this error."

"Naram-Sin, don't do this." Kasiru had looked up.

He shifted to glower at her. "If you had ever loved me, you never would have engaged in such treachery. Do not speak my name again."

Enkidu took a step forward. Naram-Sin was sincere, he

was sure of it. Gilgamesh didn't take slights well. He couldn't slaughter one of his loyal soldiers because the man was young and perhaps foolish. Gods, love made fools of all —kings included. It was foolish of Gilgamesh to throw away his legacy for Enkidu's sake.

Before Enkidu had reached a second step, Gilgamesh spoke again. "You would vow on the names of Inanna and Ninsun that you are loyal to me, Naram-Sin?"

"Of course, Lugal. With no hesitation. The gods may strike me dead if they see even a shadow of disloyalty in my heart."

"Then it would be a waste to lose your head. Rise."

The man stood, staring at the King. Enkidu turned towards him as well. Gilgamesh reached out and placed a hand on the warrior's shoulder. "Take this lesson and learn from it. Do not make a mistake like this again."

"I won't, Lugal," he said, his voice breaking.

Naram-Sin had fought as viciously and fearlessly as any of Gilgamesh's men in Umma. Yet he trembled before his king, scarcely fighting back tears. It wasn't the soldier who captured Enkidu's attention, however. It was the King who released the man's shoulder. He'd forgiven the man.

Enkidu's heart might burst from the love he felt for him.

Gilgamesh returned his attention to the musician, his eyes skimming down her cowering form. He didn't speak for some time. Shamhat shuffled up beside him and whispered in his ear. His eyes lifted to meet Enkidu's anxious gaze. For a moment they looked at each other, the room fading. A corner of Gilgamesh's lip lifted, and he nodded, like he understood whatever Enkidu wouldn't say aloud.

He turned towards the soldiers holding the musician. "Take her to Inanna's temple. Inform Our Lady in Heaven that this musician crafted a conspiracy against my family in

Inanna's name. We know the goddess who holds us under her wings' protection would never harm us so, and because of our deep faith in her, we leave it to the goddess' judgment what should be done with her. Also, inform Our Lady that we fear others may be involved, but we trust her to provide answers."

The soldiers bowed, then dragged Kasiru from the room. Naram-Sin watched her go, his eyes misting.

Gilgamesh thanked the attendants, other soldiers, and guards, then dismissed them all. He bid Shamhat good night, pressing a kiss to her cheek. When the room stretched empty, the lamps dimming until only cool light washed around the shadows, he approached Enkidu.

"Once again you've saved my son."

Enkidu shrugged and failed to form the words he wished to speak. *Once again you've reignited my love for you.*

"Follow me?" Gilgamesh asked.

He'd done that so many months before in the courtyard when Enkidu had been overwhelmed and lost. Just like then, he nodded and walked behind his king.

They stepped outside, climbed a ladder, and lay down together on the roof. Gilgamesh reached out and twined their fingers together, laying them on his chest as he stared up at the heaven's immense intensity. Enkidu found the stars fascinating, but not as much as the man beside him.

"I'm proud of you, Gilgamesh."

The King grinned. "Expected me to punish her brutally, didn't you?"

"Expected you wouldn't. Feared you might."

Gilgamesh laughed and nuzzled Enkidu's fingers with his lips. "You've taught me a great deal. There's much space between not addressing an issue and becoming a beast myself."

"If Inanna lets her off, will you regret it?"

"Oh, she won't do that. Imagine if someone came here with a person who witnesses claim attempted to assassinate the Pharaoh's son in my name? Imagine if the city—no, the entire world—watched to see my response? I couldn't ignore it without turning people against me." He took a deep breath. "You know, Inanna is likely to punish her harshly then kill her? She can't let others see her as weak."

Enkidu closed his eyes. Usun's startled expression flitted across his mind, the innocence in his voice when he asked Kasiru if she'd planned to kill him. "Yes, I understand. I wish this world weren't so cruel. Perhaps the Great Below is better."

Gilgamesh shifted. "No, legends say it's dark and cold and miserable there."

Emotions swelled up Enkidu's throat. Soon Gilgamesh might go there because of their foolishness. The misery hanging on Enkidu returned, but he choked out a response. "I suppose we enjoy the life we have now as much as we can, then."

"Hmm. Yes." Gilgamesh tucked his head into Enkidu's shoulder. "When I was a boy, I would climb onto the palace's roofs all the time. I longed to be closer to the heavens. I thought I belonged there."

"What about now?"

Gilgamesh watched the stars for another moment. Then he raised his face to Enkidu and lifted their hands to kiss Enkidu's fingertips. "Now, I think I'm right where I belong."

A smile unfurled Enkidu's lips.

"I'm not afraid anymore," Gilgamesh said. "I don't want

you to be either. Let's enjoy one another as long as the gods allow. Please, would you do that for me?"

Enkidu's lips parted, but for a dozen heartbeats he couldn't speak. The way Gilgamesh looked at him, as though he could see his soul, stalled the words, dissipated them. He'd fallen into the same trap Gilgamesh had lived in —his focus on the future so he couldn't enjoy the present.

He drew closer to the man and rested against him, mindful of his horns. Gilgamesh rearranged to pull him into his arms. They lay there together, watching the heavens as the gods observed them in return.

Ninsun had Enkidu created to love her son, and if he did nothing else in life, that would be enough.

He curled into the man's arms and refused to let his thoughts drift towards the future again.

CHAPTER TWENTY-SEVEN

UNBREAKABLE WORDS

Time was a strange thing. At some moments, it would drag like a tunic caught on river rocks. Then it would rush ahead, tumbling a being along so they scraped their knees and bloodied their nose.

Gilgamesh felt the latter's speed as weeks slipped past him. He used the time as well as he could—working harder than he ever had during the day, spending time with Shamhat, then passing blissful evenings making love to Enkidu, listening to him talk, and wishing it could last forever.

One evening they joined Shamhat, Meritkara, and Akkiru for dinner. Usun showed Kara's daughter a string trick that made the girl giggle until tears swept down her curved cheeks. Enkidu joined their laughter then turned to continue his conversation with Akkiru. The Queen, who sat beside Gilgamesh, rested her head on his shoulder.

For a moment, Gilgamesh's heart filled with such warmth it hurt.

He wished it was a pain that would last forever.

When the day finally came, Gilgamesh's hands only

trembled slightly as he privately exchanged the vows with Enkidu, the man's blood warm against his skin.

He'd expected Inanna to appear at once and end him. But she didn't.

The day roared on, and they threw a party that matched the promises Gilgamesh had given. Their staff passed food and alcohol around the entire city like they'd discovered an endless supply. Musicians played until the notes grew sloppy. Even Akkiru joined in with a group while Shamhat and Meritkara lounged together and watched him with sunny smiles.

The entire city—Enkidu and Gilgamesh included— were warm and loose from the alcohol and late hour by the time the party ended. Gilgamesh grasped Enkidu's fingers and led him through the palace grounds towards the private courtyard near the back.

Before slipping through the gate, he nodded at the guards. He planned to give extra gifts to all the soldiers and guards who'd eschewed the party to secure the palace for the night. But that was something he could worry about the next day.

When he made it into the courtyard which he'd assured was kept empty, he pushed Enkidu against a vine-covered wall and kissed him.

Enkidu laughed, his lips slipping away. "Here?"

"Why not?" Gilgamesh nipped his ear, sesame oil stinging his tongue and warming his gut. "I want you in the wild again."

Enkidu groaned a hot breath on his neck and dragged his tunic back to expose his chest. Gilgamesh fumbled as he slid his hands under Enkidu's clothing to find the fine hair and muscles beneath. He stumbled and everything blurred. The alcohol had gone to his head—damn he'd drank a lot if it outpaced his god's blood's ability to burn through it.

He smiled at his clumsiness and found Enkidu's soft lips again. The man was warm and relaxed and glorious beneath his searching hands. He didn't need sobriety to finish the celebration how he'd imagined.

Gilgamesh cherished Enkidu more than his life. He'd saved Uruk and bound himself—forever—to the man he loved.

Their kisses were clumsy, wet, landing on each other's mouths as often as cheeks or necks or chests. Warmth radiated through Gilgamesh as he clenched his hands into his vowed partner's hip, feeling muscles tense beneath his fingers. He was so happy he nearly wanted to giggle. Enkidu might think him ridiculous for such a reaction except they were both floating in the intoxication of aged wine and love.

A blood-curdling screech tore through the night air and stalled Gilgamesh's hands. Hair raised on the back of his neck.

He turned and sobered up faster than he would have imagined possible.

Inanna stood before them, twice her normal height, her wings spread, her eyes so pale they lacked color.

Gilgamesh shivered. The moment had come.

He bowed. "Inanna."

Enkidu, who was still fumbling to pull his tunic back into place, gasped but inclined himself as well.

"How dare you," the goddess seethed. She stepped closer and her talons broke tiles. One crack spread across the courtyard, climbed a wall, and shattered the mosaic of his father. Colorful tiles rained onto plants below them. Inanna's eyes flashed. "You sent that foolish girl to me knowing I'd punish her because I cannot overlook slights to me, yet you affront me far worse then throw a party to celebrate doing so."

"I'm sorry." The words surprised Gilgamesh as they left him, breathy and still tinged with alcohol's sweetness. He realized he was. All his life he'd chased after godhood when it wasn't his fate. To break that, he'd shamed a goddess, and he was sorry. For all the good it would do in the face of her fury. "People serve the gods. That's what your father crafted them for. The human throne should belong to mortals. We should remain servants, not become gods." Enkidu had shifted behind Gilgamesh, barely touching him. Yet it was the greatest comfort.

Inanna bared her teeth. "One of your filthy magicless sons, then?"

"I don't care who my throne passes to." He grabbed Enkidu's hand, needing the steadiness of his touch. "But we can't put someone with god-like strength on the throne. What if they rise in their powers and act against you in the future?"

Inanna blinked then her taloned foot shot out. It gripped Gilgamesh's neck and slammed him into the wall, ripping his hand from Enkidu's. The man cried out. Talons sliced into Gilgamesh's shoulder, and she'd cut his breath off. He didn't fight, though. This was his fate, and he was prepared to take it. He wished he and Enkidu could have finished making love one last time before he had to face it, but he'd accept it without fighting.

"Stop!" Enkidu cried. "Please."

Inanna's grip loosened enough for Gilgamesh to gasp a breath. She turned her attention on Enkidu as though she noticed him for the first time that night.

All Gilgamesh could manage was shaking his head as he

met Enkidu's eyes. Those forest-wild, compassionate, burning eyes. He mouthed, *go. Please, run. Don't get yourself killed as well.*

Inanna shifted her gaze between the two of them. She frowned but released Gilgamesh. "Death is too easy a punishment for you, oh great King of Uruk."

She turned and flew away. Enkidu hurried over and helped Gilgamesh to his feet. Blood trailed down his arms, and Enkidu worried over it, but Gilgamesh grabbed his hands. "You're a fool, do you know it?"

Enkidu bowed his forehead until it touched Gilgamesh's. "I vowed to stand at your side until the end, and I meant those words."

Gilgamesh sighed and melted into the man, grateful to still hold him. Thunder cracked across the sky. Lightning sliced the heavens which shifted to a deep crimson. The earth shook.

A winged bull swept down through the storm, landing before them.

Its hoof crashed into the courtyard's wall, smashing a dozen cubits of brick and tile. The creature snorted, and Gilgamesh lifted his face to take the beast in. The bull of heaven. This was Anu's creature.

The supreme god meant to punish Gilgamesh for his slight against his daughter.

He shoved Enkidu behind him. "Run."

The creature bellowed and slammed its horns into the wall, ruining another length of it. Shrieks and cries echoed from the palace in the distance. They were away from the palace's main building, but if that beast drew any nearer, it could take thousands of lives with a few stomps of its hooves.

"No, we can fight this," Enkidu said.

Gilgamesh turned where he could see Enkidu without losing sight of the beast that had its attention fixed on destroying the courtyard. "I can't let you get hurt again."

A softness entered Enkidu's beautiful eyes. "We can't let it hurt everyone here. What of our family?"

Our family.

The dinner they'd had with Shamhat and her partners and their children rang through Gilgamesh's mind. That's how it had felt—they were family. They belonged to each other. Gilgamesh nodded. He wanted to spare Enkidu, but perhaps he'd damned them both.

"I'll keep it distracted," Enkidu said. "You attack."

"The closest weapons are in the soldiers' practice area." In a less dire situation Gilgamesh would label that as close, but with a monster descended on the palace and the man he loved about to face it, it felt desperately far.

"Then I'll lead the bull there. I understand creatures. Trust me."

Gilgamesh shivered, and his eyes stung. His dream— the one he hadn't had since the first time he'd made love to Enkidu—returned to him. How he'd howled and wept over the broken rock. He knew it would be true now. If the Bull of Heaven killed this man, Gilgamesh would never recover from his grief.

The bull had decimated one wall and turned towards them. Gilgamesh snatched Enkidu's face and kissed him hard and quick.

"I love you," Enkidu whispered.

There was a goodbye in his words. He could have stabbed him and hurt him less.

"Tell me that later," Gilgamesh replied before turning to run as hard as he ever had. They'd already defeated one god-crafted creature so maybe it wasn't impossible.

Gilgamesh wouldn't hesitate to throw himself in danger's way to protect their family. Gods, he finally had something worth protecting and his arrogance and foolishness might steal it all away. Once again, Inanna chose her desires over the good of Uruk. She didn't care if the bull destroyed half the city. She'd point a finger in Gilgamesh's direction then demand the people rebuild and make more sacrifices to appease her anger.

He reached the weapons storage closet and kicked the door, breaking it down. Swords were polished and hanging in holders. He grabbed two and ran back out.

Enkidu had found a drum and banged it wildly, drawing the bull away from the palace.

Gilgamesh slowed his pace as he approached. Enkidu's eyes darted to him then returned to the towering bull who snorted and stomped a hoof that was nearly as large as the man. With two quick slashes, Gilgamesh warmed his muscles then charged.

He'd been too hesitant with Humbaba. Now, with the Bull of Heaven staring Enkidu down, he didn't care. The bull tensed like it was about to charge, and Gilgamesh slammed a sword into its calf. It screamed as he weaved through its legs and tossed a blade to Enkidu.

An ache pierced his ears, and he clenched his teeth. Perhaps he'd lose his hearing again by a monster's voice. Reaching the bull's tail, Gilgamesh grabbed hold of it and held on even as it thrashed about. The creature bucked and Gilgamesh hit a wall with a thud that stole his breath but didn't loosen his grip.

Enkidu used the bull's distress to change directions. He began banging the drum again then waving his sword wildly around. The creature dropped to all four hooves with a crash.

Gilgamesh climbed, reaching the beast's massive back.

Others had woken. Torches flickered to life, and soldiers flooded into the courtyard, but they fainted, falling to the earth. The creature had god's blood powers.

Only Enkidu and Gilgamesh could overthrow the beast.

Enkidu lifted a rock and chucked it at the creature. He snatched another and threw it. He kept taunting it, drawing it farther from the palace and the city. Soon they'd reach the river. Perhaps they'd avoid massive casualties because of Enkidu's quick thinking.

Enkidu tripped and landed on the ground.

The bull snorted and charged.

Gilgamesh froze.

Enkidu looked so small below—a speck against dark earth. One step from the bull, and he'd crush him into the Great Below and beyond Gilgamesh's reach.

"No," the King whispered.

Gilgamesh ran as well, his feet pounding along the bull's spine. He raised his sword.

Never had he been a devoted or spiritual man. He'd grown up amongst the gods and wanted to become one. Why should he worship another? In that moment, his pride was stripped bare. He lifted his face to the moon.

"Nanna, if I've ever done anything to please you, if I've ever been a loyal servant of the heavens, tithed to your temples even though you don't live in our city, expanded the study of the stars, and done anything to exalt you, then hear me now. Help me defeat this enemy, and I'll credit all victory to your name."

Strength surged through Gilgamesh, and a million twinkling stars rushed over his vision. He leapt like he flew across the heavens. The blow landed with more power than Gilgamesh possessed.

It sliced through the bull's neck amid a final bellowing cry.

Hot blood cascaded like a waterfall.

Gilgamesh fell.

He tucked his chin and bent his arms and legs.

Hitting the ground snapped something, and pain seared through his body, spreading everywhere so he couldn't determine what he'd injured. Enkidu clambered over the bull's head, slipped through the blood, then dropped on his knees beside Gilgamesh.

Gilgamesh kissed him.

Enkidu tasted like blood, and he didn't care.

He was alive, and they were safe.

Soldiers who had found their feet and followed, cheered. They chanted Enkidu's and Gilgamesh's names. As soon as the King could find words, he'd have to correct them. Nanna's name would be exalted.

Thank you.

The moon gleamed brighter for a moment, and Gilgamesh tucked his face into Enkidu's shoulder and listened to his heartbeat.

The bull had destroyed a small section of the palace but nothing major. Builders could repair it within a few months and the cost would be modest compared to half the city being ripped asunder. There were no casualties Gilgamesh was aware of. And Enkidu was alive and unharmed.

Inanna flew down out of the sky and landed with a flash of light that knocked his soldiers down.

Enkidu huddled closer to Gilgamesh as they fixed their eyes on eternity, on the hands that held their souls.

Inanna looked at the bull then returned her focus to Gilgamesh, her voice as sharp as the jewels decorating her temple. "You have crossed me twice now today."

"You attacked us," Gilgamesh yelled. He was over reverence and apologies. She clearly wouldn't hear them and perhaps he'd crossed her too many times for them to be worthwhile. "You attacked my home and the city you protect."

"You broke your vow to me." Inanna's voice boomed but it was cold. Calculating. Lightning flashed across her eyes and her hair blew about.

Gilgamesh rose with Enkidu's help, cradling his broken arm to his chest. "It was no vow, Inanna. I never wished to agree. You take without permission that which isn't yours to have."

Inanna stepped closer, her size shrinking. When she spoke, it was no longer the howling of a storm but the whisper of a drought coming. "You forget who I am, mortal. I'm a god." Her eyes flicked to Enkidu. "Everything in this realm is mine." A slow smile crawled up her face. "You've taken my desires from me today. I shall grant you the same."

Gilgamesh's heart tripped around itself. Having Enkidu with him was a mistake. He should have insisted Enkidu run. He was too brave, though, and too loyal. Never would he have abandoned Gilgamesh or their city to a monster. Gilgamesh tightened his grip around him.

Inanna's smile grew, her eyes turning an eerie pale green, and she shifted to Enkidu. "I curse you." Gilgamesh's mouth snapped open, and he clenched Enkidu so tightly it had to hurt the man though he didn't move. "On this very day next year, you will die and worms will eat your body. I allow you this time so your lover may look you in the eyes every single day and know what he's done to you."

Enkidu released a ragged breath, and Gilgamesh

released him. "No!" He dropped to his knees before the goddess. "I will give you anything. Please."

"You are a fool, Gilgamesh." Her talons dug into the earth. "And your offer comes too late."

She disappeared in a crackle of static-filled light.

Gilgamesh choked over a sob and turned to face Enkidu. He sat perfectly still, wide-eyed and beautiful and cursed. Ninsun's words returned to the King.

You will gain what you desire but lose what matters most in the end.

Gilgamesh stumbled towards Enkidu and traced his uninjured hand over his face. "No. No. This can't happen."

Enkidu blinked rapidly and pressed a kiss to the King's cheek. "It's okay. I was never meant to live forever."

"No." The word turned hot, flames meant to burn. "I won't allow this. I will find some way to break this curse."

The King tucked his body over the wild man's and pressed the vow into his heart. No matter what it took—he'd find a way to save him.

BONUS CONTENT

You can find bonus content with three pieces of free character art and a behind-the-scenes world building guide here:

The Legacy of Gilgamesh duology ends with the second book, Among the Cursed and the Divine.

ACKNOWLEDGMENTS

I dedicated this book in the memory of my sister Anna. She was so proud of my books and such a champion of them. For some time I thought I wouldn't be able to publish this book knowing she wouldn't be here to post about it. Thank you, Anna, for loving me so hard. I miss you every hour of every day.

My mother always has an expression for everything and many of those she inherited from her father. One is, "a good bull marks his calf." When Gilgamesh reflects on Usun favoring him and thinks this it was a direct nod to my Grandpa Dickens.

A tremendous thank you to Dr. Andrew George, who not only authored the Penguin Classics translation of The Epic of Gilgamesh which was one of the most helpful translations I read before writing this book, but who also took the time to answer some of my questions about the world building for this story.

For my editors Milly and Natalie, thank you both for your thoughtfulness and energy you poured into this project. My books are always stronger after having passed through your hands.

To Chaim who always makes the beautiful maps in my books, thank you. And thanks for being willing to zigzag when I had the idea to change the border. You are so talented and I appreciate you sharing some of that talent with my books!

To Stefanie & Florian who designed the cover and the weapons for this book, thank you. This book has a stunning cover and I love having Gilgamesh's epic axes on it.

A huge thank you to M. D. Cooper who helped me rework the blurb for this book. (She also said to me: doesn't it make you wonder if there's only a certain number of stories we tell as humans that must mean that there is a limit to the experience of what makes us human? I have yet to stop thinking about that.)

To Daniel and Chera, my readers who requested this retelling, I hope you both have loved the characters and story as much as you'd hoped. Thank you for requesting it. Getting to step into Gilgamesh's world has been a joy for me.

I have a handful of ARC readers who have been with me from my earliest series. They champion my books in dozens of different ways and have continued with me for fifteen books now. It's with your wonderful support I'm able to continue doing this. A tremendous thank you to: Julie, Brandyn, Taryn, Cheyenne, Jason, Kelsey, Sarah, and Chris.

Thank you Megan for proofreading this book! (And for the hilarious comments you sent me along the way.)

A huge thank you to my husband who is one of my best friends and greatest supporters. And thank you to my family and friends who love, support, and encourage me so greatly.

To Jacki and James who listened to endless drama about me deciding the cover for this book, thank you! I love you both.

Finally, I want to take a moment to thank the researches, archeologists, professors, translators, and authors whose research and work helped me shape the world building for this series. A tremendous thank you to:

Andrew George, Amanda H. Podany, Stephanie Dalley, Paul Kriwaczek, Zainab Bahrani, Susan Ackerman, Tate Paulette, Gerda Lerner, Massimo, Maiocchi, Marcelle Duchesne-Guillemin, E. Douglas Van Buren, Joan Goodnick Westenholz, Irving L. Finkel, Larua Feldt, Rivkah Harris, Tzvi Abusch, Aaron Shaffer, Serdar Yalçın, Benjamin R. Foster, Stephen Mitchell, Sophus Helle, Stephen Langdon, and John D. Harris

www.ingramcontent.com/pod-product-compliance
Lightning Source LLC
Chambersburg PA
CBHW070409310726
48977CB00003B/611